TWELVE ROOMS WIT~~H A VIEW~~

Theresa Rebeck is a leading American p~~laywright~~. ~~She~~ has also been a producer on *NYPD Blue* and *Law and Orde~~r: Criminal Intent~~* and has written for a number of major television serie~~s including~~ *~~B~~rooklyn Bridge*, *L.A Law* and HBO's *Dream On*. She and her hus~~band and~~ children live in New York.

Visit www.theresarebeck.com for exclusive updates.

Praise for Theresa Rebeck:

"Theresa Rebeck is so slick that Gucci wears *her* shoes"   *New Yorker*

"I was charmed—and I won't be the last"   *New York Observer*

"Hilarious first novel . . . Rebeck shines when Amelia gets cast in a ridiculous off-Broadway play . . . her insider's look at the theatre world is spot on and uproarious"   *Publishers Weekly*

"A wickedly enjoyable exposé of modern celebrity"   *Kirkus*

"An experienced playwright who has also toiled in the television industry, Ms. Rebeck has intimate knowledge of the pathologies bred in smart, seemingly well-adjusted men and women by the surreal polarities of success and failure"   *New York Times*

"*Three Girls and Their Brother* is a brilliant fiction debut. Rebeck weaves such an atmosphere of excitement and turmoil. I felt genuinely close to these characters—all three sisters and their brother. The insider's look at the life of young models and the way instant success can upend everything resonates in hilarious and heartbreaking ways. I found it impossible to put this book down"   Carol Goodman, author of *The Lake of Dead Languages*'

"Playwright Theresa Rebeck is known for black comedy and hyper-intelligent heroines, and both figure in her first novel, *Three Girls and Their Brother*—a fizzy satire of celeb-obsessed NYC about flame-haired teenage sisters who get photographed for the *New Yorker* and soon become megastars"   *Entertainment Weekly*

Also by Theresa Rebeck

Three Girls and Their Brother

THERESA REBECK

Twelve Rooms
with a View

HARPER

Harper
An imprint of HarperCollins*Publishers*
77–85 Fulham Palace Road,
Hammersmith, London W6 8JB

www.harpercollins.co.uk

This paperback edition 2009
1

First published in Great Britain by
HarperCollins*Publishers* 2009

A catalogue record for this book is
available from the British Library

ISBN: 978 0 00 725633 4

Set in Bembo by Palimpsest Book Production Limited,
Grangemouth, Stirlingshire

Printed and bound in Great Britain by
Clays Ltd, St Ives PLC

Mixed Sources

Product group from well-managed
forests and other controlled sources
www.fsc.org Cert no. SW-COC-1806
© 1996 Forest Stewardship Council

FSC is a non-profit international organisation established to promote the
responsible management of the world's forests. Products carrying the FSC
label are independently certified to assure consumers that they come
from forests that are managed to meet the social, economic and
ecological needs of present and future generations.

Find out more about HarperCollins and the environment at
www.harpercollins.co.uk/green

For Jess Lynn

I was actually standing on the edge of my mother's open grave when I heard about the house. Some idiot with tattoos and a shovel had tossed a huge wad of dirt at me. I think he was more or less perturbed that everyone else had taken off the way they're supposed to and then there I was just standing there like someone had brained me with a frying pan. It's not like I was making a scene. But I couldn't go. The service in the little chapel had totally blown, all that little deacon or whatever he was talked about was God and his mercy and utter unredeemable nonsense that had nothing to do with her so I was just standing there and thinking maybe there was something else that could be said while they put her in the earth, something simple but hopefully specific. Which is when Lucy came up and yanked at my arm.

"Come on," she said. "We have to talk about the house."

And I'm thinking, what house?

So Lucy drags me off to talk about this house, which she and Daniel and Alison clearly had already been deep in conversation about for a while, even though I had never heard of it. Which maybe I might resent? Especially as Daniel obviously has an interest but no real rights, as he is only Alison's husband? But I'm way too busy trying to catch up and get something resembling a shred of information out of them all while we crawl to Manhattan from Hoboken through the Holland Tunnel.

This is what the conversation is like, in the crummy old beige Honda that Daniel insists on driving because even though the thing is ugly it still works:

"The lawyer says that it's completely unencumbered. She died intestate, and that means it's ours, that's what the lawyer says." This from Lucy.

"What lawyer?" I ask.

"Mom's lawyer," she says.

"I have a hard time believing that that is true," Daniel says.

"Why would he lie?" Lucy shoots back at him.

"Why would a lawyer lie? I'm sorry, did you just say—"

"Yes I did. He's *our* lawyer. Why would he lie?"

"You just said he was Mom's lawyer," I point out.

"It's the same thing," she tells me.

"Really?" I say. "I've never even heard of this guy, and I don't know his name, and he's my lawyer?"

"Bill left her his house," Lucy tells me again, staying on point. "And since she died without a will that means it's ours. Mom has left us a house."

This entire chain of events seems strangely impossible to me. I'm always so chronically broke and lost in a kind of underworld of trouble that a stroke of luck like an actual house dropping on my head could only be true if it were literally true, and

2

I was about to find myself like the Wicked Witch of the East squashed to death under somebody *else's* house. Surely this cannot actually mean that. To get to the bottom of it all I continue to repeat things people previously said. "Bill left her his house?"

"Yes! He left her everything!" Lucy snaps.

"Didn't he have kids?"

"Yes, in fact, he did," Daniel pipes up. "He had two sons, two grown sons."

"Well, didn't he leave them something?"

"No, he didn't," Lucy says, firm. Daniel snorts. "What? It's true! He didn't leave them anything!"

"The lawyer said it wouldn't matter whether or not they agreed to the terms of their father's will," Alison notes, looking at Daniel, trying to be hopeful in the face of his inexplicable pessimism about the fact that somebody left us all a house.

"If the lawyer said that, he's a complete moron," Daniel informs her. "I called Ira, he's going to take a look at the documentation and let us know what kind of a mess we're in."

"It's not a mess, it's a house," Lucy notes, sort of under her breath, kind of peevish. She doesn't like Daniel. She thinks he's too bossy. Which he is, considering that we didn't *all* marry him, just Alison.

So we take a left out of the cemetery and go straight to the lawyer's. There was no brunch with distant relatives and people standing around saying trivial mournful things. Which I didn't mind being spared and I don't know that we would have been able to find anybody who knew Mom anyway, but truly I did think that at least the four of us were planning to stop at a diner and have some eggs or a bagel. But not the Finns. We get right down to business. Before noon there we were, squashed around a really small table in a really small conference room in the saddest Manhattan office you ever saw. The walls were a nasty yellow and only half plastered together; seriously, you could see the dents where the Sheetrock was screwed into the uprights. The tabletop was that kind of Formica that vaguely looks like wood, in somebody else's imagination. Honestly, I was thinking, this is a *lawyer's* office? What kind of lawyer? There was an overweight receptionist who wore a pale green sloppy shirt which unfortunately made her look even fatter than she was, and she kept poking her head in, the first time to ask us if we wanted any coffee, and then a couple more times to tell us that Mr Long would be right with us. Then he showed up. His name was Stuart Long, and he looked like an egg. Seriously, the guy had a really handsome face, with a good head of brown hair, and then the rest of him looked like an egg. For a moment it was all I could concentrate on so I was not, frankly, paying full attention when Alison interrupted him in mid-sentence and said, "Can you tell us about the house?"

She's not usually that aggressive, that's more Lucy's turf, but she was so nervous she couldn't stop herself, apparently. "I think we all would just love to hear about the house," she explained, immediately apologetic for having been so tentatively forceful. Daniel put his hand on hers and smiled like he forgave her.

"The house?" said the lawyer, seriously confused for a second. And I thought, Of course, they got it wrong, of course there is no house.

4

"Bill's house. The message you left on our machine said Bill left Mom his house, and that the house would be part of the settlement. You left this, didn't you leave this—"

"Well, I certainly would not have left any details about the settlement on a machine—I spoke to your husband, several times actually. Is that what you mean?"

"Yes, we spoke, and you talked to me about the house," Daniel interrupted, all snotty and impatient, like these details were really beneath him. I could see Lucy kind of stiffen up, because Daniel clearly *had* told her and Alison that he got "a message", when in fact he had been having long conversations with this lawyer which he had no right to have, much less lie about.

"You mean the apartment," Egg Man insisted.

"Yes, the apartment." Daniel was still acting all above it all, like he was the one who had the right to be annoyed.

"So it's not a house," I said.

"No, it's an apartment. Olivia had been living there. Up until her recent death."

"Recent death, that's an understatement," I said.

"Yes, yes, this is I'm sure overwhelming for you," the lawyer said, kind of nicely. He had very good manners, compared to everyone else in the room. "But I take it from your questions that you've never actually seen the apartment?"

"Bill didn't like us," I said. "So we weren't allowed to come over."

"He was reclusive," Alison corrected me. "As I'm sure Mr Long is aware."

"Mom told me he didn't want us to come over, because Bill didn't like us," I said.

"That's ridiculous," said Alison.

"Could we get back to the point?" Lucy said. "What about this house—this apartment? We're inheriting this place, right?"

"Yes, well—the apartment was directly willed to your mother," Egg Man agreed. "Because her death came so close upon her husband's the title was never officially transferred, but that will most likely be considered a technicality."

"But it was her house," Daniel reminded him. He was really stuck on this idea that it was a house.

"Technically it is, as I said, specifically included in the estate," our round lawyer repeated. "Why don't you let me walk you through this?"

"Why don't *you* just tell us how much the place is worth?" Lucy threw in.

Mr Long blinked, but otherwise ignored her poor manners. "Obviously it's not possible to be specific about the worth of the property until we have a professional evaluation," he informed the room.

"You really don't know?" Lucy persisted. "Like, it could be worth ten dollars or ten thousand dollars, or it could be worth a million dollars, but you don't know?"

Before Egg Guy could answer, Daniel tried to rip control of the meeting back to his side of the table. "She's just a little impatient," he explained. "Sweetie, maybe we should let Mr Long—"

Lucy actually rolled her eyes at this. "Just a ballpark, Daniel *sweetie*," she shot back.

Mr Long cleared his throat, clearly uncomfortable. "Well, I guess I could—"

"Yes, why don't you," I said, trying to be nice because frankly

6

I was starting to feel a little embarrassed that they were acting like this. Also, like everyone else in the room, I really wanted him to give up a number. "Just a ballpark," I said, smiling with as much adorable charm as I could muster under the circumstances. I thought Lucy was going to gag, but it did the trick.

"A ballpark. A *ball*park," he said, smiling back at me. "I don't know. Eleven million?"

There was a big fat silence at this.

"Eleven million?" I said. "Eleven million what?" I swear I know that sounds stupid, but what on earth was he talking about? Eleven million pesos?

"Eleven million dollars," he clarified. "That is of course almost a random number, there's no way really of knowing. But it is twelve rooms, with a view of Central Park, on a very good block. I think eleven million would be considered conservative. In terms of estimates."

So then there was a lot more talk, yelling even, people getting quite heated and worried over things that hadn't happened and might not be happening but maybe were happening and had happened already, and the solution, apparently, to all these things that no one understood was for me, Tina, to move into that big old eleven million dollar apartment, like right away, like that very day.

So it was complicated, how that happened? But that's where I ended up.

CHAPTER ONE

This is the thing you have to understand about these big old apartments in New York City: they are more completely astonishing than you ever thought they might be, even in your wildest hopes. When you walk by them, like, just walking along the edge of Central Park at sunset, and you look up at the little golden windows blazing and you think Oh My God those apartments must be mind-blowing, who on earth could possibly be so lucky that they get to live in one of those apartments? My mother and her husband were two of those people, and they lived in an apartment so huge and beautiful it was beyond imagining. Ceilings so high they made you feel like you were in a cathedral, or a forest. Light fixtures so big and far away and strangely shaped that they looked like bugs were crawling out of them. Mirrors in crumbling gilt frames that had little cherubs falling off the top; clocks from three different centuries, none of which worked. So many turns in the hallways, leading to so many different dark rooms, that you thought maybe you had stumbled into a dwarf's diamond mine. The place was also, quite frankly, covered in mustard-colored wall-to-wall shag carpet, and the walls in one of the bathrooms were papered with some sort of inexplicable silver-spotted stuff that you couldn't figure out where that shit even came from, plus there was actual moss growing on the fixtures in the kitchen, no kidding, *moss*. But none of that was in any way relevant. The place was fantastic.

There was nobody there to let us in—we had to let ourselves in, with the keys that the nice round lawyer handed over, telling us about six different times that he didn't think it was "necessary" that we take immediate ownership. Seriously, he was so worried about the whole idea—that I would just up and move into this huge old empty apartment where my mother had died—that he kept repeating himself, in a sort of sad murmur, "There's no need to rush into anything. Really. You must all be overwhelmed. Let me walk you through this."

"But you said there might be some question, about the will," Daniel reminded him.

"No, no question—well, no question about Mr Drinan's will. Your mother, as you know, does not seem to have left a will," he pointed out, trying to drag us all back into this nonsense. But now that the words "eleven million" had come out of his mouth, none of us were listening.

"We'd really like to just get a look at the place," Daniel announced.

"Before we lose the light," Lucy said.

Sometimes I am amazed when she pulls out lines like that. She just says this stuff like she really means it even though she already said maybe a second ago that we needed to get over there and get Tina moved in so that it was clear right away that we were taking ownership because if there was going to be any contention or cloud on the title we would need to have already established a proprietary right to the property. She's not even a lawyer; that's just the way her brain works. She figures out the meanest truth, gets it out there, deals with it, and then a second later pretends that really what is worrying her is some weird thing about the light. It's spectacularly nervy and impressive. And maybe Daniel doesn't like it, because Alison is the oldest, which means in his imagination that they should be calling the shots? But as I already noted, he just married into this situation, and there is no way around how smart Lucy is.

I, meanwhile, am the problem child who doesn't get a vote. This is the reason, I guess, they don't explain anything to me. Why bother? She's caused too many problems; she doesn't get a vote anymore. Even when it comes down to the question of where is Tina going to live, Tina doesn't get to vote. I didn't care. The truth is I didn't have anything better to do anyway than let my sisters move me into my dead mom's gigantic apartment on Central Park West. At the time, I was living in a trailer park, for God's sake, cleaning rich people's houses out by the Delaware Water Gap. I didn't even have a bank account because I couldn't afford the monthly fees and I had to borrow the fifty bucks for the bus to the funeral from my stupid ex-boyfriend Darren whose bright idea it was to move out there to that lousy trailer park in the first place. Oh well, the less said about the whole Delaware Water Gap fiasco the better, as it was not my smartest or most shining hour. So when Lucy leaned back in her chair and said, "We probably should take ownership right away, just to be safe. Tina can stay there," I wasn't about to put up a fight. Move into a palace—why not?

So we got the keys, crawled through traffic to the Upper West Side, actually found a meter four blocks away from the promised land, and there we were, before the light was gone, while the sun was setting and making those windows glow. The building itself was huge, a kind of murky dark brown with the occasional purple brick stuck in the mix. Above, strange and gloomy gargoyles snarled at everyone from the cornices three stories up. Two gargoyles guarded the entryway as well, on either side, serious-minded eagles with the tails of lions. While they didn't look like they were kidding around they also didn't look like they intended to eat you or spit molten lava at you, with the ones higher up, you were not quite so sure. Plus there were actual gas lamps, the old Victorian ones, burning by the heads of the eagle lions, and another one of those gas lamps, a really mammoth one, hung dead center over the door, right above a huge word in Gothic type that said EDGEWOOD. In fact all of the windows on the first two floors had additional scroll-work and carving and additional inexplicable Latin words inscribed over them. It all added up into a kind of castle-type Victorian abode that was quite friendly while simultaneously seeming like the kind of place you'd never come out of alive.

The foyer of this place was predictably spectacular. Marble floors, dotted with some kind of black stone tiles for effect, vaulted ceilings and the biggest crystal chandelier you've ever seen in your life. A huge black chair which I later found out was carved out of pure ebony sat right in front of an equally enormous fireplace, and improbably, the chair actually had wings.

12

Two more of the giant eagle-like lions stood on either side of the fireplace, which was filled with an enormous sort of greenery arrangement I later found out was plastic but which was convincing and impressive nonetheless. The doorman's station, a nice little brass stand piled with FedEx packages and a couple of manila envelopes piled on top of it, was empty. And then behind that there was a tiny bank of two elevators.

"Wow," I said. "Check out the chair with wings."

"We'll have time for that later," Lucy told me, giving me a little shove toward the elevators.

"We should wait for the doorman, shouldn't we?" I said, looking around. The place was deserted.

"Why? We live here," Lucy announced, pushing the elevator button, pressing her lips together, like don't mess with me. She kept tapping at that stupid button, as impatient as Moses whacking the rock, like that might hurry up God instead of just pissing him off.

"Seriously, we can't just go up there," I said. The whole situation suddenly seemed so dicey to me. Alison started pushing the elevator button too, pressing it really hard. Both of them were in such a rush, like rushing through all this would be what made it okay; it was just like Darren and the whole Delaware Water Gap Story—things happen too fast and you end up stuck out in the middle of nowhere with a complete shithead and a shitload of trouble. I was just about to hopelessly attempt to explain this to my two sisters when the elevator dinged and Daniel swung open the outer door.

"You guys, come on," I said. "We should wait for the doorman."

13

"Who knows where he is?" Daniel said. "We're not waiting."

And since no one showed up to stop us, I got in.

According to the set of keys the egglike lawyer had given us, Mom's apartment was number 8A so we took the elevator to the eighth floor, where it disgorged us on a tiny, horrible little landing. Green fluorescent lighting flickered from an old strip light and didn't make anyone look good, and the speckled linoleum tiles on the floor and Venetian blinds were so old and cracked and dusty even a hapless loser such as myself would have to find it offensive. The door to 8A was triple locked, so it took Lucy a long minute to figure out how to work all the keys. I was in a little bit of a bad mood by this time. I really did think we should have waited to at least tell the stupid doorman we were there, and I was worried about what might happen if a total stranger showed up and said, "Hey! What are you doing?" There was one other door, just behind the two elevators, which had been painted a kind of sad brown maybe a hundred years ago, and next to it another door, painted a gorgeous pearly grey, with heavy brass fixings which announced "8B". The 8A on our door was just a couple of those gold and black letters that you buy in the hardware store that have sticky stuff on the back. It made you wonder all of a sudden: Eleven million dollars? For this dump? Which in fact had not even crossed my mind, up to this point.

And then Lucy figured out the locks, and there was a little click, and then a sort of a breeze, and the door to the apartment swung open.

You couldn't tell how big that place was right away. The blinds were drawn and obviously nobody knew where the switches

14

were, so we all stepped tentatively into the gloom. It smelled, too, a sort of funny old people smell, not like someone died in there, but more like camphor, and dried paper, and mothballs. And then somewhere far off, in with the mothballs, there was something else that smelled like old flowers, and jewelry, and France.

"Hey, Mom's perfume," I said.

"What?" said Lucy, who had wandered into the next room, looking for a light switch in there.

"Don't you smell Mom's perfume?" I asked. It seemed unmistakable to me that that's what it was, even though she hardly ever wore the stuff because it was so ridiculously expensive. My dad gave it to her on their wedding night, and they could never afford it again so she only wore it once every three years or so when he had an actual job and they got to go to some cocktail party, and we would watch her put her one black dress on, and the clip-on earrings with the sparkles, and the smallest little bit of the most expensive perfume in the world. Who knows if it really was the most expensive in the world, I rather doubt it, but that's what she told us. Anyway there it was, way back in that huge apartment, lost in with a bunch of mothballs, the smell of my mother when she was happy.

"It's that perfume. What was the name of that stuff?" I asked, taking another step in. I loved that apartment already, so dark and big and strange, with my mother's perfume hiding in it like a secret. "Don't you smell it?"

"No," said Alison, running her hand up the wall, like a blind person looking for a doorway. "I don't."

Maybe I was making it up. There were a lot of smells in

15

there, in the dark. Mostly I think it smelled like time had just stopped. And then Daniel found the light switch, and turned it on, and there was the smallest golden glow from high up near the ceiling, you could barely see anything because the room was so big, but what you could see was, of course, that time actually *had* stopped there. Somewhere between 1857 and 1960, things had happened and then just somehow stopped happening. The ceiling was high and far away with sealike coves around the corners, and right in the middle of this enormous lake of a ceiling there was the strangest of old chandeliers, glued together out of what looked like iron filings, with things dripping and crawling out of it. It seemed to have been poorly wired, because it only had three working fake-candle 15-watt bulbs, which is why it gave off so little light. And then on the floor there was this mustard-colored shag carpeting, which I believe I have mentioned before, and then there was like one chair, in the corner. It was a pretty big chair, but seriously, it was one chair.

"What a dump," said Daniel.

"Could we not piss on this before we've even seen it, Daniel?" called Lucy, from the kitchen. But she said it friendly, not edgy. She was having a pretty good time, I think.

Alison was not. She kept pawing at the wall. "Is this all the light? There has to be another light switch somewhere," she said, sounding all worried.

"Here, I've got one," said Lucy, throwing a switch in the kitchen. It didn't really do much because the kitchen was a whole separate room with a big fat wall in front of it, so then there was just a little doorway-sized window of light that didn't actually make it very far into the living room, or parlour, whatever you wanted to call this giant space.

"Oh that's a *big* help," said Alison.

"Wow, this kitchen is a mess. You should see this!" yelled Lucy. "Oh God, there's something growing in here."

"That's not funny," Alison snapped.

"No kidding," Lucy called back, banging things around in there in a kind of sudden, alarming frenzy. "No kidding, there's something growing—ick, it's moving! It's moving! No wait—never mind, never mind."

"I am in no mood, Lucy! This is ridiculous. Daniel! Where are you? Tina, where did you go? Where is everybody! Could we all stay in one place please? *Daniel.*" Alison suddenly sounded like a total nut. It's something that happens to her, she just gets more and more worked up, and she truly doesn't know how to stop it once it gets going. No one is quite sure why Daniel married her, as he's pretty good looking and seriously could have done a lot better. Not that Alison is mean or stupid; she's just sort of high strung in a way that is definitely trying. Anyway, right about now was when that apartment literally started to drive her crazy. She kept slapping the wall, looking for another light switch, and Daniel was just ignoring how scared she was; he was heading all the way across that gigantic room into the gloom on the other side, where that one chair sat, next to a big hole in the wall. Well, it wasn't a hole; it was a hallway. But from where we all stood it looked like a hole, and the sloping black shadow that used to be Daniel was about to disappear right down it.

"Daniel, just wait, could you wait please?" Alison yelled, completely panicked now. "I cannot see where you are going!"

17

"It's fine, Alison," he said, sounding like a bastard, just before he disappeared.

"Daniel, WAIT!" she yelled, almost crying now.

"Here, Alison," I said, and I pulled open one of the blinds.

And then we were all showered with light. This incredible gold and red light shot through the window and hit every wall in that room, making everything glow and move; the sun was going down so the light was cutting through the branches of the bare trees, which were shifting in the wind. So that big old room went from being all weird and dreary to being something else altogether, and it skipped everything in between.

"Wow," I said.

"Yes, thank you, that's much better," Alison nodded, looking around, still anxious as shit. "Although that isn't going to be much help when the sun is gone."

"Is it going somewhere?" I asked.

"It's going *down*, and then what will you do? Because that chandelier gives off no light whatsoever, it's worse than useless, all the way up there. You'd think they'd have had some area lamps in a room this size."

"You'd think they'd have had some *furniture* in a room this size," I observed.

"Okay, I don't know what that stuff is, that's growing in the kitchen," Lucy announced, barging into the giant empty parlour, now filled with the light of the dying day. "But it's kind of disgusting in there. We're going to have this whole place professionally cleaned before we put it on the market, and even that might not be enough, it might be, oh God, who knows what that stuff is. And it's everywhere. On the counters,

18

in the closets. Who knows what's in the refrigerator. I was afraid to look."

"There's really something growing?" I asked. Her dire pronouncements were having the opposite effect on me; the worse she made it sound the more I wanted to see it. I slid over to the doorway just to take a peek.

"Is it mold?" Alison asked, her level of panic starting to rev up again. "Because that could ruin everything. This place will be useless, worse than useless, if there's mold. It costs millions to get rid of that stuff."

"It doesn't cost *millions,*" Lucy countered.

"A serious mold problem in an exclusive building, that's millions."

"You've never had any kind of mold problem in any building, Alison. You don't know anything about it," Lucy informed her.

"I know that if the rest of the building finds out, they could sue us," Alison shot back. "We would be the responsible parties, if mold in this apartment made anybody in the building sick. It could be making us sick, right now."

"Let's not get ahead of ourselves," Lucy said, looking at me and rolling her eyes. Seriously, everybody rolls their eyes at Alison behind her back, even if she might be right. She's just so irredeemably uptight.

"Holy shit," I said, finally getting a good look at the kitchen.

"What, is it bad? It's bad, isn't it?"

"No, no, it's not that bad," I lied. The whole kitchen was green. Or, at least, most of it. "And I don't think it's mold. I think it's moss."

19

"Moss doesn't grow inside apartments," Alison hissed. "We have to go now. We have to leave immediately, it will make us all sick. It's probably what killed Mom, truth be told."

"Mom died of a heart attack," I reminded her.

"We have to leave now, before we all get sick. *Daniel. We have to go.*"

"There's another apartment back here!" Daniel yelled.

"What?" said Lucy, heading after him into the black hallway.

"There's a whole second apartment, like another kitchen and another living room or parlour—there's like six bedrooms and two dining rooms!" he yelled.

"How can there be two dining rooms?" Lucy muttered. And then she disappeared. I looked at Alison, who was standing very still, her arms down at her sides. I completely did not want to contribute any extra fuel to the coming conflagration. But I did want to see the rest of that apartment.

"It'll be okay, Alison," I said. "It's not mold. It's moss! And Mom died of a heart attack. Let's go see the rest of this place. It sounds awesome." Realizing that I sounded like an utter fool now, I bolted.

But the place *was* awesome. The hallway was dark and twisty, and there were rooms everywhere, which all hooked onto other rooms and then hooked back to that twisty hallway further down. Seriously, you sort of never knew where you were, and then you were someplace you had gone through six rooms ago, but you didn't know how you got back there at all. And while some of those rooms were as empty and lonely as that giant room at the front of the apartment, some of the others were cozy and interesting; one was painted a weird shade of pink

20

that I had never seen before, with no furniture but with framed pictures of flowers all over the walls, except for one wall that had like the most gigantic mirror on it that you have ever seen in your life. No kidding, you thought that room was six times as big as it was because of that mirror and then you also jumped because as soon as you walked in you thought someone else was there with you but it wasn't someone else, it was just you. Another room had little bitty beds that were like only six inches off the ground, and there were these old crazy solar system stickers stuck on the ceiling. One of the walls had a giant sunset painted on it, someone had actually painted a picture of the sun setting over the ocean, right on the wall itself. One room was painted dark purple, and there were stars on that ceiling too, and a little bitty chandelier that had glass moons and suns hanging from it. There was no furniture in that room either.

Twelve rooms is a lot of rooms. It's something I had never thought about; twelve is such a low two-digit number it's almost a one-digit number, and so you think in general that twelve of anything is frankly not all that many. But twelve rooms is actually so many, it seems almost to be the same as a hundred rooms. That apartment felt like it went on forever, before I got to the second kitchen and two dining rooms, which is where Lucy and Daniel had ended up and were figuring things out.

"This is where they lived," Lucy observed, looking around.

She was right; it was the first thing you noticed. There was actual furniture in these rooms, a couple of chairs and a couch that stood across from a television set, and a coffee table with a clicker and some dirty plates on it. On one side of this room there was the so-called "second kitchen" but it was really more

21

kind of a half-kitchen dinette sort of space. It had the smallest sink imaginable, a very skinny refrigerator and an old electric stove top and a tiny oven, all jammed right on top of each other. It was kind of doll-sized, frankly, but at least it wasn't covered in moss. And then on the other side of this TV room/kitchen area kind of thing, there was an archway through which you could see an old bed, with two little bedside tables, and a chair that someone had thrown some dirty clothes on. The bed wasn't made.

"Jesus," I said, and I sat down. Compared to the rest of that great apartment, this little TV/bedroom/kitchen space seemed stupidly ordinary. So of course this would be where they lived. They lived in the most amazing apartment ever, except they just holed up in the back of it, and pretended they lived in a sort of boring normal place like the rest of us. It was overwhelming. Alison, arriving behind me, took a step forward.

"Look," she said, pointing to the coffee table. "Fish sticks. She was having fish sticks, when she died."

"Oh, for crying out loud," said Lucy, and she reached over, grabbed the plate and turned back to the tiny kitchenette, where she proceeded to bang through the cabinet doors.

"What are you looking for now?" I sighed, laying down on the hideous couch. I could hardly keep my head up, at this point.

"It's disgusting," she snapped. "That's just been sitting there for days. I can't believe no one cleaned it up."

"Who would clean it up?" I asked.

"Someone, I don't know who. Who found her? Wasn't it a neighbor? What did they do, just let the EMS people pick up the body and then just leave the place like this, just dishes and food left out in the open? It's disgusting. It could attract bugs, or mice." Lucy started looking under the teeny little sink for a garbage can. "Oh God, if there are mice I'm just going to kill myself," she muttered. "It's going to cost a fortune to take care of that mold issue; I do *not* want to have to deal with exterminators."

"Relax," Daniel told her, turning slowly and taking it all in with a kind of speculative grimace. "We won't have to do a thing. What'd he say, eleven million? This place is worth more than that, as is. With mold and mice and fish sticks on dirty plates and a shitty economy. This place is worth a fortune. We won't have to do a thing."

"Oh, well," said Alison, apparently having something approximating a philosophical moment. "She had a good life."

"She had a shitty life," I said.

"Look, there's actually some things in the freezer," Lucy announced, swinging open the refrigerator door, and moving on. "Some hamburgers and frozen vegetables. The ice cube maker seems to work . . . plenty of food. You'll be all right at least for the next couple of days, then we'll have to spring for some groceries I'm guessing, because you are, as usual, completely broke, is that the story?"

"That's the story." I shrugged. "Look, seriously, Lucy, maybe we should wait a day. For me to move in? So that we have time to like tell the building super and stuff, so they know I'm here?"

"There's no reason you shouldn't move in right now," Lucy said. "You need a place to stay, my place is too small and so is Daniel and Alison's. Where else are you going to go? By your own account you can hardly afford a hotel room."

"This is—it's just—"

"It's our apartment. Why not stay here?"

There was a *why not*, obviously; there was a good reason to slow things down, but not one of us had any inclination to mention it. Even me. You split eleven million dollars three ways, even after taxes? Every single one of us suddenly has a whole new life. I'm fairly certain that was the sum total of all the thinking that was going on in that apartment when they handed the keys over to me, and told me to sit tight.

CHAPTER TWO

I can't say that I was sorry to see them go when they finally left.

The first thing I did was take my boots off. Alison would have thrown a fit if she saw me do it. She had already managed to moan about how dirty the place was and who knows what was lurking in that crummy shag rug, like I think she thought there might be bed bugs or worms or slime from distant centuries just oozing through it all, waiting for some idiot's bare foot to come in contact so it could spread fungal disaster into your system. She really has that kind of imagination; sometimes talking to her is like talking to someone who writes horror films for a living. But I didn't care; my toes were so hot and tired by that point and I just felt like being flat on my feet before I started checking the place out. As it turns out the carpet was kind of dry and it seemed clean enough, just a little scratchy. It really was a pretty hideous color but I think that honestly is the worst that could be said about it.

By then the sun actually *had* gone away, as predicted, so

I didn't have a lot of light to explore the place with. I decided to just head back to the boring little area where Mom and Bill had more or less camped out, and then I slipped out of the one dark blue skirt I had brought for the funeral, pulled on the jeans I had stashed in my backpack, and took a look around. Lucy had already cased the refrigerator so I knew there were fish sticks. A little more casual probing in the cabinets yielded something like sixteen packets of ramen noodles; and then I noticed that on the teeny tiny counter there was half a bottle of wine, open and useless, next to three empties. The search continued, and sure enough, when I poked around the laundry room—which was right behind that little kitchenette—there was a pile of clothes on the floor which really looked like nothing until you nudged it with your foot and found that it was stacked on top of two mostly full cases of red wine. So I was feeling so good about that, I just kept looking, and wouldn't you know, I hit the mother lode: Up in the freezer of that little refrigerator, back behind the ice cube machine, there was a huge bottle of vodka, with hardly a dent in it.

Knowing my mother I also knew that would not be the only bottle out there. She liked to have it in reach, so I was pretty sure I'd find something squirreled away in several other thinly disguised hiding places. By the looks of the two cases of pricey red wine, Bill was also a bit of a drinker himself, so for a second I did think, well, at least she finally hooked up with someone who could pay for the good stuff, as opposed to the truly undrinkable crap she was surviving on the rest of her life. Seriously, I felt a little better about their utterly inexplicable marriage when I saw all the bottles. Which I'm not saying drinking yourself into an early grave is a good thing? But on the other hand, I honestly don't see much point in judging the dead.

Anyway, in the door of the refrigerator I also found a half a jar of ruby red grapefruit juice, which meant I could have an actual cocktail instead of trying to down the vodka straight or over melted ice. So I made myself a drink, put the water on to boil for the noodles and turned the television on for company. They only had basic cable so I found one of those stations that runs endless documentaries all the time and started to look around.

The bedroom was not really a bedroom, even though there was a bed in there. There were huge pocket doors which were clearly meant to shut the room off, but they had been left open for so long they were stuck on their rails. Another set of enormous pocket doors made up the entire wall on the other side of the room, but they were stuck closed and the bed was shoved up against them. Then there was a little cove that had been built into one wall, with fancy plasterwork up the sides and a crown at the top. That had a little dresser in it. Other than that there were no closets—just clothes everywhere on the floor— which in addition to the huge pocket doors made it clear that this room was not in fact ever meant to be a bedroom, and was more likely intended as a dining area. Daniel had said that there were two dining rooms but I don't think there *were* two, I think this bedroom was really the dining room, and the room behind it with the television was supposed to be the original kitchen, and the servants would cook back there and then come in with the food, through the pocket doors, which presumably opened and closed at some previous point in history. Well, honestly, I had no idea what was supposed to be what in this crazy apartment in the other century when it was built. But that's what I thought.

I also thought, I wonder where Mom's perfume is? Because back in that sort of freaky half-bedroom-half-dining room you smelled it everywhere; it was in all the clothes and the blankets and the sheets, along with the red wine and the cigarettes and dirty laundry and mothballs. I kind of had it in my head that I might find that little black bottle and snag it before Lucy turned it into some big issue for no reason whatsoever. Seriously, you just never knew when she was going to get all twitchy and start making lists and arguing about everything, and Alison sometimes goes along with that shit just because in general it's not really worth arguing with Lucy. Then the next thing you know, Lucy's telling everybody that we have to put everything smaller than a paperback into a box and sell it all together because that's the only way to be fair, and then she's handing it over to some thrift store for ten dollars or something, not even enough to buy a pizza. It made no sense to me to let Lucy try something like that, so I started looking. I was pretty sure if I found that little bottle first I could stick it in my backpack and no one would ever know.

The first place I checked was the dresser in the alcove. It seemed to me that that was probably the only place where Mom might have put anything of value to her; the rest of the room really was nothing but piles of clothes, a chair, a couple of books on the floor, and the unmade bed. Besides, the dresser really did look like she might have been using it as a vanity; there was an old gilt mirror glued to the wall above it, with the feet of half a cherub hanging down from the top. The top of the dresser had a few things on it—a hairbrush, a comb, a couple of empty glasses with some dry little well of alcohol stuck to the bottom. Then there was a completely tarnished little round silver boxlike thing, with curlicues and a big French fleur-de-lis right on top that when you opened it there were a whole bunch of keys and an old wedding ring and three little bitty medals inside. One of them said CHEMISTRY on it. In addition to the round silver box there were a couple of really old photographs in really old frames of no one I knew, and then there were a couple photographs unframed, behind them, with the edges curling toward the middle. One of them was of me, when I was about fifteen and going on the first of many disastrous dates with Ed Featherstone. He was a mighty jerk, but at fifteen who knew? But seriously it is a bit of a shock to see yourself seventeen years ago, with your arms around someone who is now seventeen years older and who made a fortune on Wall Street back when everyone was doing that, got out while the getting was good and now owns lots of property in Connecticut. Whatever. I set aside the can of keys, which I thought might be useful for future exploration, and then I looked in the drawers.

The top drawer had her underwear in it, lots of sad bras and panties, several old pairs of neutral-colored support hose, and a quart bottle of good vodka. Then in the other drawer, just beneath it, was Bill's underwear, gigantic pairs of white and light blue cotton briefs. I so did not want to go pawing through that stuff—I mean, really, I wanted to find that little bottle of perfume because I wanted to have it and honestly I didn't think anyone else would want it, but I was quickly losing my nerve. I had never even met this nutty alcoholic; who knew what lurked in his underwear? Rather than just give up, I pulled the drawer all the way out of the dresser and upended it. There was nothing in there except all those huge pairs of underwear, and a wallet.

A wallet; there was a wallet, and the guy who owned it was dead, and everything he owned got left to my mom, who left everything she owned to me and my sisters. I figured that gave me some rights, so I sat on the floor and looked through it, and lo and behold there were three receipts from a liquor store, a couple more pictures of people I didn't know, and a lot of money. A serious wad of money, the bills smooth and neatly pressed together, like they give it to you at the bank, if you are the sort of person that a bank will actually give money to. So I thought, Oh thank God, and I took it out to count it and those crispy new bills were all fifties and hundreds; Bill had seven hundred dollars in that wallet, which would I think be a significant windfall to pretty much anybody, but was a virtual miracle to a person of my limited means. I pocketed the cash.

When I leaned over to sort of half-scoop the now empty wallet and all that underwear back into the drawer I also happened to notice the no-man's-land under the bed, which was crowded with boxes. These turned out to be really hard to get to, because they all were just a little bit too big for the space which meant they were really squashed in there. They also each weighed a ton, as I discovered, since they were full of used paperbacks, most of them mysteries. After about twenty minutes of dragging those boxes out of there I was ready to completely give up, until I got to the very last box, which was up by the headboard on the far side of the bed. That one was not full of books. It was full of junk, a crummy handbag, a little red change purse, two pairs of reading glasses, and an old cedar jewelry box filled with fake pearls and junky necklaces, another quart-sized bottle of vodka, nearly empty, and a tiny bottle of French perfume.

It looked just the way I remembered it, pitch black, and shaped like a heart. The ghost of the word *Joy* ran across one side, in elegant gold letters. And then of course, as much as I wanted it, it suddenly just seemed unbearably awful to me. That perfume started with her at the beginning of her past, when she thought that lots of glamorous things were in store for her. I know that's why she was so careful with it; she was waiting for her life to be as exciting as that bottle of perfume, and the closest she ever got was a couple of cocktail parties with my father, who hardly ever had a job, and whose temper was the bane of her existence. I tipped the bottle to one side, trying to figure out how much perfume was still in there, after thirty-seven years. It was impossible to say.

It was not, of course, until this very moment that it occurred to me that I had left a pan full of water boiling this whole time on the stove top. Which I have done several times in the past, in different apartments, to more or less disastrous results, so I jolted myself out of this mournful and useless reverie and ran back to that lousy kitchenette, where I put more water on to boil, then made another cocktail, cooked up some noodles, had another drink, watched the end of a documentary about Egypt, and had a good cry. Then I thought about just passing out on that couch in front of the television set, which seemed like a really poor idea, because that is the sort of thing that leads one to think one might actually be an alcoholic like one's mother which was a thought I didn't particularly want to entertain that night. So then I stood up, definitely wobbly, but didn't judge myself because Mom was dead and I was feeling hideous, and then I thought about climbing into her bed, and that was just not an option, so then I wandered back through that maze of rooms until I found the one with the stars and planets on the ceiling and the little beds on the floor, and one of those beds was made up with a couple of pillows and a kind of a kid's coverlet that was dark blue with rocket ships all over it. And then I slid off my jeans and got under that cover and I cried a little more, and then I went to sleep.

"Who the fuck are you?"

That's the next thing I remember. Two guys standing in the doorway, staring at me. One of them had flipped on the overhead light, so I could see there were two of them, two fucking huge guys, staring at me sleeping in that little bed on the floor of that little room.

"What?" I said, blinking. "What?"

"Answer the fucking question. Who the fuck are you, and what the fuck are you doing here?" The first guy, the one standing inside the room with his hand on the light switch, was drunk. You could tell that right away.

"What time is it?" I said. I didn't know what else to say. And I really wanted to know what time it was. I was completely confused.

"Who gives a fuck what time it is? Who the fuck are you?" the first guy said again.

"Shit," I said. Which, it may not have been the brightest thing to say? But this guy was scaring me.

"Answer the fucking question. And get out of that bed. Get up. Get up!" Now he was barking orders and it was totally freaking me out. I was still blinking and trying to wake up and figure out what time it was and how much of a hangover I had, and this huge guy was reaching over to grab me. Honestly, I remember thinking, what a fucking drag. I'm in a total mess again and this time it isn't even my fault; me staying here was Lucy's dumb idea, I was just doing what Lucy wanted, and here I am now in a total fucking mess. I squeezed myself back against the wall, ducked my head down and threw my arm across my face because it was taking me so long to wake up and I was scared. Oh what a drag, I thought, what a complete hideous drag.

"Stop it, Pete. You're scaring her," said the other guy.

"Good. I want to scare her. Breaking and entering is a fucking crime, she should be scared," said Pete, still coming at me, like he was going to drag me out of that bed.

"I didn't break and enter, excuse me, *excuse me* but do you think I could put my pants on?" I yelled. "Get away from me, JESUS BACK OFF YOU JERK." I smacked Pete's hand away before he could touch me, and surprisingly he actually did back off. Feeling suddenly cocky I continued yelling. "Turn around, would you please TURN AROUND?"

Okay, why this worked I have no idea, but it did; both of these guys did as they were told. I mean I was freaked out because seriously these were two huge guys, both of them maybe six two or six four and I'm a little bit of a peewee so I totally

33

did not expect them to do as I said. But they did so I grabbed my jeans off the floor and slid them on fast. Being half naked was not going to be an advantage in whatever this situation turned out to be, that much was certain.

"Who the fuck are you guys?" I said, trying to sound angry and sure of myself. I was totally scared out of my mind so I had to keep the upper hand as long as I could.

"We're the ones asking questions here," Pete started. "I hope you're dressed because that's as much privacy as you're going to get." He turned around just as I finished zipping up my pants, and when I looked up I noticed that he was taking a hit off a beer bottle. No question: they both were tanked. This was a very bad situation. "So what's your name?" he demanded.

"I don't have to tell you my name. You tell me your name," I said.

"You're sleeping in my fucking bed, so yeah, you do have to tell me your name," Pete countered.

"Forget it. Let's just call the police," said the other guy.

"I am the police," Pete told him, annoyed. "You can't call the police when the police are already here."

"Well, who cares who she is?" asked the other guy. "Just get her out of here." He looked back toward the back of the apartment, like he knew what was back there and it made him sad. Pete looked like he wanted to argue about this, but then all of a sudden he was too tired to do it, so he looked back at me and reached out again, like he was going to grab me. I backed up. He didn't get mad this time, though, he just moved his hand, like that little gesture that means, *Come on, let's go.*

And that's what he said. "Come on, let's go. I don't know

34

how you got here and I don't care. Count yourself lucky. Just get lost." He wasn't even looking at me by now, he was half following the other guy, who had already headed down the hall. He took a hit off his beer, looking totally wiped and also like all he really cared about was finishing the one beer and finding another. Now that he wasn't screaming at me I could see that he was not bad looking; he needed a shave, and he was a little paunchy around the middle, but he had great eyes, dark brown, kind of shrewd and sad, which made his whole face look like a worried kid, even while he was being mean. Under the circumstances obviously I wasn't falling for it, plus, I truly didn't get what was supposedly going on here. These guys had barged in and woken me up maybe a minute ago. And now what, I was supposed to leave? Who the fuck did they think they were? I mean obviously I was grateful in the moment that they didn't turn out to be rapists, but after the initial terror some sense of reality was setting in. What the hell?

"I'm not going anywhere," I told Pete. "This is my apartment. I live here. And and and I think it's a good idea to call the cops because you're the ones who what the fuck are *you* doing here? Who the fuck are *you*?"

"You *live* here?" he said. "You live here?"

"Yes," I said. "This is my apartment. I own it."

"You own it?" he replied, taking a step back and calling down the hall. "Hey Doug! Get back here! This chick says she owns this place!" He turned and looked back at me, angry again, but in a calmer, nastier way. He also seemed to find my claim, that I owned the apartment, sort of quietly hilarious. He took a step back into that teeny bedroom. "Maybe you should tell me your name after all, sweetheart."

"I don't, I don't—you tell me *your* name," I insisted. I shoved my hands into the back pockets of my jeans and felt the hard edge of those bills I had stashed there. I was glad I had taken the precaution of pocketing that stuff right when I found it; it was starting to look like I might need it sooner rather than later. "I mean this is like my house and you're like, you're like . . ."

"Your house?" said Pete, half laughing. "Your house. That would make you—what was your name again?"

"Tina Finn?" I said. Okay I shouldn't have caved like that, making my name a question at the last minute, but it just wasn't so easy, keeping up the act that I was on top of this situation.

"Tina *Finn*," he said, smiling now. "Tina Finn. One of the daughters of Olivia Finn. Would I be too far off the mark, assuming that?"

"Yeah, actually, she was my mom, and she just died two days ago, and and and—"

"Yesterday was the funeral."

"Yes, *yesterday* was the *funeral*."

"Yesterday was the funeral, and you still managed to slime your way into our apartment the same night. How very resourceful of you." This was a creepy guy, smart and wily and drunk and way too fucking good looking. He was the kind of guy who knew he could get away with complete shit, and say and do completely shitty things because he *was* both great looking and smart. I wanted to get away from this guy as fast as I could, but I couldn't give any more ground, none at all. If I did, there was no question I was going to be kicked out of there, and where was I supposed to go?

"Okay, you got my name, how about you give up yours?" I said. "Somebody Drinan, yeah? Pete, that's your first name? So that makes you Pete Drinan. Bill was your dad?"

"Give the little lady a prize," he smirked.

"Well, listen, Pete Drinan," I said. "I'm not going anywhere tonight. Now that you know who I am, maybe you should just piss off."

"Maybe you should stop thinking you have any rights here."

"Maybe you should stop thinking I don't."

"And what gives you rights again? Your mother conned my father into marrying her, which gave her rights for a while, I guess, but you, I'm guessing not so much."

"He left her this place. That doesn't give me no rights," I said.

"Really," he said back, like what I said just meant nothing. He took another hit off that beer.

"Yeah, really," I said. "He left it to her, and she left it to us."

None of this seemed surprising to old Pete Drinan, but it didn't seem like he was totally familiar with the story either. He made that little wave with his hand again, like, *Let's go.*

"I'm not leaving," I said. "I don't have to leave."

"Well, that's debatable, but I'm not asking you to leave. Hey Doug!" he yelled, heading down the hallway toward the back of the apartment. "Listen to this!" Then he yelled back to me again, without even turning around. "Come on, Tina Finn, I think it would be really great for you to explain this situation to my big brother. Come on."

What a jerk, I thought, and boy does he know how to order people around. I followed him back to television land, to see what fresh hell this great-looking asshole was about to cook up for me.

His older brother was sitting on that sad little couch, in front of the television set, sort of slumped over, looking at the empty bowl of noodles and the half-empty glass of vodka and grapefruit juice. He glanced up when I entered, and I got a better look at him this time; he had the same pair of tired, smart brown eyes as his little brother, but they didn't scare me as much for some reason. It might have been the rest of his face; his mouth was thinner, and kind of kept in one line, like it was so used to being disappointed all the time it didn't even bother, anymore, to find another shape. His hair was thinning, too; I could see the beginnings of a bald spot dead center on the top of his head, and he had one of those hairlines that has crept so far up the dude just looks startled all the time. So somehow Doug Drinan managed to look shrewd, old, startled and disappointed. It happens to some people, I guess.

"There's hardly any furniture left," he observed, kind of to no one. "I wonder what he did with it all. You think he sold it? He must've sold it, but why?" It sounded like what it was: a very good question. Pete was on his own track, though. He turned to me and tipped his head, like I was some kind of circus animal he could order around with these little gestures.

"Tell my brother your name," he said, all arrogant and smug.

"Why don't you do it for me, you seem to think it's so funny," I countered. He really was the kind of guy, instead of

38

doing the simplest thing he asked, you'd really rather just irritate the shit out of him.

He grinned. "Oh, no, I don't think it's funny at all. Tina Finn. Her name is Tina Finn, and she has just shared with me a few truly remarkable facts," he said. Then before Pete could get around to narrating these fascinating facts, he glanced into the next room, the bedroom, which was as I had left it: an unmade bed, piles of clothes on the floor, underwear and books and empty boxes everywhere. The place looked absolutely ransacked because in fact I had ransacked it. "What the fuck?" He looked back at me, all angry again. "What the fuck. You went through his stuff. You went through my father's shit?"

I blushed like a teenager. "I didn't, I was just—um . . ."

"You were just what?" he asked, tossing underwear at me. "You were just casually going through my father's underwear drawer?"

"I'm sorry, I was looking—my mom had this old bottle of perfume and I was—"

"You were looking for a bottle of perfume in my father's underwear drawer and what you found was—his wallet." He unearthed it, looked through it swiftly. "And, oh look, there's nothing in there now, is there?" He closed the wallet and tossed it to the other guy, who was still sitting on the couch.

"I didn't take anything from your dad's wallet," I said.

"That's a lie," he noted, correctly.

"It's *not* a lie," I said, continuing to lie. "Yeah, I found it in there, but I mean there was nothing in it." It was, as I said, already clear that this guy was one hell of a bully but I was pretty sure he wouldn't get around to actually frisking me so

39

there was no way to prove that I had the cash, which by the way I was not about to give up. "I was looking—"

"You were looking and looking and you also found—the vodka!" he exclaimed, picking up the bottle off the coffee table, where I left it.

"Knock it off, Pete." The other Drinan stood, shaking his head, like he was used to this nonsense from crazy Pete but not in the mood. "I'm sorry for your loss," he said to me. "You must still be in shock."

"Oh," I said, surprised. Doug Drinan expressing sorrow for my loss was frankly the most consideration I had gotten out of anyone, all day. "Thanks. I mean, thanks." I said.

"It was sudden, yes? I mean, she wasn't sick," he said.

"No, they, they said it was a heart attack. I don't know."

"That makes it hard."

"Don't make friends with her; she's not staying," Pete advised his sad big brother. He had pulled the cork out of the vodka bottle and started pouring it into a dusty glass which he seemed to have located in one of those cabinets.

"You're going to regret that in the morning," said Doug.

"I'm going to regret everything in the morning. I regret everything now," Pete informed him. "But since you're so interested in making friends with our little intruder, maybe you should hear what she has to say about the apartment, and why she's here." He took a hit off that straight vodka. For a second I was hardly listening, I was sort of suddenly desperate for a drink myself and wondering if there was any way to make one without losing anymore ground. Doug looked at me with a puzzled weariness, like he was sincerely

40

curious what I might say in response to Pete's nasty prodding, but also like he didn't believe, really, that anything horrible was going to come out of my mouth. Seriously, he was just such a tired and sad person. It was like he'd already been through so much bad luck that he didn't think anything, really, could get any worse.

"I . . ."

"According to Tina Finn, who claims she is not a thief, evidence on hand notwithstanding, Dad left the apartment to her mother, you remember the oh so lovely Olivia—"

"Jesus, Pete." Doug looked away, disgusted and embarrassed. "Knock it off, would you?" He stood and grabbed the bottle of vodka, heading for the kitchenette and the little freezer full of ice cubes. The drinking was apparently going to continue with both these fellows.

"I'm just getting to the good part. Dad left the apartment to Olivia—"

Doug turned at this, confused and concerned, and about to interrupt, but Pete had more up his sleeve.

"And Olivia left it to her daughters."

This stopped Doug in his tracks. He turned and looked back at me, sceptical but wary. The whole idea was clearly so ridiculous that he couldn't take it in.

"She didn't actually leave it to us," I said, embarrassed as hell. "I mean, she did leave it to us. She didn't make a will and there's this, you know, she died intestate. And that means—"

"I know what 'intestate' means," said Doug, going for the ice. "This would explain what you're doing here."

"Yeah," I said.

"Is your mother even in the ground yet?" he asked, a sort of edgy tone underlining the question. No more friendly expressions, so sorry for your loss, now I had to tough it out with both of them. To hell with it. If they were both drinking, then so was I.

"The funeral was yesterday morning," I said, grabbing my half-empty glass of vodka and grapefruit juice and following him into the kitchen, defiant. "So we went from the cemetery to the lawyer's and then we came here."

"Very efficient." Doug nodded. He dumped some ice in my glass and handed me the vodka bottle.

"Well, we didn't, it's not like, I mean I had no idea about any of any, you know, they didn't even tell me until after, I was standing there at the graveside, you know, honestly, when they told me about it."

"'They' being . . ."

"Me and my sisters."

"Right, there are several of you," Doug reminded himself. "Four of you?"

"Three. Me and Alison and Lucy. And Daniel, he's Alison's husband. But no kids. None of us managed to, I guess."

"Fascinating," Doug nodded. "And someone told you . . ."

"This lawyer, he said he was my mom's lawyer."

"That idiot Long," stated Pete. He was lying on the couch now, spread out the whole length of it, so now there was nowhere else for anyone to sit in this dreary little room. He had the little jewelry box on his lap, the one that had Mom's perfume bottle in it. In fact he was actually looking at the perfume bottle. "And he said you inherited our apartment. You inherit all my mom's stuff, too?"

"That was my mom's," I said. I wanted him to give it back.

"That was not your mother's," Doug informed me, cold. He was just considering me now, like he was trying to decide what to do with me, like maybe he was thinking he could just lock me in a closet and leave me there. I started to wonder if maybe he was not the nice brother at all; maybe he was just a little less sparky than the other guy.

"Yeah it was too," I said. "She had it her whole life. So I just, that's why I was looking through their stuff, I knew it was in there and I wanted to have it." I set my drink down and walked over to the couch, reached out my hand to take it from asshole Pete. He closed his fingers over it and dropped it back into the jewelry box and shut it.

"Everything's up for grabs though, isn't it? Isn't that what Long told you?"

"No, that's not what he told me. What he told me was everything was ours."

"Everything of ours is yours, that's what he told you?"

"He told me, he told everybody—"

"Oh, look at this!" Pete found the little tarnished silver box, with all the keys in it; he had been lying on it, on the couch. "You take a fancy to this too?"

"I wasn't stealing anything!" I said.

"Except our home," said Doug. He leaned up against the wall, looked out the window.

"Oh look, my mom's wedding ring," Pete observed, picking it out of that silver box. "Glad to know you weren't stealing that."

"Look, you guys are mad. Okay, I get it," I said.

43

"Like her mother, a regular rocket scientist," Pete murmured.

"My point being I'm not the one who fucked up this situation. That would be your dad, right? Didn't he tell you he was leaving the apartment to my mom? Didn't he even tell you that?"

"Who are you again?" said Pete, really pissed now. "Have we met? Do I know you? Then what the fuck are you doing here in my apartment? I grew up here, with my family, and my mother. My father was happily married to my mother for twenty years, not *two* years, *twenty* years. This is our apartment! What the fuck are you doing here, sleeping in *my* bed? What the fuck gives you rights?"

"Well, apparently some document that your father signed gives me rights."

"He was a fucking drunk!"

"Yes, that's real news. I was here for fifteen minutes I figured that out."

"Because booze was the first thing you went looking for."

"No—"

"Just like your mother."

"Go tell the judge. Go tell Stuart Long. What are you yelling at me for? You think I'm making this up? You think I wouldn't be here if they hadn't given me the keys?" I snapped back at him. "Go yell at your father. Oh, sorry. Guess you missed that chance."

That shut old Pete up. He glanced at Doug, who looked at him for a second then looked out the window. It was pretty fast but there was no question.

"Holy shit, he *did* tell you, didn't he?" I said. "You knew.

44

That he was leaving her the apartment. He told you. That's why you're so mad. Because you knew." They both looked at me real surprised for a second, like it hadn't occurred to either of them that I might actually put that together.

"You don't know anything," said Pete, deflated as hell all of a sudden.

"Well, I don't know a ton, but I'm learning as we go," I retorted. "What'd you do, piss him off? That's just a wild guess."

"Don't push your luck," he said, but he was tired now.

"I don't think we should be talking about this," Doug observed, instantaneously cool as a cat. Seriously, these two were a mixed set, they were like salt and pepper shakers. They maybe fit together? But they were not alike. Both of them knocked back their vodka at the same time, but I could see it wasn't going to bring either of them any peace. Oh well, like vodka brings anybody peace, ever.

"Let's get out of here," said Doug.

"What, we're just going to let her stay?" Pete asked, offended by my very existence now.

"Unless you want to take her home with you, I don't know what to do with her," Doug said, shrugging.

"You know, you guys don't actually get to decide what to do with me," I said, all snarky and defiant again.

"Don't count on that," said Doug, rapidly moving into first place in the asshole competition that we all had going on by this point. "And don't get too comfortable." He set his empty drink down on the kitchen counter and headed for the black hallway. Pete slammed back the rest of his drink, and picked up the jewelry box as he stood.

"Listen," I said.

"What?" He looked at me. There would be no listening tonight.

"Nothing," I said.

He nodded and turned, following his brother down the hallway, taking my mother's little black bottle of perfume with him as he went.

CHAPTER THREE

I called Lucy first thing. She was not in the least bit impressed with my story about Tina and the night visitors.

"They were going to show up eventually, that was a given," she announced.

"They were pretty pissed," I told her.

"Did you think they were going to be delighted to hear that they've been disinherited? I didn't."

"Man, Lucy, do you always have to be so mean about everything?" I said, already sick of this. Lucy, she's, no kidding, it's very impressive how capable she is but honestly sometimes I think she just thinks everybody should sleep on rocks. Plus I had a whanging hangover. I was in no mood for all this steely resolve.

"Just because I knew they were going to show up, that doesn't mean I'm particularly happy about it," she replied. "I think this could get pretty complicated pretty quickly and I don't see any point in being naïve about that."

"Yes, yes, *okay*," I said. "Actually what I meant was couldn't you be like a little worried that I was stuck in this apartment by myself and these two big guys showed up and scared the shit out of me?"

"They frightened you?"

"Well yeah of course they did!" I said. "I was sound asleep, all of a sudden there are two big guys in this empty apartment with me, I didn't know who they were, it was terrifying."

"Did they threaten you?" Lucy asked, only idly curious about this.

"They were both drunk and, yeah, they threatened me; they threatened me a lot," I said. This cheered her right up; she went from being vaguely interested to downright perky.

"That is absolutely unacceptable," she said. Now I could hear her typing.

"Are you taking notes?" I asked, kind of wanting to strangle her.

"I just want to have everything on paper, for the lawyers. We're going to have to have a paper trail, if they get aggressive. No point in putting it off," she said.

"One of them is kind of good-looking," I admitted, apropos of nothing.

"Great," Lucy acknowledged. "Listen, I have to run into a meeting."

"You're running into a fucking meeting? What am I supposed to do if they come back?"

"Tell them to call our lawyer," she reported. "Let's see— Long, tell them to call Stuart Long, you met him yesterday, he was Mom and Bill's lawyer, he put together the will."

"Yes, I remember, but I don't have his number."

"They'll know who he is, Tina," Lucy said. "Listen, I really do have to run."

"Wait a minute. Would you wait a minute?" I said. "There's some-body here." And there was, there was somebody in the apartment.

"Who is it? Is it them?" she asked.

"I don't know, but it's someone," I whispered. I was all the way in the back, on that little couch and television island where Bill and Mom had drunk themselves to death. But it was like all the air in the back of the apartment was moving differently, like someone had opened a door far away and that affected the whole place, like the wind comes just before the train in a subway station. And then I could hear somebody moving somewhere far away, but inside. I could hear it.

"Tina, go find out who it is, and then if there's a problem, call me back," she instructed me, only half interested. "I'll tell my assistant to come get me out of my meeting if you really need me. All right?"

"Can you just hold on a minute?" I said.

"No, sorry, I actually can't. For heaven's sake. It's not like it's the middle of the night and they're walking in and threatening you. I can understand why that upset you, but this should be easy. Handle it, would you? You're not a child."

"Look, don't talk to me like that, okay?" I said, really annoyed now. "I don't appreciate it. We're all in this together."

"That's my point. If you need me call me back." Okay, she said that, and then she hung up. No kidding. She hung up on me, without saying goodbye.

"I hate my family," I said to myself. I knew calling Alison would be useless in the complete opposite direction: she would just get all uptight and start freaking out and have no idea what I should do and then she and Daniel would come by and he'd

49

try to take over everything. I was not terribly interested in that option, so I just thought I'd better head back to the front of the apartment and see what the hell was going on.

I heard another sound, kind of like pots banging in a kitchen, six miles away. "Hey!" I yelled. "Who's in here?" Which was not particularly sly, but I wasn't looking for the surprise element since I assumed it was just those two boneheads, or one or the other of them. "You need to get out of here!" I yelled. I was charging through the maze of rooms now, all determined and cocky. The apartment looked considerably friendlier in the morning light. Even though there wasn't much furniture and the carpeting was shitty, the walls were really all painted beautiful colors, which glowed in the morning light. It gave me courage, which was good because I didn't have much else to go on. "Get out of here and call your stupid lawyer and stop bothering me!" I shouted, charging into the giant room at the front of the apartment.

"Helllooooo," said a man. "Who are you?"

Okay, I practically jumped out of my skin. Because I turned the last corner and there was a man, a different man now, standing in the middle of that giant empty room. This one was not tall, he was actually quite short, and he was very tidy, like a tidy little person in clothes with dirt all over them. I half expected him to evaporate but he didn't evaporate, he just stood there and stared at me until I recovered the part of my brain that wasn't completely hung over and flipped out.

"Who am *I*?" I said. "Who are *you*?"

"Oh wait, oh wait," he said. "I know who you are. You're Tina! Alison, Lucy and Tina; you're Tina. Olivia showed me pictures. I've seen pictures of you."

"You've seen *pictures* of me?" I said.

"Look at you, you're pretty, you're much prettier in real life, you don't photograph well. I think that's strange, don't you, how some people look just lovely when you meet them, and then you see them in pictures and you think, Well that just didn't *translate*. Well, anyway. I'm Len! Your mother . . . didn't . . .? Didn't she?"

"Didn't she what?"

"Nothing," he said, kind of sad. "Oh well. She said you didn't talk; I didn't realize that meant you didn't talk at all. You didn't talk at all?"

"Listen, Len, I don't . . ."

"No, of course, not my business! Not my business. And honestly it's not that we spent a lot of time on it but she seemed, much more so than Bill, to have a kind of yearning, you know you should have called her, you really, oh well. You don't have to answer that; I know things were complicated. She didn't blame you, so who am I?" He seemed to think this was a point well worth making, but at the same time he didn't seem to want to continue our conversation. He glanced over toward the kitchen, distracted.

"Look, could you, you know . . ." I was starting to get really annoyed with this guy. I was getting frankly annoyed with just about everyone: Lucy, those shitheads who barged in on me in my sleep, my mother, my ex-boyfriend Darren, everyone in New York City, the universe. "I think, you know, whoever you are, Len, I think uh this isn't a great time for me to maybe visit, and I'm not sure what you're doing here."

"Sorry." he smiled, suddenly looking down and dusting himself

51

off, like he remembered something about how actual people behave. "I'm being ridiculous, you're right to be upset. Did you stay here last night? You must have done. I'm so sorry for your loss, it must have been a terrific shock. Well, it was for all of us. Such a shame. She was really a terrific person. I'm Len Colbert, like I said. I was a friend of your mother and Bill, I live in the penthouse here on the top floor. Well, of course it's the top floor, that's where penthouses are, aren't they?" He laughed at himself, bemused by this astonishingly obvious statement of fact. "I'd shake your hand but mine are not presentable, I'm a, well, it's complicated what I do," he sighed. "Not complicated. I'm an anthropological botanist, I was, that is, I don't teach anymore. But the uh—the kitchen here—have you seen the kitchen?"

"The moss?" I asked.

"Yes, the moss." He smiled. No surprise, this elflike character had a fantastic smile, charming and self-involved and devilish as hell. He also had the most alarming blue eyes I'd ever seen, dark edges but sky blue around the middle. For a second I was seriously grateful that that dude was at least thirty years older than me because in spite of the fact that he was so odd I could see the appeal of eyes like that. "Bill and I had an arrangement. He rented me his kitchen," Len the blue-eyed elf continued. "He lets me, that is—both he and your mother—they let me use it as a kind of greenhouse. My own greenhouse, up on the roof, is obviously untenable for a mossery, not that I didn't try, but to maintain the habitat, the hydration alone, not that, it may be possible that we just didn't solve it. But people were not enthusiastic overall, you can imagine. The terror of a few bryophytes!

Anyway it was finally impossible. I investigated the possibility of renovating the plumbing, you know, to provide the additional, and there was no support from my fellow tenants. None whatsoever. One may even say, open hostility. At least, lawsuits were threatened. Anyway you'll have to come see it."

"See . . ."

"The greenhouse. It's a rarity to find one in the city, but the light, as you can imagine, so far up, utterly spectacular, even, the views, not to mention what you can accomplish. With that much light? I am I think not unduly proud. I'd love for you to come up; you should take me up on this. But it is absolutely useless for moss. Our solution—Bill and I—to our mutual needs—was as you see." He made an elegant gesture toward the kitchen behind him. "Actually it's a bit of a secret. There's a lot of misunderstanding, in the building, about moss. This confusion between moss and mold—it's ridiculous. They're not even the same species. Bill and Olivia were very understanding. And discreet." He smiled at me and nodded, apparently finished with this unintelligible explanation.

"So you have a key?" I asked.

"Oh yes. They spent most of their time in the other half of the apartment, it wasn't any kind of, as you can see this part of the apartment has not been in use for years."

"Well, okay, but it looks like I'm going to be living here now," I said.

"Reeeeallly?" Len asked, cocking his head at this, as if it were the most extraordinary news. Actually, he made it sound like such extraordinary news that it was just the slightest bit too extraordinary to be believed.

"Yes, until the will is settled. I'm staying here."

"And what do the boys have to say about that?" Len the elf asked, sort of half to himself.

"I'm sorry, what did you say?" I asked him, edgy.

He smiled at me, clearly amused by my tone. "The boys," he repeated. "I ran into them last night, in the lobby. They didn't mention to me that you would be living here. So I'm just surprised to hear it. As I assume they were." He folded his hands in front of his chest, with a sort of odd little gesture of delight, and smiled at me again, as if I would find his clever little bit of deduction charming.

"Look, you're going to have to go," I said. "I don't know anything about this, and you know, you want me to be discreet and everything but I don't know, this is clearly some sort of illegal thing you got going here."

"Moss is not a controlled substance," he informed me, laughing.

"Oh sorry, I maybe misunderstood you, before," I said. "Because you said something about how people in the building got all mad when you were trying to grow it up there on the roof, so I was just thinking maybe they wouldn't like to find out, so much, that instead you decided to grow it on the eighth floor, like in the middle of the building, where it might actually *spread*."

"Ah," said Len Colbert from the penthouse. "I understand why perhaps you thought I said that."

"Yeah, it sounded a little like that, like people maybe wouldn't be so thrilled to hear what you were doing here."

"That's not what I was saying," he said.

"So I don't actually need to keep my mouth shut about this?"

Elfman laughed again, to himself this time.

"What's so funny, Len?" I asked.

"Nothing, no, nothing," he replied. He looked back at the kitchen, this time with real longing. "Do you like moss?" he asked me.

"Honestly, I never thought about it that much," I said.

"It is a rare spirit that appreciates moss," Len told me, as if this were news. "There are seventeen different species in this particular mossery, some of them exceedingly beautiful. The curators at either of the public botanical gardens in the city would give their eye teeth. Frankly, it's actually a bit of an achievement that I could do what I've done, and under these conditions? Please. Let me show it to you."

"That's not necessary, Len," I started.

"Please," he said, holding out his elegant and dirty hand, like a prince at some ball, waiting to sweep me into a dance.

"What the hell," I said.

So for the next hour this strange guy walked me through the intricacies of moss, gametophores and microphylls and archegonia—that's the female sex organ of moss, who knew—and how much water moss needs to fertilize, and how long it takes for sporophytes to mature. He talked about liverworts and hornworts; he had mosses in there that were actually only native in the Yorkshire Dales moorland, and he had mosses that only grew in cracks in city streets, and he had mosses that only grew in water. As it turns out, in World War II sphagnum mosses were used as dressings on the wounds of soldiers in Europe because they're so absorbent and they have mild antibacterial properties. Also some moss can be used to put out fires, don't ask me how they would do that but apparently it's historically accurate.

Old Len knew a ton about moss, and he made sure that I knew how great his mossery really was, and how no one builds them anymore, and what a tragedy it would be if anything were to happen to his mossery.

"That would be awful," I agreed. I looked around the transformed kitchen. Len had even hung a picture of an old medieval tree on one wall, presumably to keep the moss company. "So how much did Bill charge you, to rent out his kitchen like this?" I asked.

"Oh," he said, looking at me kind of sideways for a second. "It was a very friendly arrangement."

"He didn't charge you rent for this? But they were broke, weren't they?"

"What makes you say that?"

"I spent the night here. There's nothing here. They were living on vodka and fish sticks and red wine," I said. "Which he paid for in cash."

"You *have* been busy, and you say you just arrived yesterday?" Len observed.

"So he really gave you this room to grow moss in, for free?"

"I didn't say that." Len smiled. "I said we had a friendly arrangement."

"Like under the table, like friendly like that?" I asked.

"Bill liked to fly under the radar," he admitted with a small shrug. "He did prefer cash."

"How much did he charge you?" I asked, direct. Len looked at me sideways and then he went back to examining one of his moss beds, poking at it carefully with his middle finger. "One thousand dollars a month," he said, raising an eyebrow.

"You know what, Len?" I said. "I think this mossery is fantastic, and I see no reason why you couldn't just keep it here for as long as you want. I'm gonna go make a phone call."

"Lovely." Len smiled. "I'll just continue my work then."

Figuring that I might need to keep the cash coming, it did seem like a reasonable idea to let this guy keep his mossery. But I also figured that this was maybe going to be a little bit of a problem, given that the first thing Lucy and Alison both said when they saw it was we have to get rid of the moss. I wasn't entirely sure how I was going to finesse this situation but I felt pretty sure something would come to me. Anyway, I went back to TV Land and picked up the phone and started dialing, meaning I made it halfway through Lucy's number before I realized that the phone was dead. There was nothing on the line—no clicks, no beeps, no dial tone, just nothing. I hung it up and tried again, and then I did that about eight more times, and then I plugged and unplugged the phone about eight times and then I tried it eight more times. Then I tried it in three other jacks, in three of the little bedrooms.

"Something wrong?" Len asked me, hanging out of the kitchen door. I mean, obviously there was something wrong; I was holding the phone out and staring at it like it was about to explode.

"The phone doesn't work," I told him. "I mean, it worked just an hour ago. Now it doesn't work."

He held out his neat but dirty hand and I gave it to him. He listened for less than one second, then nodded. "Well," he said. "I need to introduce you to Frank."

Frank was the doorman. Len took me downstairs to the

57

front lobby, and there he was, Frank, a kind of good-looking Hispanic guy with a beard and really long hair, in a beige uniform with little gold things on the shoulders. He had one of those weird haircuts that are short in strange places, with a crazy zig-zag lightning bolt running down the back of his head. With the dopey uniform it looked really nuts, but he seemed nice enough.

"Hey Len, what's up?" Frank asked.

"This is Tina Finn, Olivia's daughter." Len made a little wave with his hand, seeming to indicate for a moment that I might be some sort of fancy dish that was being served up. I felt like bowing.

"Nice to meet you, Miss Finn," said Frank, reaching out and shaking my hand politely. "I'm real sorry about your mom."

"Thanks," I said.

"Tina is going to be staying in the apartment for now, while they settle things up with the estate," Len informed Frank. It was genius, seriously; coming out of Len, "she's staying in the apartment" sounded pretty good. At least, Frank the doorman had no problem with it.

"Well, welcome to the Edge," he said. "If you need anything, you let me know."

"There is something," Len nodded. "It looks like her phone's been cut off. Could you put a call in about it?"

"Sure. Who's your carrier?" asked Frank, reaching for the phone receiver on his desk.

"You know, I'm not sure who they had," I said.

"Well, let's see then, maybe I'll put a call in to Doug—that's Bill's son," he told me. "There's probably just been some mistake, he cut the phone off maybe. Did he know you were going to be staying up there?"

"Yeah, we talked you know, we just talked yesterday about it," I said. "Look, you don't need to bother him, I'll call him myself."

"I got it right here," Frank said, dialing. "It's no bother." He was dialing away when Len tapped him on the shoulder.

"It's probably better to just give her the number," Len said under his breath, like he was trying to keep me from hearing what he said. Frank looked at him, a little confused, and Len did that thing with his hands, opening them up, apologizing to the universe for the stupidity of the human race. "There's got to be a lot going on, Frank. You probably don't want to put yourself in the middle of it." It sounded so much like he was taking care of Frank there that for a minute I forgot he was actually taking care of me.

It was, however, starting to occur to old Frank that maybe this story didn't add up. "But you did see Doug last night?" he asked, a little worried now while he rooted around for a pen.

"We hadn't figured out what we were doing last night, when we talked. Everything was such a mess. With Mom's funeral, I was kind of a wreck and we hadn't actually thought about the practicalities. I mean I was just like crying and crying so I really didn't get the details straight," I fibbed.

"I know what that's like." Frank nodded. "I lost my mom fifteen years ago, I still miss her." He looked at me and I swear to God, in that split second you could see the sadness rise up in his face, nothing too much, just enough to make his cheeks flush a little and his eyes well up. He got embarrassed right away and looked down, like he was still searching for that pen even though it was in his hand, and because that hideous uniform looked so terrible on him it made me feel a little bad to be lying like this. I mean, he was significantly nicer than Len, who probably was just taking care of me so that I didn't mess with his moss. But this guy Frank was just a nice person who missed his mom. His little haircut was so sweet and stupid I thought my head was going to split.

"Well . . . thanks Frank," I finally said. "I'll go call Doug right now and make sure he knows everything about me staying there and all that and you know make sure that he knows not to turn anything else off." I turned away a little, so that Frank would have a moment of privacy to collect himself. And then there was old Len, at my elbow, showing me to the door, like a friendly undercover agent. "There's a Verizon store two blocks up and one over, on Columbus," he informed me cheerfully, under his breath. "They sell those throwaway phones. You don't need a credit card, you can just pay cash, isn't that convenient?"

"Very," I agreed. "Thanks for the tip, Len."

A throwaway phone was exactly the thing, of course, because I had no cell phone and no credit card and now no landline. So Len was right to suggest it, and while I was out putting his sensible suggestion into action I also poked around a couple of clothing stores so that I had something more than one skirt, one pair of jeans and one sweater in my wardrobe. I could have called that bonehead Darren and asked him to put all my clothes in a box and send them, but I had no reason to believe he would actually do that, even if he said he would. So I ducked into a couple of really cute little shops where I learned that my seven hundred dollars, minus one throwaway phone, might buy me one pair of excruciatingly expensive blue jeans and half a tank top, which seriously annoyed me until I found a Gap, where there was a whole lot of stuff on sale which fit fine and looked cool enough and cost quite a bit less. Then I was hungry and I had a burger in a seedy sort of deli place, and then I needed underwear, and honestly I couldn't find anyplace to buy it except one of those really cute little shops and that cost a complete fortune but there was nothing else to do. So the seven hundred dollars was more or less whittled down to two by the time I decided to head back home.

That was the first time my head said that, "Let's go home," and I know it sounds kind of ridiculous that I thought of it that way? But no kidding, I was already in love with that place. The stuff about my mother drinking herself to death there, and my sisters being so uptight and bossy, and crazy drunk guys showing up in the middle of the night—that seemed like just not so serious, when I picked up my eighteen packages and thought about going home. I kind of half wondered, What are you going to do when you get home? And then I thought, Well, maybe I'll just make myself a cup of tea and read a book or something, there are at least a thousand used mysteries still shoved under the bed in Bill and Mom's bedroom. So on the way home I stopped at one of those little shops and I bought myself some fancy tea, and I was well on my way to becoming a totally different person— the kind who lives on the Upper West Side and drinks tea in the afternoon while reading mystery novels—when I got back to the lobby of my fabulous new apartment and found out that I was still the same old Tina I had been just a couple hours ago.

The place was packed. I had only been to the lobby twice before, but the first time me and my crazy little family were the only ones there, and the second time it was just me and Len and Frank the doorman. This time there were a lot of people milling around, a bunch of kids in school uniforms clustered around the elevator, arguing with each other and hitting the buttons on the elevator bank, and a woman in a bright red jacket with a fur collar trying to get Frank's attention at the little brass podium he sits at. Frank was talking to two big guys and they were all kind of yelling at once, which sounded loud because it wasn't the biggest space to begin with, but the ceilings were so high and curved the sound bounced around in it. The lady in the red jacket was clearly supposed to be somehow related to the kids, because she would occasionally yell, "Stop it, Gail! All of you, would you just wait until I see if your father's package has arrived? Frank . . ." But the other two guys were talking on top of her, and Frank was totally dealing with whatever they were saying, which I couldn't hear because of the other noise. Then there were two more ladies behind the one in the red jacket, who were waiting a little more patiently, but not much. Both of them were spectacularly thin, and wearing the kind of clothes you only see in ads in the *New York Times*, everything tight and fitted and slightly strange, like no one really wears clothes like that except the people who do. I couldn't see their faces right away because their backs were to me; all I could see were those strange fashionable outfits and that one of them had the most astonishing black curls tumbling down her back while the other one had white hair that was kind of short and flipped around her head. Then the one with the black hair turned for a second, like she heard something just behind her, and she turned out to be one of those people who are just so idiotically beautiful that you think you're on drugs when you see them up close. Her eyes flicked in my direction, but then the other woman she was with was yanking at her arm.

"This is ludicrous," the other woman said. "I'll hail my own cab."

"That's what I said ten minutes ago," said the younger, spectacular-looking woman. She turned around and headed right for the door. But the older lady didn't follow her, in spite of the fact that the whole idea of hailing your own cab for once was hers.

"We will get our OWN CAB, FRANK!" she announced, in quite a loud voice. "And I'm going to call the management company, do you understand? This chaos is NOT ACCEPTABLE."

"I want to talk to management as well, you get them on the phone," said one of the guys who was arguing with Frank at the front.

"Maybe you could just take a second to look through the deliveries, we'll just get out of your hair, Frank," said the lady in the red jacket at the same time, trying to be nice but also trying to get her own way too, sort of poking through the stuff that was piled on the console. The kids continued to scream as the furious white-haired lady turned, muttering to herself about how nuts it all was.

Poor Frank was now apologizing to everyone at the same time. "I can do that, sure, let me—sorry Mrs Gideon, I am so sorry, so sorry Julianna," Frank called after the ladies heading for the door. "If you give me just a second here—oh she's here!"

he said, suddenly, looking both harried and relieved at the same time. And then the lady in the red jacket knocked all the packages off the top of the podium.

The whole scene was so complicated that it took me a second to realize that Frank was looking at me, and talking to me. "She says she's living there now, and that you met last night and that you spoke about it—I'm not sure, but that's the young lady, she said that you know each other," Frank told the guy at the front of the line. "Tina, there's some kind of confusion here with Doug about the locks. He says he needs to change the locks but you didn't say anything about that so I just got a little . . . Can you come talk to him while I deal with this? Hang on there, Mrs Gideon, let me get you a cab. You can go ahead and look through all this, Mrs White, but I didn't see anything." Frank rushed by me, opening the door for the infuriated Mrs Gideon and her fabulous daughter Julianna. Mrs White continued to yell at her children while she poked through the packages on the floor. Doug Drinan turned and gave me a total dirty look.

Obviously this moment, for me, was a bit of a drag. The Upper West Side glamour plates were pushing by me while I tried to grab up my Gap bags, apologizing like a loser, "So sorry, sorry, sorry . . ." Frank practically shoved me aside while he raced after them, trying to do his job. Those loud and insane kids finally managed to get the elevator to arrive but their mother was not yet ready to pile into it with them; she was too busy giving me the once over, like she thought I was someone who was trying to break into their building. Which in fact I was.

"The doorman seems to be under the impression that you're living in my father's apartment," Doug announced. "And he thinks that I somehow agreed to this."

"Well, we did have a conversation about this last night, Doug, and I don't think you could have been really surprised that Frank told you that," I announced back. We were both being polite but too forceful to actually have it count as polite.

"Last night we were decent enough not to kick you out onto the street," he told me. "The understanding was you'd be gone in the morning. You have no right to be here—your mother actually had no right to be there either, after my father died."

"That's not what my lawyer tells me."

Okay, this for some reason caused old Doug to really lose it. He was suddenly furious, his face going all red, and he actually grabbed me, right up at the front of my shirt, and yanked me toward him to do what I wasn't sure. I was totally not expecting it, obviously; even last night when he showed up with his brother totally wasted and they were both really mad and reactive, nobody put their hands on me. I had one of those terrible minutes where I thought, Oh no, this is one of those guys who's worse when he's *not* drunk; all that disappointment and sadness and his thinning hair is just too much for him in real life.

"Let go of me, let go let go," I said, real nice real fast. I didn't want to find out if he actually had it in him to hit me; I truly didn't.

"Look, I got a bunch of other jobs. Is this going to happen?" the other guy asked. He had kind of a bad leather jacket and jeans on, and one of those old tool kits, and he looked really bored by all this. Somehow you knew right away that he saw this stuff all the time, people arguing about who had the right to own the locks to some house or apartment or whatever, and that it wasn't all that earth-shattering, which made me realize that I probably was not going to get hit. Anyway, he sure didn't think so. He sort of looked away, like he didn't give a shit who won this battle, but also like he was pretty sure that whoever won this battle it was not going to be me so there was no use even acknowledging that I existed.

In any event, the little interruption gave Doug a chance to recover. He let go of my shirt, giving me a little push, like he couldn't believe he actually touched me. Then he turned and yelled back at Frank, who was all the way outside, still trying desperately to hail a cab for the fed-up Mrs Gideon and her babelicious daughter. "We're going up!" he announced. Frank didn't even notice. Doug and the locksmith headed for the elevator but there was no way they'd get in as it was full of all those kids in school uniforms and the lady in the red jacket. But Doug was on top of his game now.

"We'll take the stairs," he announced, heading for the other end of the lobby. Locksmith guy followed him. I did not. I finally got a clue, pulled out my brand new throwaway cell phone and called in the Marines.

CHAPTER FOUR

"Oh, for God's sake," said Lucy, all annoyed as soon as I got her. "Where have you been?"

"They cut off the phone," I told her.

"No kidding. I tried calling you three hours ago and got the message that the phone had been stopped," she said. "Where have you been?"

"I went out to get a cell phone—"

"You've been out buying a cell phone for three hours?"

"Well, I needed some other stuff too and—"

"I thought you were broke. What are you using for money?"

"Would you listen to me, Lucy? They're here! At least one of them is here and he's trying to change the locks. He has a locksmith here and he says I have no rights and—"

"Relax. I'm two blocks away, I'm taking care of it," she told me.

"What do you mean you're two blocks away? I called you at work," I said, all confused again.

"And my assistant patched you through to my cell," she informed me.

"So you're on your way here? How did you know to come?"

"Tina, when the phone got cut off what did you think was going on?"

"I don't know. I thought I needed to get a cell phone."

"Well, I thought a little harder than that. Just stay right there in the lobby; I'll be there in two minutes."

She hung up on me, just as Frank trotted back in. He looked a little shell-shocked, but in a more or less delirious kind of way. I thought he was going to be mad at me because I had basically just caused a huge scene, resulting in utter chaos in his little lobby, with people threatening to have him fired and all sorts of unpleasant bullshit. Frank, however, seemed to have barely noticed. He was actually humming a little tune, as he headed over to his podium and started picking up the packages which were still all over the floor. I thought for a moment that he was one of those strange sad people who need a little action to feel alive, but then I took another look, and it was like he was glowing a little bit, around the edges, you could almost see little beams of light coming out of his cuffs and collar. I thought, Oh, he's in love, Frank is in love with the unspeakably beautiful Julianna Gideon. And he just got to be near her, he got to hold the cab door open for her for half a second.

"She's pretty, huh," I said, testing out my theory.

"Oh my God," he agreed, as if I had just spoken straight to his interior monologue. "I can't even, when I look at her,

I can't . . ." He glanced out the door, taking pleasure in just seeing the place he had last been allowed to look at her.

"Does she know you like her?" I asked him.

"What?" That was a bad question; it shook him out of his fantasy and he remembered how much of a right he had to be mad at me. "Did you get things straightened out with Doug?" he asked, suddenly kind of stern. "He was quite certain that you are not supposed to be living up there in 8A. I didn't know what to say. This has put me in a very awkward position. I put a call into building management and I don't know what they're going to do. There's already been so much controversy around that apartment, I'm sure they're going to want to talk to both of you about whatever this situation is," he told me. He was trying his best to sound really mean, but the guy didn't have it in him. He was reading me the riot act, and he just sounded like he was apologizing.

"I'll try to keep this out of your hair from now on," I said.

"I would appreciate that," he said, but he didn't sound angry, he actually sounded like he would really just appreciate that. Which is about when Lucy showed up, wearing a great gray suit and heels, carrying a big briefcase and looking like the queen of the universe.

"Lucy! Hey, this is my sister Lucy," I told Frank. "She'll have this solved in five minutes, I guarantee. You don't have to talk to building management."

"I'm sure they know all about this already," Lucy announced, a little clippy. "Tina tells me there's some confusion about the locks?"

"Confusion, I should say so," Frank said. "Doug Drinan— he's Bill's son?"

"I know who he is." Lucy nodded, trying not to make that little sign with her hand that means can we hurry this up please.

"Well, he's up there, having the locks changed. He says he doesn't know anything about you all having a claim on the place. I didn't know what to tell him. Tina tells me she's staying there. I got no reason to doubt her but Doug was Bill's son—"

"And we are his wife's daughters." Lucy smiled, completely professional. "No worries. We'll clear this up in no time." She took a couple of smooth steps over to the elevator bank and pressed the call button; as far as Lucy was concerned, this was as good as done. Frank smiled at me, relieved. When she isn't just annoying as hell, Lucy does in fact have that effect on people. You know who's in charge.

Doug Drinan and his pal the locksmith were sadly not quite as easy to snow. We more or less fell out of the elevator up there on that eighth floor landing—that is, I fell out, with all my packages, while Lucy popped out like a genie and presented them both with a huge stack of documents.

"Mr Drinan? Hi, how are you? I'm Lucy Finn, Olivia's daughter. It's a pleasure to meet you after all this time," she announced, talking quickly. "As you are aware, our mother just passed only a few days ago and so obviously we are reeling, completely caught off guard, so I'm sure this is our fault. But I think there's been some confusion about the status of the estate. We spoke with Stuart Long just yesterday, he was in possession of your father's will; have you seen it? I brought an extra copy in case you hadn't." She handed it to him and kept talking. "Anyway there is some real question about who the beneficiaries of the estate are, at this time. Your father seems to have expressed in no uncertain terms that our mother was to inherit everything, that largely meaning the apartment, it's unclear what else is included, but in any event I'm going to have to ask you to hold off on changing the locks for now. Until we get this sorted out." She smiled at him, very pleasant, but there was a definite don't-fuck-with-me edge behind it all. She works in PR. It's very daunting.

Doug Drinan unfortunately didn't get on board with anything she was saying. He barely glanced at the papers she had handed him and just sort of tossed them to one side, on top of the old radiator that was hissing in the hallway. "I'm aware we're going to be in a holding pattern for a little while, with regard to the dispensation of the will," he told her. "Which is why I thought it important to secure the apartment. Obviously we can't have just anyone wandering in and out, disturbing the effects, before we've even begun to probate this situation. I hate to say it, such a sad time—I mean really, condolences on your loss—but anyway it sounds to me like this is going to get pretty complicated. This is just precautionary. Don't want things to get ugly down the line or anything."

Okay, the speech was good, but in general he really was not as good as Lucy. He pressed those thin lips together, like he was trying to smile and explain things like a nice guy, but it came off like he couldn't be bothered to really pretend all that hard, so it all sounded like what it was, condescending and mean and like he was even kind of enjoying messing with us. Which maybe he was, I'm not sure. The more I saw of this guy the less I liked him. His hair really was kind of dirty, and he had too much disappointment in him. Sometimes those are the worst people to deal with because they aren't even thinking anymore, they're just hoping that they can make you as miserable as they are.

Lucy didn't care. Honestly, she has ice water in her veins so ultimately this guy and all his unhappiness were just no match. "I completely agree," she said. "That's why we felt it was best to have Tina camp out here for the time being, just so there was someone on site, making sure nothing untoward happened to the property while we sorted this all out. For instance, I think you and your brother stopped by in the middle of the night, last night, and removed some items?"

Doug Drinan stared at her, aghast at her nerve. She just looked at him. "My mother's wedding ring," he said, finally, like the righteousness of the situation would mean something to her.

Lucy shrugged. "We have no way of ascertaining that."

"Except that she saw it." Drinan turned his cold stare on me, like I was the one who was fucking with him.

"I never said it wasn't. I didn't—ah—" I started.

Lucy raised her hand, fearless, and cut me off. "Tina, your actions are completely blameless in this matter," she informed everyone.

"How do you figure that one?" asked Drinan. "We got there, she'd already completely cased the joint."

"I was looking for my mom's perfume," I explained again.

"You went through my father's underwear drawer," he sneered. "You managed to find his wallet, which was conveniently empty by the time we got there."

"I didn't—"

"It doesn't matter what you were doing, Tina. The point is, you did not remove anything from the premises, nor are you—or I, or Alison—doing anything at all except insisting that we hold to the status quo until our lawyers, and your lawyers, have a chance to work through the documents and finalize the legal status of the estate. That's all we're trying to do. Protect everyone's rights."

"Look, I don't know what any of this is about?" said the locksmith. "But somebody's got to make a decision about what we're doing with these locks. There's a kill fee. You call to have your locks changed and then you change your mind, that's a fifteen-dollar charge."

"Not a problem," Lucy said, reaching into her purse.

"I don't agree to that," Drinan snapped. He put his hand out, stopping the locksmith from even thinking about heading for the elevator bank. "I want the locks changed and I have every right to change the locks."

"You legally have no right to change the locks," Lucy said. Man she was so cool headed, through all of this, there was no way the locksmith was not going to do what she told him to. But he did feel bad about it.

"Listen, man, I'll wait downstairs and let my boss know what's going on. If the situation changes I can come back up and do the job. But I can't get involved in something that might, you know. Be illegal."

"This is my apartment. I grew up here, this is my apartment." Drinan's temper was fraying again.

"Unfortunately we have a whole stack of legal documents

which indicate that there is a very real chance that, in fact, it is not your apartment," Lucy said, not quite so nicely anymore. "And if you insist on pursuing this course of action I will in fact be forced to call the police."

"Go ahead. My brother is a detective with the NYPD, and you want to know something? They take care of their own."

"Listen, buddy." The locksmith was really desperate to get out of here by now. So was I. Bringing up the cops made everything just that little bit more icky.

"Wonderful. Your brother works in law enforcement, and I work in publicity. He can bring in his friends, and I can bring in mine. I know several writers for several highly prominent newspapers who would be only too happy to write about the NYPD superseding the law and forcing people from their homes."

"This isn't your home," said Drinan, clearly astonished, finally, at her nerve.

"It is *Tina's home,*" she told him, in no uncertain terms. "Our mother died here, and every legal document I have studied so far tells me that this apartment is now *our* apartment, and she had no place to live, and so for now she's living here, and it is her *legal right to do so.*"

"I don't even know you people," Doug observed, like that was going to matter.

"I suspect we will have plenty of time to get acquainted," Lucy said, kind of mean. She looked at the locksmith, like she couldn't even believe he was still standing there. "If you want to call your boss, now would be the time. I think we both know what he's going to tell you."

"Yeah, I don't have to call him; I'm not getting involved in this," he said. "But I do need that kill fee."

She reached into her purse, lifted out a neatly folded bill and handed it over to him. The whole move took three seconds. "Keep the change," she announced.

"Thanks," he nodded, and he ambled back to the exit sign, pushed through that crummy brown door and slipped down into the stairwell. I didn't blame him. I wouldn't want to hang around waiting for an elevator, under those circumstances.

Drinan didn't want to wait either. He picked up his little pile of legal documents and followed the locksmith.

"Perhaps you'd like my card," Lucy cooed, holding one out to his back.

"When I need to talk to you I'm not going to have any trouble finding you," he said, as the door to the stairwell slammed shut behind him.

"What a charming character," Lucy said, putting the card away. "I thought you said he was good looking."

"The other one, the one who's a cop," I told her.

"What does this one do?" she asked. "Run a charm school? Let me have the keys."

I handed them to her. "I don't know what this one does. Last night he didn't say much," I told her. "They were both drunk."

"You should write down everything that happened last night. Have you done that yet?" she asked me.

"No, of course not. Why would I write it down?" I said.

"Well, we're going to need a paper trail on everything, Tina. This isn't a joke. I want it established that we are keeping records.

Things are going to happen really quickly, and obviously the Drinan brothers have no compunction about playing hardball. We need to be prepared, as much as we can, for whatever they throw at us. What the hell is this?" We had stepped into the front room, which was filled with light from top to bottom. In spite of that hideous wall-to-wall shag rug, and all the crazy trouble with Doug Drinan, that room was really gorgeous so I got distracted for a minute just staring at it, and didn't know what she was talking about, again. "Tina, hellloooo," she said, waving her hand in front of my face and snapping her fingers.

"What?" I said.

"What," she asked, impatient, "is this?" And with her toe she nudged a small wooden tool kit, which had been placed neatly against the wall, next to the doorway which led to the mossery.

"Oh, that's Len's," I said.

"Len," she repeated, looking at me like I had of course once again slept with someone I shouldn't have.

"He was a friend of Bill's, and Mom's. That's his moss in the kitchen. They let him grow it there. He's some kind of botanist kind of person. He lives in the building," I explained. "He was here when the phone got cut off, and he, you know, he said I should go get a cell phone for now." Lucy flipped the light switch. Nothing happened.

"Yes, I see." She sighed. "And what did you do, once you bought the cell phone? Did you call me at work, as I asked you to, and say, Lucy, the phone has been cut off and they're probably going to try to cut the electricity as well, and maybe change the locks, could you come over and help me handle this? Did you do that?"

"No, I didn't do that," I started.

"No, you didn't," she said, continuing to flip the useless light switch for effect. "You went shopping."

"Why would I assume this guy was going to do all that stuff you said? We don't even know these people."

"Tina, honestly, would you try to *think* for once? Hello, Monica, hi." She was on her cell now, firing on all jets. "I'm going to need you to call Keyspan *and* Con Ed, the gas and electric got turned off in my mom's apartment and we need to get it turned back on right away and I mean now. My sister is living here and she obviously can't stay if there's no gas or electricity, so if you need to run down to their offices then do it. I left three copies of the will on my desk; take them with you so if they give you any trouble you can prove we have the right to put the accounts in my name. Here, you can also give them the number of the building, tell them the doorman can verify that we've taken possession. What's his name?" She asked me.

"Frank," I said.

"Frank," she said to the phone, and then she rattled off the phone number of the building, which of course she knew even though I did not. She finished up the call by snapping her cell shut and then continued explaining things, just continuing the story as if there had been no interruption at all. "I checked in with that Long person, the lawyer, from yesterday?"

"I remember. Lucy, could you not talk to me like I'm an idiot?"

"Don't get snippy, Tina. You almost completely blew it today—"

"I told you, I didn't know."

77

"No, you didn't *think*; you just took off for three solid hours on a *shopping* spree, and I'm not going to ask you where you got the money because honestly I don't care. But you should rest assured, while I don't think Doug Drinan has any sort of legal claim on this apartment, I don't necessarily think that he is a *liar*. Did you find money here?" She waved her hands idly at the many shopping bags I had dumped on the floor.

"I didn't have anything to wear," I said, trying to get to the beginnings of a defence here. She was not interested.

"You listen to me," she snapped. "If I hadn't gotten worried about not hearing from you, and showed up, what would have happened?"

"I don't actually care what would have—"

"You'd be locked out. We all would be locked out. We would not have access to the apartment or the building, for that matter, for months. We'd have to go to a judge to get an injunction to get permission to even get a look at the place, by which point the Drinan brothers will have filed to legally contest their father's will, which depending on how long that takes to get through the courts? Cuts us off for years. *Years.* I checked this out with Daniel's friend, the real estate lawyer, who assures me that, contrary to what that idiot told us yesterday, a scenario like that leaves us with virtually no standing whatsoever. If they can prove that Bill was of unsound mind, and Mom was of unsound character, and none of us had ever met Bill and had never even set foot in this apartment, it is not that far a leap to making the claim that Mom *tricked* him into changing that stupid will, and that we have no claim upon this place. And that is what they are going to try to do. So do me a favor and don't make their case for them, would you? We put you here for a reason. Stay put."

"You expect me to never leave."

"Not unless you pick up your handy new little throwaway cell phone, and call me first, and let me know that you need to go out for two hours and that Alison or I need to come by and be on site while you are off traipsing about."

"Well, so how long—"

"As long as I say! If you don't like this deal, let me know. Let me know, and you can go back to Darren and the trailer park and the Delaware Water Gap now, instead of later. Because if you don't help me make this work? That is where you're going to end up anyway."

Now even though I thought Lucy really was overreacting and being obviously a total nightmare, this argument made a relatively significant impression on me. Even though I couldn't fully follow the dastardly legal turns she had already worked out for herself, in terms of where this situation maybe could go? It was pretty clear that me getting booted out of there, and back to cleaning houses in Delaware, was in the cards if we didn't pull this off.

"Okay okay okay," I said.

"Not okay okay okay!" she snapped. "I don't want to hear some sort of snotty okay! I want to hear, Yes Lucy I Will Do Whatever You Say."

"Well, I'm not going to say that," I snapped back. "I'll do it, but I'm not going to say it."

"Fine," she said, clearly sick of me. "Now, what's the story with all this moss? This is actually here for a reason?" Which, look, I find it impressive when she does that. In the middle of

79

all that arguing, she still remembered the one thing I told her about the moss.

"Len, it's Len's moss. He lives on the top floor," I said.

"Well, Len is going to have to get his moss out of here," she said, shoving his little tool box with one of her slick black heels.

"I don't have his number," I said. "But I could go downstairs and get that doorman to buzz up and see if he's there."

"That's a good idea," she said, only half paying attention again.

"Maybe I should get the keys copied, while I'm down there."

"Now that, actually, would be useful," Lucy noted. She was dialing her cell, then she popped it to the side of her head while she held out the keys. I took them. "Listen, don't panic, there's nothing to get upset about," she said, by which I knew she was talking to Alison. "But I'm over at the apartment. There's a lot going on."

Okay, now you do have to wonder why people like Lucy believe people like me when we suddenly cave and agree to all sorts of nonsense in the middle of an argument. Because really I had no intention of calling Len and telling him he had to move his moss. Instead, I went downstairs, waved to Frank, walked over to Columbus and found the one inexplicable bodega which actually hovers there, and I bought myself a box of Dots. Then I walked around the block, ate the Dots, and thought about what it was that I was going to do next. Then I wandered around the Upper West Side some more and I found a crummy little hardware store, where they made some new keys for me. While I was there I bought a few more choice items. Then I went back home, and more and more I felt I had every right to think of it that way.

CHAPTER FIVE

"The moss guy isn't in. Frank buzzed him about eight times but he wasn't answering," I told Lucy. "So I asked for his phone number, but it's unlisted and the doorman isn't allowed to give it out. Anyway, I left him a message with the doorman to call as soon as he got in, so when he does I'll tell him that we need him to move all that stuff. Here, I got a set of keys for you and then also an extra one, in addition to the ones I have." Soaring right through the lie about Len, I started fumbling with the keys. She didn't even look up as she took them from me.

"You didn't leave my number as well?" she asked, pecking away at her laptop. She had set it up on that little coffee table back in the apartment side of the apartment and there was a whole mess of documents and file folders kind of falling out of her briefcase on the couch. She clearly had decided to spend the rest of the day back there. I felt like I had been invaded.

"He and I got kind of friendly so I just thought it would be better for him to call me," I said.

"You thought it would be better if I let *you* handle it," she said, making this sound like a stupendously idiotic idea. I looked at the floor and acted like I was really sorry that I was such a stupid person, which worked, because that's what she thinks I am anyway. Smart people are easy to fool about really stupid things. It's all about the assumptions.

The door to the bathroom behind the little laundry room swung open and a woman appeared. I just about jumped out of my skin, but Lucy kept on typing.

"Fantastic," the woman said, smiling at me like we were old friends. She had very tight hair, blonde and tight to her head, and she was exceptionally tanned. She also wore a tight beige microsuede pantsuit—pants and a jacket made out of synthetic beige polyester—and then she also had on actual panty hose and a kind of boring-looking pair of low brown heels. I'm sure that everything she was wearing cost more than I made in a month of cleaning houses, but frankly I don't fully understand why people dress like that.

"This place is *fabulous*," she informed me, striding over and holding out her hand for me to shake. "Hi, I'm Betsy Hastings. Did I hear you saying something about the moss, in the front kitchen?"

"We haven't been able to get hold of the guy who owns the moss," Lucy announced, "but it's being handled."

"No worries, no worries," said Betsy Hastings. As opposed to my sister, she couldn't have been nicer. "This whole place is amazing. It's incredible when a place like this comes on the market. Just thrilling."

"You're the real estate person," I guessed.

"A lot of people are already interested, Tina," Lucy informed me. "And there are a lot of questions that need to be answered. Things are very preliminary at this point."

"No question, no question," Betsy agreed. "I would love it if you would let me handle this. I have a number of corporate clients who would pick it up immediately, as is. I mean, I don't think you need to worry about anything, the moss, the carpets, the appliances, you're in a situation where you can completely let the buyer take care of all of that. Even in this market, which obviously has cooled considerably in the past couple years. But you don't have anything to worry about; this place is *amazing*."

"We've noticed," Lucy observed.

"Absolutely. Absolutely." Betsy Hastings nodded, running her hand over the pocket doors. "A property like this, my advice would be to let a professional pick it up and do the renovation, even at eleven or twelve million it's going to be considered undervalued, which is good; you want them to see the potential for a fast turnaround and a big profit. You don't want to get involved in the level of renovation that a place like this would need, to pull in the really big numbers. There are agents out there who will tell you that you could take in twenty or even twenty-two on this, but that's going to require enormous investment on your part up front and I really would let someone else take care of that."

"Why don't you put together a strategy and call me tomorrow," Lucy nodded, not even looking at her. She held out her card. She did everything but tell Betsy to her face that her wild enthusiasm had completely put her out of the running.

"That's not to say, if you're looking for the bigger numbers, I can work with that too," Betsy explained, taking the card with a little shrug. "This end of the market, it's always a question of how long you want to wait. If you can afford to take the time and put a few million into it yourself, then we're talking about significantly larger numbers. It's just a different approach. As I said, I'd love to work with you on this. Really, it's a great place. Just the size of it, and the details! I love it when these old places open up. New York. There's no place like it, there really isn't, you just get such a sense of history. Fantastic. I'll give you a call tomorrow, we can go over a couple of different plans." I had to give it up to that old Betsy Hastings; it was pretty inspired bullshit. I mean, everything she said was true, and she really did have a kind of excitement about the apartment which I totally agreed with. But obviously she was mostly talking about money, which also obviously contributed to the fact that everything she said sounded pretty phony.

So Betsy took off, and then this young kind of swank Indian character showed up and he went into overdrive explaining how if we could take a year and sink a million into the joint and break it down into three separate but spectacular *separate* apartments we could pick up twenty-two easy. Which made me actually kind of like Betsy even better, because she totally called that, that some other agent was going to show up and tell us this version of events, and then that actually happened like within the hour. And then this older white guy came by, wearing an extremely expensive suit, and he just looked around and acted like the place really wasn't so great after all, and that the fixtures were all just inappropriate, and the appliances were from the seventies, and he would have to think about whether or not he was interested in taking this on, even if we could work out the legal difficulties. He was the only one who brought up the "legal difficulties" which, perversely, it seemed to me, cheered Lucy up quite a bit; she just shrugged and said something like, "That would be up to you." He was really pretty snotty, and they were quite snippy with each other, and his approach may have been a posture that he thought would make us want him more, but I'm not sure why he thought that because clearly we were sitting on the mother lode, in real estate terms, legal difficulties or not. Anyway it was all very nerve-wracking by the end of the day, when Daniel and Alison came by so we could have a powwow over Chinese food.

"There's no way we're going to be able to push through a sale before they slap a cloud on the title, if that's their intention, and it sure as hell would be mine," Lucy explained as she picked pieces of chicken out of one of those little cartons. "It's going to cost a fortune and the legal tangle will be considerable. What'd your friend tell you, inheritance taxes are due within the year?"

"Six months," Daniel nodded. "Although it's apparently not much of a problem getting an extension when the will's being probated. We can get Wes to file for us if it becomes necessary."

"When," said Lucy. "When it's necessary; there's no use being naïve about this."

"How much is this going to cost us?" asked Alison, all worried as usual.

"Much more than we have," Lucy admitted. "The only way we're going to be able to afford this is to get into a partnership with a real estate agency. I'm going to talk to Sotheby's about it tomorrow."

"That guy from Sotheby's was an asshole. He was the least interested of anybody," I pointed out.

"That's how I know he wants it," Lucy said, spearing a shrimp with slashing efficiency. "We need someone who's going to be willing to work around the legal problems. Those other two were too spooked to even mention it. Losers."

"What if Sotheby's gets behind the Drinan side of this?" I asked.

"I sent over a packet of the documentation. They'll look at it and decide, but it's pretty clear we're going to win." Lucy shrugged.

"How can you be so sure? I just don't know how you can talk about all of this like you know what's going to happen. How could anyone know what's going to happen?" asked Alison. "You keep acting like this is all going to just work out and I don't see how you can know that." I thought this was a pretty good point but Lucy didn't even respond. Daniel reached for some beef and broccoli thing, and he didn't bother answering Alison either. "These legal situations aren't sure. They never are," she persisted. "And if we spend all our money, if our money isn't enough to cover the costs, costs can go through the roof and instead of everything what if we end up with nothing?"

"*Alison,*" Daniel finally said, impatient. "I spent the day on the phone with four different lawyers; all of them gave us the same answer. This is a no-brainer. We're in the clear."

"If it's so totally clear that we're going to win this, how come it's all such a surprise to those Drinans?" I said. "I mean, they knew that he was leaving it all to Mom."

"They told you that?" said Lucy. "Wait a minute. They *told* you that they knew he was leaving the place to Mom?"

"They didn't say it. I just kind of figured it out," I said, eating. "Anyway, they definitely knew."

"That he was leaving the place to Mom."

"Yeah, they knew that part. But they totally didn't know the rest, that then we would show up and get it. Like, why would they know that part but not the other part?"

"What else did they say?" asked Daniel. He sounded even more uptight so I looked up from the Chinese food finally, and they were all staring at me. For a second I considered lying some more, because I was beginning to feel like Lucy and Alison and Daniel were acting like such unbelievable sharks, that's what they deserved. But I didn't see any point in protecting those Drinans either. It was hard to know whose team I was on, already. And we had only been at this for a day and a half.

"They were just sad and drunk and kind of mad, that's all." I shrugged, opting for a vague non-answer for now. "One of them talked about all the furniture being gone like it was so sad. Like he was a little surprised, I think, that so much of it was gone."

"Why would that surprise him?" Alison asked.

"Not totally surprised. But sad. Like they hadn't seen the place in a little while, like they knew what it was like in here but not all the way. Sort of like that."

"They probably weren't allowed in very much." Lucy stared into her spicy shrimp, putting it all together. "By all accounts Bill was a Howard Hughes-level freak. Then when he died, if Mom didn't want them around, she didn't have to let them in.

Maybe she was afraid they'd try and kick her out. They prob-ably *would've* tried to kick her out; they haven't been exactly civil, have they? Anyway it was only three weeks ago, they didn't exactly have a ton of time to figure out a game plan. They prob-ably didn't even know they needed a game plan. Most people don't think ahead."

"What was only three weeks ago?" I asked.

"When Bill died."

"Bill only died *three weeks ago*?" I blurted.

Okay, I honestly do not know why I didn't know this. But I didn't know; the whole situation with my mom was that screwy. One day she was living in Hoboken and working at some H & R Block office, filing tax returns, then all of a sudden she was getting married and moving to Manhattan. Then it was done before we even knew it, practically, when it became "Bill's private, he doesn't see a a lot of people," or "We're really busy this month, maybe the fall would be better." I mean, before she went off and married this guy it's not like I saw that much of her anyway. Mostly we communicated through phone messages: the man who lived underneath her got a dog and it was barking day and night, or the phone company screwed up her billing and they were just driving her crazy, or she was trying out a new recipe and did I ever hear of Asiago cheese? It makes my head hurt now to think of how lonely those messages were and that obviously I should have tried a lot harder to see her, while I could. I'm not saying that all of us had abandoned her. Alison saw her more than me or Lucy, I knew that Alison would come out and see her and Lucy saw her too. But not all that much. So when she went ahead and married a guy who didn't want us around it didn't make a huge impression.

The truth is last time I even spoke to her was almost a year and a half ago, when the three of us took her out to dinner. Mom suggested it. I think she felt guilty because none of us had been invited to the wedding. So there we were, six months after our mother went and married a total stranger, arguing over where we should take her to celebrate. Bill of course was not coming, but she made kind of a big deal about not going too far from home, because he might get uptight if she went too far. Then Lucy got bent out of shape about whether or not it would be a place we could afford, as she assumed we'd be "taking" Mom and she didn't want the bill split two ways between her and Alison because she really got the short end of the stick in these situations since "Alison" covered Alison and Daniel which meant that she, Lucy, was stuck paying for me as well as half of Mom so expensive places got really quite expensive really fast, from her point of view. She was completely blunt about all this, as usual, which I took exception to, because even though I'm consistently strapped it's not like an occasional nice dinner out is a complete impossibility. But of course Lucy was right—we ended up at a place that charged $22 for a plate of spaghetti with red sauce, which made everyone, especially me, uptight.

So that more or less set things off on an unfortunate foot. Mom had a vodka tonic which I think cost $12, and the rest of us drank tap water. Lucy as usual totally monopolized the conversation, blathering on about the big corporations she did PR for and how difficult it was to work with corporate jerks and none of them really want to talk to a woman and how they're all in love with themselves and their own power and she really thinks they're all closet cases anyway. Alison never actually got over the prices on the menu, and she kept letting us know how worried she was about how much things cost, and then she got Daniel to keep a running tab on the paper tablecloth, which he did methodically, with a mechanical pencil. I told them all I was going to move out to the Delaware Water Gap with Darren, and how he had this business plan set up, that so many really wealthy people had summer homes out there now and he was putting together a company that did caretaking year round and he already had six or seven clients and I was going to help him with the bookings and also do sort of personal services for people like shopping, say.

So that was the dinner. And Mom was fine, really. Kind of a little too perky, maybe, like she was trying too hard to seem happy. But I don't know, how can you know something like that? She never said anything at all about Bill, or how it was going with him, even though Lucy made a couple of stabs at it.

"So are we ever going to meet our so-called stepfather?" she asked, sipping her cappuccino. Since nobody had wine with dinner Daniel and Alison had relented and let people order cappuccino and biscotti after the expensive spaghetti was cleared away.

"You're all grown, you don't need a stepfather," Mom said, laughing a little and looking at the last traces of her second drink.

"Wait a minute. You guys haven't met him yet?" I asked. This fact somehow had gotten by me. I assumed the reason I hadn't met Bill was that I was out of town too much. The fact that

90

Lucy and Alison, who lived so close by in Brooklyn and Queens, hadn't met Bill did actually catch me off guard.

"He's so private, I told you, sweetheart. That's just the way he is. Some day we'll make it work out," she said, patting my hand.

"You live like right around the corner from here, right?" Lucy noted. "Let's do it now. He's home, right?"

"I don't think he'd like that."

"We won't stay. We just want to come by and see where you live!" she persisted.

"I'll tell him. Maybe we can work something out for next month."

"Is it a dump? Are you living in some sort of crazy dump?"

"No, not at all. He's just private, you know that."

"He's crazy, is what it sounds like."

It was pretty uncomfortable, frankly; the fact that Lucy was putting it out there to Mom in front of me and Daniel and Alison made the situation really sound as creepy and weird as you kind of worried it might be. Mom just shrugged a little bit and looked down and then she sighed, like this was all too much.

Lucy took offence. "It's a fair question, Mom," she pointed out, kind of edgy. "You've been married to this guy for six months. Why can't we meet him?"

"He doesn't want to, is why," Mom said. And she wasn't apologetic about that at all.

"But he's nice to you, right?" I said.

"You don't have to worry about me, sweetheart, I'm fine!" she said, and she smiled at me and squeezed my hand. Which okay is maybe why it finally occurred to me after she was dead that maybe what she meant was worry about yourself you dingbat; you've just agreed to go to Delaware with another loser.

It also occurred to me that maybe she was ashamed of us, that's why she didn't want Bill to meet us. A year and a half later, sitting there on the floor of that ridiculous little television room, eating Chinese food out of cartons, and trying to figure out how to screw over the two guys who grew up there, and whose Dad had died just three weeks before our Mom died, it certainly did occur to me that maybe we weren't acting so well.

"Are you crying?" Alison asked me, suddenly.

"It's this Kung Pao chicken. I bit into one of the peppers," I said. "I wonder if there's any Kleenex around here." I stood up and looked around, confused. Lucy held up a wad of those lousy paper napkins that they dump in the carry-out bag, and breezed on with her clever plan. "I'll have the Sotheby's guy call Long in the morning. Eventually he's going to have to transfer the files anyway, and they'll have a better sense of how soon that needs to happen. Surely they know how to work this so we can start to proceed with the sale even though the property's still in probate," she told us, licking her fingers like a cat. "There's no question they'll fight it, but we could get at least a little bit of a jump on those Drinans. Potentially we could leave them in the dust."

"They're already in the dust. Their father just died," I reminded her.

"Their father, who disinherited them," she retorted.

"Precisely," I said. "Precisely."

"You're not going to get all moralistic about this," Lucy said, looking up from her docs finally. "Oh, no no. This is not a situation of our making."

"You're sitting here—plotting!" I said.

"Plotting to make you rich. Oh, a couple million dollars, that would suck. You might have to give up cleaning houses."

"I wasn't cleaning houses," I told her, suddenly feeling peevish as hell. "I was *managing properties*."

"Well, my way you can own the properties you manage, how's that for a thought," she said, starting to close up the Chinese food cartons. "And you can go back to college and finish your oh-so-useful degree in pottery, and you can start your own little pottery shop and throw clay around for the rest of your life and never worry ever ever *ever* about whether or not you make one red cent off any of it. That's what can happen to your life, Tina, if you just sit still and let me make you rich."

"That was mean," I said.

"What?" she said, looking at me like I was nuts. "That was *mean*?"

"Yeah, mean. You're being mean to me again, Lucy."

"We're all tired. It's been a long couple of days," Daniel chimed in, soothing. He was being Mr Good Brother-in-law now, asking quietly supportive questions and making sure Lucy knew that We Were In This Together. "Lucy's worked hard to protect us all, and I for one appreciate it." He smiled at her, oh so appreciative. I wanted to smack them both. Instead, I smiled wanly and nodded my sheepish little head.

"I'm sorry," I said. "I'm still shook up about Mom."

"We all are," Alison said, like she thought maybe I was being a bit too morally superior about this after all.

"I know I know, I mean, what I mean is I didn't get much sleep last night." I nodded, fully in retreat mode because what other option did I have? I rubbed my little eyes for effect. "I think I'd better go lie down."

"Be my guest," Lucy shrugged, continuing to clean. Which was her way of letting me know that this wasn't my apartment, it was her apartment, and I wasn't calling the shots. As if I ever called the shots with this crew. In any event, I went and hid in the bedroom with the futons on the floor, and I stared at the stars on the ceiling and waited for my so-called family to leave. Which they did not do for what seemed forever, or at least long enough for me to start worrying that maybe they were out there plotting about what they were going to do to cut me out of my share of the loot once we got our hands on it. And once it occurred to me that that was probably what they were doing, I got myself worked into a complete paranoid frenzy, and I almost went back out there to just hang out and make sure they knew that they weren't pulling any fast ones on me, and I was a full member of this little tribe of pirates, and there would be no sneaking around and cheating anybody out of anything. Then I thought that I probably shouldn't be so confrontational, that that would make them think I was paranoid and weak, and that the smartest move actually would be sneaking through the pink room and into the empty room next to the television room, where I could hide behind the door and find out about their diabolical maneuverings with a clever bit of eavesdropping.

I was actually about to put this idiotic plan in motion—I mean, I was literally sneaking to the door of the pink room, and easing it open as silently as I could—when I heard them coming down the hallway. So then I had to sneak back and slide into the futon against the far wall, so that when Lucy looked back through the crack in the door she could see me sleeping peacefully and tell herself that I was a mess, but not a problem. Her shadow hovered in the doorway for a moment, watching my back, curled against the light in the hallway. Then she thought whatever it was she needed to think, and she left.

I lay there for a good five minutes after I heard the door thump shut, and the three different tumblers turn in their locks. And then I waited another five minutes. I didn't want anybody coming back and interrupting me, which was a complete possibility, given the devious mind of my older sister. But after fifteen minutes I was fairly sure that they had in fact driven away, so I turned the light on and I pulled out the sack I had hidden underneath all the clothes that I had bought that afternoon, and then I retrieved my afternoon's purchases from where I had stuffed them in my backpack.

So this is what I had: one Philips-head screwdriver with exchangeable heads, one zinc-plated steel four-inch spring-bolt lock, and two brass chain door guards. Both the spring bolt and the chain guards came with their own set of screws, but screws are cheap so I bought an extra half dozen just in case.

And then I spent the next fifty minutes locking myself into that apartment.

I knew it would piss off absolutely everybody that I was doing this—Lucy, Alison, Daniel, those Drinans, maybe even Len the moss lover and Frank the doorman, both of whom had really been so nice to me. Nobody was going to be happy that

I had figured out a way to be the one who said who could come in and who couldn't. But honestly I didn't see that I had much choice. In case you hadn't noticed, in spite of the fact that I was totally invaded the night before, not one person all day actually had spent one second figuring out how I was supposed to protect myself, given that those Drinan brothers had keys and also that they clearly thought it was well within their rights to use them at any given moment, and that they actually had badly frightened me, twice. Lucy was spending all her time cooking up plans to pull a fast one and get one over on those guys; well, if you ask me it wouldn't take a brain surgeon to figure out that they were doing the same thing to us. I needed protection. I needed a spring bolt, and two security chains.

CHAPTER SIX

I was right. I mean, I was like, immediately right. Like within ten minutes of finishing the installation process. I was back in the kitchen pouring myself a tumbler of vodka grapefruit surprise when the yelling started. You could hear the guy all the way back there, he was that mad.

"What the fuck? HEY. WHAT THE FUCK," he yelled, starting to pound the shit out of the door. Then he started yanking and pulling at it, and pounding some more. It was enormously satisfying.

"GO AWAY!" I yelled in return, while I sauntered back up to the front of the apartment. "I'M CALLING THE COPS!"

"I AM THE COPS!" he yelled. "OPEN THE FUCKING DOOR." By this I knew it was the other Drinan, the cop with the sexy eyes. Not that I was surprised.

"I'M SLEEPING IN HERE AND I'M NOT BOTHERING ANYBODY. GO AWAY," I yelled.

"OPEN THE FUCKING DOOR," he yelled back.

"What, you got like three sentences, is that all you know

how to say?" I asked him, through the door. "Open the door, I'm a cop, what the fuck, is that all you know how to say?"

"I'd open the door, Tina Finn," he warned me.

"Oh yeah, why?" I said to the door, kind of bold and cocky. It was weird; all of a sudden I felt like I was flirting with someone in a bar. "What are you going to do to me, officer?"

"I'm going to arrest you," he announced.

"I'm not the one trying to break in and harass an innocent citizen in her home, dude," I retorted. "If I put a call in to 911, you're the one who's in the shithouse."

"There's a stay on the apartment, Tina," he informed me, through the door. "No one's allowed to fuck with the locks. You're in violation of the law."

"Except I didn't fuck with the locks, Pierre," I informed him back. "I put in a spring bolt and some chain guards. The locks are fine. When I'm not here? The locks work just fine. When I am here? YOU'RE NOT ALLOWED IN."

There was a pause, and then a kind of bump, right at my shoulder. "Shit," I heard him mumble. He must have been right up against the door. For a second I thought, Wow, this door is thin, I can hear everything and if I can hear everything he can probably pry it open with one of those little battering ram things cops carry with them, whether or not I have the spring bolt in place. And then I thought, Is he the kind of cop who carries those things? What kind of a cop is this guy anyway? Does he have a gun on him? He didn't have a gun, or a uniform, the last time I saw him, but obviously since I wouldn't let him into the apartment there was no knowing if he any of those things—gun, uniform, battering ram—right now. I took a step

98

back, because it did occur to me that if he started whacking at the door all of a sudden I didn't want to be leaning up against it. But whacking at the door did not seem to be on his mind. For the moment, at least, he was quiet.

And then someone else started talking, someone who wasn't him.

I couldn't hear at all what the other person was saying. The other voice was much softer, more from a distance; it was a murmur, and a question. He answered it, only now I couldn't hear him, either; he was practically whispering all of a sudden, to whoever else was out there. This should have been good news to me—let's face it, having an angry cop screaming at me to let him into my apartment in the middle of the night was not anything like an ideal situation—but the whispering voices actually made me more anxious. I stepped back to the door, and put my ear up against it, to see if I could hear what the other person was saying, or what my angry friend Pete Drinan was saying. But while a second ago I felt like Pete was practically in the room with me, now I could barely hear him. He wasn't up against the door anymore; he was down by the elevators. The other person asked him another question, that I couldn't hear, and he answered again, and I couldn't hear the answer. I thought he might be talking to his brother, that would make the most sense, but it didn't really sound like him; whoever this person was actually talked more carefully, and Drinan was talking carefully back. I truly couldn't tell what was going on.

Given my options I decided I'd better go for it, and slid back the spring bolt quietly and carefully. Which was exceptionally difficult; those spring bolts hold together pretty tight, what use would they be if they didn't? Luckily Drinan was far enough away now, and the conversation was apparently riveting enough that he wasn't supernaturally attuned to the sound of a spring bolt being slowly scraped back into the unbolted version of its identity. He had already thrown the tumblers in the three door locks, so all I had to do then was make sure the chain guards were in place and open that door as silently as possible, and find out who the hell was out there with him. I cracked the door.

He was past the elevators, his back to me, and he was talking to whoever it was who lived in the other apartment, 8B. Of course he was! It made so much sense when I saw it that I almost laughed out loud about how paranoid I was being. The lady—I could see it was a lady, with kind of messy brown hair—was standing in her doorway, like all the yelling had just woken her up, and she needed to come out and complain about what-ever nonsense we were involved in, just across the hall from her doorway. But she didn't seem to be angry. She had her hand on Drinan's arm and every now and then she would pat it, like she was comforting him, and he would nod, and look at the floor. He had a bottle of beer in his left hand that he was kind of holding behind him, like a teenager who doesn't want his mom's friend to know that he's got a beer back there. His thumb was hooked into the top to make sure the fizz didn't go.

They didn't know I was there listening, so they just kept talking. "God rest her soul, I miss her every day," said the lady.

"I do too," he told her, quiet.

"It would have just killed her to see this, just killed her!

100

Oh my God when they were selling the furniture, all I could think was this would have just killed Sophie, the way Bill is just letting everything go."

"Actually she hated most of that stuff," Drinan noted.

"So many beautiful pieces. Worth a fortune! And then the paintings, I thought I would just cry when the paintings—"

"She didn't like them either." He sounded like on every line he wanted to take a hit off that beer bottle, but she wasn't giving him an opening.

"Your inheritance, it was all your inheritance, gone, that's what she wouldn't have liked. Your father should be ashamed of himself."

"Yeah, well, he never was."

"God rest his soul you got that right. And he never asked me. If I wanted them? I thought at least ask, I would have been happy to step in, and keep them in the building. I would have done that for your mother, God rest her soul. I told him! But you couldn't talk to him. Well, you know that."

"Yes." He shifted on his feet and for about fifteen seconds I got a better look at the woman, who had a very good face, underneath that big head of messy hair. I was sort of not liking her much until I saw her face, then I wasn't so sure, because she seemed sort of sensible, even though she was saying slightly dotty things and clearly was just cranky that she couldn't get her hands on those paintings and all that furniture. She also had on some kind of silk robe, sage green with a burnt orange stripe; the bit I could see hanging off her shoulder suggested it might be spectacularly beautiful if I could get a better look at it. Drinan shifted again, and I lost the sightline.

"Well, thank you for your thoughts, Mrs Westmoreland," he started. His hand, holding the beer, was getting a little slippery, plus I could see from the way his shoulders were scrunching together that he was getting pretty desperate for that drink. Before he could take a step backwards and turn to take a fast hit off it she touched him on the sleeve again, and held him there. Ai yi yi, I thought, this is getting interesting.

"But these people, who are these people?" she asked, all concerned. "Coming and going, acting like they own the place. Frank says that one of them has moved in. I'm horrified." I went back to not liking her. What on earth was she complaining about, she was "horrified" about me living in an apartment I had every legal right to live in? She was just some Upper West Side snob who had the hots for a dude half her age, that's what I decided, on the basis of admittedly hardly any information at all.

"It's something to do with Dad's will." He shrugged. "He left everything to Olivia."

"You're kidding!"

"Look, it's fine, it's going to be fine." You could hear that he was already kicking himself for letting go that much. And it did seem, in fact, to be a terrific and instant mistake.

"He left everything to *Olivia*? He barely knew her!"

"They were married two years," he corrected her.

"Did you know he was doing that? Did you agree to it?"

"He didn't actually ask us to agree," Pete said. His voice was starting to get real uptight. "He told us. Doug tried to talk him out of it. But Dad wanted to do something for Olivia."

"That's ridiculous."

"Yeah, well, he was worried she wouldn't have anything if he died. That's what he said."

"She didn't deserve anything!"

"Well, that's what he felt, anyway. He, you know, he knew he was dying and he wanted her to have some security after he was gone."

"Surely you could have put a stop to this."

"We had a big fight about it. Doug was, you know he pretty much felt what you were saying. Dad got real mad about it. It wasn't . . . we didn't really talk much after that."

This was so much more information than I'd ever had about Bill I was momentarily thrilled. I was once again delighted to find how successful snooping at doors could be. I was also happy to have a shred of good feeling for Bill since he did the right thing by Mom in the face of opposition. He was instantly transformed, in my imagination, from a selfish drunk into an eccentric recluse who had lousy kids.

"But Olivia is dead now. And these other people, what rights do they have?"

"I don't know. Honestly, I just don't know." Pete trailed off, clearly wanting to get out of this hideous conversation. But she was a sharp one. And she was as completely fascinated as I was by what he had told her already.

"He didn't even know them, he refused to meet them!" she told him. "He was afraid of just this scenario, that complete strangers would come after his property, that's why he told her they were never to set foot in the building!"

"She told you that?"

"She did! I asked her one night. She had just come back in

from having dinner with the rest of them, apparently. It was so rare that you ever saw either one of them leave the apartment, so when I saw her in the lobby I said, 'This is a treat! You and Bill don't go out much, do you?' and she said, 'I was having dinner with my daughters,' and we rode up in the elevator together, and I said, 'Are we going to meet your daughters?' and she said, 'Oh no, Bill prefers to keep me all to himself!' And I said, 'Well, that hardly seems fair. You must miss them a lot.' And she said she did, very much, and that she had tried to speak to him about it but he was very worried, these were her own words, he was worried that other people were after his property, and he had to protect it. Those were her exact words. And then I saw him one day, not long after that—I actually saw him, putting trash in the bin, which he never did—and I said, 'Why, Bill! There you are!' He looked terrible, I don't need to tell you that, he was sick for a long long time and I know he refused to see a doctor—"

"Yeah, but you said you talked to him?"

"I did. I took the opportunity. I said, 'Bill, Olivia tells me you've never even met her daughters. Aren't you curious to even meet them? She's your wife!' I was reluctant to say anything to him at all, I couldn't believe he brought another woman into your mother's apartment. It was the Livingston mansion apartment, it is an historic property! He should have let it go, is my opinion, when your mother died. He should have sold it to someone who might take care of it, someone in the building who would appreciate it. He never appreciated it. She was the one."

"But he said something? About these daughters?"

104

"He said, yes, he said they were trash. He said, 'Those daughters are trash and I'm not meeting them.' That's what he called them. *Trash*. And he wouldn't meet them. All they wanted was his money." At which point old Bill went back to being an alcoholic asshole, in my imagination.

Pete Drinan thought about this. It was not an uninteresting bit of information to him. "Was he drunk?" he finally asked.

"Well, I only saw him for a moment, so I couldn't really say," Mrs Westmoreland admitted. "I know he did like to drink."

"Yes, he did." Pete sighed, his hand curled around the beer bottle behind his back. "Listen, Mrs Westmoreland—would you be willing to talk about this? To our lawyer?"

"Oh, a lawyer . . ." She sighed, all worried, but excited too, like she was secretly happy to be asked. "You mean, officially?"

"Well, yeah," said Pete. "It might make a difference—that you spoke to him directly and he told you that he didn't want the property going out of the family. That that was his intent? That's what she said, huh, that was his intent?"

"That was my understanding. But if this is an official situation—I don't know. Do you want to come in, have a cup of tea? I want you and your brother to have your inheritance. But obviously I don't want to get into some complicated legal mess. But I did love your mother. Maybe, do you want to come in and have a cup of tea?"

"Oh," said Pete, his fingers twirling around the neck of that beer bottle. I started thinking about how that beer was probably getting all warm and flat, and then I thought, Well, if I'm thinking that I bet he is too. And sure enough he leaned back on his left leg, ready to edge away again. But she was not letting go. She actually had her fingers twisted in his jacket sleeve now. Her door had swung completely open by this point. What little you could see of her place from my vantage point was gorgeous.

"Your mother was my neighbor for thirty years. This whole story breaks my heart," she explained, leaning up against the doorway.

"Mine too, Mrs Westmoreland." He nodded, leaning back.

"Good heavens, Peter." She sighed. "After all this time I think you could consider calling me Delia."

"Yeah, well . . ."

"Come in, let me get you that tea. Or a drink! Maybe a whiskey. That sounds like a policeman's drink!" she said with a smile.

He turned, to finally take a hit off that beer bottle, and stared me straight in the face. We looked at each other, through the crack in the door. He looked tired. And then he kind of remembered, I guess, what was going on, and he took a fast step in my direction, and I remembered too, and I slammed the door and slid the bolt back in place. I thought he was going to start pounding again, but he didn't, he just waited. I could hear the woman from 8B start to gripe again, about how awful it all was; I couldn't really hear the words but the tone of her voice was not complimentary. He didn't say anything back to her. I stood at the door and listened, and he didn't say anything at all. I wasn't sure what was going on, if he was going to try and bust the door down with one of those sticks, or what. Finally the woman from 8B stopped talking, and things were really quiet. I thought maybe he was gone. And then a little white card slid under the door. At the last second, it kind of wafted, like he had pushed it. After another second I picked it up. It was a really plain business card, with the NYPD shield on one side, and his name, Detective Peter Drinan, right in the middle, and a cell number on it. I turned it over. On the back, written in ink, in teeny little block letters it said, CALL ME WHEN YOU'RE READY. I thought about that for a second, and I kept listening at the door. He was still out there; in fact, from the shadows it looked like he was sort of hovering down there near the floor to see if I had actually picked the card up. So I took the paper bag that they gave me at the hardware store, and I looked through my backpack, which was still right there where I had dumped it, and I found a pen, and I ripped a piece off the paper bag, and I wrote on it: OKAY. And then I shoved that through the door. And then I watched, through the crack, while he picked it up. And then I heard him laugh. The lady in the other apartment squawked some more questions at him, and he said something else to her, but then I heard the elevator ding, and the door close. And when I went out there, in the morning, he was gone.

CHAPTER SEVEN

Len's greenhouse was so big it had rooms: the deciduous room, the desert room, the rainforest room, the heirloom plants from other centuries room, the plants that only grow on other plants room. Some of these rooms were apparently subsets or extensions of rooms, and some of the rooms overlapped before growing into new rooms—like the plants growing on other plants room turned into the orchid subset of a room, which evolved into the spectacularly gorgeous and weird plants room, which turned a corner before becoming the poisonous plants room—so that the whole place seemed actually to be growing, itself; it covered the roof and threatened to crawl down the side of the building, in some places. It was truly the only greenhouse I have ever seen that is big enough to get lost in. I told old Len that I thought it was pretty surprising he could get enough water up there to make a greenhouse that big—especially since it had a rainforest in it—but he couldn't get enough water up there for a little bit of moss. He said, "I know, it is surprising, isn't it?" By which I knew he really was full of shit, and there was no reason that he had to stash the moss in my apartment, except for the fact that he had run out of room in his. That, and there really was quite a bit of sunlight. He got light on six sides up there. It was like being on Mount Olympus, with a whole bunch of plants.

As much fun as it had been to talk to Len about his moss, it was nothing compared to hearing him go on about plants. He started out delivering information sort of like a university lecturer, which he had been at some point in his life. Everything was all about the genus and the species and the Latinate name and the common name, and the historical derivatives of the names. But he couldn't hold on to the formality of it all, frankly. In no time flat he was talking to the plants, checking out the texture of the leaves, telling the pretty ones how pretty they were, telling the ones that were all spiky and weird looking that looks didn't matter, the pink coleus is just a slut for showing off like that, beauty comes and goes so quickly and she was only an annual anyway. He thought the cactuses were sly and devious, he called them the "tricksters of the desert", which I didn't quite follow because I have to admit all those spikes didn't look so sly to me, they were pretty direct, in fact, but when I pointed that out Len just laughed, like there was so much about cactuses that I just didn't know. Which of course how could you argue with that, I actually *don't* know anything about cactuses, I was just making an observation. And then he took me into the orchid room and I got an earful about the orchids. He had truly more than a hundred different kinds, each one stranger than the next. Some had spots all over them, which I had never seen before on any flower. They were pink and purple and yellow and white, and dark red with black centers, and there was one that was black everywhere, which was strangely frightening, to see a completely black flower. There were some that looked like stars and some that looked like butterflies, some that looked like tarantulas, some that looked like hornets or some other kind of stinging animal, and then of course there were just dozens that looked like sex organs. Seriously, all of those flowers looked like they want to have sex with humans. It was a bit creepy, honestly. I was somewhat afraid to touch them.

This turned out to be a good impulse on my part, as Len sort of casually informed me once we were done with the orchid room.

"Some of them are poisonous," he admitted. "The pollen, the ovules, the nectar, this little darling here—don't touch—not that it would really hurt you permanently, but you very well might lose all feeling in your arm, for at least a day."

"Come on, Len," I said.

"Do you want to try it?" he asked, raising those eyebrows at me.

I didn't. "But if orchids are poisonous how come everybody has them in their houses?" I asked.

"Only certain species, Tina. Use your head," he told me, pulling out a very small pair of clippers and snipping some extraneous vines away from a line of bright yellow star-shaped flowers which wound down the side of a tree. "Please don't touch that."

"You can't touch any of them?" I asked.

"Until you know which ones are poisonous, and which aren't, no, in fact, you can't touch any of them."

"How did you find out which ones are poisonous?"

"The hard way," he informed me. "I studied."

The place smelled like growing things, and sounded like water. He had little fountains in corners, and strange pools suddenly appeared behind tree trunks, or alongside a hillside of ferns. That greenhouse was so big it had hills—small hills, but there were definite undulations. And everything was green, a thousand different greens, each one more subtle than the next. In spite of the pink coleus and the startling sexuality of the many-colored and poisonous orchids, green was what you saw, everywhere. And sky. You forgot, honestly, that you were in a building, in a city, on an island. I don't know where you were, but it was not where you thought.

And then all of a sudden you turned a corner and you were back in his apartment. His apartment was quite small. You would say that it was quite small in comparison to the size of the greenhouse, but the fact is that it was quite small in comparison to anything; it was one little room, right at the center of the roof. There was a linoleum counter and a kitchenette, completely cluttered with pots and pans and a blender and lots of mismatched dishes on open shelves. And then across from the counter there was a wall with a lot of books, all about plants, and a chair and a little table, and then to one side of that there was a big overstuffed blue couch that had magazines and books piled all over it, and then behind that, in a corner, there was an unmade bed. And then next to the bed there seemed to be some sort of closet, and then at the back of the closet, or to the side, actually, there was a very small bathroom that had a skylight and lots of plants in the bathtub. And then on the other side of the bathtub there was one of those Plexiglas walls they sell you in fancy bath stores, and just beyond the Plexiglas was the room with all the ferns. Seriously you could step out of that bathtub and into the greenhouse. I mean, Len had walls, he did have actual walls in some places, just not as many walls as most people have. So that the greenhouse actually did seem to grow out of that tiny apartment, and then it just kept growing.

"Would you like a cup of tea?" Len asked me. "Or a cappuccino?" He gestured gently toward a large silver contraption which took up the entire counter space between the very small stovetop and the equally small refrigerator unit. The only thing that wasn't utterly minuscule in the entire kitchen was the cappuccino machine, and it was enormous. Len considered it with an air of bemused resignation, like it was an old but hapless and worrisome friend. "I have this wonderful machine someone gave me, I can never get it to work," he admitted.

"If you can't get it to work, why are you offering me cappuccino?" I asked him.

"Well, I was thinking that if you wanted a cappuccino you could try to make it yourself, and then if you were successful you could show me how to do it," he admitted, offering up that dazzling smile.

"Fair enough," I said. "Where's the coffee?"

"Oh, coffee . . . oh," he mused, looking around that tiny kitchen.

"Never mind, I'll find it," I said, and I started poking around. Frankly that kitchen was so small there weren't that many places to look. I landed on the stuff my first try: it was in the freezer.

"You know you're not really supposed to freeze your beans, it dries them out," I informed old Len, looking over the bag to see if I could spot an expiration date. "How long has this been in here?"

"Oh, not long. A week? My daughter brought it by. She brought me one of those baskets of food they give to invalids in hospitals. I think there are chocolate biscuits somewhere." He started poking around the bookshelves, like there was a possibility he had hidden the biscuits in with the books.

"You have a daughter?" This was real news, as far as I was concerned. I mean, it was hard to imagine this strange person having any human relations. I thought he was half plant himself, by this point.

"Oh yes, she's, well, you know, she's my daughter, you know what that's like," he replied, seemingly thinking that all girls with parents somehow shared the same frontal lobe. "I can't find the biscuits."

"Here they are," I said, pulling them out from behind the cappuccino machine. Len looked at them with a sort of stern surprise, like the biscuits had done something really pretty offensive, locating themselves in such an unusual spot.

"What are they doing there?" he asked.

"Maybe your daughter put them there," I suggested. "Maybe she was trying to clean up your kitchen for you a little bit and she thought it was, you know, a good spot to stash the cookies. You know, by the cappuccino machine. What's her name?"

"Oh, who remembers," he sighed, suddenly bored to the point of apathy. "Her mother always called her Charlie. I dislike it when girls have boys' names, it's all confusing enough as it is without things like that."

"Is that the name on her birth certificate?"

"What? No. Do you think I'm crazy?"

"Well, yes, a bit," I said, looking around.

"Her given name is Charlotte. We named her *Charlotte*," he informed me, with some heat.

"Well, why don't you just call her that?" I asked, pouring a bunch of coffee beans into what seemed to be the grinding part of the machine; at least, there was a clever little chute that opened up off one side which implied that beans might go there.

"I rarely see her, so I don't call her anything," Len informed me, increasingly annoyed with this line of questioning.

"Why don't you see her?" I said, looking for the switch.

"Well, let's see, Tina. Why would a parent and child become estranged? Let's speculate on that, shall we?" He ducked his head into the refrigerator. "You'll need milk, I think."

"This is a very nice machine, Len," I told him, flipping the switch. Nothing happened. He set a red and white carton of whole milk on the cluttered counter between us and watched as I flipped the switch again.

"Stop it. It makes no sense to keep flipping that switch all around like that. One try is plenty. It doesn't work, I told you. I've had that machine for years and it doesn't ever work."

"So why don't you get another one?"

"Oh, I don't really like cappuccino anyway," he sighed, opening the tin of cookies.

"Then why am I making it?"

"Well, you're not, as far as I can see. You haven't gotten that thing to work anymore than I did," he observed. "And now you have to figure out how to get the beans out of there. You're going to have to turn the whole thing upside down, and doubtless the beans will simply go everywhere. And no one has even begun to make the tea. It's a complete waste of time."

"Wait," I said, plugging it in. "Hang on." I flipped the switch. The machine started to hum and rumble as the beans swirled in the chute.

"Oh," said Len, arrested for a second. Then ground coffee began to spit all over the counter. "Well, that is—interesting."

It took another twenty minutes to figure out how to get the ground coffee into the other part of the machine, steam the espresso and then steam the milk, but the whole thing was frankly pretty entertaining and relaxing, compared to the other stuff that had been happening to me for the past three days. Len had a lot to say about everything except his own personal history; as long as you were willing to stay off the subject of his daughter Charlie and her mother, he was a complete motor mouth. He left a lot of things out, but if you didn't push too hard and let him just keep yakking, there was plenty of information, which I was happy to have, as I had become insanely eager to fill in the blanks left by the tantalizing conversation I had spied on several nights before.

"So what's the story on the lady who lives on the same floor as me?" I said, serving up a perfect cappuccino—which, as it turns out, Len liked a lot.

"You've met Delia Westmoreland!" he noted, admiring the foam on his coffee cup. "How was that for you?"

"How was it?"

"Yes, did you find her charming? She can be, if she likes."

"But not, if she doesn't like?"

"I didn't say that. Where are those cookies?"

"We finished them, but there are some cheese twist things here," I said, finding another little foil bag from a fancy food store. "Is this all you eat, gourmet snack food?"

"I have a hard time in grocery stores, they confuse me," he admitted. "Delia Westmoreland. She's a very strong personality, I would say. And she had very strong ties to the previous tenants of your apartment."

"Yeah, I noticed."

"You noticed? How so?"

"One of them came by a couple days ago, the Drinan who's a police detective or something?"

"Yes, I know who he is," Len responded drily.

"Anyway, when he couldn't get in he stood out in the hall and yelled, and she came out and talked to him. She's pretty oo la la for a lady her age," I observed.

"She's sixty, darling. It's the new seventeen," Len informed me. "Although 'oo la la' does cover it. Why did young Mr Drinan find himself stuck out in the hall yelling in the first place? It was my understanding that neither you nor the Drinans were allowed to change the locks."

"Where'd you hear that?"

"Everyone in the building is talking about it, Tina. You'll have to get used to it, the walls have ears in a co-op. Either one of you is going to need a court order, at this point, to change those locks. You didn't do something foolish, did you?"

117

"I didn't change the locks myself, if that's what you mean. I just put in a couple of chains and a deadbolt, so that people can't barge in whenever they want."

"Oh," said Len, startled at this idea. "Oh! That's clever. Good for you."

"He didn't think I was so clever. He was pretty pissed off," I noted.

"Well, legally you're not allowed to forbid them access to the apartment until claim to the title is established."

"I didn't say he couldn't come in, I just don't want him barging in while I'm sleeping there."

"Well, you put yourself in that situation, darling."

"My sister put me there."

"Oh yes, I see," he said, raising his eyes.

"What?"

"A girl who knows how to put in a deadbolt and two chain guards is hardly a victim, Tina."

"I didn't say I was a victim."

"Didn't you? I thought you did."

"Could we get back to this horny Westmoreland character, who lives on my floor?"

"Horny? Why do you say that?"

"She was coming on to Drinan, big time. She kept trying to get him to come into her apartment and have tea."

"You're up in my apartment, having cappuccino—do you think I have designs on you?"

"No, you have designs on making sure nobody bothers your moss," I told him.

"Well, along those same lines allow me to inform you that

118

Delia Westmoreland does not lust after young Mr Drinan. She lusts, but not after human flesh."

"She said she was mad that they wouldn't sell her all the stuff in the apartment, when they started selling everything off," I remembered. "But now it's all gone. You've been in the place—there's nothing left there for her to want, is there?"

"Things of the flesh are not what she's after," he told me, eating one of those cheese twists. "No, darling; she wants the same thing everyone else in New York is pining for: square footage. If she could get her hands on the Livingston Mansion Apartment, she would own the entire eighth floor. Minor renovation and she's sitting on one of the most spectacular apartments in the city. She's been trying to buy that place for years. She literally hounded Bill about it."

"She wants to own the whole eighth floor."

"Of course she does."

"I thought, I mean, she kind of—doesn't she live alone over there?"

"There's the occasional visit from estranged nephews, but yes, for the most part she lives alone."

"Well, how much room does she need?"

"It's never about need, when it comes to real estate," Len informed me. Which to a girl who at one time lived in a mobile home in a trailer park did not completely make sense, but he was dead serious.

"So, if she bought it—she'd have like—how big an apartment would that be?"

"Twelve thousand square feet."

"That's a lot."

"With park views and walk-in closets? All those freaks over in 10021 will commit collective suicide out of sheer envy if Delia manages to pull off a coup like that. A place like that would be worth forty million dollars in any market."

"So she's like mega loaded."

"Not particularly, no."

"Come on, she's got to have some money. She lives in this place."

"She inherited. Her husband's parents bought their apartment in the twenties for something ridiculous, thirty-five thousand or something, and then they died—this was some time in the late eighties, just before the market tanked and I managed to grab the roof here—which is a whole different story—anyway, that's how she got in. He was in finance, but he was never a major player, so in some ways they actually were just scraping by. I think she's got twelve or fifteen million on a good day in the market, apart from the apartment."

"So she's worth, like, twenty-five million. And that's not loaded."

"Well, it's certainly not enough for her to make a grab on 8A, unless she leveraged her place, which may be her thinking. If she puts up two, let's say, she should be able to find a bank to lend her the rest. Another million goes into the renovation and voilà!, for the upfront price of three million dollars she owns an apartment worth forty. But my suspicion is, she hopes to lay her hands on that place for nothing at all."

"How's that supposed to work?"

"Well, I'm not saying it will work. But if she can convince a developer to put the money up front, in exchange for right

120

of first refusal to buy the place from her estate when she dies, that might be something that was of interest to any number of speculators."

"People do that?"

"That's actually a fairly tame and sensible scenario. For instance, it doesn't involve an actual homicide, although if Delia makes it into her nineties I am sure there will be some discussion of poison at that time. Even in the most catastrophic of markets, a twelve-thousand-square-foot apartment with park views on the Upper West Side will never depreciate. It's win win win win win for everyone. Oh yes, I'm sure that all of these options have been considered by now. And not merely by her."

"Who else?"

"It's an old and elegant building, Tina. People have lived here a long time."

"What does that mean?"

"It means it's an old and elegant building and people have lived here a long time," he repeated, mysteriously.

"Well, if any of these 'people' want to buy it they should call Sotheby's. Why is this woman sucking up to Pete Drinan in the middle of the night, if what she really wants is to buy the stupid apartment?" I was getting a little peevish all of a sudden. I turned back to the cappuccino machine, thinking I'd make another round, even though I was already so caffeinated I thought my head was going to explode.

"Is something wrong?" asked Len.

"I just, all these rich people make me nervous. She has a zillion rooms herself, and she wants our place too? But she doesn't want to have to pay for it? That's just, that's incredible, is what that is. Plus you should have heard her going on about how horrible it all was, we're horrible, Mom was horrible, like we're just crazy—skanks from Jersey, or something—and meanwhile she has all these rights, to like take over our apartment, she has the right to do that just because she lived on the same floor for a bunch of years. That's classic, it really is."

"It wasn't your place at all, as I might remind you, until six days ago."

"It was my mom's. When she died the deed was in her name, was it not? Was it not?"

"So I'm told," said Len.

"So I'm told, too. By *lawyers*. My mom lived there, oh and by the way she died there, too. That doesn't give us rights?"

"I don't imagine that Delia Westmoreland thinks so, no. I don't believe the Drinan brothers think so either. And I have a suspicion that the co-op board also will not feel that it gives you rights."

"Well, they don't get to say, do they? The *law* says. The *LAW* says we own, it's ours by *law*."

"That's not going to do you any good if you can't sell it, Tina. And if you can't sell, how will you pay the inheritance tax? Have you asked yourselves any of these questions?"

"We are going to sell it."

"Not if the co-op board can stop you."

I truly didn't know what he was talking about, but it had that peculiar sound of a true thing. "Okay," I said, trying to not get too worked up now. "Okay, so tell me what the problem is with the co-op board. I don't even know what a co-op board is."

122

"They are the twelve residents of this building who will inform you and your sisters—repeatedly, I am afraid to tell you— that even if the courts tell you that in fact you do own that apartment, and you very much have the right to sell it, that in fact they will not permit you to sell it."

"They can't do that."

"Alarmingly, yes they can."

"Why would they do that?"

"Because they don't know you. You're an outsider, your mother was an outsider, it's an offence to everyone here that you and your sisters think you can just come in and take over that beautiful old apartment. You and your sisters can talk to Sotheby's all you want; every offer that they put on the table will be rejected out of hand, until someone, or more than one person inside the building, has been permitted to make an offer. An offer so low it will amount to, let's call it—theft."

"They can't do that. They said, that lawyer said, there isn't a cloud on the title. It's means, that legally means—"

"I know what it means, Tina, and I'm afraid that there is very much a cloud on the title, whether there is a cloud on the title or not."

"I have to call Lucy," I said, digging into my pocket for that cell phone I'd bought the day before.

"She knows all about this, Tina, I'm sure."

"No, she doesn't."

"Does she tell you everything?" he asked me, pointed. I looked at him. He was considering me like I was some kind of interesting plant that was growing in odd directions, or that my leaves were drooping and grey, and he couldn't quite understand why.

"Why—why are you telling me all this?" I finally asked him. Truly, none of this was good news, but it wasn't like he was trying to scare me off. If he had had a watering can at that point, I was pretty sure he would have been shaking it over my head.

"Well," said Len, looking around. "You did fix the cappuccino machine. And you know your mother, I had pneumonia last year, and I ended up in the hospital for two weeks, and she took good care of my moss. There aren't many people who would have bothered."

"You're nice to me because my mom saved your moss?"

"There are worse reasons, Tina Finn," he told me. "She was a nice woman. She was a caretaker at heart. I'm sorry you didn't know that about her."

"I did know it," I said.

"Well, then you should have visited her more," he replied, turning back and putting our dishes in the tiny sink. The air from the greehouse drifted through the kitchen, a little chill now, and he looked up, like someone had spoken. "Oh, the rain drip mechanism is off again in the deciduous room. I'm sorry, you'll have to go," he told me.

"But—"

"I just have a lot of work this afternoon. Thank you for coming up and telling me about the spring bolt; when I need to come down I'll be sure to check in, so that I don't startle you."

"You don't startle me," I told him, a little confused at the change in him. "I just—"

"I'm sorry but I really do have work. Is there something *else*

124

you need?" He was seriously impatient with me now. I had no idea what had happened. We had been doing so well.

"Why are you mad at me?" I said.

"I'm not angry. I have no feelings at all," he said, like that was going to make it better. "Are you *crying*?"

"I just don't know what to do," I said, and the fact is I was crying. Just a little bit, but I had most definitely teared up. It was really mortifying. "If everybody hates me, just because I'm here, what do I do?"

"Oh for heaven's sake. Get a grip," he said. "If nobody likes you the thing you need to do is *make friends*."

CHAPTER EIGHT

The Whites lived on the ninth floor, directly above me. Their apartment, like mine, had way more rooms and closets and hallways than you could possibly figure out or follow, but unlike my apartment there were people in all of them. There was Mrs White, who dressed in really cute little jackets and skirts and hose and short heels, so she looked great while she ran around like a lunatic, shouting at everyone and carrying things everywhere, books and piles of laundry and stuffed animals and spoons and forks and empty juice boxes. Then there was a cook, actually two cooks, but they came on different days, and this Polish woman named Anna who was always doing laundry, and a Hispanic woman, Magda, who seemed to be always cleaning bathrooms, and then there were lots and lots of girls, little girls and big girls, mostly wearing plaid pleated skirts and dark green cardigan sweaters. The Whites had six kids, and all of them were girls. Since there were six of them it took me more than a few days to learn all their names. They were: Louise, Jennifer, Gail, Mary Ellen, Katharine and a two-year-old named Barbie. They actually called the kid Barbie, which I thought was a mistake, but she was so little I figured the chances were that ultimately she would grow up and tell them to cut it out and that would be the end of that.

When I went up to 9A to introduce myself to the chaotic Whites, I had no idea what I might find there. After Len kicked me out of the greenhouse I went back to my apartment and poked around the kitchen and the laundry without really knowing what I was looking for. I put a call in to Lucy, but her assistant told me that she was in meetings all afternoon and would not be able to return calls until tomorrow. I thought for a second about arguing with her and telling her that there was an emergency around the apartment but I was pretty sure that Lucy would not consider my musings about the devious co-op board and the greedy Mrs Westmoreland an emergency so I just said thanks and hung up. Then I thought about calling Alison, which didn't seem likely to calm me down either, and then I picked up the clicker for the television and thought about channel flipping for the rest of the day, as in fact I have in previous times spent entire days aimlessly trolling basic cable for traces of common sense or answers that never appeared. Then I considered throwing the fucking clicker against the wall, and then I decided against it and started to set it down again, on the coffee table. Which is where I found the card for Stuart Long, Esq, who actually got on the phone as soon as his receptionist told him I was on the line.

"Hello, Tina, how are you?" he asked, all kind and concerned. "Are you still in the apartment?"

"Where else would I be?"

"Well, I heard from the Drinans that they'd prefer that you stayed elsewhere, as they are planning to litigate," he observed sagely, as if this were big news.

"Listen, Mr Long, I actually called about a slightly different question. The co-op board over here, they may or may not make it difficult for a sale to go through, when we try to sell this place, is that right?"

"They will have to approve the sale, if or when it gets to that point, of course," Long agreed. "I don't think it's anything you need to worry about now, though. You have a lot of hoops to jump through before that."

"That's not what Lucy thinks. She's already had realtors coming through here. She thinks we're all good to go," I informed him.

"Your sister is clearly someone who likes to move quickly; I noticed that when we met," Long agreed. "Nevertheless I'm sure she doesn't expect for this situation to resolve itself overnight. Even probating a simple will takes months, and this is far from simple. The courts have not yet probated Mr Drinan's estate, and the deposition of that will directly bear on your own situation."

What he had said made next to no sense to me, so I stuck with the subject at hand. "Yeah, well, what about the co-op board?" I asked.

"Have they contacted you?"

"Is that what happens next?"

He paused for a moment, with that kindly concern. "Tina—your sister indicated that you are employing other counsel. Are you aware of that?"

"No, she didn't mention that either. Sorry, Mr Long, I didn't know, I'm so—uh look, could you just tell me who's on the co-op board and I'll take it from there?"

"Well, that information is included in the documentation about the apartment which I gave to your sister."

"So you don't have it anymore?"

"Of course I have it. I represented Bill Drinan for thirty years. I have everything on file."

"Could you give me those names?"

"You don't want to ask your sister for them?"

"I just, I have you on the phone so I thought it made more sense just to get them from you." I did not want to get into a discussion of my problematic sister with this nice man, especially if he wasn't going to represent me anyway. What would be the point?

There was a little silence on the end of the line, and then he sighed. "Let's see what we have," he said. "Here we are. There are twelve people on the board. It's a rotating board, of course, but this slate was just elected last spring, so it should be current. Alice White, apartment 9A. Roger Masterson, 5B . . ."

Twelve people to suck up to and make friends with. One of them was Len, something I did think that he might have mentioned when he brought the whole thing up in the first place. Even though I found that to be a worrisome oversight on Len's part, however, I couldn't dismiss the common sense of the theory that maybe I should try and present a good face to the people in this fancy building and start pretending to the neighbors that I really did belong there. I grabbed a bottle of Bill's good wine and started with the Whites because they were the closest, just one floor away.

"Hi, I'm looking for Mrs White," I informed the edgy teenager who answered the door. She was wearing a plaid skirt and a green cardigan sweater, which looked terrible on her, as they would on any reasonably attractive person.

"Mooooom!" she yelled. "There's some lady here!"

"Louise, don't shout, *please,*" shouted Mrs White from two or three rooms away. Louise shrugged and walked away from me; I had no choice but to just let myself in and watch her pass by her mother in the hallway. Mrs White was carrying a baby, and had another crying child glued to her leg. In spite of this, she wore a really cute little pink suit, which looked terrific on her.

"Who is it?" she asked, looking back toward the other end of the apartment, as if I might be back there. I think she was just confused for a moment about where the front door was.

"I don't know her name. I think it's that lady, who moved downstairs," said curt Louise, not even bothering to pause in the hallway as she answered the question.

"Oh, that's ridiculous," said Mrs White. "You didn't ask her name?"

"It's Tina Finn!" I called, trying to be all friendly. "My mother was married to Bill? My mother was Olivia? Did you know my mom?"

Mrs White was too startled to answer this at first. She just stared at me. I took a step in and held up the bottle of wine, like a trophy. "I wanted to come introduce myself and say hello. I'll be staying downstairs for now. So I wanted to say hello." I was hoping it didn't sound as ridiculous and dopey as it seemed to, in my head. If it did, Mrs White's manners were really just too good to let me know.

"Of course!" she said, trying to unpeel the kid from her shin and take a few steps toward me in the foyer. "Yes, I did see you the other day, didn't I? Downstairs in the lobby, I think—Sweetie, let go of my leg. Mommy needs to just say hello to the lady."

"Tina," I repeated.

"Yes, Tina, it is—lovely—to meet you," she agreed, reaching a bit so that she could shake my hand. I took the last few steps in, to make it easier for her. At which point the kid on the floor backed up, bumped into a side table, and knocked everything on it onto the floor.

"Katharine, be careful—Katharine—oh, thank you, thanks," Mrs White said, as I started picking up books and mail.

Katharine the unfortunate started to tear up. "Sorry," she said. "I didn't see it!"

"You never see it, Katharine," sighed Mrs White. Then, to me, "Thank you, that's not necessary—"

"No problem," I assured her, stacking the mail smoothly into a neat little pile.

"Wow, that's your name, Katharine?" I asked the kid. "Hi, I'm Tina." The baby started to wail.

"Katharine, don't bother her. Thank you for the wine," Mrs White started again.

"She's not bothering me," I offered, ignoring her not-so-subtle hint for me to leave. I had made it through the door; it was much farther than I ever thought I'd get and I wasn't going to give up ground so quickly. As the baby was really going at it, wailing and writhing with that peculiar rage that comes out of nowhere to really little kids, Mrs White was suddenly helpless.

132

"Barbie—Barbie—oh, for heaven's sake. Sweetie. Barbie! Would you mind waiting just a moment while I get Barbie her bottle?"

"Barbie?" I said, not realizing right away that Mrs White was talking about an actual person, which would be the baby. "Oh, I mean, sure. Hello, Barbie."

"I'll be right back," said Mrs White. And she scooted off leaving me with the other kid in the front hallway. We stared at each other for a moment.

"Do you want to see my toys?" Katharine asked.

"Sure," I said. I followed her down another hallway, to a soft yellow room so far back in the building I would not have even guessed that it was there. There was a comfortable kind of day bed covered with a pink and yellow bedspread up against one wall, underneath an enormous cross-stitched quilt of little pictures of things that started with the different letters of the alphabet. And then there was a rug with a big rainbow on it. Itty bitty wooden and plastic people were everywhere, clumped in small groupings, like they were having sort of discreet parties in every corner of the room, around tiny plastic toy playground sets, or, in one corner, by the side of a little wooden castle. "Wow," I said, flopping on the day bed casually so I could sneak a glance out the window. It looked out on an alleyway that I had never even seen before, which convinced me that in fact there was another room somewhere in my own apartment that I had not yet found. "Is this your room? It's so cute."

"This is my bed, and these are my animals," Katharine informed me, pulling about seventy stuffed animals out from under the sweet little trundle bed that sat tidily in the opposite corner. "This is Blackie. This is Lulu. This is Betty."

I climbed down to the floor to get a closer look at the dogs and cats and rabbits and bears and ponies and ducks and sheep and llamas that were now pouring out from under the bed, and we were deep into some game that had to do with little animals living in the forest when someone finally found us all the way back there. It was one of those teenagers, not the one I met at the door, but one who seemed slightly younger and even more unhappy about wearing that hideous school uniform. This one had hair that drooped all over her head, like she couldn't be bothered with it, which was a shame because it was that great sort of dark blonde color with streaks of red in it that only teenagers get to have, and only for a while. She also had pretty gray eyes, but they were sort of narrowed together, under suspicious eyebrows. The kid definitely needed a makeover.

"Who the fuck are you?" she asked, a tad hostile, from the doorway.

"You said the f word, you owe me a dollar," Katharine announced, without looking up.

"Fuck fuck fuck. Fuck," hostile teen replied.

"Jennifer!" Katharine gasped, truly appalled by this outrageous breach of decorum.

"It's better for you, now I owe you a five," Jennifer announced, and she picked the kid up and kissed her, then set her down back into the middle of her animals with a move that was both careless and careful at the same time. "Are you the person who moved into 8A?" she asked me, flopping on the day bed.

"Yeah. My name is Tina," I started.

"I know your name," she announced, utterly bored. At least

134

she was certainly acting bored, but I know enough about teenage girls, having been one, that I was well aware that she was in fact completely desperate for information about me and the empty apartment beneath our feet.

I was only too happy to share. "My mom died, so yeah I just moved in. Downstairs, I guess I'm right downstairs." I tried to smile, decided that was too much, so I turned back to the game. Katharine was in the thick of it, waving a spotted pony in my face. "No, no, go away!" she yelled.

"I'm gonna get her," I informed her, picking up the unicorn and pretending to eat it. She started laughing, completely beside herself with glee. Seriously the kid was the easiest audience I had ever had, which I appreciated in the moment.

"Yeah, but you're not like staying there," Jennifer informed me. "I heard they were kicking you out."

"Who told you that?" I asked.

"Everybody," she shrugged.

"Everybody who?" I pressed.

"Just people." She shrugged. I knew I'd get nothing more from her until she felt like it.

"We'll see, I guess." I shrugged back. "Do you want to see it?"

"See it?" she asked, not quite getting me. "You mean the apartment?"

"Yeah, you want to come down and see it?"

The possibility of this stroke of blind good luck had never even occurred to this sullen teen. She was, however, far too well versed in the etiquette of cool to acknowledge any excitement. "Are you *allowed* to let people in?" she asked, choosing to completely dismiss my invitation rather than express any interest in it.

"I have the key," I pointed out. "My stuff is there. They haven't kicked me out yet."

"But isn't it just like this place?" She suddenly and cleverly decided to feign a kind of phony indifference, pretending to be bored with the possibility of seeing no-man's-land. "It's the same layout and everything, it's the same apartment, right?"

"Are you kidding? Your place is more like normal. You should come see my place, it's pretty weird. Like they were selling off all the furniture so there's nothing in there but light fixtures and moss, and some clocks and then some of those crazy mirrors from like the nineteenth century? All sorts of cracked stuff."

"Moss?" said Jennifer, disbelieving this. "I mean, like, are you kidding? What is it, like mold?"

"No, it's really moss. The guy who has the greenhouse up on the roof needed a place to put his moss."

"You know that guy?"

"Len? Yeah, he was a friend of my mom's; he's great. Have you ever seen his greenhouse?"

"No," she said, an edge of sullen jealousy creeping into her tone.

"It's amazing. If you want I'll take you up there." I knew this all sounded quite unbelievable, so unbelievable in fact that she was tempted to believe it. "Anyway, you have to at least come by and see the moss. He's got like twenty different kinds in my kitchen. One of the kitchens."

"You have two kitchens? 'Cause we only have one."

"Yeah, it's different down there. The layout is completely different. Like, this room, the one we're in right now? It's not there."

"Well, where is it?"

"I don't know. Maybe it's part of the Westmoreland apartment. Do you know her, Delia Westmoreland?"

"Do *you* know her?"

"Not really."

"She wants that apartment. She's been trying to buy it for something like fifteen years," she informed me. "She's going to try and get you kicked out. She's hell on wheels."

When Jennifer wasn't pretending to be bored with the universe she got a kind of curious beam going, right inside her eyelids, like there was a spectacularly intelligent person in there who was perfectly capable of utterly devious behaviour.

"I'm not going anywhere," I announced, feeling far less sure of this than I sounded. "You want to come down?"

"I'm not allowed." She shrugged.

"Come on, it's only one floor," I persisted, trying not to sound too desperate. The idea of having an idle teenager to show off my cool apartment to was suddenly very enticing to me.

"Seriously, I'm not allowed," she said. And the devious person went away again.

As it turned out, Jennifer was in fact telling the truth. When Mrs White showed up two minutes later, she shooed Jennifer back to her room and explained the facts of life to me, as they were lived in 9A.

"Their father is very strict," Mrs White explained, as she politely ushered me back through the many hallways to the front of the apartment. Their place was easier to navigate than mine but it was unquestionably a bit of a maze nonetheless. "Raising six girls on Manhattan, you can imagine how that

137

would be necessary. The things that go on in the private schools, you don't want to know about."

"Drugs, boys, blow jobs?" I asked her, kind of all concerned and quiet.

She shot me a look, none too pleased with my slightly too careless display of insider information about things like drugs, boys and blow jobs.

"Of course you would know about this," she observed, smiling a little too tightly.

"Oh, I just know what I've read. It's all over the web," I countered, fast. "Isn't it? I went to Catholic school in Jersey. All girls, only nuns. We didn't even have priests. Well, and thank God for that! I mean, what the priests turned out to be up to, a kid would be safer in prison."

"You went to Catholic school?" This seemed vaguely interesting to her, so I was glad that I had made it up.

"St Ignatius, over in Jersey City. They finally closed it a couple years ago, which is too bad. I got a great education there." To my own ear I sounded like a pretty desperate liar by this point, but she was dealing with a writhing baby and wasn't paying full attention to my tone. "Your girls are in Catholic school, right?"

"St Peter in Chains, up on 98th." She nodded.

"St Peter in Chains!" I said, smiling at her like I knew it well. "I love their uniforms. They look so cute."

"Well, it certainly makes life simpler. With six girls you can imagine what kind of chaos we would have to deal with, in the clothes department, if we didn't have the uniforms," she agreed. "And my husband wants them to learn a broader system of values."

Eying Mrs White's gorgeous pink outfit, I felt a sincere moment of sympathy for all those teenage girls who were learning a broader system of values. I mean, their mother was running all over New York City in designer suits, and they had to throw on the same hideous pleated skirts every morning before heading uptown to hang out with a bunch of nuns all day. It seemed like a pretty nasty fate, especially considering that they lived on Manhattan, where I would have thought that nobody, and I mean *nobody* goes to Catholic school to learn values.

"Well, I know I loved my uniform, maybe not every day of high school, but afterwards, definitely," I said. "I come from a family of girls too. Not as many, there were only three of us, but obviously we were in something of the same boat, in terms of the clothes, I mean. My mother was always up to her eyeballs in laundry." I was definitely starting to sound like a suck up. Mrs White, mother of teenage girls, finally recognized the sound, and as soon as she did her already chilly attitude became loga- rithmically less friendly.

"Thank you for coming," she said, shifting Barbie to her other hip and opening the front door of the apartment. Behind her I could see Katharine, standing in the hallway, watching. Off in the distance teenage voices suddenly raised, in heat; Jennifer and Louise sniping at each other over shoes, or hair clips, or who was hogging the phone, and then a third voice chimed in, topping them both, and I thought for a second about the two other girls out there, whose names I didn't know yet, two more girls who I hadn't even laid eyes on. Mrs White turned for a second, impatient.

"Girls, no yelling! Gail! Louise! NO YELLING IN THE HOUSE!" she yelled. And then she looked back at me, clearly waiting for me to just go.

"I have two sisters," I repeated.

"Yes," she said. "So you said."

"I'm the youngest," I said. "We didn't live in a very big house so we were really on top of each other all the time. And we would argue about everything, sometimes I think about the stupid things we argued about and wonder how my mother didn't go stark raving mad just listening to us. Did you ever meet my mother? She lived downstairs. She died just a few days ago. It feels like a long time already but it was just a few days. I mean, it was a shock to everybody, we had no idea she was even, well, I guess that's how heart attacks work, nobody sees them coming. And maybe it was good for her, to go that way, just fast like that. If you're going to die that would be the way, right? I just worry. I'm staying down there and I'm seeing all her stuff which there wasn't much of, I'm telling you, she— did you know Bill? Because we didn't, they didn't—anyway I just hadn't seen her in such a long time. I think she maybe was lonely. It's nice to meet you. It's nice to meet your girls. I'm happy to be here."

Don't ask me what I was trying because I didn't even know. I just didn't want her to think I was whatever she thought I was. Katharine was still watching me from behind her mother. I gave her a little wave, low, so she knew I could see her. She waved back. The voices of the girls far back in the apartment rose again, unyielding in their fury. For a moment a few words shook themselves free of the sound and made the argument

140

comprehensible: shampoo. They were mad at each other over shampoo.

"GIRLS, HONESTLY YOU DO NOT WANT ME TO COME BACK THERE!" Mrs White hollered. "I'M NOT KIDDING. DO YOU WANT ME TO TELL YOUR FATHER ABOUT THIS?" Silence bloomed instantly around the question. She turned back to me, newly determined. "Well," she said. "Thank you for coming by." She raised her hand, but with the palm up, so it was more like an offering and less like she was actually pointing at the door, which in fact was what she was doing.

"I would love to babysit some time, if you need anybody," I said.

"We'll give you a call," she said, politely shutting the door right in my face.

Okay, so that didn't go exactly the way I wanted, but since I hadn't put a ton of thought into the plan before trying it I decided not to take it personally. Besides I had made definite inroads with two of the kids, and I had left the dangling possibility of cheap and local babysitting in the back of Mrs White's busy brain. Even though she had more or less slammed the door in my face I decided it might be worthwhile to capitalize on the introduction, so I immediately hopped in the elevator and went down to the lobby, where Frank was leaning on his podium, head in hands, talking quietly in Spanish to someone on the other end of the line who was clearly bugging the shit out of him. He didn't raise his voice, ever, but the speed of the conversation kept increasing until Frank was careening through sentences and thoughts so fast you couldn't help but expect him to crash and burn any second. But he didn't. He just looked up, saw me standing there and switched into English.

"I got to go," he said, and he hung up the phone.

"*Hay una problema?*" I asked, in friendly, lame Spanish.

"*Dos problemas. Dos hermanos, dos problemas* not as big as the problem with *mi padre*, but what can I do for you, Tina? I heard you were maybe moving out today," he said.

"Ohhhh, not yet," I said. "Who'd you hear that from?"

"Well, who you think?" he said, starting to sort mail. He was really a lot less friendly to me than he had been before, but having come down from Mrs White, who was downright rude, I didn't take it personally. It just made it clear how right Len was, that I had a lot of work to do if I was going to try and stay where I was. I stayed away from rumours of the co-op board, who were doubtless paying Frank's salary, and stuck with facts.

"Yeah, I heard that Doug wants me out but I think Pete's okay with it, isn't he?" I asked. "Did you talk to Pete?"

"No, I talked to Doug. He said you were moving out," Frank repeated.

"No, not yet," I repeated back. "Listen, Mrs White asked me if I could babysit for her some time, so I said okay, but I didn't know the number of my cell phone because I just got it? So is there something I can write it on, and you can maybe give it to her with her mail?"

"You're going to babysit for the Whites?" He looked up at me, surprised, and I could see that his eyes were kind of red and sad around the edges. Then he looked away again, fast, and I thought, Oh hell, he's not mad at me, he's upset, those problemas on the phone had really upset him. He took a second to press his eyes, like he was pretending to have a headache, but really so that the tips of his fingers could catch the tears before they actually existed. Then he started sorting the mail with extremely fierce attention, so I knew I'd better say something fast or it would be impossible for us both to keep pretending that I didn't see him almost cry.

"Yeah, I went up and said hello because my mom always talked about how much she liked Mrs White, and we talked about me babysitting, but I didn't have my phone, so I went back to the apartment and got it and then I was going to just run back up with the number but you know they were in the middle of homework and stuff when I left, and I thought it would be easier to just leave it for her with you, and you should have it too anyway," I said, acting all casual and sticking my fingers in the back pockets of my jeans, pretending I was looking for something there. "And of course I'm so retarded I don't even have a pen. Do you have a pen? Do you have anything I can write on?"

"Yeah, I don't know, here, here's a pen," he said, handing me one of those old skinny ballpoints that nobody really buys anymore, but cheap bosses get in truckloads and then give out to people they don't care about. He went back to sorting the mail, but then he stopped himself and said, "There's paper too, hang on, I got a notebook here under the mail." And he lifted up the whole pile, which was quite an awkward maneuver, and I saw a spiral notebook under there which I slid out before he could drop something. The whole move was so complicated that by the time we were on the other side of it we were both in the clear, and I was writing my cell phone number down

143

and he was putting it in with Mrs White's mail, as if that was the only thing that was going on anyway.

So we were busy with all that when Vince Masterson showed up.

There is almost no point in describing Vince Masterson. When you first meet him he seems to look like nothing, his features are so normal that he really just doesn't look like anybody. He's about thirty, you think, and he looks kind of normal. Then he starts to talk, and you realize that his eyes are just a perfect light blue and his nose is long and beautiful and he's tall and just jaw-droppingly gorgeous, in fact. And then he keeps talking and you realize that he's actually kind of an asshole and he doesn't really know as much as he thinks he knows and he's not that handsome after all. And then he keeps on talking and you think, Wow what a gorgeous guy, maybe I'm wrong, maybe he does know all this stuff, and I'm the one who's stupid. And then he talks some more and you think, What an asshole. And then you think he's handsome again, but maybe not really. It's like that.

So this is the first time I've laid eyes on old Vince. He announces his arrival nicely enough. "Hey, Frank, how's it going?" he calls from the doorway. Frank and I both turn, and I have the initial experience of thinking, Oh it's just some guy, some average guy who knows Frank, stopping by to say hello.

"Hey, Vince," says Frank, holding up his hand in a polite, friendly wave.

"Anything in there for me?" asks Vince, and he saunters over, sticks his hands in his pockets and leans over the podium to watch what Frank is doing. Because I am in fact standing there right in his way, his arm more or less brushes my shoulder and

I take half a step back. He's tall, I'm short, and when he stands that close that fast, it becomes immediately clear that I would fit perfectly right under his arm. He smiles down at me and I'm thinking, Holy shit, this guy is gorgeous.

"Hi," he says.

"Hi," I say, and I swear to God, I turn all red. Seriously, that's how great looking Vince sometimes is: you just go all red.

"I got a couple days worth here," Frank mentions. "Hang on a second." His head disappeared under the podium. Vince continued to smile down at me, but he didn't say anything. The effect was insanely flirtatious.

"Hi, I'm Tina, Tina Finn." I suddenly got it together and held up my hand, to shake. "I just moved in. Do you live here? I'm in 8A."

"Oh, the Drinan place. I heard about this. You're squatting there."

"I'm not squatting there, no, I, no," I said, now both flustered and defensive. "My mother was, she left the apartment to me and my sisters. It's our apartment."

"That's not what I heard." Vince shrugged. "Thanks, Frank." He took a slender pile of mail from Frank and stood there, ignoring me again, while he glanced through it.

"Most of it's for your dad," Frank offered. Vince looked up at this, with a fast flash of annoyance, and I had a horrible moment of feeling glad that he didn't get any mail and that the mail was all for his dad.

"Yeah, thanks, Frank, I'll get it to him," he said, and he tossed the junk mail back onto the podium, right on top of what Frank was doing, sorting everyone else's mail. It was so condescending that I had another horrible moment of dislike for this handsome guy, because you could tell that he really thought he was better than Frank and he didn't care if Frank knew it. I mean, obviously people do that to me all the time, and I don't love it, but it doesn't actually piss me off as much as watching people be mean to people like Frank.

"Here, I'll take care of that for you, Frank," I said, and I grabbed the junk mail before he could reach for it. "He's the doorman, not the garbage man," I informed horrible Vince with a smile, as I carried it across the foyer.

"It's okay, Tina," said Frank, a little confused and nervous. And why not, I was being unspeakably rude on his behalf.

"Are you up or down, what's your name, Tina?" Vince said, looking me over again, sort of like he was skinning me alive.

"What?" I said, shocked.

"Up or down?" This time it sounded like he was talking about sexual positions. He smirked, like he knew I was thinking that. "Are you on your way up, or have you just come down?"

What a creep, I thought fast, and I was about to say something completely inappropriate and aggressive and arrogant when I glanced down at the junk mail which I was about to dump into the trash can, and caught the name there: *Roger Masterson*. Roger Masterson. One of the names on the list, one of the kings of the co-op board.

I took a breath and dumped the junk mail in the trash. "I'm on my way up," I said. "Want to share an elevator?"

CHAPTER NINE

Vince Masterson hates his father. He lives in his father's apartment, which is quite nice but small, compared to, say, my apartment. Vince also has a trust fund which pays him thousands of dollars a month, which his father set up, so Vince gets a check in the mail for many thousands of dollars—more than fifteen, as it turns out—from his father *every month,* while he lives in his father's apartment and hates his father. Vince talks about how much he hates his father easily and exhaustively. It is his favorite subject.

"It's not even his money. That's the thing you really have to remember." We were in the big room, swigging red wine. Vince had by this point taken his gorgeous but slightly uptight jacket and tie off, and he had also managed to unbutton the top three buttons of his shirt, without me even seeing him do it, while I gave him a tour of the place. "He *inherited* it, and it's not like he inherited a small fortune and then was such a blinding genius at investing it that it grew into a significant fortune, that's not what happened," he explained, as he launched into what I would come to learn was his favorite subject. "He just got it handed to him from my grandfather, who had it handed to him, and God let me tell you it's not like either one of them added to it; it just *sits* in the *markets*. Someone else, some completely anonymous but clever underling at Goldman Sachs or Morgan Stanley or Chase Manhattan or what*ever* moves it around or leaves it where it is, for years, these anonymous financial peons keep their eye on it and tend to it and it does grow, even in a shitty market it just keeps growing in these underground vaults and every so often dad or grandpa or great-grandpa or great-great-grandpa will go and lop off a wad of this stuff and then go out and blow it on something ludicrous like a house in Palm Beach or East Hampton, membership at some ridiculous club where no one has anything to say to anyone. So that's the family business, spending money, even though in my family there is no way to spend it that means anything. Know what I mean? It just *spreads*. It's like this: No one *does anything*. It's that amount of money. Because if you *did* something with it, other than just buy things I mean, you would either have to *be* someone, you know, actually be someone that people *dealt* with on a cultural or political or even global level, I mean, really, you'd be a *player* even though I hate that word you'd have to risk that, the having of real power, you know what I mean, or—and honestly I think this is even the better option—you'd lose it, seriously, you'd have to risk losing it and then being yourself that person, the person who lost the fucking family money but you'd *also* be yourself." At this Vince took a huge swig of wine and looked out the window, over the park, posing like a model in a fashion shoot. It was quite a performance. He sounded both like a complete idiot and a broken-hearted old soul. "And that's what scares him!" he exclaimed, turning back to me with complete heart-break in his eyes. "The man is so utterly terrified of his own existence he can barely speak. You say 'Hello Dad' and he looks at you like you're a total insect, seriously, that is precisely what he means to communicate, complete and utter *contempt*, but it's not contempt, it's terror that is driving him, trust me, the *contempt* is just the cover and not a very good one at that."

The heartbreak careened into superiority. "All the sneering and spending and *womanizing*, it's positively mun*dane*," Vince explained, as if I could follow this. "I have not two but three stepmothers, all of them utterly identical, you know I can't keep their names straight quite frankly and he's cheated on them all with women who look just like them. A couple of them completely tried to take him to the cleaners but the money's tied up, as you can imagine; the lawyers aren't letting anyone walk away with anything meaningful, much less a trophy wife, no matter how big a shit my father is. But what I don't under-stand is the endless repetition. Honestly, why trade in one for the other if they're exactly the same model? And what on earth do they talk about? Seriously, you can't fuck all the time, I don't actually think he fucks them at all if you want to know the truth, these women are not getting laid, every last one of them has this look of pinched terror hovering around the corners of their bottom lips although that could be the plastic surgery or the fact that they're all fucking starving to death. Has anyone ever thought about that, the irony of all these ridiculously wealthy white women who are literally starving themselves to death on the Upper East Side of the richest city in the richest country in the world, because the instant they look like anything healthier than a fucking holocaust survivor their husbands will divorce them? Although trust me I waste no sympathy on any of the brainless twigs who married my father. Christ, the whole thing is so *stupid*, it's so fucking *stupid* I can't even bear to talk about it. What a fucking waste of time. Is there more wine? You know this stuff is actually quite good. And there were just cases of it lying around? That had to be a nice surprise."

He carried his half-empty glass of wine loosely in his right hand and poured with his left, not even glancing down to make sure he didn't spill anything. It was simultaneously reckless and completely assured; he didn't lose a drop. While I found the guy utterly annoying I also couldn't help noticing that he had a great chest, because of the way the top three buttons on his shirt had sort of magically come undone at some point during the rant.

"So what's under here?" he suddenly asked, kicking at a tuft of the mustard-colored shag.

"I haven't looked," I said, looking at his chest. He smirked like a thirteen-year-old and I turned red. "I mean, we haven't had much of a chance to do an inventory or anything like that."

"I heard you already had the place appraised."

"Who'd you hear that from?"

"I'm asking the questions, Ms Finn. Did they give you an estimate?"

"Yes they did. We got three separate estimates. One from *Sotheby's*." I held my glass out, opting suddenly for a stance of deliberate and overt sexuality. It always works. He came to my side and refilled it with sloppy generosity, finishing off the bottle.

"Well, so how much did they tell you you'd get, without even bothering to glance under the rugs?" he asked, coolly appraising the place himself.

"I don't know you well enough to discuss my personal finances, Vince."

"We just drank an entire bottle of red wine together in under twenty minutes, Tina. I think you know me pretty well, or at least you will within the hour." I couldn't help it, it was so cocky I had to laugh.

"What's so funny?"

"You're just a really good flirt," I tossed at him.

"Thank you," he said, following me around the room like a dog on a leash. "I appreciate your appreciation. Must be this place. Down in the lobby I could have sworn you didn't like me."

"I don't like you," I said. "That doesn't change the fact that you're really a really good flirt."

"You're not so bad yourself," he said, with a dazzling smile full of smug self-assurance. And why not, he really was beautiful, especially standing in front of a view of all of Manhattan with his shirt half open. Vince glanced over my head and out onto the spectacular expanse of Central Park visible from all six windows spanning the length of the big room's front wall. "Christ, this place really is amazing. It's got to be six thousand square feet, and this view! What did Sotheby's tell you? Come on, I want a number. Everybody in the building is guessing you'll get at least ten for it, if they let you sell it, that is."

"Are they going to try and stop us?"

"I'm still the one asking the questions today. Come on, what did they say you'd get?" Wandering back across the room, Vince stuck his head in the kitchen and jumped. "Holy shit, what's this? There's mold everywhere in here. Have you called the super?"

I laughed at him. This time he glanced back at me, flushing with annoyance, and you could see that mean streak flare up. Mean, handsome, hyper-sensitive, rich, arrogant, sexy and drunk; there was no question anymore where this was going. I followed him back across the room, and passed him in the doorway of the kitchen, where he hovered like a scared rabbit. "That guy who lives in the penthouse, Len? The botanist? He had a deal with my mom, she rented the kitchen to him," I told him. "It's a *mossery*." I even leaned on the word to make it sound a little bit like I thought he was stupid.

"A what?" He followed me in but stayed behind me, still completely and obviously creeped out at the sight of all that moss. I flipped the wall switch. The place started to glow; Len had tucked itty bitty light fixtures into odd corners amongst the moss that made it look like you really were lost in some gnomic netherworld. There were also three separate fountains which propelled tiny streams of water through the various stands of bryophytes. The pump that kept the water running hummed, so the dark mossy room seemed to vibrate a little, and shift in the unusual light. I took a step in and reached by Vince, to show him one of the species that Len had showed me the first day he came, the tiniest of small purple blossoms skimming the surface of that particular tray of moss.

"It's a mossery," I repeated, whispering in the gloom. "They used to have them all over the place in the nineteenth century.

People don't do them so much anymore except for places like botanical gardens. But Len wanted to build one, and he gets too much light up there in the penthouse, so he rented the kitchen here. Look at the cedar plank boxes, he built them himself. And some of the moss—like this one—grows on concrete. But mostly he had to create an environment that approximates the floor of a deciduous forest." Len had told me some of this stuff but mostly I was making it up. "Here," I said. I put my hand on his, lifted it, and moved it onto a particularly dense thicket, pushing his fingers into the softest part of the growth. "Feels weird, doesn't it?"

Vince looked down at me. "Fantastic," he said.

No surprise, Vince knew exactly what to do in a situation like that. He just leaned down and kissed me hard right on the mouth. His right arm went around me, he tossed his wine glass up onto one of the moss beds without even looking at where it landed, and then he had my back up against the wall while his other hand moved easily up under my shirt, pushing it out of the way so that my skin was right up against his two seconds later when his half-buttoned shirt was somehow suddenly completely undone. I mean, both of us still had our clothes on, but who could tell? His tongue was so far down my throat I was seeing stars. I thought about coming up for air and decided I'd rather faint, if it came to it. Seriously, I knew it was bad news, how good this guy was at making a pass at someone he barely knew, but he was so good you really couldn't care. He kept me pinned against the wall, with both hands on my waist, and then he slid his fingers down into the tops of my jeans and I almost leapt out of my skin. I could feel his erection pressing against me and he made a little sound in the back of his throat, like he knew he was an animal and he assumed that so was I, and he wasn't going to give me a chance to pretend otherwise. I mean, it was one hell of a kiss. Vince made out the way he talked, with so much reckless confidence, it didn't really matter that everything he said was bullshit.

By the time we stopped kissing we were both gasping for air. He set me down, took a step back and leaned against the opposite wall, setting the picture of the tree askew and knocking over a pile of wooden trays that Len had stacked there next to a bag of some kind of plant food. The trays went flying. He reached out to stop them from collapsing into the room, and somehow bumped into something else that bumped into something else that knocked his wine glass off the counter and onto the floor, where it shattered with a loud crack.

"Holy shit, the moss is attacking me," Vince muttered, shoving the trays back against the wall with his foot. "It seems to be very protective of your honor."

"Too late for that," I laughed, sounding way too shaky. Vince looked up from the broken glass and considered me from the darkness of the other side of the room.

"Thanks for showing me the place," he said. "Maybe we should take another look at the bedrooms."

"You know, now is not a good time," I said. "But thanks for stopping by." I turned out of the kitchen and headed for the front door. Which surprised him; there was no hiding the fact that I was dying to just leap on him a second time and let it take me wherever it would. But I thought it was a bad idea, to give him the satisfaction. He had too many character flaws and

I knew most of them already. "So maybe I'll see you around the building," I said, turning the locks on the door with casual determination.

"I'd like that," he said, at my shoulder.

I turned to smile a goodbye to him, I really did. My hand was on the spring bolt. But before I could get the door open he grabbed me at the shoulder, flipped me around and got his tongue down my throat a second time. I considered resisting for about half a second but honestly it is not always easy to consider consequences at moments like that. So much for walking away from this, I thought; my hands were going after the top button of his jeans. He already had mine unzipped, when someone started talking.

"Tina? Are you in there? Tina?" There was a little rapping on the door, the sound of keys. I stopped.

"Yeah—Lucy—just give me a minute." None of this made even the slightest impression on old Vince, who was wrapping his arms around my waist. I very weakly tried to extract myself. "Put your clothes back on, come on," I whispered, while I dragged him away from the doorway.

"Tell her to go away," he murmured in my ear, as his fingers continued in their determination to undress me.

"She doesn't do what I tell her, or I would," I said, shoving him. The locks were flipping. I was not going to have Lucy find me in a clinch with old Vince Masterson with my clothes half off.

"She can't be your mother, your mother's dead," Vince laughed, as I desperately slid the button on my jeans safely into place.

"She's worse, she's my sister," I told him. He laughed again, and leaned against the wall, completely amused now by my predicament. Lucy stepped through the door. Her eyes swiped over us, then raked the room, finding the empty red wine bottle in the middle of the floor, where Vince had simply dropped it. She looked back at us, and didn't say anything. She didn't even set her briefcase down. Vince stifled another laugh. I elbowed him.

"Ow, what'd you do that for?" he said, acting like a frat boy. "Hi, I'm Vince Masterson. I live on the fifth floor, Tina was just showing me the apartment. It's fabulous, congratulations. What did you say your name was?" All his sexual and class confidence merged into one dazzling bit of arrogance and he ignored the utterly disheveled state of his clothes, holding out his hand to shake. Lucy looked him in the eye before glancing down at his hand, trying to decide if it was clean enough to touch because it was not clear, in fact, where his fingers had recently been. I wanted to hit her.

Vince just laughed, and brought his hand up, touching her carelessly on the elbow as if that had been what he intended to do all along. "Terrific meeting you," he said, smiling. "Tina, you were just showing me out, weren't you?"

He looked back at me and held out his hand. I obediently reached for it, and let him drag me to the front door, which was still standing open. He leaned down and kissed me on the cheek. "I feel like I got caught in the back of the schoolhouse with the parson's daughter," he murmured in my ear.

"It was *so* great to meet you, Vince," I said, loud.

"Likewise," he agreed. "Give me a call."

I shut the door and turned to find Lucy picking up the empty wine bottle. She held it out to me.

"Do you think you could put this in with the recycling? I don't want this place turning into a dump," she said.

"It's one empty wine bottle," I told her, with deliberate indifference.

"It's trashy," she informed me. "And we're not going down that road this time, is that understood? It's not happening!" Okay, and then she shoved me. Presumably she just meant to poke me in the shoulder for emphasis but her anger got the better of her and she *shoved* me. It really hurt.

"Hey," I said. "What's your problem?"

"*You* are my problem. Jesus—I would just, I would just like to fucking kill you!" she hissed. Seriously, I did not particularly enjoy the fact that she had walked in on me making out with a cute guy, but this was somehow strangely out of control.

"Chill out, will you?" I said. "That guy—"

"I don't want to hear about that guy."

"He lives in the building."

"He lives in the building! Terrific! Is that enough of a reason to bring him up here and have sex with him?"

"I didn't have sex with him! I was trying to make friends with him—"

"Well, you seem to have succeeded. Well done, Tina. And what's this?" She looked at the inside of the front door, where my rigged-up set of spring bolts and door chains sparkled in the afternoon light.

"It's my security system," I said. "Too many people have keys to this place and seem to feel that they can let themselves in

157

any time they want. We're not doing that anymore. If I don't want people to come in, I'm not going to let them in."

"I don't agree to that."

"I don't give a shit if you agree or not," I said, heading back for television land. It was rough coming down from near sex with a really hot and deeply problematic guy, to getting yelled at by your bossy sister. I needed more wine.

"Don't you dare just walk away from me," Lucy snarled, at a dead heat, over my shoulder.

"Relax, would you?" I said. "I'm getting myself a glass of wine."

"Don't you think you've had enough to drink?" she asked me.

"No, actually, I don't," I told her. "Want some?"

"No," Lucy countered, tossing her briefcase onto the couch. It landed right next to Vince's jacket and tie. "Oh look. Your friend who you're not sleeping with left his clothes."

"Yeah, great, I'll get them back to him. It'll give me an excuse to go up to his place and not fuck him there," I said. I headed for the laundry room to score another bottle from the stash back there. She stayed where she was and just shouted.

"This is no joke, Tina!"

"Lucy, if you want to sell this place, we have to get by the co-op board," I informed her, returning with the fresh bottle. "And they can stop a sale if they feel like it, and right now that is how they feel. They don't like us. Oh wait! No, wait. One of them likes us. Vince likes *me*."

"He wants to have sex with you. It's not quite the same thing."

"For most people it's close enough. And if you had sex on

anything remotely like a regular basis, you might know things like that."

"Thank you for once again elevating the conversation. Really, it's quite a boon to have you around to put things in perspective," Lucy said. She stood there in her tight grey suit, not even looking at me, her thumbs moving restlessly through the air above her ever-present BlackBerry, and I knew that nothing I said, sensible or otherwise, would make an impression.

"Look, is there a reason you're here?" I said. "Is there some dazzling legal maneuver you're about to pull, or did you just stop by to make me feel shitty?"

Lucy took a good long pause before she deigned to answer. She kept reading her BlackBerry, decided she was done with that, pocketed it, and reached for her briefcase before glancing in my direction. "Well, let me just tell you this much: We don't have to worry about the co-op board for now," she finally said. She snapped the clasps on the cover of her briefcase and flipped it open, reaching inside for a pristine manila envelope which she then tossed onto the coffee table. I could tell by the way the thing hit the wood that there were freshly minted documents inside.

"What is that?" I said, again with the indifference. I actually was interested, because I was pretty sure it was something big, but she was really working my nerves so I thought I'd return the favor.

"You can read, right? I mean, you did acquire that skill before you dropped out of college so you could run off with some loser, didn't you?"

"Yes I can read, but since I'm so stupid it takes me a real

long time. Maybe you could just summarize in ten words or less and tell me what I'm supposed to get myself all upset about today."

"We have a court date."

"A court date for what?"

"The Drinans are objecting to the will."

"Well, what does that mean?"

"They're claiming that their father was mentally incapacitated when he made his will, and that Mom used undue influence, and that we came into possession illegally, so they're suing for damages."

"Well, they are damaged, but whose fault is that? Not mine."

"They're suing you for it. And they're suing me, and they're suing Daniel and Alison to the tune of twenty million dollars."

"Come on."

"You asked me to summarize."

This sounded so bizarre I couldn't believe it. I decided it might be smart to take a look at the documents myself so I opened the envelope. Lucy went back to attacking her BlackBerry.

"There's a preliminary hearing in Surrogates Court on December 7th," she informed me. "That's three months away. It's unheard of that they could get a date set that quickly, so they're clearly pulling strings. They also went judge shopping while they were at it; we're scheduled to be heard by the one judge who thinks she can do whatever she feels like with the law. The one who's a cop, he probably had enough clout in the legal system to put this where they wanted it. The other one is some sort of principal at the Dalton School, he knows absolutely everybody as well. In any case they pulled strings." I paged through the papers in front of me and tried to make sense of them. They seemed utterly incomprehensible, and for a moment I thought, Maybe Lucy's right. Maybe I never really did learn to read properly.

"They're suing us, like *suing* us, for money?"

"That's a separate action. They're just trying to scare us. They want us to make a counter-offer to make this whole thing go away."

"What kind of counter-offer?"

"Well, let see, what do they want? The apartment! I think if we offered them the apartment, this would all go away."

"What if the judge gives them the apartment?"

"We're not going to let that happen."

"But they're suing us? So we could lose the apartment and then if they win the lawsuit we'll have to pay them money too?"

"You're not going to have to worry about that, Tina, as you are to my knowledge as usual completely without resources. That's right, isn't it? Do you have any money left, from the stash you found in Bill's wallet?"

"Some," I admitted.

"How much?"

"Maybe two hundred?"

"You're going to have to use it to buy some decent clothes. And I do mean decent, none of this boho loser chic stuff you think is so cool. A skirt and a blouse, and ugly shoes. You're going to have to stop dressing like a slut."

"Anything else, Mein Führer?"

"When there is, I'll let you know." She picked up her briefcase and looked at me, sprawled on the couch, watching her with my best sullen disregard.

"Before you take off can you at least tell me who my lawyer is? You said you maybe were going to replace that nice egg man; did that happen?"

"We have a new and very good lawyer, yes. His name is Ira Grossman. He's very experienced in these kinds of litigious inheritance situations."

"Can I call him?"

"No, you can't call him! Every time you call him it costs a hundred dollars which you don't have!"

"Yeah but—"

"Tina, just, I don't have time to hold your hand on everything today. If you have questions about your legal status in this situation, read the pleadings."

"I can't understand this shit!"

"No? Then I guess you're going to have to rely on me and Daniel and Alison to tell you what to do. Get that shit off the door, buy some decent clothes and keep this place clean. Oh, and tell that guy to come down here and get rid of the moss. Sotheby's has agreed to represent the apartment as a historic property and no one is going to understand a roomful of moss, when they start to show the place."

"How come—"

"That's all you have to worry about. Okay? Okay?"

"Okay."

She smiled, like she found that was satisfactory, to hear me say "Okay," but she honestly didn't look satisfied. She looked like her suit was too tight, and she wasn't eating enough red meat, and her shoes hurt. There were little grey smudges under her eyes and she had pulled her hair back into a bun, which was an extremely bad look for her, and usually she knew better than to try it. Her mouth was pinched together, bitter and worried, and for the first time I saw what Vince had seen instantly underneath the skin of my smart, ferocious sister: an old schoolmarm in a rage because the world had overlooked her.

"Hey, Lucy," I said, just feeling completely lousy all of a sudden. "No kidding, Lucy. Maybe we should just offer to split it with them. Even split five ways we'd all end up with a ton of money. Has anyone offered to split it?"

"I don't believe that's been discussed, no!" she said, with a kind of infantile brightness that had yet another sneer behind it.

"Yeah, I guess that's pretty stupid," I said. "Sorry. 'Compromise.' What a boneheaded idea."

"You said it, not me," she murmured, under her breath.

She left. I let her go. I decided to stop asking a bunch of questions nobody had any answers for anyway, and let things happen as they would.

CHAPTER TEN

Two days later, when Len came by to check in on current events, he was not particularly happy with the state of his mossery. He found the fact that someone had been messing with his trays, knocking over bags of mulch and tossing shards of glass all over the floor thoroughly appalling. During our abortive but completely memorable make-out session, Vince and I had also, it seems, damaged one of the displays which contained a delicate species of hornwort, several large sections of which had turned a distressing kind of mottled grey as a result. The picture of the tree on the wall was so far askew it looked like it was about to fall off the wall.

"For a thousand dollars a month, I think it's understood that the mossery is protected space," he informed me, straightening the picture with annoyed precision. "Your mother took great care with it; you I see do not have her touch. I'm going to have to ask you to refrain from even entering my room unless I am here to supervise you."

"It's not your room, Len," I reminded him, a tad defensive since I knew he was right. "You're just renting it."

"Renting it from whom, that's the question," he said, smiling at me with a sharp little nod of contempt. He leaned past me to open the tiniest sliver of a closet door which was squashed between the refrigerator and the wall, where he retrieved a whisk broom and a dustpan which had been hung just inside the door, at eye level. I watched as he swept the shards of glass together, disposing of them carefully into the plastic dustbin which stood to one side of the sink. Then he swept the floor again, and then he did it a third time. Each time you could see him pick up ever more delicate pieces of broken glass, until he reached above his head, pulled a roll of paper towels out of the cabinets above the moss, and dabbed carefully at every corner of the linoleum, finding little sparkles of glass dust everywhere. He neatly folded the paper towel, put it to one side, and considered the dirty red stain of the wine that had spilled and set in ugly blotches seemingly everywhere. Len glanced up at me, his face a mask of disappointed annoyance. "How long has this been here?" he asked, exhausted by my incompetence.

"Just a day. I was going to clean it up. I just forgot," I said, trying a little too hard not to sound like a ten-year-old.

"And how did all this happen?" he asked, coolly disinterested in my peevish excuses.

"I um, I met that guy, Vince Masterson? He lives on the fifth floor?"

"Yes, I'm aware of who he is," Len agreed, even more coolly disinterested, as if that were possible.

"He wanted to see the apartment. So I invited him up. And I was showing him around and he dropped, he had a glass of wine and he dropped it, so—anyway, I met the Whites, too. I might be doing some babysitting for them," I told Len. Len considered this possibility while he ran a paper towel through the faucet and started working on the red spots on the floor.

"Babysitting?" he said, raising his eyebrows, as if he'd like to see that one.

"Yes," I said. "I'm good with kids. And, you'll be stunned to hear, I could use the money."

"Your mother never had any money either," Len told me, glancing up from the floor. "Bill didn't either. I used to ask them about it. They were both eligible for social security. But, Bill wouldn't cash the checks. There was some sort of pension out there but Bill wrote to them and told them he moved. So those stopped coming too. Neither one of them had any money, really, at all."

"They didn't cash the checks?"

"Bill wanted to live off the grid."

"He lived in New York City!"

"Nevertheless. His need for privacy was beyond any other concern in his life. Except, perhaps, his love for your mother. If you had any real interest in the details of their life here together—"

"Of course I'm interested!"

"You might have put two and two together and realized that for Bill privacy was everything. *Everything.*"

"Why are you so mad at me?"

"Why are *you* letting people parade in and out of their home?"

"Well, the Drinans parade in and out because they think it's their—"

"Which you are determined to dissuade them of, the fact that they were both raised here notwithstanding."

"The only other people parading in and out are my sisters."

"And?"

"And okay the real estate people, but what am I supposed to do about that?"

"And?"

"And you, you're the only other person 'parading' in and out. I don't know what you're talking about."

"Stop acting like a child."

"What is the big deal! It was one person!"

"A trustworthy person, I'm sure. Someone with unassailable character. Who will treat this apartment and its history with the respect it deserves."

"You were the one, you told me to make friends—"

"Whatever you say."

"Oh for crying out loud. You're a guy who talks to plants!"

"Then why do you care what I think?"

He turned back to check in on his hornwort. He was right; I did care. I so did not want him to be mad at me.

"I'm sorry," I finally said. "I mean it. I won't do it again. I didn't know. I mean, I knew that they were, that Bill was, privacy was big with him, but how was I supposed to, I mean people knew they were in here! Didn't they? They went out and stuff!"

"They did not."

"But they—they weren't really off the grid. In the middle of the city? You can't live off the grid in New York City. They had heat and water and telephones, and television."

"Bill set up a trust that was taking care of that through his lawyer. The rest was absorbed by the building."

"Absorbed by the building?"

"Honestly, Tina, I don't have time to explain everything to you. Just do me a favor: Next time you have friends in, to take a look at this wonderful and very private old place, please do not let them in the mossery. It is officially off limits to you now. Is that understood?" He actually tried to shoo me out of the room, so that he could continue cleaning up in peace.

"They want you to get it out of here. Lucy says you have to take it out by next week."

"Quite frankly, I don't believe you'll be here that long," he informed me.

"I wouldn't bet on it if I were you." I leaned against the refrigerator and watched him work. The place was almost back to normal by this point. The floor was spick and span, the cedar boxes were re-stacked and the half-spilled bag of mulch had been tidied and tucked back into its corner. Now that Len had bent his attention to the tiny tray of hornworts his anger had cooled, and he was murmuring comfort to the thing.

"You're okay. Oh, no no, this isn't a tragedy. We'll fix you right up," he cooed. Seriously. The guy was talking to *moss*.

"I'm not kidding, Len, Lucy is dead set on you getting this stuff out of here as of now," I told him. He looked over at me, annoyed again. "Yeah, I'm sorry to interrupt," I said, "but you can't just boss me around and expect this problem to go away. I'm going to need a little more help than that."

"How about two hundred," he said, suddenly. "Will that help?"

169

That wasn't what I had been going for, but given the life I lead I am never averse to taking money. "Yes, I think that will help me figure out how to solve this. I really do."

"Why don't you let me finish up here," he said, turning his gaze back to his wounded moss. "Maybe twenty minutes?"

"Great," I said. "I'll go take a shower."

After Len had finished tending his moss, and I had dried my hair with the thirty-year-old hair blow dryer I found underneath some sink, we headed upstairs to the greenhouse, where Len apparently kept piles of hundred-dollar bills hidden in corners.

"Seriously, you have that kind of money lying around?" I asked him, impressed.

"You live in New York City, you have to expect that someone may come along and try to extort you any time of the day or night," he explained. "As you seem to have noticed today, Tina."

"Come on, Len, you offered," I started, lame.

"Are you saying you don't want the money?"

"We got a court date. I need some decent clothes," I explained.

"And of course I would be responsible for that," he replied, not impressed with my logic. The elevator dinged, he slid the grill back and pushed the outer door open, stepping out onto the landing. I stepped out behind him and slammed right into him because he had stopped; he just stood there, holding the elevator door open, and he stopped moving.

"Hey, Len, is there a problem?" I asked, trying to look over his shoulder.

"No, no problem," he informed me, but his voice had fallen back from the bossy exasperation he had come to use as his regular tone with me into a kind of effortless chill I had come to recognize as bad news.

"What is it?" I said. He still hadn't moved. I had a feeling he might shove me back into the elevator and send me off, so I suddenly turned and nudged him with my shoulder, just a little but hard enough to get the right side of my body past him and into the hallway. He looked at me, annoyed.

"That hurt," he announced.

"Well, why are you just standing there?" I asked.

"Hello, Dad," said the person leaning against the door to the greenhouse. Len smiled at me, tight and unamused, and waved his hand toward the person in the door, with his little elfin flourish.

"Hello, Charlie," he said. "This is my friend, Tina."

"Hello, Tina," said Charlie. She was tall, much taller than Len, but she had his air of earthen capability. She also had his strange blue eyes, and her light brown hair was pulled back in a pony tail, all of which plus the height made her look even more like an elf than he did. Although, unlike Len, she behaved like an actual human being. She reached out, smiled, and shook my hand, as if she believed that we might be friends soon.

"Hello," I said, smiling back at her. Len bristled beside me. "Are you okay, Len?" I asked.

"I'm just surprised, I'm surprised to see you, Charlie, very surprised, and I think you know I don't particularly like surprises and I'm busy, now, I think you can see I have a guest and we're very busy."

"It won't take long, Dad," she told him, completely ignoring how rude he was being. "I have something I need you to look at. Benny, this is my dad, who I told you about." She turned back to the doorway, where there was yet another person hidden, a boy, it looked like, maybe ten years old, in jeans and an old dark red T-shirt with some sort of ad about an insurance company on it. His skin was so black you could barely see him in the shadows and he was so shy you could barely see him in the light. He looked up at Charlie with complete bewilderment and utter trust.

"Show it to him," she said.

Benny looked down and you could see that he carried something in his hands. And then he held it up, dutiful, so that we could see what it was. It was a plant, a small plant in a small white plastic cup, with some dirt in it. I hadn't noticed it at first because I was trying so hard to make out the kid, who still struck me as being the most nearly invisible person I had ever seen in my life. But Len sure saw it. He took a step forward, finally, and reached his hand out for it. The boy lifted the plant, to hand it to him, and I saw Len's fingers curl and shake for a moment, they went all bony with greed. I think I may have gasped, because he turned to me, sharp, as if to tell me to shut up, when in fact I hadn't said anything. In any event, Charlie wasn't going to let him just grab the thing and scare the kid like that; she stepped forward and folded her arms across her chest, like a soldier. Which, I discovered later, she was.

"Let's go inside," she said. "There's not enough light here."

Inside the greenhouse there was plenty of light. Len pushed into the kitchen quickly, impatient to get a look at that thing, leaving Charlie behind him to hold the door for me and the kid, who stopped in the doorway and gasped, completely and instantly overwhelmed at the sight of all those plants. Charlie glanced back at him, surprised, but then she remembered he had never seen it before, and she herself looked up and around her with the same wonder; she smiled at all those plants like they were old and best friends.

"I told you," Charlie said, as if she was hearing the thoughts in his head. Then she carefully took the little plastic cup out of the boy's hands and ushered him over to the kitchen, which was still relatively tidy from the cleaning I had given it three days before. "Place looks good, Dad," she noted, letting her eyes brush over me. I don't know what she thought was going on, but she didn't much care. What she cared about was that kid, and the plant in the plastic cup.

"Okay, Benny brought this to me over at the Botanic Gardens. Someone told them that I might know what it was. He grew it on his window ledge, didn't you, Ben?" She smiled at the kid, who smiled back, shy; there was some great achievement, apparently, in growing this plant on a window ledge. "And then he looked through all his books, and he couldn't figure out what it was, so he got on a bus, and rode all the way in from Crown Heights to find me in the Botanic Gardens and see if I knew. And I wasn't sure. But I told him I knew someone who would definitely know. So I brought him here, Dad. Do your stuff." She was sensational, this woman. She kept her hand on the kid's shoulder, and let him know he was safe, and she was taking care of him and his plant, and even though her own father was being so rude he could barely look at her she didn't seemed to notice.

"Where did he get it?" Len asked, completely focused on

the plant now. Charlie made sure there was enough space at one end of the counter, so that people could get a good look at it from all sides. She set it down and held her arm out, warning Len that he was not yet allowed to get too close to it. For now, all she was going to do was let him look.

"Tell him where you got it, Benny." Benny gazed up at her, really not sure whether or not that would be a good idea. "He won't tell anybody, I *promise*," she said, and then she laughed. "Trust me. My dad is not going to want anybody anywhere to know about this."

"So you do know what it is," Len murmured, half to himself.

"I think I do, but I didn't think it was possible," she admitted.

"Let's not get ahead of ourselves," Len said, wiping his palms on his gardener's apron. Charlie took the boy's hand and led him a little bit further into the greenhouse, reaching up and touching a hanging leaf as she moved, checking the texture of its surface, like it was something that you just did. She pointed at a plant with enormous leaves and showed Benny something at its roots. He was mesmerized. Len kept staring at the tiny plant on the counter before him. These people really were their own tribe.

"Where did he find it?" Len asked, sudden. He turned his eyes back to Benny, and considered him with more interest. "Where did you find it, young man? What's your name, Benny?"

"Yes," whispered Benny. The kid was overwhelmed, and who could blame him? *I* was overwhelmed, and it wasn't even my plant.

"Did someone give you the seeds for this, or did they bring you a cutting from another plant?"

174

"It was some seeds," he said.

"And who gave you the seeds?"

"It was some friends of my mom's," he said.

"How many seeds?"

"Little bag. Maybe six or seven."

"Can I see them? The seeds?"

"That's the only one that growed."

"You planted them all."

"Well yeah."

"You should see where he lives," Charlie said with pride, putting her hand on the kid's shoulder, like he was her own. "Every corner of this shitty little apartment, he's got plants growing everywhere, his mother's hardly ever home from what I could tell. He's got two older brothers, who knows what they're up to, so he's almost on his own there. And the place is just filled, things, Dad, you can't believe what he's gotten to grow in rooms, no light, no air practically, he's a miracle worker."

"I'm impressed already," Len nodded, smiling at the kid. "Now, these seeds. Where were they from? Did they bring them from Africa?"

"That's what they said."

"And why did they give them to you?"

"I don't know. It was one guy, my mom knows him. He saw I liked plants."

Len tilted his head and tore his attention away from the plant to look at the kid, who was now looking at the ground, completely overwhelmed with shame. It wasn't too far of a stretch for anyone in that room to know he was lying. Charlie crouched down next to him, so that he was taller than her, and kept her arm around him. She looked up at Len. "Some friend of his mother's took their welfare check. He told Benny he would trade the seeds for the check. Benny got into a lot of trouble for it, even though it wasn't his fault."

"And how old were the seeds? Did he tell you?" Len asked, not giving a rat's ass about Benny and how much trouble he got in for letting this friend of his mom's con him out of their welfare check.

"He said they were magic," Benny admitted. "I wanted to see if I could make them grow."

His eyes filled with tears at the admission of his own stupidity. Len turned back to the plant. He didn't give a shit about Benny's stupidity, either.

"But he didn't tell you how old the seeds were, or where exactly they came from?"

"No, sir."

"And you didn't save even one? You planted them all? Did you plant them all like this, in separate trays?"

"You mean the cups?"

"Yeah, the cups, you planted each one in a separate cup, yes? Did any of the other ones come up at all?"

Benny nodded, still miserable, but regaining his equilibrium now that they were back on the subject of plants and seeds. "Two sprouted but never flourished, they just turned yellow and got some brown spots, then they shriveled up and that was it. The other ones never even sprouted."

"Did you save the unsprouted seeds?"

I didn't think this was in the least bit likely, and neither, I could tell, did Len. There was a sort of hopeless moment of expectant disappointment, as we waited for the kid to tell us that he had just tossed the other useless seeds. But you never know what's going to happen, honestly; you just really never do. Benny reached into his pocket and took out a rolled-up paper towel. "Yeah, sure. I dug 'em up to see how far they gestated."

Len looked up, startled, and caught Charlie smirking at him. She had known that the kid had the other seeds all along, and she had also known that Len would underestimate him. So I guess as many things that you don't know are going to happen? There are just as many that you do. Len didn't waste any time on Charlie judging him, though. He turned back to the kid and held out his bony, greedy hand.

"Good for you, Benny. You saved the seeds, to see how far they gestated. That was the smart thing to do," he said. "May I see them?" Benny handed him the rolled-up paper towel, and with the care of a jeweler revealing a trove of uncut diamonds Len opened the towel to consider the second half of this apparently unheard-of treasure.

"I see, I see," he said. He reached over and plucked a pair of tweezers out of a pencil tin that was hidden somewhere in the mess on the phone table, and delicately picked up something that looked like a fossilized raisin. "Wonderful," Len whispered. He set the raisin back down and turned his attention back to the tiny plant, which looked like a small twig with pale green stars growing out of it. "Wonderful," he said again.

"What is it?" I asked.

It was a mistake; I can see that now. In the extreme excitement surrounding the kid's apparently extraordinary plant, all of them had completely forgotten I was even in the room. Announcing my presence with a completely boneheaded question more or less shattered the dream.

"What are you doing here, Tina?" Len said. He seemed to mean it, too; he had utterly forgotten why I had come up to the greenhouse with him.

"Well, we were—you were down at my place checking in on the moss, Len," I reminded him.

"What moss?" asked Charlie.

"She's just a neighbor I was doing a favor for. We will have to talk about that later, Tina." Len swiftly held up his hand to silence me, and then just as swiftly he went over to the desk, turned his back to us so we couldn't see what he was doing, then he quickly made the few steps back to the door and opened it. "This I think covers it," he said, shoving a few bills into my hand. "Thanks for the help."

"What's going on?" I said to Len, under my breath. "What's with the plant?"

"I'll tell you when I know more myself," Len said, utterly polite, as if he barely knew me. He took my arm, pushed me politely out the door, and closed it.

The elevators are beautiful in the Edgewood. Up on Len's floor, the penthouse, they are especially magical. The original walnut doorways are still there, and while at some point they were apparently covered in thick black varnish which clings in the crevices of the molding, years ago they were stripped and restored and now you can see every nuance of the swirling wood. You open the door of the elevator and the grating is just as intricate, with leaves and vines crawling up the sides of the

178

wrought iron. The floor, of both the elevator and the landing, is also original to the building; it's the same simple marble and obsidian pattern that's in the lobby where Frank stands alone at his podium. So, in terms of landings, Len really did hit the jackpot. And of course he improved the space by putting foliage everywhere. Or maybe it was just overflow from his apartment-greenhouse. In any case, his landing was exceptional, and I just stood there and looked at it for a full minute, trying to get up the nerve to knock on the door with some sort of excuse that might persuade them to let me back in. But there was nothing in my head. Grabbing that extra two hundred from Len seemed embarrassing and trashy, the two things Lucy was always calling me. There was no way to pretend Len and I were friends now, that I was someone he might include in the cool secret surrounding that plant. You don't extort your friends. You don't do it.

Depressed by my own horrible behaviour, I went home. I got off the elevator on the eighth floor, and at first glance it was just the same old boring landing that was as ugly as Len's was beautiful. The linoleum floor needed a serious scrubbing, and the plastic plants frankly didn't just need to be dusted; they needed to be tossed and replaced with something you could actually water. The blinds covering the one dirty window needed to be replaced as well. I had a rather desperate and gloomy moment which suddenly erupted into hope. I can do this, I thought. I used to clean houses for a living, out there at the Delaware Water Gap; a bucket of water, a tub of Lysol, some new blinds and thirty bucks worth of plants would really make all the difference here. I could make the landing a better place and then see what happens next. I can *do this*. So I was actually contemplating the possibility of being a better person, I really was, when I heard a door creak behind me. Not my door, the other one. I looked over and saw that it was open, just a few inches, and there was someone there watching me.

"Mrs Westmoreland?" I asked. "Hi, I'm Tina Finn. I'm living in 8A."

The door stayed cracked, it didn't close, but it didn't open any further either. I could see just a little of the entryway; its marble floor was polished within an inch of its life. Further in, you could see the end of a couch, in the living room, with a perfectly folded throw, in gold and orange, hanging off one side. It was exceptional—perfect, serene—nothing like my crazy apartment, but I took a step forward with determination. "My mother was Olivia, she was married to Bill? Anyway I, uh, I'm living in the apartment until we can get everything sorted out with the wills. I wanted to introduce myself." I was talking way too loud, but I just kept going. "Anyway, I just wanted to say hi, and I was thinking, you know, I was just looking at the landing and thinking I might clean it up a little, get rid of the plastic plants, get some new blinds. Would that be okay with you? You wouldn't have to do anything. I just think it might make the place look a lot nicer if I maybe took a scrub brush to everything . . ."

"You got to go."

"What?" Mrs Westmoreland had finally answered but her voice was so soft I could barely hear her. I leaned in, to listen.

"You got to get out of here." The person on the other side of the door was whispering. "The cops are here. You got to go."

"The cops?" I said. The door shut quickly as behind me the door to my own apartment opened. I turned, not quite knowing what to expect, but I was beginning to get a clue. A uniform officer stood in front of my apartment. He was young and buff and kind of mean looking. I'd seen his type before.

"You Tina Finn?" he asked.

"Who's asking?" I gave him back.

"This your stuff in here?" He held up my backpack and a pair of my underwear.

"Is that my 'stuff'? You mean, is that my underwear? Yeah, that's my underwear. You got a reason for breaking into my apartment and going through my underwear, officer?" I mean, I know you're supposed to shut up and just do what you're told when they come at you like that; believe me, I have been warned. But sadly I always seem to forget.

"Could you come in here, please?"

"Yeah, you bet, whatever you say, officer. I'm sure your reasons for pawing through my underwear are excellent." The sarcastic tone is also not a good idea when talking to belligerent police officers. What can I say? I walked back to the doorway and looked at him with what can only be called disgraceful disregard, considering the fact that we both knew what was coming.

"You're going to have to step aside," I said. "You're so big and strong and scary, I just can't squeeze by you."

"You think you're helping yourself here, Miss Finn?" the guy asked.

"Would that be even possible, officer?" I asked. Behind him, there were two other uniforms waiting for me.

181

"I don't think so," he said.

"Then I don't give a shit," I responded. "Could you step back, please?" He did, and I stepped into the apartment.

"You're under arrest," he said.

"I'm stunned to hear it," I replied.

CHAPTER ELEVEN

When Officer MacDowell read the charges, it turned out that an injunction had in fact been issued by some court and it was subsequently received by one Ira Grossman, Esquire, who was acting on behalf of Alison and Daniel Lindemann, Lucille Finn and Christina Finn of a lot of different addresses. The injunction stated in no uncertain terms that we were not permitted to trespass on the premises of co-operative apartment numbered 8A in the Edgewood Building, address 819 Central Park West. Service having been accepted on my behalf, the legal system assumed that I had been duly informed that further trespass upon the premises would be treated as an unlawful act and I would be persecuted for such to the fullest extent of the law.

So that's what happened. The arresting officer informed me that I had violated the injunction and that they were hauling me into the precinct, and then I smirked and said "Yes, sir" like I thought he was a complete idiot, and so he asked me if I had a problem and so I said, "No, officer. You're so big and strong and mean I'm just terrified is all!" Which more or less was as usual not the right thing to say, because one of the other officers said, "Phil . . ." like a warning, because you could see Officer MacMean go seriously red around the corners of his face, like he had a spectacularly shitty temper, which anybody could see just by looking at him, but then he said he was fine, grabbed me by the arm and shoved me through the door with significantly more force than might be necessary, considering the fact that he weighed probably 240 pounds and I come in under 115. I mean, he didn't insist on handcuffs, because he couldn't— I wasn't technically resisting arrest; I was just tossing around attitude—but he did make sure that he hurt my arm.

I don't know which precinct I actually got taken into, but since it was the Upper West Side it was actually not too bad, as police precincts go. It was alarmingly ugly, with fluorescent lights, linoleum floors and weird green plasterboard walls, and they also did that thing where they put Venetian blinds on inside office windows, which made the whole place look a little bit like a third-rate medical clinic. But, trust me, the fact that there wasn't a layer of grime on the walls and floor put it in a whole different league from the other police precincts in which I'd had the pleasure of being arrested. The mean cop was still a little too rough, so one of the other two guys kind of stepped between us in a very casual way, like that wasn't what he meant to do; he was more just showing me the direction I needed to go to get myself processed. He didn't actually give me any eye contact either; he just leaned over and said, "You're going to have to leave your valuables at the window," but then he stayed where he was, and started to trade greetings with the guy at the front desk, which effectively stopped MacMean from shoving me around anymore. So then I waited for the lady cop to show up, because that's what they always do, they pass you off to a female officer, who takes your valuables, puts them in an envelope, gives them to the guy behind the window, and then leads you to the back of the precinct for your interview. Then if they decide they're going to hold you, someone comes and takes you off to the holding tank for girls. In my experience, the procedure is frankly pretty straightforward and consistent.

This time, though, they didn't take me to the little room for the interview. The lady cop—black, slightly overweight, only a little bit but it was just enough to make her look horrible in that uniform—walked me down a crummy hallway straight to the holding tank.

"Don't I get an interview?" I asked.

"What are you going to tell them, you weren't there?" she said.

"There might be extenuating circumstances," I suggested, while she turned the bolts in the barred door.

"I'm sure your lawyer will make that clear," she noted. And then she shut the door and threw the bolts back in place. Which, in spite of the notable differences in procedure up to this point, had an unfortunately familiar ring to it.

But the holding tank was not bad, as these things go. Except for the bars on one side, it could easily have passed as the waiting room in a hospital. There were rows of blue plastic chairs stuck to the wall, and it was apparently a slow night for crime on the Upper West Side as there was only one other woman in there, a kind of sorry-looking teenage girl who had black hair and a lot of tattoos. She also wore a ripped T-shirt and a kilt, which is a look which honestly works for no one, but what can you do, some trends take forever to die. She glanced up at me with tired eyes, and you could see that at some point earlier in the day they had been lined with the blackest eyeliner out there, but however many hours in a holding tank had taken its toll on her makeup, so now she just looked like an eighteen-year-old kid who had done something dumb.

"I'll be back in a second so you can make your call," the lady officer informed me as she tossed the bolt.

"Hey, can I have another call? I need to make another call. Can I have another one?" the kid said.

"You only get one call," the police lady said.

"I need to make another call! I called my friend and she's not coming, I need to call somebody, I need to call my mom!" Police lady didn't even seem to hear her. She disappeared down the icky hallway, so bored that you could see it in her walk. Goth girl leaned up against the bars, squeezing her eyes shut in a completely concocted rage that she clearly hoped would keep her from crying.

"Is this your first time?" I heard myself saying. I didn't mean to sound like some sort of jaded old creep; it honestly just came out of me. Goth girl tipped her head back and actually looked at the ceiling with her mouth open, as if she seriously could not believe that she was stuck in this holding tank with an idiot as colossal as myself.

"So you're like an old hand at this," she said.

"Not an old hand. But it's not like I've never been arrested before," I admitted.

"Good for you," she mumbled, looking off through the bars again, dismissing me entirely. The phone, a huge old industrial model that looked like it may have been designed by the army corps of engineers, hung on the painted cinderblock wall three feet away. "This is so fucked," she told herself. "I have to get home. This is just fucked. I am so fucked." There was no way to reach the telephone from where we were, but you could see that she was barely stopping herself from shoving her arm through the bars and uselessly trying to grab it.

"When the public defender shows up, they can call people for you," I offered, leaning against the bars. I had no idea how long I was going to be stuck there so I had no interest in sitting down just yet. Plus, those seats looked fiendishly uncomfortable. It is quite maddening to see those individual plastic seats because you know they only do that—put in separate seats like that—so that people can't lay down, which you can do when there are benches.

"I've been waiting for four hours for the fucking public defender! When's the fucking public defender supposed to fucking show up?"

"Sometimes it takes a while," I admitted.

"This is so fucked," the girl repeated, glancing down the hallway. The lady cop was coming back now, with her slow, bored walk. I couldn't figure out why she left in the first place, and decided she probably had to go to the bathroom.

"So who we calling?" she said to me, as she handed me the receiver through the bars. This was more the usual drill; they give you the receiver, you tell them the number you want to dial, and then they dial it for you, and you talk. I thought for a second about my so-called lawyer Ira Grossman, who I had never even met. I thought about calling Lucy. Then I thought about calling Alison and Daniel, who would just call Lucy who would then call the lawyer. And then I'd have to go home with one of them, because I wasn't allowed to stay in the apartment anymore, and if it was Lucy I'd have to listen to her bitch at me all night even though this clearly wasn't my fault, and if it was Alison and Daniel I'd have to listen to them hang out in their tiny kitchen and whisper about how long it was going to be that I slept on their crummy couch, and whether or not Lucy would be able to put me up, and wasn't there anyone else out there who Tina could stay with, and why doesn't Tina ever have any money or seem to be able to hold down a job. I had already lived through this delightful conversation more than once, truth be told, and I was not looking forward to hearing them again. The thought of it made my head hurt.

"Hey, Kilt Girl," I said. "What's your mom's phone number?"

"What?"

"Is that who you want to call?"

"She's not allowed another call until the PD shows up," the lady cop informed me, irritated.

"Yeah, but I get a phone call," I said.

"You want to call my mom?" the kid asked.

"Isn't that who you want to talk to?"

"Yeah, but . . ."

"So what's her number?"

The girl looked at me. The cop looked at me too. She was moving out of irritated and more firmly into pissed off. "Look,

188

this isn't up to you," she told me again. "She's not getting another phone call."

"It's not her call, it's my call," I said.

"You aren't getting another call. You call this kid's mother? That's your call."

"I know that's my call."

"You call her, you're stuck here," she said again, like I wasn't getting it.

"What's your mother's phone number, kid?" I asked.

"And she's not allowed to talk to her."

"She's not going to talk to her; I'm going to talk to her. Kid, what's the number?"

The kid spit out the number so fast I almost didn't get it. I mean, this sudden stroke of good fortune had definitely commanded her attention, and she had no time to affect disinterest or suspicion. "Tell her that I really need her to come down," she said. "Tell her that they said I was doing drugs but I was totally not doing them at all, it was totally three other kids at this party I was at? And it's a total mistake."

"I totally will tell her that," I said. Now that she had a shred of hope that someone was actually going to help her out here, the kid was sort of charming in a way that made me suspect she was not in fact eighteen. Someone picked up the phone.

"Hello," said a kind of tony fake voice on the other end of the line. You could practically see the whole apartment from the sound of that voice.

"Hi," I said. "I'm a friend of . . ."

"Collette," Kilt Girl said, fast.

"I'm a friend of Collette's," I said, thinking this kid looks nothing like a Collette. "Is this her mother?"

"Yes, I am her mother," said the voice, getting a little worried now, but also kind of exhausted too, like the sound of someone who was already exhausted by Collette's recent shenanigans, and not looking forward to a new chapter.

"Well, I'm afraid Collette, unfortunately she's having some trouble with the police right now, nothing serious—"

"It's a mistake, a total mistake," she dictated.

"A total mistake," I repeated. "But she does need for you to come down to the precinct and pick her up."

"Oh my God. You're kidding. She's at the police station?" said the tony voice, raising an octave. "PAUL! COLLETTE'S AT THE POLICE STATION! What is it? Has she been arrested? Is she all right?"

"Oh yeah, she's fine, she's just, you just need to come pick her up," I reassured the voice.

"It's a little more complicated than that," the lady cop sneered.

"Maybe, maybe not," I told her. "What precinct is this again?"

"The forty-ninth."

"We're over here at the forty-ninth precinct. I don't know the exact address but it's on 83rd Street. Oh, and can I ask— how old is Collette again?"

"How *old* is she?" asked the voice, all frosty now. "She's sixteen. Why?"

"Okay, you might want to mention that to the guy at the front desk. When someone gets picked up between the ages of ten and seventeen they're actually not allowed to hold them, unless there's an adult present. Collette may have lied about her age, so I wouldn't be too mean about it? But you know, it's not legal for them to hold her, without you being here."

"Who is this again?" asked the voice.

"Okay, see you," I said, and I handed the phone back to the officer. She stared at me.

"You're quite the expert on juvenile arrests," she observed, hanging up the phone.

"Yeah, weird, huh," I said. "I'm going to need a PD."

In about twenty minutes she came back and picked up Collette, which I thought was a good sign—I mean, it's not like her folks made her sweat down there; they just came right away and got her. She didn't even look at me, she just followed that lady cop down the hall. "You're welcome," I yelled, but then I didn't watch to see if she even flinched. Some people are young, and some people are just stupid, and I wasn't all that curious to find out which that kid was. So then Kilt Girl was no longer someone to share the cell with, and I was stuck there by myself. I sat down for a while in one of those blue plastic chairs, which was ridiculously uncomfortable, and then I tried to lie down across three of them, which was truly back-breaking, and then I thought about lying on the floor, which even though that place was clean was still relatively disgusting so I didn't do that either. I ended up sitting on one of the corner chairs and stretching my legs out to the second chair in the row across from me, which actually turned out to be a just barely comfortable enough position for me to actually sleep in, once I took my sweater off and figured out how to lodge it between my head and the cinderblock wall in a kind of weird angle that held up my neck. Then of course as soon as

I managed to pass out a different lady cop, this one Hispanic and skinny, woke me up.

"HEY!" she yelled. "Tina Finn! You Tina Finn?"

"Yeah," I said, picking my head up way too fast, given the crazy position my head was in. My poor neck felt like it was in pieces and one of my eyes seemed to have glued itself together, so I decided I had slept for longer than it felt like, but it was clearly one of those odd sleeps where you pass out so thoroughly you don't have any sense, when you wake up, of what day it is.

"What day is it?" I said.

"They want you in interrogation," she answered. I nodded and grabbed my sweater, which had fallen on the floor while I tried to reorient myself, and then I followed her back down the hallway to the interrogation room. Because the fluorescent lights are always on in those places it really is impossible to tell what time of the day it is, so I had utterly no clue until I got into the interrogation room and spotted a clock, which informed me that it was a little past two in the morning.

"It's two in the morning," I said to the officer.

"That's right," she admitted.

"Well, the PD isn't coming at two in the morning," I said, still feeling kind of stupid and like it was taking too long to wake up.

"This is interrogation, they want you for interrogation," she said, and then she left, like this made any sense at all.

"How come they didn't interrogate me when I got here?" I said, but the door was already closed behind her. So there I was stuck again, in this totally empty room.

The whole thing was starting to seem completely surreal to me, and I'm someone who has a relatively high tolerance for strange adventures. I looked around for a minute, thinking about the shit that goes down in places like that. There was no sign of it here—like everything else in this too-clean police precinct, there wasn't a shred of interest; the walls gave up nothing at all. I felt like I was trapped in one of those science-fiction movies where they make everybody work in identical cubicles where they bore you to death and suck your brain out until everyone is a complete automaton; seriously, I was getting significantly creeped out by this fluorescent precinct when the door opened again, and Detective Pete Drinan walked in. At which point, nothing seemed surreal at all.

"Oh, it's you," I said. "Such a surprise."

"Yeah, how you doing?" he asked, tossing a manila file folder on the table. "You want anything, a cup of coffee or something? You want a Coke?"

"A Coke sounds kind of good, sure," I said. Drinan went to the door and leaned out, yelling, "Hey! Can somebody bring me a Coke?" It seemed so much like cops on television I almost started to laugh. Nobody answered immediately and after glancing up and down the hallway for a minute he just disappeared again, letting the door swing closed behind him. Then I was alone again for another three minutes, during which time I got bored so I picked up the manila file and started to read it.

The door swung open again. "Hey, what are you doing? Don't do that," Drinan said. He came over behind me and took it out of my hand, impatient. "What's the matter with you?"

"What's the big deal? It's my record," I said. "It's not like it's a big secret."

Detective Drinan took a seat and gave me a look. "You always act like this when you get arrested?" he asked.

"I do when the cops are acting like jerks," I told him.

"Most people would have the sense to keep their mouths shut when the cops are acting like jerks, Miss Finn," he said. He tossed my file back on the table and ran his hand over the back of his neck, like he was trying to figure out some big annoying puzzle. "What happened to your arm?"

I looked down, to see what he was talking about. You couldn't tell when I had my sweater on, but since I had taken it off to use as a pillow in that uncomfortable holding cell it was still in my hands, and all I had on over my jeans was a tank top. In that horrible green light you could see that my arm was elbow to shoulder covered with bruises from where the somewhat too aggressive arresting officer had been shoving me around. I suddenly felt so embarrassed I didn't even know what to say. My face turned red, which was even more mortifying, and then I was so surprised by my own embarrassment and also exhausted in general that for a second I thought I might actually start crying. Drinan was really watching me now, so I stared at the broken corner of the table top and tried to focus. The rounded edge of the table was Formica, and the top was fake wood, and I wondered, silently, why everyone kept trying to get plastic to look like wood when even a half-wit like me knows that that's just not possible.

The door to the interrogation room opened again, and the skinny Hispanic lady police officer stuck her head in.

"You wanted this?" she asked.

"Yeah, thanks," Drinan said, and he reached out to take the can of Coke which she held out to him. While his back was turned I picked up my sweater out of my lap and wrapped it around my shoulders, fast, so you couldn't see as much. When I looked up Drinan was watching me with those sad brown eyes, which at the moment registered nothing more than a mild detective-like curiosity. He shrugged a little, put the can of soda on the table and popped the seal with one hand. Then he held it out to me, sat down and started reading my file, while I drank my Coke. It tasted pretty good, frankly.

"Don't bolt it," he advised. "I'm not going to get you another one."

"I'm thirsty," I said. "I've been here since I don't even know, a long time."

"4.37 p.m.," he said, reading it off the front page of the arrest report. "You resist arrest?"

"It doesn't say that," I said.

"'Belligerent and provocative' is actually what it says, right here." He held it up briefly, to show me.

"We're not allowed to talk back?"

"No, in fact, you are not allowed to talk back to your arresting officer. What are you, a moron?"

"I come home and find my apartment full of police officers and I haven't done a fucking thing and I'm not allowed to have an opinion about that?"

"It's not your home," he informed me.

"Far as I can tell it's not yours either."

He paused, without looking up, like he was thinking about

195

responding to that, but got more interested in the question of why I persisted in my stupidity. "You might want to watch your mouth," he finally suggested.

"Yes sir," I said. He looked up at me now, but he wasn't annoyed by my problematic tone of voice. Now his face was bent around the question of the words that actually came out of my mouth.

"Wait a minute. What did you say, before? You came home and found them there?"

"Yes sir."

"So what, you opened the door and found them in your apartment, so-called?"

"No."

"So what happened?"

"I got off the elevator and I was going to go in, when Mrs Westmoreland told me that the cops were in there and I should get out of there. So—"

"You know Mrs Westmoreland?"

"I saw her that night she was trying to get you to come in and have a drink with her."

"That night you were spying on us."

"Yeah, that night."

"Well, maybe you heard that night, she's not actually someone who's necessarily going to go out on a limb and do you any favors. And now you're claiming what, that she *warned* you that there were police officers there, who were looking for you? Why would she do that?"

"I don't know. Maybe it wasn't her, maybe it was someone else."

"She lives there alone."

"Well I don't know who it was. I told you, she was standing behind the door."

"And whoever this person was said get out of here the cops are here?"

"Yes."

"So then what did you do?"

"Well, then the arresting officer—"

"The one who put his hands on you?"

"Yeah, that guy, he stepped out into the hallway and said, 'Could you come in here please?'"

"Did he put his hands on you then?"

"No, he just told me to come inside."

"So that's what you did."

"Yes."

This seemed like bad news to Detective Drinan. He was in a completely pissy mood now, you could see it in his face. His eyes were hooded and his hand covered his chin, which made it look like he was trying to be businesslike while he looked at those docs. But he was also biting the inside of his lip, like there was a canker sore in there that was giving him hell. He shifted in his seat and looked up at me.

"You knew there was an injunction barring you from the apartment and that there were cops waiting in there for you, and you walked over and stepped into the apartment anyway?"

"I didn't know there was any injunction."

"You were served."

"I wasn't served."

"Your representation was served. Your legal representative

accepted service on your behalf two days ago." He leafed through a pile of documents in another manila folder and shoved one across the table to me. I couldn't even read it.

"I was served?" I said, sounding really stupid all of a sudden, like someone who was completely exhausted and hadn't eaten in twenty-two hours.

"What's the matter with you?" he asked. "Was this deliberate? That why you went in there and mouthed off at Officer MacDowell, so you could provoke him into shoving you around a little bit? We going to see all this in the newspapers tomorrow?"

"Oh, knock it off. This isn't my fault," I said.

"The hell it isn't. You walked right into this. You defied a court order and forced an arrest—"

"You're the one who got this fucking injunction."

"Yes, I did. That's right, I did. I fucking well did."

"You said you'd wait. You said let me know when you're ready, you'd come by when I was ready to let you in, and then you sent a bunch of creepy police officers to arrest me."

"You wanted to be arrested."

"Oh yeah, I love being arrested. It's just a total blast having police officers manhandle you."

"According to your record you have something of a problem with men shoving you around. Maybe you enjoy that type of thing a little more than you like to admit."

"What did you say? You think I like it when men hit me. Did you just say that?"

Now it was his turn to go all red. He didn't say anything for a second, like he was thinking about what to do next, and then he just shrugged. "Sorry," he said. "I apologize."

I had no idea at this point where this was all going. He wore me out, Pete Drinan, he really did. I looked up at the ceiling and saw that there was a fan up there, and while it twirled around I tried to keep focused on one of the frets and watch it spin, so that I could see them all individually, instead of just watching them blur together. I suddenly felt so tired I thought I was going to fall over. It probably had more to do with bolting down that Coke than anything else, but who's to say.

"You didn't use your phone call," Drinan finally observed, still consulting my file.

"What?"

"There was some kid in the holding tank. You called her mother, told her to come get her?"

"Yeah?"

"Why'd you do that?"

"I don't know. It was stupid."

"Yeah, it was stupid. Now you're stuck here until some useless PD shows up and gets your bail posted and calls your sister for you. And I got to be honest, Ms Finn, you strike me as a lot of things, but I wouldn't put stupid on the list."

"Is there a question in there?"

He bit back a snappy response and tossed down the file. Then he rubbed his eyes. "Yeah, okay," he said. "Here's the question. Did the arresting officer ask you to step into the apartment before he arrested you?"

"Yeah, he did. I just told you he did!" I said, standing up finally. This whole situation was really making my head explode. "I told you—I told all of you—I . . ."

"Relax, just relax, Tina," he sighed. "Sit down." Then, "Are you all right?"

I really wasn't. I felt exceptionally sweaty all of a sudden, and like my tongue was stuck to the inside of my mouth; fireworks were erupting in my brain. "Oh, shit," I said, and I keeled over.

CHAPTER TWELVE

When I came to, I was lying on the floor of that hideous interrogation room. My sweater was off again, and that Hispanic lady cop was waving her hands around my face in some strained attempt, apparently, to stir up a breeze.

"What are you doing?" I asked, trying to shove her away. My arms didn't seem to work. "What happened?"

"You fainted," said Drinan's voice, somewhere behind me. "Here, can you pick your head up?" A couple of hands I couldn't see lifted my head a few inches off the linoleum and then cradled it, briefly, before shoving something that turned out to be my sweater underneath it.

"I'm okay," I said. I wanted to sit up but I was afraid to try it, and frankly I was still pretty confused about what I was doing on the floor. "I just got hot."

"They been working on the heat for three months and nobody still knows what the problem is," the Hispanic officer agreed. Up close she was kind of pretty; her hair was pulled back too tight but she had crazy eyebrows that looked like some sort of unusual piece of punctuation. She was still flapping her hands in my face but I didn't think it was so annoying now; she was so matter-of-fact and determined, it seemed good natured and odd at the same time that she was just trying to fan me off like that.

"Maybe we could prop the door open," Drinan suggested. The lady cop stood and went to prop open the door, and for a moment his hands came back and stroked my hair away from my forehead, even though my hair wasn't on my forehead. A breath of air moved across the floor. I hoped I didn't look too stupid, spread out on the floor like that, but I was pretty sure that I did.

"Could you go get us a bottle of water?" he asked the lady cop. Then he leaned over so that I could spot his face in my line of vision. "You think you can sit up if I help you?" He didn't wait for me to answer; he just put his arm under my shoulder and lifted, but then stopped carefully when we were only halfway up. It was a good thing too, because the whole room started to spin again, and I almost fell over a second time. "Hold on, hold on," he repeated, holding on. I was really having trouble with the air.

"I'm okay," I said. "Seriously, I'm okay. I just drank that Coke too fast."

"Yeah, a cold can of soda, that makes everybody pass out," he observed. We just sat there for a moment, while he propped me up and I leaned against his chest, trying to breathe. "When was the last time you had anything to eat?" he finally asked.

"Who knows," I said.

"They give you anything, when you got here?"

"You mean like carry-out?"

"Yeah, like that," he said. "Never mind."

He stood me up very slowly. Then he took me into the hallway, where he leaned me up against a wall and watched while I dutifully took sips from the plastic cup full of lukewarm water Officer Martinez of the Extraordinary Eyebrows eventually delivered. It was something of a major thoroughfare, as hallways go, so even though it was about three in the morning by then there was a good deal of foot traffic. Mostly it was the night-shift officers who were taking a bathroom break in between falling asleep at their desks. But then another detective came through with a couple of younger officers who were dragging some perp who got picked up on something or other. As they cut through, he nodded to Drinan.

"Hey, Pete," he said. "What are you doing over here?"

"Just talking to a witness," he said.

"Out in the hallway? Some hospitality," the other detective said. "You want to use my desk, it's free for at least twenty minutes."

"Yeah, thanks, I might do that," he said. "See you, Mitch." He looked back at me as Mitch disappeared down the hallway with his arrest. "You feeling better? You want to sit down?"

"So this isn't your precinct, huh?" I asked.

This actually made Drinan laugh. "Jesus," he said. "You don't miss a trick. How many times have you been arrested anyway?"

"Not that many. Three."

"Is this three or four?"

"I haven't been processed yet, so I can't tell."

"Yeah, well, you're right, it's not my precinct," he admitted. "Come on, let's go. I'll buy you a burger."

"I'm not allowed to just leave, you moron," I said, although I didn't lean on the "moron" so it didn't actually sound that bad. "I'm under arrest."

"Thanks for explaining the rules," he said. "Now, could we get something to eat before you pass out a second time and we have to put you on an IV?"

He stood up from where he was leaning against the wall, and turned but took a step back, like he was in charge and I was of course just going to do what he said, but he was also going to be a gentleman about it. "There's an all-night diner around the corner, on Broadway," he said. "It doesn't look like much but the food is okay. Burgers, omelettes, fries, that sound all right?"

"Boy," I said. "Who knew that fainting was so effective?"

"Yeah," he agreed. "You figure out how to do that on cue, the world's your oyster." He put his hands in his pockets to make it look like he was less in charge of this march, but stayed just the tiniest bit behind me, so that there was still no question in anyone's mind. I was in fact completely starving by this point so I was losing interest in my own perpetual impulse to argue just for the hell of it. I let him nudge me toward the entryway of the precinct house.

"Can I have my sweater back?" I asked, as we neared the front desk.

"You cold?" he asked.

"No, I just want my sweater," I said.

"Then why don't you let me carry it for you," he replied.

204

He waved to the officer manning the desk. "Hey, Randy, how's it going? Pete Drinan. We met last year at the Mets game with Jimmy Marks and Brian Cahill, you remember? They were playing the Royals, Jimmy scored those seats off some reporter he did a favor for over at the *Daily News*."

"Sure sure sure," Randy replied. "How's it going, Pete? What are you doing here, this time of night?"

"Tommy MacDowell brought in a witness on one of my cases," Detective Drinan lied. "She's been hanging out here all night. I need to get her something to eat! Tina Finn, this is Officer Bohrman."

The guy behind the desk, a huge black man with a nice smile, stood, which made him eight times as big as me and Detective Drinan combined. "How you doing, young lady?" he asked.

"Great," I said. "Just a little hungry."

"My fault, entirely," Drinan said, still the perfect gentleman. "She's been waiting for me all night. Whoa! Tina! What happened to your arm? Randy, look at this! She's covered in bruises!"

Randy behind the desk glanced at Drinan, then glanced at my arm, then glanced back at Drinan. "That is a shame," he said, cool and formal. "You need to take better care of yourself, Ms Finn."

"Thank you, officer, I will, I will do that," I said.

"See you, Randy," Pete said.

"You take care, Pete," the guy behind the desk replied. And with that, Drinan put his hand on my back and steered me right out the front door.

"So what was that about?" I asked him twenty minutes later, when I had an enormous, dripping hamburger in my hand. Actually there was less than half a hamburger in my hand by then. I was so hungry I couldn't even talk until I had consumed most of it, in addition to two dozen enormous and fairly mediocre fries. Drinan was picking at a piece of apple pie.

"What?" he asked me, pouring sugar into his second cup of what had to be truly shitty coffee. The place he had taken me to was linoleum central. There was one waitress propped up against the fry window, and apparently one person back there somewhere; the whole place was barely more populated than my apartment. But the burger was good.

"With Randy at the front desk. 'Oh Tina, what happened to your arm?' You practically made him take a picture of it," I said.

"Are you complaining?"

"I'm asking a question."

"You want to end up in the Tombs for the rest of the week?"

"Is that what you do to people who ask questions?"

"Why didn't you call your sister? Why didn't you call your lawyer?"

"Oh, for crying out loud."

"I'm giving you an opening here, Tina. You might want to consider taking it."

"You were the one who had me arrested in the first place."

"You let yourself get arrested. You saw MacDowell standing there and you let him arrest you. Why'd you do that?"

"Maybe I wanted to see you."

"So, you got your wish. Keep this up, you'll also see the

206

inside of a jail cell for a second time tonight. Or, you could go home."

This was news to me, honestly. I could tell he was feeling vaguely lousy about the fact that I got roughed up and nearly starved to death by his friends in the local precinct, but it had not frankly occurred to me yet that this might amount to a get out of jail free card. At the same time, as soon as he said it I couldn't help but wonder what good a get out of jail free card is to someone who has nowhere to go.

"What's the matter?" he asked. "You look like I just killed your dog."

"I'm just surprised," I said. "So how come you arrested me if you're just going to let me go?"

"How about we pretend that I'm asking the questions for a little while, Ms Finn," he said. "Why'd you walk into that arrest?"

"I didn't, strictly speaking," I said, going for the dregs of my Coke.

"Didn't strictly speaking *what*?" he said, waving to the waitress to refill my drink. "Strictly speaking, I didn't know about this injunction," I told him.

"You said that before. It won't stand up; they served the papers legally."

"I don't know. But they didn't tell me. I don't know why."

"I find that hard to believe."

"Look, it's what happened. You guys never make mistakes? They didn't tell me. I mean, that it was illegal, that I could get arrested. They never told me."

"You sister never told you?"

"You think she knew?" This honestly had not occurred to me,

207

that Lucy would know something like that and just not share the information. It suddenly sounded so plausible that I turned all red. I mean, Lucy sometimes behaves in questionable ways, but would she set me up to be *arrested*? "Come on," I said, trying to shrug this off, but I sounded, honestly, like I was just being an idiot about the truth. "There was just a screw-up some-where."

Drinan was listening to all of this with a sort of vague boredom. He reached over and took a limp fry from my plate and doused it with salt, then he licked the salt off the fry and went after it again with the salt shaker.

"That is really gross," I said. "You're going to give yourself a heart attack."

"I'm touched by your concern."

"Well, what are you doing? You're acting like some wild boar at a salt lick. That's gross. Stop it," I told him, slapping his hand and taking the salt shaker out of it.

"There's something else I'd like to know."

"I told you everything. There isn't any more." I sighed. "Come on, you've been grilling me for hours. This is stupid."

"No," he said, finally tossing the excess salt off his disgusting french fry and dropping it on his plate. "Even if this was all just a technical screw-up, you still haven't said why you didn't call anybody. Why spending a night, or a day and a night, or a week, in jail, is preferable to calling one of your sisters and asking her to come get you out."

He picked up the paper napkin that was sitting next to his coffee cup and unfolded it carefully. He hadn't used it yet, really, so it was perfectly white and pressed, except for a single brown circle which showed the one time he had made a mistake and set his coffee cup down on it instead of in its saucer. He looked up at me while he wiped off his fingers, and his eyebrows went up, just a little, like, You think I'm going to let you avoid that one? Which of course I never did. I'm just not sure why everyone thinks that saying the true thing that's in your heart is ever really going to get you what you want or need.

"I can't," I finally said.

"Can't what?"

"I can't, I don't . . . There's no place for me. Lucy won't let me stay with her, and Alison and Daniel don't want me. So. It's like that," I said.

He sat there and waited, like that wasn't going to be good enough, and I was going to have to give him all of it.

"They think I'm a loser," I said. My voice was getting steadier. It didn't sound so bad, honestly, when you just said it. "They don't want me. I'm not allowed to stay in their apartments. And I don't, I don't have any money and I don't have friends here, I don't live here. Seriously. I got no place to go. So what the . . . why should I call Lucy and let her come down to the precinct and make a big deal like she's doing me some huge favor, and then act like her shitty couch is too good for me? Why let them all just keep acting like I'm some huge hideous problem that they always have to deal with? Why not just stay in jail?"

"You ever been in jail? I mean, I can see you've been arrested,

209

but you ever actually spend a night anywhere other than a lock-up?"

"You mean like jail jail?"

"Yeah, 'jail jail', Miss Smartypants. You ever actually spend any time there? Your so-called record says three arrests but no actual jail time. Is there something I'm missing here?"

"No."

"Okay, then stop acting like it's an option."

"You want me to call Lucy?"

"I'm not going to tell you what to do." I couldn't tell if he was bothered by my lack of self-regard, or disgusted with the lot of us. He finished wiping off his fingers, and set down the crumpled napkin, then he checked out his nails, like it had just occurred to him that second that they might be filthy, which in fact they were not. He leaned back into the vinyl of the booth and seemed to be thinking about what I had just said, but at the same time I could see that his eyes were checking out where the waitress might be, because he needed to ask her for something, more bad coffee, or the check. I had an inkling that he probably was a pretty good detective because even though I kept mouthing off and acting like I was running the show all night he had in fact found out everything that he wanted to know, and I hadn't found out anything at all.

"You ever even meet my dad?" he finally asked. Over my head he caught the eye of the waitress and tipped his chin just a little bit, like some sort of strange sign language. He reached for a toothpick, even though he hadn't eaten anything other than sugar, coffee and salt, while I pigged out on that enormous burger. Good looking, mean, and he doesn't eat; maybe he's a vampire, I thought.

"Hey, are you with us?" he asked.

"What was the question? Did I ever meet your dad? No, I never did. Did you ever meet my mom?"

"A couple times."

"You did, you met her?" This suddenly seemed like really great news to me, that he had seen my mother after she went away from me, and into this other world, up there in that beautiful strange apartment with that strange old crazy drunk. "What was, what—wow. I didn't know you met her," I admitted.

"Before they got married, when she was cleaning house for him. I met her a few times."

"She was cleaning *house* for him?" I asked.

"You didn't know that?"

Why is the news that your mother had been cleaning houses the worst news you could get, when in fact it's exactly what you were doing? I had let her go so far from me for so long that I thought the guilt of such a distance had burned itself out. But she had still lived in the world, and she found herself cleaning houses. And this sad-eyed detective had seen her, with buckets and rags, on her hands and knees, and I had not.

He wasn't volunteering any more information. I started to hate the way you had to pry facts out of this bonehead. "Did you see her often?" I asked.

"Just a couple times."

"So how did she look?"

"I didn't pay much attention, until he married her," Detective Bonehead stated.

"Were you at the wedding?"

"No, I was not invited," he declared. "My brother and I were not in fact consulted about the marriage. We were told about it, after the fact."

"So what happened then?"

"You know as much as me about that part."

"I *don't* know as much as you. I don't know anything. I think *that's* pretty obvious. Which is why I'm asking. I only saw her the one time which you already know about from Mrs What's Her Name who was *spying* across the hall, because we weren't allowed, your dad—we didn't—oh fuck it." I moved almost instantaneously through losing my cool to picking up a phony version of it, as it had occurred to me fast that I had to keep my mouth shut about how Bill was keeping us out of his life. Lucy had warned me about this sort of thing: Don't let them know how much he didn't want us around, it'll hurt our chances to walk off with all of it. I remembered the rules and stopped myself from giving up any more information, I really did. But I still wanted to know what he knew. "Did they, so, what, did they have a wedding dinner?" I asked.

"No," he said, laughing a little at the very idea.

"Well, when did he tell you? That they got married?"

"A couple days later."

"Did you see them?"

"Yeah, we did. We were over at the apartment, and we saw them and they told us."

"And they were happy?"

"You know, it's hard to tell about people and happiness, Tina. That's one thing you learn in police school." He looked down and I could see that he had at some point pulled a small wad of neatly folded bills out of his pocket which he rifled through swiftly, counting ones to himself like a little kid.

"What does that mean?" I asked, trying again not to get mad. He wasn't objecting to the fact that I was asking questions now, so I didn't want to piss him off with my famously bad attitude, but my nerves were really running on fumes by this point. "I mean, did you see them? What did they, wow. Okay. Okay," I stumbled. "When was the last time you saw them?"

He looked up at me from his counting, caught by the question, like he couldn't immediately remember the answer. "A long time," he admitted with some shade of something that looked like sorrow, or reluctance. "I don't know. A couple years maybe."

"A couple years, like two years?" I asked.

"Yeah, like two years."

"Like when they got married, that's when you stopped seeing him?"

"Yes, that's when I stopped seeing him."

"So he married my mom and he told you and you guys had a fight and that was like the end of it for you, like how could he have married my *mom* and so then you just—stopped even talking to him, that's how horrible it was for you and your brother, you cut yourself off from him because he married her? Is that what happened?"

"Something like that."

He looked down, still trying to count those bills, a task which was mysteriously beyond his ability all of a sudden. "Look, she was cleaning his *house*," he said, and he sounded truly pained, somehow, that he was the one who had to tell me this. "And then he married her? What were we supposed to think?"

"Just whatever you thought, I guess. Whatever your thoughts were that you were having. How do I know?"

"Exactly."

"Look," I said. "Look. She was a really nice person." Somehow I thought this would make a difference. It didn't. Detective Bonehead raised an eyebrow, as if he were impressed, not really, with my loyal little burst of sentimentality. Then he went back to asking questions.

"So how come you abandoned her?" he said.

"I didn't," I said. "I didn't. I didn't."

My assertion that my mother was a nice person did not get through to this guy, but the idiotic desperation behind those three denials apparently did. He shrugged. There was a mournful pause, where we both considered how pathetic I sounded. "Well," he said, with a truly hopeless edge entering his voice. "I didn't abandon them, either."

"No, I get it," I said. "I do. Here, let me do it, you're like—retarded all of a sudden." Before he could argue I just reached over and took the ones out of his hand, and started counting. "How much is it?"

"I don't know," he admitted, looking around helplessly. We had been abandoned by the waitress.

"We just had a burger and a Coke and pie and some coffee,

it can't be that hard to figure out," I noted, counting out about twelve bucks. Somehow everything had shifted, and now we were just two people talking about our fucked-up families. And it was late.

Drinan sucked in his breath, controlled, and then he blew it out slow, like someone taught him that once in the one yoga class he ever condescended to take when some hippie girlfriend actually got him to go before he became a cop. But he still remembered the breathing, and so he did it, sitting there in that booth, like that one good yoga breath was going to put him back in control of his whole fucked-up life. His face looked like four in the morning. "Yeah," he said. "Let's go."

"Oh, wait, hang on," I said, remembering what my situation was. My heart started pounding way too hard. "Jesus, wait, hang on." Reality was setting in; I wasn't actually going to be spending the next three days sitting in a booth in a shitty diner; I was going to jail. I suddenly felt as old and tired as he looked.

"Relax, Tina," said Detective Bonehead. He stood and dusted the crumbs of salt off his mediocre suit jacket. "I'll take you home."

So then Detective Bonehead drove me back to the Edge in a shitty old blue Buick, and then I sat in his car for a long minute, trying to figure out what to say.

"Are you going to get out of the car?" he finally said.

"Yeah, I'm getting out," I said, "Sorry. Yes, sorry, I'm just trying to figure out what this all means. Does this mean I can stay in the apartment?"

"It means you can stay tonight," he told me.

"What about after tonight?"

"After tonight is tomorrow," he said.

"And after that?"

"You know what, Tina," he said, and he tilted his head quickly to the left, and to the right, like he was working some bad kink out of his neck. "I'm not going to try and tell you what happens the day after tomorrow. Nobody knows what's going to happen. If you think you do, you're wrong."

I was looking down the street, past a couple of drunks who were staggering up the sidewalk toward us. The sky was starting to turn that strange dark purple that meant the night was on its last legs. "Well," I said. "The sun's coming up, I know that much."

"That's just an educated guess," Drinan said. "Listen. If anyone tries to arrest you again? You might want to mention that you got roughed up the first time. That sergeant at the desk, his name is Randy Bowen. Randy Bowen, you think you can remember that?"

"I think so," I said.

"They're not going to bother you. That's just in case."

"Thanks," I said.

"I'll see you in court." He was gripping the steering wheel now, but he didn't seem angry; he seemed more like he was trying to stay awake.

"Look," I said. "You want to come up?"

He tilted his head away, like that thing in his neck was just not going to let him alone. Then he glanced back at me with a weary, cop-like regret. "That won't be necessary," he said. I turned all red yet again.

"I didn't mean that," I said. "I just meant, since you haven't seen it. In so long. Just that one time. And you were drunk, that night, and I thought . . . Do you want to come see it. Just see it. Oh whatever. Whatever!" I said. I think I yelled it as I started to get out of his stupid loser car. "That is just classic, and you know what? I'm too tired to even be embarrassed by you thinking that I'm trying to come on to you right now. Like, I'm so tired, I'm not even awake enough to think, What did he say? This moron thinks I want to sleep with him even though he tried to have me arrested? He thinks I want to have sex, twenty minutes after eating a pound of hamburger and six dozen french fries? Men are such geniuses. I'm so tired I can't even articulate any sarcastic bullshit for you, Detective. So when you want to see the apartment you grew up in—when you want to see your old room and what's left of your mom's crazy paint job—you'll let me know."

I was almost all the way to the door of the building, when he yelled after me.

"What did you say?" he yelled.

"Oh, man," I said. "I'm not kidding. I'm done. I'm going to bed."

"About my mom's paint job."

"What about it?"

"How'd you know it's my mom's?"

I couldn't remember. I couldn't even remember what I said about his mom, and I had just said it like seconds ago. "Come on, man," I said. "It's four in the morning."

"Yeah yeah yeah, okay," he said. He looked back at his

hands on the steering wheel, and he sat there for a second like something else was occurring to him to ask me about. Before he could ask it, I went inside and I laid down and I didn't get up until Lucy appeared and told me to get out of bed.

CHAPTER THIRTEEN

It took me a second to catch up. She was hanging in the doorway, watching me, impatient, while I fumbled around with the covers, groggy. The little bedroom I had adopted has two windows, but they overlook an exhaust shaft, so there's very little light even when the old pull-down shades are up, which they were not at the time. So it truly was pitch black in there. "What time is it?" I asked.

"It's three-thirty, what is the matter with you?" Lucy asserted, stalking in on her low sensible heels, and yanking the shades up. "Are you hung over?"

"No, I'm not hung over," I said.

"Right," she replied, all pissy as usual.

"I don't have a hangover, Lucy," I said. "I was arrested yesterday afternoon, so I spent the night in lock-up thank you very much because *some*one forgot to *inform* me that there is a fucking *injunction* on this place."

That did get her attention, although she was completely unapologetic. "You were arrested?" she asked, with more than a shred of disbelief.

"Don't give me that," I said, disgusted with her. "You knew all about it. And don't even bother lying to me about it—"

"I am not—"

"You forgot to inform me. You and that lawyer, although my bet is he told you and you told him that you would tell me but then you didn't even bother to tell me."

"I am not sure what you're accusing me of here, Tina. But if you were arrested—"

"What do you mean, 'if'? Do you think I'd make something like that up?"

"I don't know what you'd do."

"Why would I make that up?"

"Well, why would I want you to be arrested? Isn't that what you're accusing me of, trying to have you arrested for some unknown reason?"

"Oh forget it," I said.

"You know, Tina, you're increasingly unstable," she noted, starting to dial her CrackBerry.

"I'm excuse me, I'm what, what am I?"

"All these crazy accusations. If you had been arrested I would know about it, wouldn't I? If you were arrested, you would have had to call me—Hi, it's Lucy Finn. Could I speak to Ira? Thanks," she cooed into the phone.

"I'm not making this up!"

"Or Alison. Or anybody. You would have had to call somebody, and they would have had to call me. Which to my knowledge also did not happen."

"I'm going to go take a shower."

"Hi!" she chirped. "I'm over here at the apartment and Tina has just told me an interesting story."

There was a bathroom right across the hall—the one with the silver-spotted wallpaper—but it really needed a good cleaning and several tiles had come up around one of the corners so it was frankly too depressing to take a shower in there. There was also a pretty capable blue bathroom right behind the kitchen off the great room, but Len had all sorts of apparatus set up in there. Then there was a really quite tidy peach-colored bathroom off the TV room, to the right of both it and the bedroom, but it had one of those chair things set in it, so people who are old and decrepit can actually sit down in the shower, which was simply too depressing to contemplate. But there was a fourth bathroom which you could get to if you walked down a hall off the TV room, past the laundry room and around a corner. It had been painted periwinkle blue at some point, and there were a whole lot of sixties-looking groovy flower stickers stuck to the ceiling. The flowers were also all over the cheap plastic door on the stand-up shower. So although it was a little inconvenient to find yourself walking a quarter mile to take a shower, it was a nice bathroom and, for me at least, worth the effort. I left my nightmare of a sister to her devilish shenanigans and went hiking to the shower, to clear my head.

By the time I got back Lucy was done with her phone calls and having a cup of tea. She glanced up at me, set the tea down and stood, then she smiled, like we were good friends who had had some sort of minor misunderstanding. "I talked to Ira," she informed me.

"Good for you," I said.

"He told me that they do in fact have a record of you being taken down to the forty-ninth precinct."

"Did you think I was lying?"

"Well, Tina—it didn't make sense. And by the way, you weren't actually arrested. They just had you in for questioning. At least that's what they have on record."

"They have anything on record about an injunction?"

"Well, that's the interesting part," she said, still smiling. "There was in fact an injunction. Ira accepted service and he did in fact tell me about it but he assured me that he didn't think it would stick."

"And then you just forgot to tell me."

"I didn't forget, for heaven's sake. No one thought they would really *arrest* you."

"So you deliberately didn't tell me?"

"This is not my fault, Tina. I am not the one who had you arrested," Lucy claimed, staying right on point. "And if you would just calm down long enough to listen it might interest you to know that the injunction is gone. Obviously it would never have held up to a court challenge, which Ira was going to file this week."

"They just dropped it? When?"

"Just this afternoon, apparently. So no worries about that, okay, Tina? Although honestly, if the police come by, you will call me, right? Even though they just took you in for questioning that is completely unacceptable and you should never *ever* talk to the police without a lawyer present. Ira got really upset when he heard that you let them take you down there and no one called him."

"I don't even know him," I said.

"But you should have called me, and I would have called him. Listen, tell me you understand this. If you're being harassed it's important that you let us know."

"Why, because you're so worried about my safety? That's why you didn't even *warn* me?"

"I'm not going to get into some long argument about this, Tina, especially when everything came out all right. I already said I'm glad that it was nothing worse. I don't know what more you want out of me, but then I never did." She sighed, looked at her CrackBerry, and started doing that little thing with her thumbs.

"Why are you here?" I asked.

"What?"

"You never just show up. You always have a reason," I said. "So what's your reason today?"

"A friend of mine is coming over."

"What friend?"

"His name is Dave. He works on the city page of the *Times*. He's going to come take a look at the apartment. He might be interested in writing about it."

"No. Come on," I said, suddenly overwhelmed. "No."

"What do you mean, no?" She said, looking up at me, sharp.

"I mean *no*. No reporters in here. No." I thought about Len talking about privacy and Pete Drinan not even stepping foot in his home for years and years, and that tender-hearted paint job in the kids' bedroom, and I just couldn't bear the thought of some fucking reporter wandering around my apartment. "No," I said.

223

"You know, I don't actually need your permission, Tina," Lucy observed with that nasty edge which somehow could not stay out of her tone. "You can just stop acting like you own the place, when you're just staying here for all of us."

"I can't believe you," I said, trying seriously for once not to just lose it. "I spent the night in jail because you—you—"

"I'm not doing anything except taking care of my interests and yours. And as to spending a night in jail, it's not the first time, so I don't know what you're making such a big deal about." She stood up, turned away from me and went to the little kitchenette, where she started wiping down the counters deliberately, like I had not done a good enough job and that that, and everything else, was as usual my fault.

"Fuck you," I said, totally sounding like a peevish loser teenager. "Fuck you. Call me when he's gone."

"He might want to talk to you," she asserted, all deliberate and chilly and mean, like some nasty old high school nun. "About being hauled into the police station. We're in the middle of a real estate war! And they had you arrested? You should tell him about it. It might help sell the story."

"Go to hell, Lucy," I said. And I slammed the door behind me, good and loud. I am sure Mrs Westmoreland heard it, and took notes.

Wandering the Upper West Side of Manhattan can be an entertaining proposition when your life is less screwed up, but when you're in a bad mood both about having been arrested and having a hideous sister who consistently behaves like a jerk, it is not all that much fun. I walked up and down Amsterdam for a while, then I cut over to the park and wandered around some more, hoping that a little urban nature might make me feel better. It was a lonely and pathetic endeavour, but over about an hour it finally started to get the job done. That section of Central Park was in fact particularly utopic; old ladies and their dogs wandered down charming and curling pathways where young boys and girls on roller blades flew by them, calling to each other with hopeful and nonsensical glee. Alongside the path, college kids lay on the grass and laughed at each other while inching ever closer to having sex. I passed a mossy lake, and a giant statue of an angel coming down to earth. There was an Arab guy at a little glass stand under a green and white umbrella, selling falafel sandwiches and cans of soda. Things were coming back into focus and the exhausting and endless night finally seemed to be a little bit finished.

Which is when I tried to buy a can of lemonade. It seemed like a sane enough idea as I had been walking and thinking for quite a while and was feeling rather thirsty. Unfortunately, I was so thoroughly peeved with Lucy when I left the apartment that I had been more concerned with making an exit than I was with grabbing my backpack. As a consequence all I had on me were my house keys and a dollar twenty-five in my back pocket, and the Arab guy in the falafel cart wouldn't spot me the quarter.

In fact he was at first dismissive. "One *fifty*. You need one dollar and fifty, young lady," he explained, which I was perfectly willing to accept, if he hadn't so quickly and needlessly worked himself into a lather over it. "What is the matter with you?" he asked, before I even had a chance to retrieve the three quarters, four dimes and two nickels I had managed to scrounge out of

225

my pocket. "Can you step aside please? If you are not going to purchase something step aside!"

"Cool your jets," I muttered. This sent him even further over the edge.

"You have no money! Step aside! Step aside, please! You have no money!"

"Could you just relax for a second," I said. "I *have* it. For fuck's sake."

"Why are you using obscenity?" the guy howled suddenly. "STEP ASIDE," he raged. I couldn't move. I was in trouble. Seriously, I was in serious psychological trouble. After the day and night I had had, there was nothing left. I was actually considering leaping onto his strange little cart and hurling cans of soda at him when some girl came up behind me.

"I'll buy her a lemonade," she said.

"It's fine," I said, trying not to sound as insane as I felt. "I didn't want his stupid fucking lemonade."

"This crazy woman is cursing me! I do not have to serve people who speak to me with this language!"

"Yeah, I'm sure you've never heard that word before," said the girl. "Relax." She reached past my shoulder and handed the guy a five. "Make it two," she said. I turned to snap at her and stopped. It was Jennifer White, my sullen teenage neighbor from 9A.

"Oh," I said.

"Yeah," she said. "You're welcome." She handed me my bottle of lemonade and turned back to reach for her change.

"Here, here is your change, now please go!" snapped the way-too-uptight Arab. "There are customers who are waiting!" Jennifer ignored him, holding her lemonade under her arm while she slowly took the two dollars off the Plexiglas top of the stand and carefully folded them into a tiny pink change purse. "Please!" he howled, but honestly he was starting to sound like he was begging now. Still ignoring him, she dropped the change purse into the side pocket of an enormous backpack, and finally stepped aside.

"I AM SO SORRY, HOW CAN I HELP YOU!" the guy shouted at the next man in line, with a kind of friendly fury.

Jennifer looked at me, unruffled. "Are you heading home?" she asked.

"I guess so," I said. "Thanks." She popped the lid of her lemonade and took a long slow sip, as if this were the most natural thing in the world. The leaves were glowing above us. We both sipped our lemonades silently, as if there were some sort of solution in this, then turned toward the pathways. Jennifer walked so slowly we were barely moving at all.

Outside, in the golden light of the late afternoon, Jennifer White looked like a young goddess. A slight breeze moved carelessly through her hair and her cheeks had the slightest lift of color in them. She was still wearing that dopey uniform, but the boring white blouse was open a little bit too wide at the neck, and the plaid skirt looked witty, somehow, like something someone might wear in a hip-hop video. Heroic-looking young men in shorts and running shoes kept glancing back at us with a fleet, happy admiration.

"This lemonade is pretty good," I said.

"It's all right," she agreed.

"I don't want to go home either," I told her.

She didn't respond to that, as it would have amounted to

her admitting something. I decided to just keep talking. "My sister is a fucking nightmare," I said. "Sooner or later she'll leave, but I can't go home until she does."

"What's so bad about her?" asked Jennifer.

"All she thinks about is money," I said.

"That's all anybody thinks about."

"Yeah I know, but trust me, Lucy is off the deep end. I think inheriting this apartment has driven her insane."

"I heard you didn't inherit it," Jennifer volunteered. She didn't sound like she was fishing, but she didn't sound like she wasn't, either.

"You heard what?" I asked, feigning equal parts boredom and fishing expedition myself.

"It's just what I heard," she shrugged, giving up nothing.

"My mom was married to Bill and he left it to her, so they say we inherited it. It sounds legal to me, but what do I know." This came out sounding snottier than I wanted it to, especially since I was thinking that maybe I had someone in front of me who could actually shed some light on a few things. "Anyway that's I guess what they're going to figure out, if we did inherit it. Nobody knows yet."

"They think they do."

"They who?"

"Everyone."

"Everyone who?"

"They're having meetings about it, you know. You are so totally not supposed to be there. It's driving them nuts."

"Them who?"

"The *building*," she told me.

228

I knew what she was talking about, but it was unnerving to hear it stated so definitively by a teenage girl.

"The building doesn't get to decide, does it?"

Jennifer shot me a bored look, like she didn't believe that a person as old as I was could also be so stupid.

"*What?*" I said, trying to laugh at her. "It's not up to them."

"They *think* it's up to them," she said. Then, "They didn't like your mom."

This last bit, offered up with no prodding or prying on my part, landed like an atom bomb on my heart. For a second I hated that bored kid in her snotty pleated skirt and her shitty little white blouse and her perfect blonde hair, but before I could figure out something cutting to say, to avenge this completely obscure and meaningless slight on the mother I barely spoke to in the last years of her life, poor Jennifer flushed, ashamed of herself. "Not me," she apologized. "I liked her. I mean, she was just always nice to me. But she was like a cleaning lady. That's what they're all hung up on. And Mr Drinan was kind of weird. And they're all kind of obsessed with that apartment. Everybody knows that it's the best one in the building and they're all just hung up, they are *so* hung up, it's so, whatever. I'm just telling you. That's what the problem is."

She felt so terrible for telling me the truth I didn't even know what to say.

"It's okay," I said. "I appreciate the information."

"Yeah, okay," she said. And then neither one of us said anything else for a little while. And then, as slow as we were going, we were there. Both of us looked up at the Edgewood, looming above us, elegant, enormous, the *building*.

"I love those lions," I said.

"They look like guard dogs to me," she replied, tossing her empty bottle of lemonade into the cast-iron trash can which stood on the street corner. She looked over at me and did one of those half-smiles which make you look like you expect people to know how unhappy you really are. It was the most human expression I'd seen cross her face.

"Look," I said. "Do you have to go in?"

"They're already probably flipping out," she said, and the half-smile evaporated. She just looked sad.

So that's how I got into that apartment again. I took Jennifer upstairs and rang the doorbell and started talking. "Hey, Mrs White," I said, all friendly and helpful. She was, as usual, wearing an absolutely glorious suit. "I hope you haven't been too worried about Jennifer. She's been with me."

"We have been worried!" Mrs White started. Her entire ensemble was the most extraordinary shade of sea green. She must have had the shoes dyed to match the suit; there could be no other explanation as to how she got the colors so exact. "I was just about to send for the police!" she announced, checking herself out in the mirror.

"Oh I am so sorry. We should have called, but she was really upset," I admitted humbly.

"Jennifer is not allowed to go off and have activities after school, certainly not with people she barely knows! Your father will be beside himself, Jennifer. You know the rules!"

"Would you relax, Mom?" Jennifer started. I reached over and squeezed her hand, her new best friend.

"No no, don't get angry. Of course your mom was worried.

She didn't know what we were doing!" I explained. Then I looked at Mrs White and smiled. "I was helping her with her math!" This was completely improvised on my part, so Jennifer looked at me with real surprise. I just kept talking. "We just bumped into each other in the lobby—I mean, literally, it was ridiculous and completely my fault because I as usual was just not looking where I was going—and her homework just went everywhere and when I was helping her get it back together she admitted that she didn't have a clue how to make it through today's problem sets. And there were so many, today, let me reassure you, those nuns are doing their job up there at St Peter in Chains, she's getting a workout in the math department. It is almost laughable how much homework she's got. Anyway she was in fact a little upset by it so I told her—well, I'm actually, you know, I'm pretty good at math." Improbably, this part actually was true. "And I felt bad, she seemed so overwhelmed. So we went to my place just to look at a couple of the most difficult problems and we seriously lost track of time down there. And when I realized how long we had been, I was appalled, and I thought about calling but obviously it just made more sense to bring her home. I'm really, really sorry." Jennifer was staring at me now. It is possible that I was laying all this on a bit thick, but I could tell that Mrs White was actually not all that interested in facts and so the more I gave her the less likely she might be to examine them too closely. Besides, there were as usual seven things going on in that apartment at once. Kids were screaming somewhere off in the distance, you could hear a washing machine chugging and then something big fell with a crash in the kitchen. Mrs White really couldn't waste a ton of time worrying about me, under the circumstances.

"Oh well, thank you," she finally said, picking up a small child and kicking a pile of coats and scarves into the floor of the closet that was right there off the foyer. "That really was kind of you. I just wish—Anna, where are you going? I have to go and meet Bob any minute. Is dinner ready for the girls?"

"Is Wednesday," Anna the cleaning lady announced, as if that were enough of an answer. She was putting on her coat.

"Wednesday?" said Mrs White. "No no, it's not Wednesday. Or I mean it is Wednesday, but we talked about this, this is the Wednesday you're staying. Barbie, please!"

"I'll take her," I said, and as I untangled the wriggling baby from her arms Mrs White tried to explain, to no avail, that Anna had in fact agreed to stay that night until midnight, as she and Mr White had made arrangements months before to attend an auction this evening benefiting the Museum of Modern Art, and his firm had bought a whole table at great expense, and there would be Korean clients at that table who it was extremely important for him to get to know, and they would not understand if his wife failed to make an appearance. Anna, the Polish cleaning lady, seemingly felt bad but it wasn't clear if she even understood English really and she didn't actually respond as if she were following the logic of Mrs White's desperation. She kept saying, "Sorry, so sorry," and nothing else, while Mrs White kept explaining to her why she couldn't leave, and that went on for a little while, and then Anna just walked out the door, leaving me and Barbie and Jennifer there as witnesses to Mrs White and her problem and her beautiful suit.

Mrs White looked over at me. She really had no options, so

232

I knew better than to push it. I kissed Barbie on the cheek and started to hand her back. "Here's your mommy," I said. "Don't mess up her pretty suit."

"You couldn't—I'm sorry, but you did say you might be interested in babysitting some time. You wouldn't be available right now, would you?"

"Right now?" I said. "Gee."

Once we got rid of Mrs White, things really started to cook up there. The first hour or so was a bit of a mess, because six sets of coats and shoes needed to be hung up and put away, the baby completely needed a new diaper and dinner had not in fact even been started. Katharine had decided that she had seen me first so she didn't fully understand why anyone else had any claim on my attention whatsoever. She would follow me around, silently worshipful but with big confused tears in her eyes while I dealt with all sorts of other nonsense, instead of going back to her room to play stuffed animals with her. The other two kids who I had not met before didn't want to eat anything, and they argued incessantly with each other over total bullshit. There were three pre-cooked casseroles from fancy gourmet stores in the refrigerator but even though they looked wildly delicious to me nobody was interested in them at all. Louise, the oldest daughter, made herself some sort of shake with flaxseed and wheatgrass, and ignored me. Jennifer sat in a corner of the kitchen, picked at a salad, and looked bored.

"Is that all you're going to eat?" I asked.

"Are you my mother?" she asked back.

"No, I'm the person who wants to know if that's all you're going to eat," I told her. She smiled to herself like she thought

233

that was amusing in a kind of minor way, and then she looked at the ceiling.

"Yeah, this is all I'm going to eat," she said.

All of this eating or not eating was going on around the kitchen table, which was apparently a real treat for everyone, whether they were eating or not.

"We're not *allowed* to eat in the kitchen," one of the middle kids said, whose name I couldn't remember.

"Your mom didn't tell me that," I told her.

"*I'm* telling you," she insisted. "We eat in the *dining* room."

"I want to eat in the kitchen. It's easier," I said.

"You don't get to *decide*," she informed me.

"Sure I do. I'm in charge," I said.

"You're not *old* enough to be in charge," she insisted.

"Don't you think it's boring to eat in the dining room all the time?" I asked.

"It's the way we *do* things," she told me.

"It *is* boring," announced Jennifer, from her corner. "This is better."

"How old are you, anyway?" asked Louise. As I said, she was the eldest, and she had been helping me feed Katharine and the baby with a sort of effortless ease.

"I'm thirty-two," I told her.

This of course made everyone stare. The two monstrous middle kids, Jennifer, Louise, Katharine, even the baby seemed startled to hear that I was as old as all that. I was startled myself.

"You're in your *thirties?*" said one of the monsters.

"You don't look that old," said the other one.

"It's just because I'm short," I told her. "If you stretched me out a little, I would look older."

"You would look *taller* maybe," Jennifer corrected me. The two monsters thought this was a riot, for some reason, and they started giggling hilariously, burying their heads in each other like little animals. Because the monsters were laughing so hard, Katharine started laughing too. Then Louise started laughing, because everyone else was laughing. The baby just looked bewildered. For a second, Jennifer's mood lifted and she actually smiled, like she really liked the fact that she had gotten the whole room to laugh, even inadvertently.

"Thirty-two, that's bizarre. That's like *old,*" said Louise, and I could see that she wasn't being all withholding and weird, the way Jennifer was, she was just a little shy with strangers.

"Yeah, I'm pretty near death," I admitted. This made the monsters laugh even harder, and things were pleasant for about ten minutes, until I told them that no, they were not going to be allowed to have chocolate ice cream and watch television unless they ate their dinner and finished their homework. Then they started whining and yelling again, and then Jennifer sighed and told them to fuck off, which pretty much put an end to all the fun. The monsters went back to their room, where they argued with each other over nothing for another hour or so. The baby fell asleep in her high chair, but she woke up screaming while I wiped her off, and Katharine started crying because no one was paying attention to her, and the kitchen ended up looking like a disaster because I didn't have time to clean it up before Louise announced that both Katharine and the baby really needed to have a bath and be in bed before eight and

235

she couldn't help me out with that because she had too much homework to do.

So that's what that was like. There was a vague moment when I wondered how much people got paid for this, as I had not in fact nailed Mrs White down on the details of the babysitting plan before she fled the apartment in her hot little turquoise suit. But there really wasn't time to think about that missed opportunity. I gave the baby a bath and then Katharine got a bath, and then she ran around the apartment naked, screaming, while I tried to put the baby to sleep, but the baby was having none of it because, I was told by Louise, I should never have let her fall asleep in her high chair even for a minute because then she just doesn't go down for hours. The two monsters suddenly came out into the hallway, declaring that they were in fact hungry for dinner but they didn't want the cold food congealing on plates in the dirty kitchen; they wanted the leftovers of the Chinese carry-out which they had had earlier in the week with some different babysitter who, they insisted, had shoved it all somewhere in the back of the refrigerator. Louise told them in no uncertain terms that Anna had tossed all the leftover Chinese food when she came in that morning, which started another unfortunate round of whining. I wanted to smack Louise because it really did seem like she was constantly full of bad news, but then she sighed, suddenly, and told me to go read to Katharine, that she would put Bee to bed. I didn't know what she was talking about for a moment and then I realized that she was reaching for the baby, and the fact that she called the baby Bee—instead of Barbie—made me like her even more than the offer of help did. And then Jennifer appeared out of nowhere and said, "I'll feed them," shoving the two hungry middle-school monsters down the hallway toward the kitchen. Which left me leading a naked Katharine back to her little yellow room, and finding her some pajamas, and looking through a pile of books with her.

Which was extremely pleasant, after all the chaos. The kid carefully and quietly picked up one book after another and considered which ones she wanted read with great care. The books all had a lot of brilliantly colored pictures of talking animals and princesses and elves and happy families who had small but significant problems, all of which got worked out by everybody being kind to each other. Seriously, the pictures in these books were so pretty and the people in the stories so decent and sensible that you wondered, honestly, how we all ended up being such assholes in real life.

Anyway, after about twenty minutes of lying in bed and paging through peaceful and lovely picture books, I was quite frankly drifting off, when Katharine whispered, "There's the ghost."

Because I was only half awake at first I thought she was talking about the story we were reading. I shook my head slightly, to clear the fog, and considered the picture, confused. The story we were looking at had to do with a talking teddy bear who got left in a large department store by mistake, and then he had a series of charming misadventures before the little girl who owned him came back and found him. "What ghost? There's no ghost," I said.

"Listen, *listen*," Katharine told me, worried. She put her small hand up in the air, like the ghost was in the room with us and that it might flee if I kept talking. We had turned off the overhead light and were reading by the bedside lamp so the room was dark. I put my arm around her and looked up, to listen, meaning to just take a moment before telling her that there were no ghosts in her room, only night and shadows.

Which is when I heard the ghost. I tensed up a little bit, so Katharine knew she was right. "See?" she said.

She was right. There was a kind of whisper, in the walls. It was a female ghost, who was upset, and talking fast in a different language in her other world, which seemed to be sort of adjacent to this one, or maybe simply in a slightly skewed dimension. It was truly spooky; it sounded like a river of dead words with nowhere to go, trapped in the air all around us, some sort of past catastrophe frozen in between worlds where things moved. Seriously, there was no way that wasn't a ghost; it was definitely a ghost. Katharine looked at me with solemn confidence. She knew that I knew that was a ghost.

"That's not a ghost," I said. "Come on, that's just some person who lives in the building."

"Then why is she on our floor? We live on this floor, and that's not us."

"It's somebody on some other floor."

"Shhhhhh," she said. "She's crying." Sure enough the ghost had stopped her mournful complaints and now she was sobbing, long pain-wracked moans which clung to the insides of the walls. It was the saddest ghost I had ever heard.

"That is not a ghost," I repeated. I sat up to go look for it, and caught sight of Jennifer in the doorway.

"You hear the ghost?" she whispered. She glided into the room and joined us on the bed.

"That's not a ghost!" I said, with so little confidence that they both looked at me like I was a moron.

"Shhhhhh," whispered Katharine. "If you talk too loud, it goes away."

"I'm not going to be loud," I said, whispering as well. "I'm just going to go listen." I left them on the bed and got down on my hands and knees, so that I might crawl silently through the wool pile of the carpet, and get to the wall without the ghost knowing I was closing in on her. She was talking again, a fast, anxious complaint of a sound, like she knew she was trapped forever and simply couldn't make peace with it. Katharine sat up on the bed, clearly worried that something was going to happen to me. She leaned into Jennifer, who put her arm around the kid in a gesture of such careless affection it wounded me to the core.

"Come back, come back," Katharine whispered, and she waved her hands at me, like I was doing something way too dangerous and I had to be ushered back to the one safe spot in the room—the bed—otherwise the ghost would get me. I didn't answer right away, I just put my ear up against the wall. The murmuring river of grief got louder; there was no question that that ghost was inside the wall. "Oh," Katharine said, really worried. "Come on!"

"Does the closet go all the way down here?" I asked, still in a whisper. "How big is that closet?"

"We've checked out the closet. The ghost is not in the closet," Jennifer informed me.

"Yeah, I know. I just want to check out something else," I murmured, and I crawled up to the closet door, reached up for the knob and carefully swung it open.

"No!" said Katharine, in a terrified little wail.

"There's no ghost in the closet, Katharine. We already went through this. The ghost doesn't live in your closet," Jennifer told her. By this point I was not so sure. The ghost's voice was distinctively louder there, and it seemed to inhabit the closet space with more authority. The walls were definitely holding on to the sound and carrying it into the room, but the sound actually did seem to be coming from the closet. I put my ear on the polished wood floor and listened. There was no question. The ghost was in the floor. I tapped quietly on the floorboards with my index finger. The ghost fell silent.

"Hey," I said. "Hey, who are you? Are you okay?" There was another moment of silence, then the sound of air, some things bumping and then the sound of a door closing. Then nothing. I turned back to Jennifer and Katharine, who were watching me talk to the floor, from the bed.

"You scared her away," Katharine reprimanded me. She was clearly not too pleased with my behaviour.

"I did scare her away. Isn't that what you're supposed to do with ghosts? Most of them are not quite so cooperative," I said. I reached up and flicked on the light switch for the closet, and started shoving around all the shoes and kid's costumes and stuffed animals that had been thrown willy-nilly around the floor.

"What are you doing?" asked Jennifer.

"I don't know, I'm just looking," I said. "It doesn't make any sense. This room is right above my apartment, right?" I said. "Would she be in my apartment?"

"You said you didn't have this room," Jennifer noted.

"No, I have this room. I just don't have this view," I explained.

"So the ghost is in your apartment?"

"It's not a ghost, sweetheart, it's a person. That's a person who's downstairs, and she's upset, and it sounds like she's in my apartment, but she couldn't be," I explained.

"You said you didn't have the room," Jennifer repeated, mostly to herself. She was virtually ignoring me now, as she dropped off the bed, got on all fours and shoved all those stuffed animals out of the closet and into the room. The floor of the closet was carpeted with more of the yellow wool. Jennifer started peeling away at its edges.

"What are you doing?" said Katharine, excited.

"I'm looking for the trap door."

"There's no trap door," I said. "I was making that up."

"There might be," Jennifer said. "There's clearly something down there. And you say it's not part of your apartment."

"I don't know if it's part of my apartment or not, Jennifer, but you can't just rip up the carpet in here. Your mother will kill me."

"She won't even notice," Jennifer muttered. By this point Katharine had crawled off the bed and was helping her pull up the carpet.

"What on earth are you *doing*?" said Louise, from the door.

"We're looking for the trap door," said Katharine, quite matter of fact. Louise looked at me as if I were completely insane.

"You told them it would be okay to take the carpet up? Mom is going to flip out," she informed me.

"I didn't tell them it was okay. We just heard something in the wall so we were looking. It's okay, Jennifer. Katharine, get back in bed, please. We're fine. The ghost is gone."

"The *ghost*?" said Louise, and she raised her eyes to heaven as if someone there might glance down and agree with her assessment of this whole mess, which was not good. "You know my parents are not going to be happy to hear that you're telling her ghost stories. It's not a part of our religion."

"I didn't tell her a ghost story. She *heard* the ghost in the *wall*. We all did. Come on, sweetie, you have to get back in bed now." I leaned over and grabbed Katharine before she could crawl further away from me, swinging her into my arms and plopping her on the bed in one swift move which left her giggling. Louise continued to watch with disapproval, but I was not letting her get to me. "Come on, Jennifer, Katharine has to go to bed. There's nothing there. I was kidding."

Jennifer looked up at me, and for the first time since I met her I saw her smile, a big, happy, excited grin. "Then what's this?" she said.

CHAPTER FOURTEEN

It didn't look like much, but there was no question that she had found something: a perfect square, about three feet by three feet. It seemed to have been cut out of the wall and then just dropped back in, tightly fitting the hole from which it had been cut. Then they painted over it, and then taped a laminated picture of Noah and the ark over that. It was pretty well hidden, but there was no question, it was there, right in the wall.

"Wow," said Katharine. "How do you open it?"

"It doesn't open, Katharine," Louise said. "It's not a door, it's just a hole, from the old crawlspace for the workers who built the building. After they were finished they built a plug for it and sealed it up. They were all sealed up ages ago." Not content to have made such a deflating statement, Louise continued droning on. "This is an old building and it has its quirks, but there's nothing more to it than that. This isn't one of your books. I don't know why you're encouraging her, Jennifer, you're not a child. And isn't it past her bedtime?" This she directed to me, with a kind of pointed superiority. Those nuns are doing a good job with this one, I thought. Louise then moved to the closet and flicked off the light with a quick, impatient gesture, and then she stood in the shadows with her hands on her hips. "Mom really wants the little kids to get to bed on time."

Jennifer stood, silent, and glided away into the hallway where, quiet as a ghost herself, she disappeared behind a door into her own room. Sanity regained its footing. One by one my charges went to sleep, and at half past twelve their parents returned, paid me a surprising amount of money, and sent me back downstairs to my own life.

I let myself in to my apartment with all my multiple keys. Lucy of course was long gone; the place was deserted. There was no sign of the guy from the city page of the *Times*, if in fact he had shown his face and prowled around and invaded the empty corners of my enormous and empty apartment. And compared to the Whites'—so cluttered with children and toys and furniture and uneaten dinners and coats and shoes and arguments over nothing— my apartment seemed especially enormous and empty. Feeling both exhausted and spooked, I went into each separate room and turned on all the lights everywhere, as if that would populate the vacant spaces. But a lot of the bulbs were dead, and the ones that worked put out only the shadow of an actual glow. The whole effect was so painfully lacklustre and grim it just made everything worse, and I started to panic. I looked around that empty apartment and I didn't know, honestly, how I was supposed to do it. After spending the night with six messy and unfinished girls who hadn't yet made a single disastrous life-altering mistake, I was not in the mood to spend any time alone with shadows. Besides which I was now somewhat convinced that there was a ghost there.

It occurred to me that even though it was the middle of the night I could at least replace a few of those bulbs. I remembered I had seen some dusty packets of replacement bulbs somewhere, during my early searches, so I went looking again, poking in a few closets in the empty bedrooms and some of the excess bathrooms. I didn't locate anything other than some empty plastic bags and a couple of old sheets at first, so I then went to check out the laundry room, where the light was marginally better than anywhere else in the apartment, and started to look through the lousy plywood closets that Bill had at some point nailed to the wall above and alongside the washer-dryer. There I found more old plastic bags shoved in one corner, next to a dozen or so crisply folded paper ones. Then a packet of bright blue sponges, shriveled together like frightened old ladies, still in their shrink wrap, and behind that an unused toilet plunger, also still in its shrink wrap. Both the packet of sponges and the plunger were covered with dust, as was an old red plastic bottle of liquid Tide, my mother's detergent of choice, and the nearly empty box of those sheets of fabric softener she used to put into the dryer because she was convinced that they actually made a difference. Behind that, there were three different kinds of stain remover, two flashlights with no batteries in them, and behind that, folded neatly and stacked one on top of the other, a pile of old sheets and pillowcases so worn and drained of color that you honestly wouldn't know they even existed if you weren't bent on emptying the whole sorry cabinet just to see if there were any light bulbs back there.

The other two cabinets above the washer and dryer yielded similarly dispiriting prizes: a half-empty bottle of Windex, some peculiar container of tarnish remover, more withered sponges, tile cleanser from the past century. It was truly dreary to find so many different kinds of household cleansers covered with so much dust, and I was starting to feel pretty sure that these plywood cubicles were never going to yield any light bulbs, but I was so wired I just kept looking without really caring what showed up. The closet that had been shoved into the corner between the dryer and the wall stretched from floor to ceiling and so of course it was full of dusty mops and a couple of broomsticks with bent yellow plastic bristles on the end. There was a folded metal footstool in there that was so rusted you couldn't open it anymore, and then more old plastic bags crumpled together in such a dirty and disgusting heap that I was vaguely afraid that something horrible might crawl out of them if I moved even one. I kicked the whole mess cautiously a couple of times and nothing scurried out, so I just reached in with both arms and started to paw it all aside, pulling it out into the room, alongside the ancient brooms and mops, and the dusty cleansers that I had already dumped into the middle of the floor. And then, because I had taken all the stuff out of it, the closet lost its ballast and almost fell on my head, because it wasn't fastened to the wall in any rational way. So I had to catch it, and wriggle out from underneath it, and somehow keep it from braining me.

And I was right all along, it seems; the layout of the apartments did not in fact line up because there was another room right there, and that cheap little plywood closet had been shoved right up against its doorway.

There it was, the extra room; it was right underneath Katharine's, and somehow a ghost had gotten in there.

CHAPTER FIFTEEN

It took me almost an hour to get up the nerve to go in there. It was quite dark and the light switch on the wall, like so many of the other light switches in that apartment, was completely useless. Eventually I found a flashlight and stepped in, and this is what I found: sixty-seven ancient cardboard boxes, taped shut, and stacked neatly on top of each other; six oil paintings in dusty and broken wood frames; six ornate oak dining-room chairs, with turned legs; an orange and yellow vinyl folded baby's high chair; an old bed frame; a giant wing-backed easy chair with torn pink upholstery fabric; an eight-foot-long solid oak Stickley dining-room table, leaned up against the wall, with the legs removed. In the far corner, stuffed between the last two rows of boxes, there was a cracked black garment bag, which held three floor-length evening gowns.

This is what was in the boxes: six Waterford crystal tumblers, three with chips in them; two dozen plastic jars filled with two dozen different colors of dried-up poster paint; four pairs of battered gym shoes, two pairs of low black pumps, one pair of bright gold four-inch spike heels; sixteen pairs of cowboy boots; a dark gray and black hand-knit Fair Isle sweater; four Indian print cotton scarves, three silk scarves, seven wool scarves and one scarf-like shawl thing with Tibetan coins stitched around one of the edges; four shoe boxes filled with dangly silver earrings, tangled up bracelets and inexpensive but sparkly necklaces; another shoebox full of Mardi Gras beads; a box full of red, blue, yellow, black and white Lego blocks; another box full of tinker toys and Matchbox cars, along with about sixty pieces of orange plastic Matchbox car track; two boxes of old phonograph albums, by bands and girl singers I'd never heard of, except for the Beatles and the Rolling Stones; two broken plastic light sabres and three plastic swords; a whole boxful of hats, a bowler, four fedoras, something that looked like a Robin Hood hat, a really well-made French beret, an equally well-made wool cap from Ireland; five leather gloves, none of them with a mate; six pairs of worn jeans, a bunch of T-shirts, eight cotton Indian print skirts, four pairs of eyeglasses; dishes; glassware; a shoe box full of expensive flatware; two table lamps with strangely carved bases and even stranger Dr Seuss-like lampshades; two broken laptop computers; three unspeakably beautiful glass vases with a kind of whorled gold and blue finish; a funny cookie jar that looked like a fat man carrying a suitcase; two half-sized mugs made out of bone china with pictures of dogs on them; a whole box full of china mugs that looked like they came from different countries all over the world; a dozen different Halloween costumes, including three pirates of different sizes; a hand-made knit blanket with six holes in it, and an enormous patchwork quilt that looked like it was big enough to cover three beds; an old Minolta SLR camera, three boxes full of dusty negatives and seventeen photo albums, filled with pictures.

That actually was not, in fact, everything; that's just what I managed to get through in three or four days. Every morning I got up, made myself a cup of coffee and some ramen noodles, watched ten or fifteen minutes of the morning news, and then I got my flashlight and let myself back into that hidden room to look around. There was no overhead light and only one dim window, buried deep underneath all the detritus in the far corner, so whenever I landed a box that looked like it might have something interesting in it—which was, in fact, all of them—I would shove it across the floor, back to the tiny laundry room, and there I would unload it, examining each separate piece before I piled them all on top of the dryer. On the second day of this I tried to rig up an improvised light source, running one of those giant orange extension cords back out into the plug in the laundry room so that I could fire up a couple of portable electric photographer's lamps which I bought at my favorite new hardware store. The lamps gave off a fierce and uncompromising amount of light which was finally too unnerving to be tolerated. This especially became a problem the second night, when the ghost in the wall started to mourn again. Honestly, she sounded like she was trapped in there, and the light was truly terrifying. So there really was nothing for it but dragging each box back into the laundry room, and squeezing the lives that had been hidden there back into the apartment they once inhabited.

It was at this moment that the precautions I had already taken in terms of my security situation actually did come in handy. Presumably sensing that I was becoming increasingly less willing to just let her push me around the Monopoly board of our lives, Lucy had decided to give me a little time off from her clever maneuverings. It was a trick she had figured out when we were kids: she would just keep pushing me and Alison around until one of us finally snapped, then she would go back to her room and wait a little while before she decided enough time had passed for us to forget how annoyed we were with her, at which point she would reappear and start up again. So I wasn't entirely surprised when she suddenly evaporated, because she did know that she had sincerely pissed me off with the injunction thing and letting me get arrested. Then after two days of peace and quiet Alison called my cell phone, leaving a tight little birdlike message about wanting to see how I was, going on to speculate that maybe she and Daniel could drop by for carry-out so that I wasn't all alone over here. The whole message was predictably phoney and manipulative so I didn't call her back. So then she called me again and left a message which was virtually identical to the first one, which I was a hundred per cent sure she only made in the first place because Lucy told her to. When I didn't return either call, Daniel himself phoned and said he was worried about me and that he and Alison were coming by later that day. So then I called Alison back and got her voicemail and left a short, cheerful message about how I was fine and everything was fine and they shouldn't come over. So then Daniel left another message about wanting to talk to me, which I didn't respond to, and then Lucy left a message saying that Daniel and Alison were coming over and that she had heard that I told them they couldn't, which was not okay because even though I was staying there that didn't mean I controlled access to the apartment and the apartment belonged to all three of us and I could not say that people couldn't come over. So then I called Lucy back and left a message on her voicemail saying I didn't think that I owned the apartment and that in fact my understanding was that nobody actually knew who owned the apartment until the courts had made a ruling, but that it really was not a good time for me and I didn't want anyone to come over right now because I had some things I was doing. At which point Lucy called back and left another message saying that that was not acceptable and that she and Daniel and Alison would all be coming over that evening, at six.

Which would have been fine—I was planning on letting them in, for Chrissakes—except that Lucy got herself so worked up over my arrogance that she decided she better just come over and yell at me some more. So she showed up in the middle of the day, well before I was expecting to have to let anybody in. And she couldn't get in, because even though she had keys to the door I had locked it from the inside with my slide bolt and two chain guards.

Because I had not predicted that she might get so offended by my defiance that she would just show up, I was all the way in the back of the apartment, crawling around inside that secret room, looking through boxes with a flashlight and trying to determine which one I wanted to go through next. I had already gone through six other boxes that day, and I had not yet thought about packing it all up and hiding it away again, so flatware and shoes and fifty-year-old Halloween costumes were in fact strewn all over the laundry room. I had just found the first box of photo albums when my cell phone, which I kept clipped to my belt loop, started to buzz. I looked down, saw that it was Lucy, and decided not to answer it. After about three minutes it buzzed again, and I ignored it again, figuring that I had already gotten a shitty message from her once that day and that was plenty for now. I mean, why listen to her snipe at me some more on the phone when I could just wait and get it in person later? So I was truly immersed in my studies when the phone buzzed a third time. Which started to seem so excessive that I decided to finally answer it.

"Yes, *what*, Lucy?" I said, annoyed as hell.

"I am out in the hall. Let me in," she demanded.

"Wait. You're what?"

"I'm in the hall at the front door and I can't get in. I told you to take those extra locks off the door. We don't need them. I'm not going to talk to you about this while I'm standing out in the hallway. Just let me in. Right now," she ordered. She was calm but furious.

"You said you were coming at six," I said.

"I don't have to get your permission to come over, Tina!" she said. "And I am not kidding around! You have to come and let me in immediately!"

Lucy is actually so good at bossing people around that sometimes I actually do start to do whatever it is she's told me to do, before I've even decided to do it. So I had already squeezed myself through the doorway of the secret room and out into the laundry area before I stopped to consider what would happen if I did let her in. I had just paused for a moment to kick aside the pile of sweaters which I had unearthed and which was now strewn all over the floor and I could see that one of them, a rather small olive green pullover, had a lot of charming cables all over it, and that one of the rows of the cable was all screwed up—it went one way and then the other and then it twisted around again, and then it kind of collapsed into a knot, and then it came out the other side and held steady for the rest of its journey up the sleeve of the sweater. And I realized then that the sweater was hand-made, and that the mother of those two boys had knitted it, and that she was a knitter.

"Tina, where are you?" Lucy snapped, because in fact I hadn't said anything for a moment, while I considered the hapless cable on the sleeve of the little sweater on the floor.

"You have to come back," I said.

"Open the door, Tina," Lucy said, surprised.

"Come back at six. I'll let you in then," I told her. And then I hung up.

Because Lucy is nothing if not persistent, she did not in fact go away. She tried to call me back three more times, and then she stood out there and pounded on the door for another ten minutes, trying the locks in between calls, pulling furiously at the door knob and hollering, "Tina! TINA! TINA!" I cautiously made my way to the front of the apartment so I could listen to the commotion for a little while, and it really did continue for longer than you would have thought, even given the fact that it was Lucy. Then I heard Mrs Westmoreland come out and say something curt to her. Lucy said something sharp back. Then there was a door slam, and then there was more pounding on my door, and then a little while later I heard the elevator ding and a moment later there was a soft rumbly voice that sounded vaguely confused and vaguely like Frank. And then Mrs Westmoreland, who had apparently returned after presumably calling Frank and telling him to get up there, said something else wounded and angry and filled with righteous indignation, and Lucy started to argue but after a little more patient rumbling from Frank she threw in the towel, because the next thing I heard was the ding of the elevator, and then the slamming of the door across the hall, and then silence.

So then I went back and I picked up the sweaters, which I had really strewn about with a ridiculous degree of disregard, and I folded them up in two piles. I kept the little green sweater out, because it seemed kind of friendly and real to me now. I held it up to my nose and smelled it, and thought that it smelled a little bit like fall air, but that may have been because there was no heat in that storage area, and so everything had been imbued with a slight timeless chill. In any event I looked around at all the sweaters and the shoes and the Halloween costumes, and I thought about all the other things stored in that room, and then I spent the rest of the day picking up everything I had already excavated, and shoving it back into the room behind the laundry room. Then I shoved the broom closet back into place in front of the door, and for good measure I also shoved one of those half-empty boxes full of expensive wine back in front of it, and tried to make it look exactly like it had looked before I had figured out what was in there.

When Lucy arrived for the second time that day she was

predictably in a state. "This is completely unacceptable," she snarled, pushing right by me as soon as I opened the door. "You are *forbidden* to deny us entrance, Tina!"

"I'm not denying you entrance; I'm letting you in," I pointed out, calm. "Hi, Alison. Hi, Daniel."

Alison smiled at me with a vague air of apologetic goodwill. I could tell she'd already gotten an earful about how horrible I was being from Lucy, who really was ridiculously worked up.

"This afternoon was humiliating. Do you know I was asked to leave the building?"

"Oh, for crying out loud." I sighed. "Would you stop yelling at me? What is the big damn deal? I'm not your apartment *slave*. I was doing something and I didn't want to see you right then! I didn't say you couldn't come in *ever*."

"This is coming off. Now," Lucy asserted, ignoring me all of a sudden and turning her attention back to my own private set of locks on the door. "Daniel, can you take care of this?"

"Well . . . I *can*," said Daniel, with a tone of such rational reluctance that we all turned and stared at him. He shoved his hands into his pockets, thoughtful, and squeezed up his face into a sort of regret-filled grimace. He's actually a fairly nice-looking guy, although his hair is thinning and prematurely grey, and he has a fondness for corduroy jackets, so even though he can be a total drip, as I believe I've mentioned, at the moment he sort of suddenly looked like an excessively reasonable father figure who was about to step in and make the girls behave.

"You *can*?" Lucy repeated. "Then please do so."

"You know, Lucy . . . I think that Tina might be right," Daniel suggested. "She's a bit at risk here. I personally can see why

255

she'd want to have some degree of control over people coming and going. Besides, she's entitled to a bit of privacy, isn't she?"

"This apartment belongs to all of us!"

"It doesn't belong to us quite yet, actually," Daniel pointed out.

"That's what I said," I started. He held up his hand, endlessly patient.

"Maybe we should take this away from the door," he suggested, waving everyone further into the apartment, where the patently nosy Mrs Westmoreland couldn't overhear absolutely every evil thing we might dream up to say to each other. It was pretty slick; in one fell swoop he looked even saner and Lucy looked even more out of control and nuts. The implication was not lost on her. But rather than snapping back, as was her clear instinct, she did as she was told.

"Of course," she said, tersely diplomatic. "Thank you. You are absolutely right."

"I just think we do have to be careful," Daniel continued, walking calmly to the other end of the great room, away from the front of the apartment. "You were asked to leave the building? That's bad. That's the sort of thing that people talk about."

"That's my point. She should never have put me in that position," Lucy asserted.

"I didn't. I told you I was busy," I volunteered.

"Doing *what?*" Lucy hissed.

"It's not relevant, Lucy, really, what she was doing," Daniel told her. I was thrilled to be on the winning side of this, but I'm not so stupid that I didn't actually get what Daniel was doing. The power plays were flying thick and fast. "It's clearly important that we maintain a presence here," he continued, sounding like the most sensible guy on earth. "So far I think that Tina's doing a good job. You told me that she's already made a lot of friends in the building. She knows some people on the co-op board. She's gotten some jobs babysitting?"

"For the Whites, yes. Mrs White is on the board," I started. Daniel's hand went up again, keeping me from drowning them all in helpful sloppy details.

"So Tina is in fact doing what we need her to do," he noted methodically. "And you want to kick her out?"

"Kick me out?" I said. "Did she tell you that? She wants to kick me out?"

"No one's kicking you out, Tina. That's what Daniel is *saying*," Alison reassured me, a little too nicely.

"You guys talked about kicking me out because I wouldn't let Lucy just barge in on me in the middle of the day?" I said, getting all worked up as fast as I could. "That is *ridiculous*."

"It is ridiculous and it's not happening," Daniel repeated, but he wasn't talking to me, he was talking to Lucy. Lucy looked him square in the face, unflinching, even though she knew she had over-reached and lost.

"Well then, maybe I'll just move in," she said. And with that she headed down the hallway, pulling out her CrackBerry, moving her thumbs over it. I looked at Daniel, reeling from the whiplash of it all and worried that maybe I had won the battle and lost the war. He shook his head and raised his shoulders in a dismissive shrug.

"Let it go. She doesn't mean it," he said. He was right. By

the time we caught up with her she was phoning in an order for sandwiches to some deli, without asking anyone what they wanted. I got stuck with salami on rye, which I have a feeling she did on purpose. But for the next two hours the conversation stayed on boring lawyer issues and everyone behaved themselves and I was happily nearly rid of them by eight, when Alison started clearing the paper plates off the coffee table. She took the trash into the kitchen while Lucy droned on about our court date and the deposition schedules and how Mr Long was going to testify on Mom's behalf even though the oppositional attorney had tried to have him barred from the proceedings because of a conflict of interest but our attorney had pulled some unbelievably clever move and successfully squashed their motions. Seriously it was so devious and boring I thought my head was going to explode, when Alison breezed back into the room and held up a little green sweater.

"What's this?" she asked.

I froze. I don't know why, as usually I am a much more fluid liar. "Oh," I said, and I could feel my face turn all red. Lucy looked at me, her antennae at full alert.

"What is it?" she asked.

"It's a sweater, a children's sweater," Alison told her. "I found it in the kitchen, on the counter."

Why I had left that thing in the kitchen on the counter is anybody's guess. It was the only thing I hadn't put away, but why on earth did I have to leave it out in plain sight? I was wracking my brain trying to figure out what I had been thinking when I left it on the counter while Alison was holding it up and admiring it, running her fingers down one of the cables and smiling. She wants to have kids so badly that even holding a piece of their clothing can make her shyly hopeful. "It looks like it's hand-made," she observed. "Isn't it sweet?"

"Adorable," said Lucy, taking the sweater from Alison and looking at it, then looking up at me. "Where did it come from, Tina?"

"I found it," I said. My brain felt like it was full of oatmeal and molasses. The secret I was now keeping from them was so large it was making me catastrophically stupid.

"I've been over every inch of this apartment and all the closets are empty," Lucy observed, not buying it. "Where was it?"

"Oh, not here. I didn't find it here," I said, recovering finally. "I took a walk over to Amsterdam and there was a stoop sale."

"You bought it at a stoop sale? Why?" asked Lucy.

"For the little girl upstairs." What a relief. My brain was starting to function again. The lies were coming thick and fast. "It was only like a dollar and I thought it might be a nice way to just, you know. Build on the relationship."

"Very smart," Daniel said, nodding to himself. Lucy handed it back to Alison, who folded it up and set it softly on the arm of the couch. And then ten minutes later she mentioned that she was tired, and they headed for the door.

Lucy did not follow immediately; she wasn't going to try to punish me anymore for locking her out, but she also wasn't going to just leave when Alison decided it was time to go. That would have looked weak, and she was tired of looking weak. So she lingered there on the couch, checking her emails yet again. I, however, jumped up, and said, "I'll walk you to the door!" Which had the advantage of both looking proprietary and affording me a moment alone with Alison while Daniel headed for the elevator bank.

"Hey, Alison," I whispered, yanking her back into the apartment for a split second. "Can I ask you something?"

She looked at me, surprised and immediately worried by my conspiratorial tone. I had tried once or twice, when we were teenagers, to get her to side with me against Lucy, and it didn't end well. Consequently her default position in times of family conflict was a sort of worried neutrality.

"It's really late, Tina," Alison informed me, as she edged toward the door. "I have to be at work early tomorrow."

"Do you know how Mom met Bill?" I said.

"She was his housekeeper. Is that what you mean?" Alison said.

"You knew that? She was his cleaning lady?"

"For heaven's sake. You know they don't call it that anymore."

"What would you call it?"

"I don't know. What did you call it, while you were out there at the Delaware Water Gap? You were a 'caretaker' or something. A lot of people do it. It's a good way to make money without paying taxes."

"She needed money?"

"She always needed money. You knew that."

"I just don't understand why nobody told me."

"Probably that was because nobody could find you half the time. Look, is there a problem?"

"Did she clean for, for other people?" I asked.

"What does it matter now?" said Alison.

"I just want to know."

"Yeah, Tina," said Alison. "She was a cleaning lady. That's what she was doing when she met Bill."

"Elevator's here," said Daniel, from the hallway. "Are you coming?"

Alison looked at the door, and then back to me, and I realized that she kind of felt sorry for me. She also maybe kind of thought I was stupid. "Look," she said. "Be nice to Lucy, okay? It's okay, what she's doing. It's what Mom wanted. She wanted us to have something."

"Did Mom tell you that, that she wanted us to have Bill's apartment?"

"Don't make life so hard, Tina, *please*. It's always so hard with you. Daniel says that if you don't screw this up we have a really good shot at winning. It doesn't matter how it happened. We could win this. We could win, Tina! We could win."

"Alison, I cannot hold this elevator forever!"

"I have to go, Tina. It's going to be fine!" she said. She squeezed my hand. "Don't screw this up! We could *win*."

CHAPTER SIXTEEN

There were lots of books about the architecture of old New York stuffed in boxes back there in that lost room, all of them with little pieces of paper taped to the pages that told the story of the Livingston Mansion Apartment, which is an important apartment, as apartments go. I personally had never thought of apartments being important, but now that I was staying in this one I could see their point. The Livingston Mansion Apartment was the grandest of the grand apartments in the Edgewood, which was the grandest of New York apartment buildings when it was built in 1879. The Livingstons were an important New York family, one of the 400 most important, or at least one of the 400 families who consider themselves the most important, and Sophie Drinan was a Livingston, the last of the Livingstons, in fact. The story of her life, as told by her photographs, is elegant and thrilling. Pictures of her childhood show a home so lavish in its grandeur it took me a while to figure out that that was in fact my deserted and decaying apartment she was living in at the time.

Sophie was a good-looking kid, but like everyone on the

planet her school pictures were horrible. As she got older her dark hair got more starched and insane, developing into corny little bouffants that were clearly someone else's idea of pretty because no seven-year-old really thinks their hair should look like that. The starched hair unfortunately followed her into high school, where I found a bunch of formal shots in which she was presented with truly insane hair, in one evening gown more astonishing than the next. There was also a tidy stack of yearbooks from the Brearly School, which had more pictures of her in plaid uniforms, but her hair looked more normal in those. They showed her acting up a storm in some school play, and giving a thumbs up to the camera after a soccer game, for which she wore baggy shorts, a T-shirt and hair in a pony tail.

The next stack of yearbooks were from Columbia University, and in those her look shifted suddenly and radically into hippie chick/Janis Joplin chic. Lots of cowboy boots and long skirts, tiny little tank tops, hair down her back and in her face, and constant boyfriends in beards and blue jeans hanging all over her. At one point she seems to have done one of those crazy perms that no one would even consider anymore, and then one other time she cut her hair down to nothing, which made her look young and frightened. The next thing that showed up were wedding albums. This was the first time I got a look at Bill, the man who had abducted my own mother and left nothing to show of it other than underwear and mystery novels and some pretty good red wine. In his wedding pictures with Sophie he looks young and nervous. He squints, he has a bad haircut, and the suit he's wearing is starting to wrinkle. The groomsmen, of which there are seven, seem a smoother but sort of unremarkable bunch, all stiff smiles and identical boutonnieres, and the bridesmaids, also seven, are equally unremarkable in narrow pink sheaths with empire waists and matching headbands. The maid of honor's dress flushes into a darker and mustier shade of rose, although her transparent complexion is actually too pale to pull it off, and so she ends up looking like a person standing inside a dress instead of a person wearing a dress. Bill looks hot and and wilted next to all of them.

In the middle of all this upscale insanity, Sophie somehow manages to look somewhat spectacular. Her wedding dress is made of pristine white satin, and it has a low, scalloping neckline and a tight bodice which comes to a perfect point at her waist, which makes it vaguely resemble the dress that Sleeping Beauty wore when she pricked her finger and fell asleep in the Disney movie. It also had miles of train and a huge tulle veil which was held in place with a ridiculous little pillbox hat, but in the picture where her maid of honor was helping her pin the veil to her head she looked like she thought the whole thing was so stupid you kind of forgave her for it. In fact, in each one of those posed photographs she looked like she was thinking about something other than having her picture taken, and that whatever it was she was thinking about was really about to make her laugh. So while everyone else seems completely empty-headed in their willingness to do whatever the idiot photographer was telling them to, she actually looks like a crazy hippie chick wearing a really dumb white dress which she clearly thought was stupid but had agreed to wear to make someone else happy.

I have to admit that by this point I really hated these people.

I couldn't believe the haircuts, the phony grins, the expensive dresses that no one seemed to wear more than once, all the smug details that money could buy, I hated all of it. The wedding pictures came in a large, white, formal book with a cover draped in white stuffed satin and it had a big heart fixed right in the center which actually proclaimed, in gold stitching, *Forever*. Seriously, the whole thing made you want to throw up and then just throw it at the wall. Instead I just dumped it back into its box and went back into the secret room to see what else I could find. Seriously, I couldn't stand these people, and I couldn't get enough of them. Sophie seemed just perfect. I hated her.

My hunt through the boxes then yielded more cowboy boots—which, having seen pictures of Sophie wearing them, now seemed almost eerie in their reality—and lots of thin stockings, the kind you wear with boots and under skirts when the weather gets too cold. I also found four full boxes of wool yarn in about sixteen different colors, some of it still wrapped tightly in skeins, some of it knitted onto needles and abandoned as half-finished pieces of half-imagined sweaters. Then I found a box full of watercolor paper stuck together at the edges, linoleum matte cutters and dried up old plastic tubes of dried up inks. Then I found the rest of the photographs, cluttered together in half-finished albums and boxes of loose prints. And then the ghost came back.

I knew it wasn't a ghost; I did. There was no question that there was somebody in the apartment next door or on some other floor even who was having a crying jag, right next to an air duct somewhere else in the building. But seriously, it sounded so much like someone stuck in time somewhere that it truly made your skin crawl. I was sitting up next to the doorway, looking through the boxes by the light of the laundry room, and the ghost was deep in the wall all the way across the room, buried by boxes that I hadn't gone through yet. Her unseen and unintelligible argument was so drenched in heartsick rage that it sounded like she wanted to kill me for going through her stuff. So I quit for the night and went back to my sorry little adopted bedroom, where I stared at the painting on the wall and wondered what happened to that woman and why my beautiful apartment was so barren and lost that there was only room for me in it now.

I lay there for a long time, wondering if the ghost would follow me, but she didn't; she was definitely trapped back there. She was trapped in the night, too. You never heard her, except after dark; during the daylight hours all was quiet. Meanwhile the legal machinations of everyone's various lawyers were off in some other cosmos, churning away, and for the moment Alison and Lucy and Daniel had agreed to leave me be. I was perfectly free to keep pawing through somebody else's stuff. So after spending a couple more days going through boxes of dishware and towels and children's toys and old ski boots, I went back to the photographs.

There were about 600 of them, and they were tossed into one box with a bunch of old negatives and three chaotic photo albums which had been put together with no concern for chronology whatsoever. In one album, which was covered with dark blue leather, there was dozens of photographs of two laughing little boys, and then suddenly pages and pages of one laughing little baby, and then pictures of Sophie pregnant, holding the hand of one of the little boys, and then just Sophie, alone, laughing at the camera, pregnant. After the strict chronology of the yearbooks and the wedding album, the chaos of photos

267

had a startling effect; you thought, Oh, I'm going back in time, and then forward in time, and then backward and forward at once. The other two albums were the same, just a mess of people's lives with no sense of order to it at all.

Sophie's boys seemed to have a pretty good time of it. She took a lot of pictures of them running in the park, eating ice cream, blowing out candles, riding scooters. In the photographs the boys would leap back and forth between ages while maintaining a brotherly goodwill for each other and the camera which was startling in its consistency, particularly given the grim weariness of the two men I now knew as Doug and Pete Drinan. Even well into adolescence both boys were blessed with what looked like wealth and happiness, cute girlfriends, fun birthday parties and an unbelievably cool-looking apartment to grow up in. Some people who may have been grandparents showed up occasionally and there were a couple of girlfriends, or cousins maybe, who were here and there. Bill was there, grumpy, a little sloppy, a lot of times with a can of beer in his hand. And Sophie would show up, looking like a hippie chick, all long sweaters and Indian print skirts and cowboy boots. At some point you could tell that she thought she was getting fat, because she started to wear big loose shirts open at the neck over a tank top, and then when she felt skinny again she would just wear the tank top without the shirt. And then she got a pair of wire-rimmed glasses at some point but either she didn't wear them all the time, or maybe all of the back and forth with the weight and the hair and the glasses were because of the pictures being jumbled up, who can say. She had a wide mouth and her nose was a little too long and she had eyes that were large and expressive, like she couldn't look at a camera without mugging a little bit. Her hair was dark brown, and it never got grey.

So that, anyway, is what their lives looked like. After all those high-school proms and cotillions and the one big wedding, there were no formal pictures of Sophie or Bill, which struck me as surprising, when I bothered to think about it. The Livingston Mansion Apartment, I had been told incessantly by those boring architecture books, was a centerpiece of old New York. The pictures in those books were unquestionably dazzling. And it's not like the Edge had fallen on hard times; everybody I ran into there seemed more or less made of money—that's why, clearly, they were so mad at my mom and me and my sisters, we were big broke nobodies and they were not. So where were all the pictures of Sophie and Bill at galas and opera benefits and smashing dinner parties? There were none. There weren't even any pictures of her in which you might say she was dressed up. Except for one.

She and Bill are holding hands and smiling at the camera. They are standing in front of a white marble mantle that has three golden glass vases on it, next to an antique black clock with tiny gilt feet. The wall is painted a kind of pearly dove grey and you can see from the elaborate carving on the mantle itself that it's the mantlepiece in the great room; they are having their picture taken in their home, before going out for the evening. The flash of the camera has caught them both slightly by surprise, but even so both Sophie and Bill look traditionally glamorous; he is in a blue suit, and she wears a tight little black dress with pearls at the neckline, and a pair of low heels. Her hair is up, in a classic knot, which shows off her neck. They look happy, and excited for a night out. Except for the fact that they are standing in the greatest apartment I've ever seen, they look just like my mom and dad. You can practically see the kids in pajamas watching in awe while the babysitter frames the picture.

It took me a couple days because there were still a lot of boxes I hadn't gone through yet, but then I thought a bit and went back to that garment bag. Sure enough the dress was there, tucked inside one of the longer and flashier dresses from her high-school days. Having been so carefully folded inside the evening gown, it was well protected, even pristine, almost as if it came straight off the rack. It was a gorgeous dress—black silk taffeta, a fitted bodice, a plunging back neckline. The shoes I found by going back through the first boxes I had looked through; they were slightly scuffed around the back of the heels and they were crushed a little because something too heavy had been placed on top of them. They were also a little dusty.

The pearls I finally found in the bottom of another box. They had been just tossed there like nobody really cared what happened to them, even though they were clearly the real thing, not fake at all like the jewelry my mom wore when she got dressed up. But there they were, curled at the bottom of the box, a double rope of perfectly matched champagne-colored pearls held together by a heavy gold clasp encrusted with real diamonds. That necklace should have been carefully laid in some dark blue velvet-lined case from Tiffany's, or Bergdorf's. But there it was, thrown into the bottom of a brown cardboard box, where it was lost in a disorderly clutter of unrelated junk: shoes, plastic dishes, everyday spoons, and more shoes.

CHAPTER SEVENTEEN

I carried those pearls out into the grim little TV room and sat on that lousy couch and wondered what to do. I was afraid to tell anybody what I had found because I knew that Lucy would insist that the stuff was all part of the estate, which meant, according to her, that it was ours, and then she would probably have appraisers from Sotheby's show up and paw through it all to see if they could find all the really valuable bits, like that pearl necklace, and then those Drinan brothers would lose everything else they had already lost, only they wouldn't even know that they had lost it again.

Even so. With the blooming awareness that I was turning into a complete voyeur, I still wanted to know what had happened there. Why the hell had Bill boxed everything up in that room? Did my mom help him do it? What happened to Sophie; what happened to those happy little boys? I looked at those pearls and I thought that the one person who might be able to actually fill in some gaps was Len. The few times I had asked he had been cryptic as hell while simultaneously tossing clues around like bird droppings. He knew a lot, and I was starting to feel like I had the right to some answers. Why I thought this was anybody's guess; it was increasingly clear to me that I had no rights at all. I didn't care; I wanted to know; I was going to ask Len.

It was then that I realized that I had not seen Len. And I had not seen Len, in fact, because he had not been there. And then I thought about the moss.

A dying mossery doesn't actually look like what you would normally call a disaster in the sense that there isn't a lot of spectacle involved, but when I poked my head in and turned on the lights there was an unmistakable air of doom hovering over all the different beds. It was as if the breath of the room had unexpectedly tiptoed away; the place felt kind of cold and dry and it was simply too silent for anything to be growing. If you had never been in there before you might not notice it because now it just seemed like an old, tired kitchen that had trays of brownish kudzu all over its counters. The air wasn't moist, and the gentle tune of the water being pumped through the teeny tiny irrigation system had gone silent. The pumps were dead, and the moss was dying.

It is amazing how panicked you can get over some dying moss. My heart started to race and I immediately started pawing around the counter to see if I could find the controls to turn the water back on. I had actually watched Len refill the pumps at one point so I had a general idea of where the switches were, running along the wall to the right of some trays that held beds of a normally purple flowering forest moss which had now turned a disturbing shade of grey. But when I located the switches and turned them on, they immediately switched themselves off with a clarity that

272

was frankly startling to find in an inanimate object. Because I was so confused and worried about the moss in that moment, the water pumps and their aggressive refusal to return to life seemed upsetting and perverse until I realized that they were turning themselves off because there was no water, there was just no water anywhere, in the trays, in the beds, in the irrigation tubes, anywhere. I hurried to the sink, picked up one of the plastic watering cans Len had lined up there, filled it from the tap and immediately started watering everything in sight. After I watered the beds, I refilled the three reserve tanks which were tucked into different corners around the room, and I tried turning on the irrigation system again. It clunked a few times, but then it started whirring and humming, and then the sound of the water running around the edges of the trays reemerged from the silence.

Once I had the water going I felt better, but there was no question that every one of those moss beds was in serious trouble. Most of them had gone brown; the previously spongy soil was hard and even brittle in places and water was now pooling in little brown puddles everywhere, instead of soaking in gently, the way it was supposed to. Len had all sorts of moss-sized gardening implements lined up on the open shelves above the sink, tiny rakes and extremely small hand shovels which looked like they might be useful in terms of breaking up the soil, and there were also several bags of plant food and fertilizer stacked under a table by the door. Unfortunately I had no idea what to do with any of it; watering was pretty much at the far end of my restorative capabilities. Besides, I thought, where is Len? I racked my brains; while it was true that I had been turning my cell phone off every day I also checked it every night, and he hadn't been

273

calling. He hadn't even called once, to say let me come in and take care of my moss. Where on earth was he?

After I checked my phone and saw again that he hadn't called, I tried to call him; he didn't pick up, and he seemed to have turned his machine off, because at this end the line just rang and rang. So then I went to his landing and knocked on his door. For a moment I thought I heard the vague rustle of movement which sounded like someone was in there, at which point I pounded even more and yelled specifically that the moss was in real trouble and that he needed to come down and take a look at it. There was no response. I called him on my cell phone from out there on the landing and listened to his phone ring endlessly inside the apartment. So then I went down to the lobby.

"Hey, Frank! How you doing?" I asked. It was strangely nice to see him—I had gotten myself so lost in time I realized sort of dimly that I hadn't actually been out of the apartment for a while, maybe even weeks.

"Yeah. Tina. Hi," Frank said, with less enthusiasm for me than I was feeling for him. He was sorting through the mail and doing a crossword puzzle at the same time. "Haven't seen you in a while."

"I've been kind of busy."

"Good for you."

It was a little troubling to have Frank bristle at me, but I was so worried about the moss I didn't have time to waste thinking about his surprising manners. "Hey, have you seen Len?" I asked, getting straight to the point.

"Not today," Frank said, still not looking at me.

"Did you see him yesterday?" I asked.

"No, Tina, I didn't."

"Well, when was the last time you saw him?" I asked.

"It's not my job to keep track of people. That is not my job description," he informed me.

"No, I know, I just—"

"And you don't have any rights here."

"What?" I said, so surprised at how direct and horrible that statement was, coming out of Frank, that I was truly hurt by it. I guess my confusion made that clear, because Frank flushed a little, like he was privately ashamed for half a second, before the mean version of himself could take over again. It took the sting out of what came next.

"I just mean you're staying here, okay, obviously no one can stop you from doing that but it's not like totally clear what's going to happen next. People want to make sure you are aware of that."

"Of course I'm aware of that."

"All right then."

"So like . . . what? Has the building been talking about us?"

Frank glanced up, and then he took a small step back, sort of like he just wanted to make sure he was a little further away from me. "Yeah, the building has been talking," he said.

This statement was so unnerving I barely knew what to say. That little step more than anything had smacked me in the heart, but there was nothing I could do about it. Frank worked for the building. He was going to act the way they told him to act. I tried to remember why I had come down to speak to him, to just get through this, and get out of the lobby, before somebody with more power showed up and really gave me trouble. "What about Len?" I said, finally. "I really need to get hold of him.

There's something he needs to know, and I haven't seen him for at least two weeks and now I can't get him on the phone."

Frank looked up at the ceiling, like he had to find the nerve to keep up the nasty edge, and it was hiding somewhere up there, in the corner maybe. In any event, he did in fact find it. "Like I said it's not my job—" he started.

"Okay, I got it, Frank!" I snapped. "Just if you see him, tell him I need to talk to him and it's *important,*" I hissed. Frank turned all red, like I had really hurt his feelings. Like most nice people he was just terrible at being mean; he didn't know how to pull it off, and he also didn't know how to not be hurt when people were mean back. So of course I felt ashamed of myself immediately. It is no fun picking on nice people; I don't know why anyone does it, ever, honestly.

Back up in my apartment, with no one explaining a thing, I did my best to fertilize and feed the dying moss. In the corner of the kitchen Len had stashed dozens of different varieties of plant nutrients—potassium, nitrogen, magnesium, something with an oxidized silicate formula, arsenic and bromides—which all had different forms and functions. His central supply of plant food came in little glass bottles with droppers, and you had to mix them up into various solutions before you infused them, literally, with this thing that looked like an IV lead, into the water supply. That only took me three hours to figure out, which I finally did by carefully following the pictures on the backs of the boxes and putting that information together with some of the things I had seen Len do the half-dozen times I had watched him work in there. I sorted through little plastic containers of strange-looking black goo which apparently was some special

276

kind of compost that was pooped out by special worms; each one had the Latinate name of a specific moss written on masking tape on the top, and since Len had also labeled the trays of the different mosses it was fairly simple to match them up and put a few little scoops of compost in each tray. Bat guano also made an appearance in a little muslin sack inside a cardboard box, but that's all it said on the box—"Bat Guano"—so I had no way of knowing what to do with it. I also, quite honestly, had no way of knowing if I was giving anything the right amount of any of these different versions of fertilizer. I had a feeling just dumping lots of plant food on everything at once was maybe not the correct approach. But since I still couldn't find Len—his phone just rang and rang whenever I tried him—I was left with my own haphazard guesswork.

There was one person, I knew, who might be able to help me. After two days of working on the moss with only mixed results I decided I'd better seek out her advice.

It's easy to get to the Brooklyn Botanical Gardens from the Upper West Side; you just take the express from 72nd straight into Park Slope, where the Eastern Parkway stop lets you off right at the front gate. When I told the person in the ticket booth that I was looking for Charlotte Colbert, he didn't even make me pay for a ticket, he just directed me to the conservatory, where another cheerfully helpful Botanical employee pointed me toward a side room, where I found her tending to a subdivision of bonsai trees.

The bonsai room was bright and hot and full of light. Long wooden tables lined the walls and presented to the world a series of bonsai trees each more surreal than the next. There was a tiny maple with a whorled trunk and perfect five-point leaves, a miniature stand of beech trees with tiny, whittled bark, a tiny juniper with elegantly twirling deadwood branches. An impossibly miniature dogwood gracefully presented fresh miniature pink blossoms, alongside an ancient bald cypress which, I was told by the metal plaque on its base, was over 300 years old. Even though there was no one else there it took me a moment to locate Len's daughter Charlie; she had drifted into a tiny alcove just off the main displaying area, her entire attention focused on a miniature pine tree which she was pruning with extraordinary care. Like every other tree in the room, the tiny pine seemed truly bizarre in its botanical precision, but I barely had time to register it because even as Charlie looked up with a plant-induced haze that I had often seen on Len's face, I realized that it, and every other tree in the room, was growing in trays that were covered in moss.

"Can I help you?" she said, not recognizing me at first.

"Hi, I'm Tina. I'm Tina Finn? I met you at your dad's apartment," I told her.

"My father?" She didn't actually perk up at this; what she did was more the opposite of perking up. She set down her pruning shears and looked down, as if she were trying to decide whether or not to say something that she might regret. She started to peel off her gloves, all business. "What about him?"

"Have you talked to him?"

"Who are you again?" Charlie folded her arms over her chest. She had Len's strange blue eyes, which had that peculiar skill of making me feel like I was a weed and not a plant. I remembered that when I first met her, in the foyer of Len's apartment, she struck me as a sort of friendly soldier. The friendly part of the equation had, unfortunately, evaporated.

"I live in his building, and he keeps his moss in my apartment, and I haven't been able to get hold of him for, well, a while," I explained, trying to be as polite as possible under the circumstances. "Have you heard from him?"

Charlie continued to consider me like a piece of stinkgrass. "No," she finally said, short, turning back to her miniature pine tree like that was all that I could possibly expect out of her.

"Well, if you do hear from him could you ask him to call me? Here, I can write my number down for you," I offered, trying not to sound too desperate.

"Look, I don't know what you think you're doing with my father," Charlie said, cutting me off. "But you've made a colossal mistake if you think I'm going to help you with that."

"Aw come on—that is just—No." I said, half to myself. "I'm not doing anything with your father. I'm helping him with his moss."

"That's the first time I've heard it called that," she said with a sneer.

"Look," I retorted. "There are plenty of people who have good reason to be mad at me, but trust me, you are not one of them. I'm telling you the truth. Who would make something like this up? The kitchen of my apartment is just covered with moss beds and the moss is dying because he hasn't shown up to take care of it for weeks, and I didn't even notice at first because I was not paying attention, but now I'm telling you, the moss is *dying*. It's dying and I don't know how to take care of it and I can't find Len. Did he go somewhere? Did he take a trip? Do you know where he is? And if you don't know where he is can you at least tell me what to *do*. There's moss on all these little bonsai trees; you clearly know what you're doing, I don't know *what* I am doing and the moss is going to *die*. My mother took care of the moss for Len before she died. She was, he told me she was a good person." This fact, blurting out of my mouth so unexpectedly, seemed simply and suddenly overwhelming to me. "She took care of his moss. I don't want it to die."

Charlie was not impressed. But she was at least listening. "So you're not some sort of hooker?" she asked.

"Why does everyone think that?" I asked her back, pinching my eyes quickly so that she couldn't see that I was crying.

"I don't know why other people think that but I think that because the last time I saw you you were hanging around my dad's apartment and he handed you hundreds of dollars and then told you to get lost. That would be why I think that."

"That was for the *moss*," I said, trying not to get too defensive about this. "Are you going to help me save the stupid moss, or are we just going to let it die?"

Unlike Len, Charlie was not much of a talker. She didn't say anything on the subway ride back to my apartment, and she didn't say anything in the elevator, and she didn't say anything even when I took her into the kitchen, flipped on the lights and showed her the catastrophic mess that once was a mossery. She took in the situation from the doorway for a moment, then took a step forward to consider each separate bed. She looked up and over, immediately spotting the open shelf with the itty-bitty gardening implements, as if she knew they would be there because that was the only logical place they might be. She picked up a miniature trowel, and turned back to the moss, gently pressing it and her fingers into the edges of the soil, searching for some-

280

thing under the surface that I would never understand. She did that for a full five minutes before I finally lost patience with the silence.

"So can you fix this or are they all going to die?" I blurted.

"You fed them," she observed, without answering the question.

"I tried," I admitted.

"Do you remember what you did?"

"I did whatever the plant food told me to do," I said. I started pulling out all the different kinds of plant food and fertilizer from under the table, and handing them to her. "He's got everything written on the top of the containers, so I tried to do what it said, but who knows, I didn't know if I should be mixing it up, or putting it on top of the moss or underneath it, or he has these little spiky things, so I thought maybe I should dig holes in the beds and then put the bat guano in the hole or something. I was kind of making it up as I went along."

"Yes, I see," Charlie said, opening one of the little plastic containers and rubbing the black stuff between her fingers. She held her finger up to her nose, breathing it in quietly, and then she tasted it with the tip of her tongue. She looked at another container in her hand, then glanced back at the moss. "Okay," she said. "Can you get me a ham sandwich?"

"A ham sandwich?"

"Yeah, I'm kind of hungry. There's got to be some sort of deli around here. I'd like a ham sandwich."

"Oh. Sure," I said. "I'm just, I guess I assumed that people like you were like, vegetarians."

"No," she said, and she went back to work.

Three hours later I was lying on the futon in my bedroom,

reading a passably interesting mystery novel about some detective who was as screwed up as the killers he was chasing. He more or less drank too much, and had trouble opening up to people, and he had a cynical weariness that came from seeing too much suffering, and he distrusted women who all found him to be irresistibly sexy. In short, he was such a dead ringer for Pete Drinan, whose personal history was now parading all over my brain, that I could not help but wonder if they taught those specific qualities in detective school. I picked up one of the photo albums I had swiped from the lost room and looked at the pictures of the young Pete and Doug Drinan, around when they were both in high school and grinning at the camera with all the money and good looks that New York privilege could buy. It didn't make sense. How could someone who grew up in the swankest apartment in New York, and whose brother was some sort of big deal egghead at the Dalton School end up in the NYPD?

"You're all right for now," Charlie announced, standing in the doorway.

"Wow! What? Wow, you scared the shit out of me," I noted, shoving the photo album back into its hiding place between the bed and the wall. Her eyes flickered as she watched me do it, but she didn't comment. Like Len, she apparently was not interested in anything in that apartment except for the moss.

"You're all set," she informed me. She took a half step through the doorway and held out a piece of lined notebook paper, with tidy rows of information neatly inscribed in tight handwriting down one side. "You need to make sure there's enough water in the pumps every morning, and then add the minerals and fertilizers according to this schedule. You did mostly a good job faking your way through this. Aside from the fact that you pretty much drowned the hornwort, and I don't know what you thought you were doing with the bat guano."

"It didn't have any instructions on it."

"So you decided to just toss it everywhere. No, I get it," she said, finally raising an eyebrow with a shred of humour.

"Then you think we can save most of it?"

She shrugged; it was a stupid question, but now she was acting like she was more or less used to dealing with me and other people who don't really understand plants. "Moss is pretty sturdy," she explained. "It goes dormant when humidity or ground conditions become hostile to growth. How long was it that the water was turned off?"

"I don't know exactly. Maybe two weeks? Len always just came down and worked in there every day and then he . . . stopped."

This was the information she was secretly after. She folded her arms and leaned against the door jamb, acting like she could give a shit, but her crazy eyes were thinking.

"And you tried to get hold of him."

"I called him and I went up there and knocked on the door a bunch of times. I think he's in there, but he didn't answer. And he's not answering the phone, obviously. I mean, I wouldn't have come looking for you if he had. Is something going on with him?"

Charlie lifted her arms into the air, clasped them backwards over her head, and let them float to her sides. It made her look really tall, like a tree spirit, standing in the doorway of my strange little room with the sunset on the wall and the stars and planets glued to the ceiling. Then she twisted swiftly back and forth at the waist and bent forward until her hands touched the ground in front of her. I couldn't tell what was going on, and then I realized that she was just doing a few yoga stretches while she considered how much to tell me.

"Look," I said, trying to prompt her. "Do you think something's happened to him? I mean, do you think he's hurt or—"

"He's up there. I came by a couple of nights ago and watched from the park, with a pair of binoculars. The lights were on and he's in there."

This was obviously a pretty interesting piece of information. "You came by and spied on him?"

"Yes," she responded, completely without apology. "He stole something from me and I need to get it back."

"That plant you brought him? That little boy's plant?"

"Do you actually not know?"

"Well—no—I mean, yes, I *don't* know," I said, trying not to sound too annoyed at yet another person acting like I was stupid. "I mean I think it's obvious I'm not actually a plant person, and since no one has told me anything about it at all, why should I?"

"It's on the wall in your kitchen," she told me. I just stared at her. "The plate. From the *Sarum Horae*. *Madrigalis antiaris toxicaria*."

"The picture of the tree?"

"Yes. That is, it's possible. We're not precisely sure. No one knows really what that plant looks like," she admitted. "No one's seen it for a millennium."

"And you think that's what those seeds were, seeds to some medieval tree?"

"It's older than that," she corrected me, ignoring my incredulous tone. "There are records of it being cultivated on the island

284

of Malta as early as the fourth century. Some people think that it was one of the psychotropic plants that were used in the Greek rituals at Elysium, which, if that is true, would make it quite a bit older than that, even."

"Psychotropic," I said. "So it's like a drug plant?"

"It is historically understood to have promoted altered states, yes," she replied.

"So what do you do, you smoke it?"

"My impulse would be to study it. No one knows how or if, in fact, the rumours about its ritualistic uses are accurate. As I said, no one has in fact seen that plant in any shape or form for quite a long time. If it is what we think it is, it's worth a lot of money, which Benny in fact could use. That's why I took it to him. My father. He knows a lot of people. He knows . . ." She drifted off for a moment, in a spasm of regret. "I took it to him," she continued, "because I thought he would be able to help us. And protect it, if it's, no one is going to want to, while everybody is going to—it's so improbable, but if it's true, we needed proctection, Benny needed—and I took that boy, who trusted me, and I told him my father would help us. And now he, apparently, he has decided . . . I don't know what he's decided," she admitted, looking off. Then, "I would like to kill him."

I didn't know what to say to this. I thought that probably she was kidding, you know, just saying that the way people do, but she was also so tall and fierce and with those strange blue eyes it certainly did sound and look like she meant it. The few times I had met them Len and Charlie and even that little boy Benny, they struck me as special, people who talked to plants,

285

but now they were beginning to sound and look like everyone else, just people who had a hole in their hearts and only one thing could fill it. For them, that one thing was a plant.

But Charlie was shaking herself awake again. She smiled at me, one of those old smiles that admit things to people you barely know. "It's my fault. I should never have trusted him," she said.

"He's your father," I said.

"Yeah." She turned around and looked at the stars on the ceiling of the little bedroom. "This is a nice room. How come you don't have any furniture in this place?"

"It's kind of a long story," I said, wishing I had enough time to tell her. "If I hear from Len, do you want me to have him call you?"

"I think it might be better if you just called me," she said. "My phone number is there." She tipped her chin up, indicated the sheet of watering and feeding instructions in my hand. "Thanks for the ham sandwich." And with that, she left.

CHAPTER EIGHTEEN

Ira Grossman and his offices were the last word in swank. His waiting room was paneled in actual wood, and he had several low black leather couches and chairs with stylishly sloped backs, plus sleek glass coffee tables which displayed international newspapers, fanned out neatly across its glittering surface. You expected to see a wealthy murderous widow draped in front of the view from the narrow, knife-like windows, which overlooked a particularly dense canyon of skyscrapers in midtown. Unfortunately, there were no wealthy widows to be found; there was just us. Although each and every one of us was dressed better than we were on the day that we buried Mom and ended up in Stuart Long's lousy offices further downtown.

Grossman himself turned out to be just as slick as his waiting room. He wore a bespoke suit, double breasted and with the thinnest of pinstripes, which was so flawlessly fitted you felt like you were talking to a magazine. His shoes shone up at you, evenly and fiercely polished to a rich meaty brown, as he crossed the room with capable purpose. Honestly, you couldn't help but notice the perfection of those shoes, it was completely distracting, so while everyone in my family was standing and greeting this killer with the usual phony confidence my eyes kept slipping back to the floor. Those dazzling shoes smiled up at me like crocodiles.

"You must be Tina," Grossman announced, reaching out to shake. I looked up just in time to catch him giving me the once over; Lucy had clearly filled him in on my questionable past, only the facts had as usual backfired on her. He held my hand about two and a half seconds longer than was strictly necessary and there was the slightest suggestion in his smile that he was thinking about licking his chops. No question, like many clever and successful men, Ira Grossman liked bad girls. "Let's get to it, shall we?" he asked me.

"That would be wonderful!" Alison trilled, annoyed. It was always hard on her, the way guys flirted with me. She was the oldest but from high school on it was clear that Lucy was destined to be the smartest, and I was going to be the one that boys liked. She ended up with the cute, stable husband while I careened from one loser to the next, but it didn't seem to make a difference, finally. Whenever creepy guys in suits started sniffing around me, Alison took it as a personal offense. Which put me in a really kind of a bad mood, just then.

"Yeah, let's get to this, Mr Grossman." I smiled, turning up the wattage. I even reached over and touched him lightly on the sleeve of that astonishing suit. "I looked through all those papers Lucy gave me and I can't make head or tail out of them. I hope you can explain to me what really is going on here. I mean, I suck at math."

"It is a bit complicated," Grossman told me, infinitely touched and turned on by my putative stupidity. "Let's go to the conference room. Would anyone like some coffee?"

"I'll take a Coke," I said, trying to make it sound like I wanted to have sex. I thought Lucy was going to gag and that Alison was going to throttle me, or at least ask Daniel to do it. I didn't care. Both my sisters were really getting on my nerves. They didn't have a clue what was going on. I was the one who was living there and I was the one who had found the lost room and I was the one who knew everyone in the building, and they just didn't have a clue. This was my oh so enlightened position at the time, or at least it was enough of an internal assumption for me to give myself permission to be snarky and superior back to them, while they were being snarky and superior to me.

Things started simply enough, with piles of paper that we were told to sign for no apparent reason, in triplicate.

"Since Lucille has been acting as Administratrix for the past two months we do need to formalize that situation immediately," Grossman announced, as we all took our seats around a conference table made of some sort of solid black metal. "There's no need to backdate the documents since we don't even have a court date yet in the matter of the execution of your mother's estate, but in the negotiations with Mr Drinan's estate it is going to be occasionally necessary for a representative of your mother's estate to make a physical appearance. She will need to be authorized to negotiate on your behalf legally as in fact."

"What?" I said.

"Just sign it, Tina," Daniel advised me, opening my docs

helpfully to the signature pages. Alison had already bent her head over her own pages and was writing her name with a schoolgirl's determination, like she was trying to teach me a lesson by following the rules loudly and to a T. Lucy was a little more subtle, but she was also doing as she was told as quickly and efficiently as possible, leaving me quite openly in the position of Problem Child as I sat there, pen in hand, not signing a thing.

"This makes Lucy *what*? 'Administratrix?'" I asked. "How come she gets to do that?"

"It's just a legal designation. She doesn't actually 'do' anything," Grossman assured me, with just enough of a conspiratorial gleam in his eye to register what an administratrix might actually "do" in private. "The courts require that the estate designate a petitioner to represent all interested parties as a matter of expediency, but if there is a discrepancy in the wishes of the interested parties you and your sister will have the opportunity to appear and object in court." Both Alison and Lucy pretended that they understood this nonsense and shoved their carefully signed documents across the table to him, which he took with one hand while passing different documents back to Lucy with the other. They all completely ignored the fact that not only was I not finished signing my set of documents, I had not even started. I had not even picked up one of the plain little ballpoint pens Grossman had so helpfully pushed in front of everyone.

"This authorizes me to act as your legal representative on your behalf in this matter," he explained, quickly moving through the docs. "This authorizes the previous attorney for the estate to forward to me all files pertaining to the estate. This authorizes a schedule of payment of monies from the estate."

"What monies? There are no monies," I said.

"There will be," Lucy replied, signing away.

"Yeah, but when? How can we hire this guy—excuse me, Mr Grossman—"

"Ira, please."

"Ira, I'm having a little trouble catching up with this."

"Which would be why Lucy is the administrator," Alison muttered.

"Sure, okay, sure, Alison, fine," I started, getting testy now. "I'm still allowed to ask a few questions."

"Absolutely. That's why we're here," Grossman reassured the room. "These situations are always complicated, and the one in which you find yourselves is obviously especially so. The fact is, however, that as the Drinans are moving ahead with the challenge to their father's will, and you and your sisters have already been designated interested parties in that action, they've already scheduled a deposition of your mother's attorney, and the likelihood is that they will attempt to depose all three of you. We're hoping to avoid that, which is why the documents need to be signed which make Lucille the point person. Otherwise all three of you will have to give depositions which, not that we think anything unsavoury or contradictory will come out of a situation like that? It's just an issue of controlling the odds."

"Odds of what?"

"The odds of something coming out," Daniel inserted, blunt.

"What could come out?" I asked.

"The Drinans are claiming that your mother kept their father in a state of constant inebriation, during which she coerced him into changing his will to one which disinherits them and leaves her the entirety of the estate."

"That's ridiculous," I said, out of loyalty. "Mom *coerced* him? He wouldn't let Mom out of his sight. She was like his prisoner, and if he had a drinking problem that wasn't her fault."

"What makes you think he had a drinking problem?" Grossman asked me, suddenly serious.

"The first day we got there, there was alcohol everywhere," I said.

"This was the day of your mother's funeral?"

"Yes," I said. "No furniture, just vodka and red wine."

"This was a full three weeks after her husband's death," Grossman said, pointed.

"Well, I don't know exactly when Bill died," I started.

"She didn't tell you?" Grossman asked.

"Not right when it happened."

"When did she tell you?"

Lucy, Daniel and Alison were all staring at me, silent, as if I was about to betray them all. "She . . ." I started, and then I turned all red, as the truth occurred to me. "She never told me that he died. I didn't know."

"What did you think when you heard that he had died? Didn't it strike you as odd that she never informed you of it?"

"I didn't actually think about it. I was upset about Mom so I, no, I was sad, I mean, when I found out that Bill had died. But I thought he died a long time ago." Lucy, Daniel and Alison kept staring at me like a jury. It was really rather creepy. "What is the big deal? Did she tell you guys? They didn't know either," I commented, defensive.

"I knew," said Lucy.

"How could you know?"

"I knew because she told me. She was very sad and she called and told me that Bill had died but that she didn't want us to come to the funeral." Lucy stared at me coolly, like this was common knowledge. Next to her, Alison stiffened her spine fiercely, like a little bird.

"Did you know too, Alison?"

"Yes," Alison whispered. "I did."

"So that would be another thing you didn't tell me."

"Mom told her not to," Lucy inserted.

"Mom *told* you not to tell me? The way she *told* you both not to tell me that she was—what she was doing, to make money, that she was cleaning houses, she told you not to tell me any of that." I looked at both of them. Lucy looked back, unapologetic; Alison looked at the floor.

"Yes, she did," Lucy informed me.

"Why?"

"I don't know," said Lucy, very plain. Alison's lips were pursed by this point. Daniel just kept staring at me.

"This is good, this is good," Grossman explained, smoothly. "It's wonderful to see you all work out the complications of this situation, in terms of communication and confusion. Death is often like this. People know things, people don't know things. My understanding, Tina, is that you were out of touch with the family for a while. But your personal circumstances—where you were, what you were doing—are completely irrelevant to the court case, and have no bearing on the details of the settlement. So you see why it would be important to keep these personal discussions out of the court record," Grossman continued, smiling at me like he and I shared a secret, even though it was clear now that we did not. "And the amounts of alcohol that your mother was keeping in the apartment even though she was the only person living there is not something that the court is going to be able to ignore, since it is at the heart of the Drinans' case."

"Bill was a big drinker," I started.

"By your own admission you never met Bill," Grossman reminded me. "And your mother did not share information with you about her marriage. Your testimony is not going to be helpful in this matter."

I was completely speechless. The thought that I might lose my claim to my apartment because Pete Drinan would go to court and tell everyone that my mom was a drunk had honestly never occurred to me.

"Please don't worry about this," Grossman hastened to re-assure me, taking the opportunity to reach over and press my hand. "It isn't much of an argument, given their own family history. The burden of proof is on them. I'm just saying we don't want to help them out if we can easily avoid it. The first step is making it difficult for them to depose all three of you. We need to name an administrator anyway. Both Alison and Lucy feel that Lucy's the right person for that job. And since you've already taken on so much responsibility for the daily upkeep of the apartment, no one wants to burden you further."

This guy was a really smooth customer. It occurred to me

that he had been flirting with me because he thought it would get him what he wanted, which was my signature, and nothing else. It also occurred to me that Alison and Lucy were lying— that Mom hadn't called anybody when Bill died, because she just didn't—and they had secretly consulted with this new smooth lawyer who told them that that was the kind of information that didn't really need to get out there, so they had agreed amongst themselves to lie about it. It occurred to me that maybe she did call Alison and Lucy and told them that Bill had died, and they just didn't do anything about it because that was their way, they were too busy with their own lives to wonder if Mom was alone and needed anything, like a friend or a kid at the funeral. It occurred to me that maybe Mom called them and told them not to come. It occurred to me that maybe she didn't call me because I was out at the Delaware Water Gap living in a trailer with another loser, and I didn't return my phone calls. It occurred to me that maybe Mom didn't call any of us because we weren't ever much comfort to her anyway.

I picked up my sorry little ballpoint pen. Lucy let out her breath with a little noise that meant "Finally!" but I wasn't actually thinking of going along with this just yet. "What is . . . what . . ." I started to ask. She snapped.

"Just do it, Tina! Alison and I have the majority vote and we can do this with or without you! Just do it!"

"Now now, no one is being forced into anything. We absolutely want to present a united front here," Grossman announced, soothing. "Tina, do you have more questions?"

I did have a lot of questions, so many that I didn't even know

295

where to start. Most of them were about me and my sisters, and why we ended up the way we did, why we all just ended up abandoning each other and Mom, why none of us meant more to the others. But I didn't think that was what he meant. I thought I'd best stick to someone else's facts for now. "When you said 'given their own family history'? 'The Drinans don't have much of an argument, given their own family history.' What does that mean?" I asked.

"Because of what happened with the first Mrs Drinan," Grossman said, nodding like that was a very good question and he was glad I asked it. "They may try to make that in-admissible, but it clearly relates to why and how the sons were disinherited."

"Didn't she die a long time ago?" Alison asked, shy and anxious. "Do we have to deal with her relatives too?"

"Not at all. The apartment did, however, originally belong to her. Mr Drinan came into possession at the time of her death. But there was no question that he was the sole beneficiary. I think there were cousins or nieces, but they had no claim, then or now."

"Yeah, but if it was her apartment in the first place, doesn't that make it more of a stretcher, that we should get the place instead of her own sons?" I pointed out.

"You might argue that, but you could also argue that they were heavily implicated in her death," Grossman announced, like he was reporting the weather. "There were apparently a lot of recriminations between them and their father about it, but there is no question that both supported him when he made the decision to have her institutionalized."

"There is no question, okay *what*?" I asked. "What did you just say?"

"I don't have the hospital records yet, and it's not clear that I'll be able to get them released, but according to Long all three of them were in agreement, at first, that she needed to be hospitalized. I'm told that all three of them signed the admission papers. It apparently wasn't until later that a lot of hard feelings emerged."

"Okay, wait, wait," I said, really trying to catch up with this. It seemed an inconceivable end to the story that was lying around in scraps in my apartment. "She was *institutionalized*? And all three of them—okay—"

"The facts indicate that all three of them agreed that she should be admitted into a psychiatric facility, and then after some period of time there—I don't know really how long— she died. Obviously the hospital itself bears responsibility for the lack of oversight, but there were never any legal actions taken. Anyway, upon her death the apartment, which was in her name, became her husband's property, which coincided with the rift with the sons, so there may have been some overlap there, in terms of what they were all upset about. Our argument would be that Mr Drinan disinherited his sons because of that situation, long before he met your mother. It's not even an argument; it's the simple truth. Your mother did nothing worse than fall in love with the man and take care of him in the last years of his life, long after his sons had abandoned him. And so he willingly left her his estate. There's no coercion involved, none that can be proven in any case."

"What was wrong with her? The first Mrs Drinan?" Alison asked, touched and curious about Sophie's troubles.

Grossman shrugged; this part of the story wasn't relevant to the cash, so it wasn't relevant to him. "Long maintains that it was some form of depression, but there's no way to say, unless we get a look at the records, which they most certainly will not permit," Grossman noted, looking through his papers. "And even then, 'depression' is one of those diagnoses that cover a lot of ground. She could have been terribly sick, or she could have just been angry."

"You can lock up people for just being angry?" Lucy asked. Like Grossman, she was not even vaguely interested; she was working her CrackBerry again. It was more a rhetorical question than anything.

"Well, that's a good question, but one that I have no jurisdiction to answer." Grossman smiled, pleasant. Having finished his gruesome history, he turned his full attention back to me. "Tina, did you have any more questions about the process? We do have a lot to cover today."

I stared at my poor little ballpoint and the pile of documents in front of me. There were three more stacks of documents at Grossman's elbow. I felt like Alice down the rabbit hole, things just kept getting more complicated, nothing got simpler, it all just got weirder, meaner, richer. We were all getting richer, inch by inch, billable hour by the billable hour.

"No, I'm fine," I said. "So where do I sign?"

CHAPTER NINETEEN

The press conference with Sotheby's was a predictably swank affair. There were a lot of minions—men in suits, women in expensive and tightly fitted dresses, all of them completely confident that they belonged at Sotheby's and that you did too. Lucy was wrong when she told me that I'd better buy myself some ugly clothing, because there was nothing ugly about any of these people. Maybe they were just a lot of normal people who worked for a lot of rich people, but we were the people they were working for now, so we sure as hell needed to look as rich as possible. And that didn't mean expensive, that meant *rich*. I wore the black taffeta dress, and the pearls, and the low pumps that went with them. The Sotheby's minions were not unimpressed.

Lucy also managed to pull off an acceptable presence; she wore her best grey silk suit, but her hair was down and she had had the foresight to put on a little blush and mascara so she did look businesslike and thin, but in a pretty way. Alison unfortunately didn't quite come up to the mark. She wore her best red wool dress, which I know she likes but it doesn't actually suit her; it bunches around the waist and clings to her stomach in a tragic way which finally makes her look bit like a dumpy middle-aged housewife. Which sadly had never occurred to her until possibly this moment, when she was surrounded by so many men and women who looked nothing like housewives at all. She kept looking around the room and smiling at everyone with such panicked eyes that I finally snuck around behind her and gave her a fast hug.

"You look beautiful, Alison," I said, holding her close.

"Really?" she said, hungry to believe me. She ran her fingers through her hair, which was sadly losing its bounce, because she had been fooling with it incessantly for the past twenty minutes.

"Absolutely, stunning!" I told her, helping carefully to put her hair back in place without messing it up any further. "That color is phenomenal on you. I wish I could wear red."

She smiled at me with that sad hope which had become more or less a continual expression for her of late. Daniel came up behind us, looking around as if he didn't even really know she was related to him. "I think they're about to start," he informed the air next to Alison, without even glancing at her. He was wearing a dazzling new suit, and he had gotten a haircut, so that it was short on the sides but sort of sexy and floppy over his eyes. All done up and standing next to Alison like that, they didn't look like they were even vaguely related. His eyes raked back to me and paused, impressed. "You look good, Tina," he mentioned.

"Oh, thanks," I said, not actually appreciating the appreciative glint in his eye. "Oh look, you're right, they're starting."

The crowd seemed to be gently and effortlessly drifting toward the other end of the room, where a small podium awaited. We ebbed along with the others, catching up with Lucy just in front of the podium. "Where'd you get that?" Lucy asked me, barely glancing at my dress, but noting it with some approval nonetheless. As long as I showed up looking like someone who should inherit fifteen million dollars, she didn't care if I looked better than she did.

"Used clothing place in my neighborhood," I said. "It didn't cost a thing."

"You look good. You look rich," she told me.

"That was the plan," I said. She actually smiled at this, and for a moment there was a sincere relief between the both of us that we were actually on the same page. I wasn't sure why we needed a big press conference before we'd even made it into court on one of these depositions or hearings or pleadings, but she and our snaky lawyer and our fancy new partner—Sotheby's—seemed to think it was a good idea. I wasn't going to argue with them; it didn't get me anywhere, and there was nowhere else I wanted to go anyway. If that meant putting on a nice dress and drinking the Koolaid at the press conference, I was happy to oblige.

Our host, one of the senior curators of Sotheby's real-estate division, approached and took my hand, helping me take the last few steps up to the small staging area they had assembled for our inaugural conversation with the public. His name was Leonard and he looked like a Leonard, all arching nose under a big head of fabulous white hair. I decided it was in fact true, men do age better than women. This guy was a skinny rich old hunk. "That piece is stunning," Leonard informed me, kissing me on the cheek. "Where did you get it?"

He was of course talking about the pearls which were draped around my neck and held there with a fourteen-carat gold and diamond clasp.

"A tag sale," I said, smiling.

"The clasp is extraordinary."

"Thank you," I said, demure.

"If you ever want to sell it I hope you'll bring it here. We'll take very good care of you," he advised me, intimate. I was about to say something sweet in response about all the attention he was giving my chest when Alison turned, sharp, and stared at me. And then the lights went haywire and the room began to pulse with a million flashes. The press conference was on its merry way.

"Thank you all for coming in on this lovely day," Leonard announced into the microphone. "I feel very sure that we can make it worth your while." He looked down at some papers on the podium in front of him and carefully rearranged them in a meaningless way so that it looked like he was doing something rather than pausing when in fact pausing was all he was doing. The small but attentive audience of reporters and real estate agents settled into an expectant hush laced with something that was either awe or greed as Leonard laid it all out for them: Not only was my apartment a gorgeous piece of real estate, it was Important, too.

"It is a rare occasion when a truly historic New York property comes on the market, one that reminds us of the very great privilege we here at Sotheby's enjoy as stewards of history,"

302

Leonard announced. "The great families of this country—the Morgans, the Rockefellers, the Clays, the Fricks—made their mark in finance, transportation, industry, the art world. They also left their mark in the bricks and stones and mortar, the heart and soul of New York. Ladies and gentlemen, today it is my great privilege to introduce to you one of the finest of New York historic properties, the Livingston Mansion Apartment, which occupies 6,000 square feet of the eighth floor of the Edgewood Building at a prime location on Central Park West. Could we dim the lights please?"

The flashes had now stopped, and the lights magically lowered upon his order. To our right there was a large white projection screen which came to life as the lights went down, revealing a stunning black-and-white photograph of the outside of my building. A horse and carriage stood in front of the front door, and women in long, sweeping gowns paraded sedately up the street. The Edge in all its glory stood alone—severe, gorgeous, Victorian.

"The Edgewood was built in 1879," Leonard informed us, "two years before they broke ground for the Dakota building a half mile to the north." A series of beautiful photographs of old New York wafted across the screen as he continued with his history, which was definitely educational but also a little boring. It got slightly more interesting when he started working in the specific history of the Livingston family, but as it turned out Sophie's forebears were just a couple of brothers who made a ton of money by cornering the market on bolted cotton fabric some time around when pre-made dresses became all the rage. So they soaked the guys who were paying teenage girls slave

303

wages to sew dresses eighteen hours a day in huge Victorian sweatshops, and then they soaked everyone who was selling fabric out in the Wild West and Ohio and Canada as well. The rest of the Livingston family history wasn't quite as unfeeling and creepy, but it wasn't inspiring either, as they all seemed to just hang around and marry other wealthy New Yorkers and then branch out in other fabric-related endeavours which also seemed to endlessly yield buckets of cash. The most noteworthy thing about the Livingstons, as far as I was concerned, was their continued inability to propagate. There were several historic pictures of my endlessly sprawling 6,000-square-foot apartment in the slide show with no people in them, and no matter how many stories Leonard told about the historically important Livingston family they never seemed to have more than one or two kids, many of whom died childless. Which is how, apparently, the property finally came into the possession of the lone Livingston heir, our own Sophie, whose dress and pearls and shoes I was wearing while the Head of Historic Properties at Sotheby's blipped over her quiet and terrible end.

"Eventually the family's prominence would fade," Leonard announced happily. "And the apartment would move into other hands. Today, Sotheby's is proud to present this jewel of New York, an apartment almost unparalleled in architectural detail and beauty, to the real estate community."

The lights were gently coming up by this point, and hands were raised. Leonard tipped his head slightly toward a youngish guy with messy hair in a corduroy jacket, who was sitting in the front row. "Who are the sellers?" Corduroy Jacket asked, getting straight to the point.

"The sellers are the daughters of Olivia Drinan, the second wife of the Livingston heir, William Franklin Drinan," Leonard replied with simple confidence.

"Can we get the names?"

"The names of the heirs to Mrs Drinan's estate are Alison Finn Lindemann, Lucille Finn and Christina Finn," Leonard replied. "All of whom are with me today." He bowed a little bit, turned and gestured toward us with an open palm. We smiled at the small crowd, as we had been previously instructed to do, and Lucy stepped forward. Leonard made an elegant little gesture in our direction and relinquished the microphone to her.

"On behalf of myself and my sisters I would like to thank Mr Rubenstein and Sotheby's for hosting us today," Lucy announced with a clear and gracious confidence. Although she's relentlessly mean in private, public relations is actually her field for a reason as she definitely knows how to pull it out. She has a nice smile when she bothers, and under lights she bothers a lot. In fact it's utterly astonishing how high the wattage can go. "It is a tremendous honor to be a part of this presentation," she proclaimed. "We are well aware that the Edgewood is one of the most prestigious addresses on Manhattan, and the Livingston Mansion Apartment has long been considered the centerpiece of the property. We very much feel the responsibility and privilege of our stewardship, in helping it move into the hands of someone who will value it as much as our mother did." What utter horseshit, I thought, but the crowd did not seem to notice that so much as the one big detail which no one had yet mentioned.

"Our understanding is that there is a competing claim on the apartment from the Livingston heirs," someone called from

305

the back of the room. I couldn't see who it was because the lights were very much in my eyes at that point, but it was some woman and she wasn't kidding around. No one else was, either; in the front you could see everyone stop scribbling and look up at us, expectant. This was the real show, as far as they were concerned. Lucy looked over her shoulder, supremely confident, and Ira Grossman stepped forward, joining her and Leonard up there. In her little grey outfit she was now framed by two handsome men in pinstripe suits. It made an extremely reassuring picture.

"The apartment legally was bequeathed to Mrs Drinan, who bequeathed it to her daughters," Grossman said simply. "The sons of the first Mrs Drinan are investigating the terms of their father's will, as it is their right to do. But as of now there is no reason to believe that there are any legal grounds upon which the will might be set aside. Our expectation is that everyone's concerns will be addressed expeditiously by the Surrogates Court, and that the sale of the apartment will not be affected."

"Is there a cloud on the title?" the invisible woman in the back continued.

"As of this moment there is no cloud on the title."

I had no idea frankly what that meant, but everyone certainly found it relevant as they all bent their heads and dutifully scribbled it down. It all sounded so calm and reassuring—Historic property! No clouds! Everything is being addressed expeditiously! I found myself feeling effortlessly confident, just standing there in a pretty dress and listening to it all. My peculiar and precarious life with everyone over there at the Edge seemed a million miles away.

"Is it true that one of the heirs is being harassed by the NYPD, at the request of one of the counter-claimants?" asked the Corduroy Jacket in the first row. Grossman nodded, all disappointed and concerned now, not wanting to spread the bad news in the middle of this elegant party. "One of the heirs, Christina Finn, is currently living in the apartment and she has experienced several harassing incidents," he admitted. "One specific incident is of particular concern as it seems that one of the counter-claimants, who is associated with the police department, used illegal influence to have Ms Finn arrested and held unlawfully in an attempt to intimidate and humiliate her." All of this was so bizarrely phrased that I didn't even know they were talking about me at first.

"Would you care to comment, Miss Finn?" Corduroy Jacket pursued. Everybody on stage turned to look at me. This is about when I got a clue. Daniel, who was standing next to me, gave me a little look under his new cool haircut, like *Tina, pay attention and don't fuck this up, please.*

"Oh," I said, stepping up quickly and unfortunately tripping slightly because I forgot for a moment that I was wearing heels. "I'm sorry, what's the question? What do I think of getting arrested? I think it sucks." Out of the corner of my eye I could see Lucy's smile stiffen slightly in annoyance but I was pretty sure that that was because I got the only laugh of the afternoon, and it was on my first line.

"Can you describe what happened?" Corduroy Jacket asked.

"Well," I started. Grossman had actually drilled a little speech into my head, in case this did come up, so I was not completely unprepared. Corduroy Jacket waited, expectant, with his crummy ballpoint in his left hand hovering over the narrow reporter's notebook in his right. The spill light from the stage hit him at a harsh angle, illuminating the lines of the wale in the dark brown corduroy and the furry edges of the suede patch on the elbow of his sleeve, and for a moment he almost looked like a statue hovering there with the light glistening off the wide place on his forehead where his hairline was receding. He wasn't even looking at me. That's what tipped me off, actually, the way he was waiting without looking, like he wasn't really all that curious, because he already knew the answer.

"I'm sorry," I said. "Who do you write for?"

Lucy actually turned her head at this. "Who do I write for?" asked Corduroy Jacket, surprised that he was being asked a question for once, apparently.

"No no, don't tell me, let me guess," I said. "You write for the city page of the *New York Times*, right?"

We were right there under the lights so Lucy couldn't snap, "What does it matter, Tina?" even under her breath. She just stood next to me and smiled, and she got a little perplexed look on her face, which she turned on both the audience and Grossman, like isn't my sister silly and adorable. But I was not feeling particularly silly and adorable at the moment; I was feeling more kind of like I'd been had.

"Yes, I write for the city page of the *New York Times*. Is that all right?" asked Corduroy Jacket, smug.

"No, sure, I'm sure that's sensational," I told him. "As far as being arrested, let me tell you, that was my fourth time, and honestly the other ones were a lot more spectacular. The one in Hoboken, in 2003? I actually slugged a cap. Although that was a complete misunderstanding so by comparison I'd give this one two stars. Although I did spend about eight hours in a holding cell, which is always a drag, even on the Upper West Side."

Corduroy Jacket nodded and wrote this down, smiling to himself. I got another laugh, but this one was a tad uncomfortable, as laughs go. Several flashes went off at once. Leonard leaned forward and spoke into the microphone, fluidly edging me the slightest bit out of the way with his shoulder.

"Are there more questions about the property itself?" he asked. Someone in another unlit corner raised her hand.

"What is it listing for?" she asked. And with that my part of the song and dance was for now over.

CHAPTER TWENTY

"Nice dress," said the note. That was all there was, the two words: "Nice dress."

"Where did this come from?" I asked Frank.

He glanced up from his copy of *Spanish People* magazine, but just barely.

"Vince Masterson, he came by for his mail and then he left that for you, said for to me to give it to you. He said you were on television." He went back to his magazine, but you could tell he wasn't really reading it. There were rings under his eyes and his uniform didn't quite fit him anymore. The corny epaulettes were hanging way too far over his shoulders as if he had somehow started to shrink inside it.

"Frank, are you okay?" I asked.

"Sure, I'm fine," he said, not much interested in the question. "I didn't get any sleep last night because my stupid brother was up watching wrestling on the television set and drinking beer until three in the morning. Other than that, no problem."

He didn't sound much like this was really no problem. There was no question that Frank was deteriorating.

"You look thin," I told him. "Your uniform's like falling off you, Frank."

"My uniform?" He looked down at the uniform, completely annoyed now, and seemingly surprised to discover that he was wearing anything at all. "It's not mine. Mine's at the dry cleaners. This is the extra one they keep in the storage closet."

"Yeah, but I'm not kidding, you look like you're not eating."

"Tina, you maybe should worry about yourself, huh?" Frank said, reminding me abruptly that my standing with the building was not sturdy enough for me to be asking him about whether or not he was eating properly. He went back to his magazine again, again not reading it. "Vince said to remind you he's up in 5B."

I could have ignored this summons from the problematic Vince Masterson and in fact it did cross my mind to do so but at the same time I was pretty curious about Frank's assertion that Vince had seen me on television. I knew there were news cameras there but the possibility that we would actually get on TV seemed pretty far-fetched to me. I mean, I know that New Yorkers are a little nutty about real estate, but is the sale of an apartment something that you would put on the evening news? Even a really nice apartment? It seemed unlikely. But at the same time I was a little relieved that someone in the building was actually inviting me over. I decided to go.

Apparently a press conference about real estate actually is big enough news to put on television, in New York City. New York One, the local public access news station, broacasts things like

312

continued coverage of city council meetings or roundtables about real estate developments in Brooklyn. They also broadcast strange and overwrought talk shows where slightly crazy-looking people scream at each other about off-Broadway theatre. This was actually the programme Vince and his eleven gay male friends were looking for when I showed up. It was the show they had been looking for when my turn in front of the cameras popped up for them.

"Well, we cheered, as you can imagine," Vince told me, pouring an icy and perfect vodka gimlet out of a silver bar shaker and expertly twisting a lime wedge over it. "I said, 'Wait wait wait, that's the *girl*, the one who's squatting in the fifteen-million-dollar apartment,' and no one believed me. And then you started talking about how many times you'd been arrested and you were wearing that incredible dress and I thought, What have you been up to, Tina, and why haven't you come by to visit me?"

"I've been busy," I said, taking my gimlet from him with both hands so that I could be careful not to spill it.

"So I gather, darling," Vince said, smiling at me. "Come and meet my friends!"

He took me by the hand and led me like a prize from the perfectly appointed black marble kitchen and into the equally well appointed living room of his father's apartment. The walls of this room—what you could see of them behind the floor-to-ceiling bookcases—were painted a deep maroon. There was an enormous blue and gold Turkish rug on the floor plus a leather couch, a coffee table, coffee-table books, two dark brown leather chairs and eleven gay men. Which would have been intimidating in any room but was particularly daunting in this one because in contrast to my apartment, which was cavernous and fascinating and incoherent, Vince's father's apartment was gorgeous, coherent, and quite small.

"We're so excited to meet you. Vince has told us all about you," one of the gay men announced, standing and reaching out to shake my hand.

"Not everything, I hope," I said, trying to laugh at this and feeling completely out of my element. I took a sip of my gimlet. It was, no surprise, perfect.

"That dress is amazing. Is it a Chanel? It looks antique," said a second.

"It's pretty old," I said. "But not Chanel. The tag says Ballen-something."

"Oh my God, it's Balenciaga," someone sighed. "Of course it is."

"Where did you find it?" asked a fourth.

"In a closet," I said, wondering how long I might be able to just tell the truth to these guys and get away with it.

"And the alligator clutch was just tucked away in there as well? Look at this, Lyle. How much is this worth?" A fifth gay man took it from my hand and held it up, waving it to someone across the room.

"Stop it!" said Lyle, making his way over to eye the clutch.

"You were hilarious at that press conference," said a sixth. "Have you really been arrested?"

"Yes," I said.

"Could someone show some manners here?" said a seventh. "Hi, my name's Jonathan." This one stopped while he was shaking my hand, put his arm around me and steered me toward one of

314

the chairs. "Could one of you ladies be a gentleman and offer her a seat?" Two more of them leapt up and offered me one of the leather chairs. I sat down and they took my shoes off, handed me gimlets and we watched the recording of the Sotheby's press conference six times. Every time I announced, on the television, "The one in Hoboken, in 2003? I actually slugged a cap," everybody cheered, and then when I said, "So by comparison I'd give this one two stars," they cheered again. I do think that most of them were a little bit drunk—I certainly was, after my second gimlet—but mostly they were just kind of fun and excitable and happy to have me at their party.

"Vincent says your place is completely gorgeous, twelve-foot ceilings and marble arches and mirrors everywhere and thousands and thousands of square footage galore," said one of them.

"That's actually pretty accurate," I admitted. "Except the arches aren't marble, they're more that kind of dark red wood."

"Cherry?" asked another.

"Walnut," Vince observed, and three of these guys moaned, like walnut doorframes were some especially appealing kind of pornography.

"Yeah, they're pretty nice," I admitted. "Can I have one of those?" There was a bag of fancy potato chips behind Jonathan's arm, on the floor.

"Absolutely. Have you not eaten?" he said, handing the bag over.

"Sotheby's didn't feed you? Shame on them," Vince tossed over his shoulder. He headed to the kitchen with the authority of someone who knew there was really good food in there, but then all he came back with was a cell phone. "How about sushi?"

he asked, dialing. People murmured some kind of assent but he wasn't really paying attention to them; he was already talking to some underling. "Hi, I'm over at the Edgewood and we're going to need a couple platters," he announced. "Just some of those big ones that you do. Tell the chef Omikase is fine. Oh, and some of those little fried chicken appetizers. Do people want Japanese fried chicken?" he asked the room. Then he went right back to the phone without waiting for an answer. "Just bring some of the fried chicken," he ordered.

"Christ, he is such a young god," Jonathan said under his breath. I looked over at him and watched him watch Vince with a kind of deeply amused wonder. Vince was leaning in the doorway with his head down, listening to the guy at the sushi joint repeat back his chaotic order, and then he turned, untucking his pale blue Oxford shirt from his dark blue wool trousers, like it was suddenly too hot or something. Oblivious to the fact that every guy in the room was staring at him—or maybe not so oblivious—Vince tapped the phone off and headed back into the kitchen. "Twenty minutes," he called back to us.

"Ooo la la," someone sighed. "I need a cigarette. I'm going out on the balcony. Tina, do you want to come?"

"Vince has a balcony?" I asked, strangely enticed and distracted by this.

"It isn't a balcony; it's a fire escape, darling," my new friend informed me. "Although I like the competitive nature of the question. Come on, let me show you Vincent's apartment. His father's apartment, that is," he said casually loudly so that Vince, returning from the kitchen, could hear all the way across the room. Vince wagged a finger in our direction, which made everyone laugh although it was a pretty edgy joke to say the least. I didn't have time to really register how annoyed Vince was, though, as my guide was already narrating in my ear.

"I know he hates that but, please, how many people get to live in the Edge for free? He should just count his blessings, of which he has *quite a few*," he observed. "Check out the closet. He has a walk-in *closet* which is bigger than my entire apartment, and look at this. Somebody painted the woodwork sage. It's genius, don't you think?"

"I do," I said. It was really relaxing listening to this stranger blather on. He had the same attitude all these gay guys seemed to have: even though we had never before met, he assumed a level of complete understanding between us which was surprisingly accurate considering the fact that I was still having trouble remembering his name.

As it turns out, the apartments on the fifth floor had been subdivided three times since the building was built, which meant that Vince's dad's apartment really was only four rooms—a bedroom, a living room, a den and a kitchen, plus the bath—which were all really rather small, even though the walk-in closet was, as my new friend (whose name turned out to be Andrew) noted, quite large. The bedroom had a sleekly square king-size bed in it which took up virtually the entire space, except for the three feet in front of an enormous flat-screen television which was screwed into the wall like a giant piece of pop art. And the bathroom was a thing of beauty. Pink and Italian tile rose up the walls and framed an actual jacuzzi which was tucked neatly into a corner so that unlike the bed in the next room it didn't take over the entire space, although it threatened to.

"A jacuzzi," I breathed. I suddenly felt completely exhausted. "A jacuzzi."

"Right?" Andrew asked, as if I had said something profound. "And he's mad because his father hasn't put the lease in his name. I'm going, *taxes*? It's not in your name so who pays the property taxes, you could also look at it that way . . . Oh, look what I've found!" He plucked something off the bottom shelf of the tiniest little teak cabinet you've ever seen, which stood next to the pedestal sink. "This looks like a bottle of bubble bath that has your name on it. Look, it says 'Tina Finn', right here," he announced, waving it madly in the air and leaning over to turn on the faucets.

I admit that it's a little crazy that I took off my dress and got in that hot tub, but by that point I was so tired and drunk on vodka gimlets it seemed like a good idea. The bubbles smelled like lavender and the jacuzzi jets were whipping them into a complete state of frenzy and those guys were being so nice to me. At first it was just Andrew, who as I said simply started filling the tub as if the whole thing were a done deal, and then Scott with the silver hair came in to use the bathroom, but then he immediately got into the spirit of the thing and started running around looking for towels. Then Lyle (short) and Roger (buzz cut) showed up, reporting that Dave and Edward *and* Christopher were *all* in love with Vince and he was driving everyone crazy and he just didn't want to watch it anymore. So they were just coming back to say goodbye and then take off, but then they thought that having a jacuzzi with Tina sounded like fun, so they decided they would stick around but that we all needed another round of drinks. While they were getting the drinks the sushi arrived, which they brought back to us along with the drinks, and then everyone took turns getting in and out of the jacuzzi but I didn't have to because for some reason they all really thought of me as somebody truly special who deserved for one night to be treated like a queen.

And they wanted to know everything. All of it. Every time I would start to explain, it would turn out that I just wasn't telling near enough. They kept telling me to back up.

"Okay, back up," said Andrew. "Let's start at the beginning. Your mother died—"

"Yes, they said that on television. You know that."

"No, back up beyond that," said Scott, slightly abrupt. You didn't take it wrong, though, because it was kind of just his manner. "Where were you when she died?"

"I was out at the Delaware Water Gap—"

"The Delaware *Water* Gap? Why?" Scott demanded.

"I had this boyfriend. He had this idea that we would you know clean houses—"

"He had you cleaning houses? Back up," said Lyle.

"It was more supposed to be like caretakers to rich people who had houses out there. But he didn't have it worked out."

"Back *up*. What do you mean it wasn't worked out?" Lyle held his hand out to silence the other three, so that he could get the information he wanted about old stupid Darren.

"Well, you know, he didn't know anybody out there, we went out there and there was no place to even rent an apartment because there just wasn't, so we ended up renting this trailer—"

"You went from living in a trailer to living in the Edge?" said Roger, clearly entranced by the magic of this.

"Don't rush her. We're not there yet!" Scott interrupted. "So then your mother died."

"Yes. My mother died."

"And when was this?" he continued.

"It was, you know, about two months ago."

"Two months?" someone murmured. "It was just two months ago?"

"It was just two months ago? Oh, sweetie. Oh, Tina. That's such a loss." All of them were silent for a moment, thinking about what a loss it is, to lose a mother. And it did seem like that, suddenly. For the first time since it happened, I knew that I was talking to people who wanted to hear about my mom.

"It was," I said. "It really was. But the fact is, I had already lost her! I hadn't seen her in so long. Years. I hadn't seen her in years."

"So you lost her twice," said Andrew, mourning that double loss quietly, with the question.

"I lost her so long ago, even before that," I admitted. "She started drinking when I was in high school. And it wasn't her fault."

"Spoken like the true daughter of an alcoholic. I see some Al-Anon meetings in your future, darling," Scott observed.

"I don't mind that she drank," I said. "It didn't make her mean or anything, it just made her kind of dopey. Honestly, I thought it made her feel better. Nobody was really very nice to her. My father was a nightmare, he was just so hideous."

"Did he hit her? Did he hit you?"

"He hit everybody," I admitted. Somehow, soaking in a tubful of bubbles, surrounded by nice gay men, that turned out to be not so hard to say.

"Did he drink too?"

"Well sure, he always drank. He drank a lot of beer. Her drink was vodka."

"God I love vodka," said Roger with a sort of spiritual sigh.

"Okay, so he was always a drinker, and then she started when you were in high school," Lyle narrated, making sure we were all on the same page.

"Yes," I said.

"It happens like that sometimes," said Andrew, the compassionate realist. "People don't know they have options and so they get dragged into it."

"Is anyone worried that we're all sitting here getting smashed while we talk about Tina's tragic and clearly alcoholic parents who both died terribly young? They died terribly young, right?" said Scott, the less compassionate realist.

"My father died in a car crash when I was twenty," I admitted. "He was forty-seven or something."

"Did you cheer?"

"No, nobody cheered. Everybody just sort of pretended this was all so sad," I remembered. "It was weird. Lucy and Alison and I were all out of the house by then—"

"You were in college," Scott supplied.

"No, I dropped out of college."

"You *dropped* out of *college*?" Roger exclaimed, as if this were really astonishing.

"Let her *finish*," said Lyle.

321

"Yeah, so I was living with, I guess I was living with this guy," I fumbled.

"Darren?" suggested Roger.

"No, a different guy. There are—several—different guys," I admitted.

"I'm sure," Scott nodded.

"Anyway Lucy and Alison—Alison wasn't married yet, so it was just the three of us. And we came back and after the funeral—there was like a little thing at the house, after the funeral." I had a terrible moment as I realized that we had a little party for my oh so shitty father, and we didn't have one for Mom. But I didn't want to stop and fill in all the ironic extra details anymore; as nice as these guys really were, I was afraid that suddenly I might drown. "Anyway, there were neighbors and some friends of his from his work, and we had like, we had—casseroles, people brought food and stood around, you know, wearing black clothes, in the house. We lived in a little duplex, one of those places that has aluminum siding on it, it was pretty nice, Mom always kept it clean. And so people were there, after the funeral, talking about how it was such a shame and what a relief that he didn't suffer, and and—then you know they all left. And Mom was drinking by then, it was like one in the afternoon and she was totally just—but she didn't ever show it, she would sort of just go into the kitchen when no one was there, and then come out with something that looked like a glass of grape juice or orange juice like pretending that that's all it was, so that she never said, 'Oh I need another drink,' she would just disappear and then come back and then eventually she would fall asleep. She would, honestly. She would lie her head down on the table and say, "No

322

matter what you do, it's never enough." I used to hate her for that. I did, I hated her. Because it was so self-pitying. She was such a quitter. So Alison and Lucy and I—she kept disappearing into the kitchen, so we all assumed she was going to just pass out, and we were getting ready to take off. Alison had put all the dishes in the dishwasher and it was running and we were leaving. And then Mom was, she just showed up in the doorway and said, 'Can you take that out of here?'" I couldn't believe I was remembering all this. I was just sitting there in all those bubbles and it seemed so clear to me, like a movie playing in my head. "And we didn't know what she'was talking about. But she sort of lifted her hand just a little because she was really drunk; she was, she was just smashed—" Okay, and then I did start crying, that just seemed like the worst detail of the whole story, that she was that drunk. "And she was pointing at his chair. He had this chair, it was so ugly, this brown plaid Barca-lounger thing that he would just, he sat there all the time and got drunk and watched stupid sports on television and it was like *him*. It was just *him*. And she said it, she didn't have to ask twice, we knew what she was asking. Just, get that *thing* out of here. Which we did, the three of us, we just went over and picked up that horrible chair and took it to the front door and I don't know how we got it out but we did, we took it out to the kerb and left it there. And it sat out there for like a week and a half and then the garbage men finally got tired of ignoring it I guess because then it was finally gone. It was just gone. Like him. Like no one could explain how it finally happened that we were all just—free."

Andrew poured some more vodka gimlet into my glass. He had a little shaker tucked by the side of the jacuzzi, on the floor.

"Thank you," I said, clutching the slippery glass. It made me concentrate hard enough so that I could actually stop sobbing, which was a relief.

"Why didn't she leave him?" Roger asked, after a short moment while we all pondered all of it. "That's what I don't understand. Honestly, what is the point of sticking *around*."

"She had three little kids," I offered, as if that answered the question. I was aware as soon as I said it that it answered nothing at all, but I was too exhausted and embarrassed and drunk by then to cop to the inadequacy of my own opinions.

"Did you inherit those pearls?" asked Scott.

"The pearls?" I felt my hand creep up to my neck, to make sure they were still there, although I could feel them laying heavy against my neck. Scott raised an eyebrow at me. He was sitting on the floor now, draped with a towel, and he looked a little like Zeus or Apollo or some severe god who was not going to be easily fooled by mere mortals.

"Yes, the pearls, Tina. Don't look so guilty," he commented. "Did you steal them?"

"Did I *steal* them?"

"Goodness, you sound so paranoid! I was joking. I just wanted to know where you got them. You know they have to be worth a fortune. Is that a Melo pearl in the clasp? How much are those worth?" Scott turned to Lyle, who was apparently some sort of expert on all things women wore.

"If you have to ask, you can't afford it," Lyle said, without seeming to notice the questions inside the question. "Although I will note that the clutch is a Rue Jacob and probably worth at least fifteen thousand. Does anyone want this last piece of sushi?"

"Fifteen—come on, for just the purse?" I asked.

"Well, that's probably what you'd pay for it, in a vintage couture shop. You wouldn't get that if you sold it. You'd get maybe five."

"And the pearls?"

"You really want to know?" Lyle said, getting closer to asking with his eyebrows what on earth I was doing wearing them if I didn't even know what they were worth.

"I just borrowed them," I said, sliding down a little further in the bubbles. The steam in the room was making everyone a little pink, so no one could see me blush. I am occasionally an accomplished liar but I didn't feel like lying to these guys. They cared enough about me to respect the truth, which made it hard. "Isn't that funny?" I thought.

"What's funny, Tina?" asked Andrew, gently. I looked at him, surprised that I had spoken the words aloud, like in one of those dreams where you can't tell the difference between what you are thinking and what you are saying.

"It's funny that Lucy and Alison are so easy to lie to, but you're not," I said. "I don't even know you. Shouldn't it be the other way around?"

Before this could lead to any more truth telling, however, our steam-filled reverie was interrupted.

"Tina Finn, in a hot tub wearing pearls, surrounded by men," said a sardonic voice. "Be still my heart." Everyone looked up, and there was Vince, his shirt hanging open as usual, lounging in the doorway. While it was true that I had been sitting in that hot tub surrounded by men and bubbles for a good twenty minutes, no one had even glanced at me that entire time with anything more intrusive than good-natured kindness or drunken bonhomie. Vince's lust curled and snapped through the room like a whip. I knew he couldn't see a thing below my breastbone because the bubbles, having been frothed up by the water jets, were insanely thorough by this point. But for the first time all night I felt naked.

"Go away, Vince," I said. "We're having a good time."

"I can see that," he returned. "I can't believe I've missed all the fun."

But it wasn't fun anymore. I looked up at him slouching in that doorway, thinking about having sex with me, and he looked like Darren hanging there, or Ed Featherstone, or Brendan Dineen, or half a dozen other guys I let myself get swallowed up by. I looked over at Roger and Lyle and they were rolling their eyes at each other; there's no mistaking a guy in heat, and if you're not the one he's gunning for you may as well not be in the room. Our little cabal had turned into some sort of hot fantasy for Vince. As far as the rest of us were concerned, the fun was over.

"Well, we were just taking off," Lyle announced. "It's great to meet you, Tina. Take care of those pearls. Those are a treasure. And so are you." He leaned over and kissed me on the cheek, dropping his towel carelessly as he did. He truly was somebody who spent a lot of time at the gym so there was no reason not to be bold at a moment like that. Scott and Andrew cheered. "Have a good look, girls," Lyle said, raising his arms with a little flourish as he squeezed by Vince. Roger, who was a little shorter and stouter, held onto his towel, but he kissed me too.

"Bye, Tina. Be a good girl," he said. And he gave me a little look, like there was no need to say anything about my past in this moment but there was also no need to pretend that I didn't have one. Scott and Andrew were collecting their clothes as well. I reached out and kind of grabbed Andrew's wet fingers, and he lifted my hand to his mouth, kissing it sweetly while he raised an eyebrow at me. Vince watched the mass exodus of gay men with a smirk; there was no question in his mind that he was going to get a turn with me in the hot tub. And then the retreating Roger threw me a lifeline. "Are Dave and Edward still here?" he called, from the next room.

This clipped Vince, right across the back of the neck. He turned, caught out somehow, and his face got all thoughtful, like he really cared about whether or not Dave and Edward were still there. "Yeah, they're in the kitchen, cleaning up, with Jonathan," he called back. There were loose towels everywhere by this point, and I had one in my hand before he had time to turn back.

"You're not getting out?" he asked, petulant, as he slid into the bathroom and closed the door. "Come on, I just got here." There was a kind of spoiled and wicked glint in his eye and his bare chest seemed to immediately glisten as it came in contact with the humidity in there. There was no question that was a dangerous, soggy moment, or at the very least it was a moment when one's weaknesses for hot, problematic men might be tested. The one thought that kept me from just doing something stupid was in fact that last sentence that good-hearted Roger had flung over his shoulder just before Vince shut the bathroom door.

"What's the story with Dave and Edward? I hear they're both in love with you," I said. Vince cocked his head, amused somewhat, and definitely checked in his approach. It gave me enough room to wrap myself in that towel and step out onto the tiles. I wobbled a little, as the floor was slippery and I was drunk— a little less drunk, fortunately, since Vince had arrived and put a straight male damper on things—but class training triumphed. Vince reached out, a perfect gentleman, and steadied me.

"Who told you that?" he asked.

"Roger and Lyle. They say that half the party is in love with you. Is it possible that you have not told those nice boys which side of the fence you fall on?" I asked.

"Not that it's any of your business, Tina, but Dave and Edward and some of the other men here have a fair amount of disposable income that they are considering investing with me. It doesn't have anything to do with fences. Or falling. You look very fetching, wearing nothing but pearls." He was hovering over me and that thing had happened, where I just fit so neatly into the curve of his arm it seemed inevitable that we were going to just end up having sex on the floor any second. His arm was curling down my naked back, and his mouth was closing in on mine. Honestly it was not the kind of situation I heretofore would have even tried to resist, but my loyalties were not to my past at this moment.

"Vince—I'm not going to have sex with you in your bathroom while you have guests in the next room, who you are by the way conning into thinking you're gay so that you can get them to give you money," I informed him. His face was right up against mine so I literally had to whisper it into his ear. "It's not going to happen, Vince. I like those guys. You shouldn't fuck around with them." I wobbled again, and wheeled myself around on my toes, grabbing onto the front of his shirt as I did. For a second he thought he was going to get lucky even though I was telling him he wasn't, but then he realized I had just repositioned myself so I could grab my dress and scoot out the door.

Which is what I did. In the bedroom Lyle and Roger and Scott had already finished dressing and moved back to the living room and the kitchen to rejoin the party which was still in process. But Andrew was there, pulling his ash-colored cashmere crew neck over his head carefully, so that it didn't stretch. He looked up and smiled at me and reached out for my dress, which I handed to him. I finished drying myself off, and let Andrew help me slip the dress back on, and then we crawled around the floor looking for my underwear and my stockings and my heels, which I had dropped carelessly in corners when I took them off. And then Andrew helped me slip them on as well, and neither of us said a thing about the fact that Vince was watching the whole operation from the door of the bathroom. You can watch all you want, I thought; this is as close as you're going to get to me, or Sophie's dress, or Sophie's pearls.

CHAPTER TWENTY-ONE

After I kissed all those nice boys goodbye, I went back to my beautiful and empty apartment and crawled into a T-shirt and then crawled into my little bed on the floor, and I had a dream. It was not a very subtle dream. I was back out at the Delaware Water Gap, standing in front of my trailer, and there was no one there. The wind was blowing the few trees around so violently that they looked like they might come down. I knew there was a terrible storm coming and so I looked around for Alison and Lucy and Mom, but I couldn't see them anywhere, so I ran into the middle of the trailer park to see if I could find them. You could see people in all the other trailers but they were just moving around inside them, you didn't know who they were, and every now and then one of them came to the door to look at me and wave me back, everyone wanted me to go back to my trailer. One lady started to yell at me and point, and I looked at where she was pointing and I could see a tornado coming, a real tornado with the funnel cloud that reached all the way down to the earth, and it was maybe not even half a mile away, it was coming right at us. She kept waving her arms like you have to go home, you have to get to safety, and so I ran back to the trailer, even though I knew no one was there and that a trailer is the last place you wanted to be during a tornado. I kept thinking you should just get down on the ground, Tina, get down, that's the only chance you'll have. But when I looked in the door of the trailer I thought there was someone there, maybe Alison or Lucy or Mom had come back, and I needed to get them and hide them with me in the ground. So I went into that terrible old plywood and aluminum trailer, and I looked inside, where it was empty and dark, and there was no one there, and then the tornado hit and I knew it was too late for me and everybody.

Which of course woke me up. I sat upright, my heart pounding the way it does when a nightmare is so upsetting that it shocks you awake, and for a terrible second I didn't know where I was. That room is usually so dark, but for some reason light coming from somewhere was spilling all down the sunset painting on the wall and then I heard someone crying, like a child, long miserable sobs, and I didn't know if was me or the dream or the ghost or someone breaking into my apartment; honestly it was disorienting as hell. So I held onto my heart, trying to force it to slow the fuck down, and then I turned to at least see where the light was coming from, because I thought that might get me to wake up the rest of the way, and then everything would be all right. So I turned and looked at the door, thinking I just forgot to turn off the hall light, that the hall light would be the explanation for everything, and there was someone there. Standing in the doorway. A child, in a night-gown, holding a club. And she was real.

"Oh my *God*," I said. "Holy *shit*. Jesus God above, what do you want? Oh my God." I don't think I've ever been so scared in my life. Truly. Over the past two months my mother had died, I'd been invaded, I'd been arrested, I'd met a ghost—and nothing tossed me into complete unblinking terror the way that kid standing there with a club did. I crept up the wall, hoping that it would swallow me up and protect me from this unholy escape from a horror flick. It didn't. But rather than enter the room swinging, the kid just stood there and sobbed.

"What do you want?" I said. "Seriously. Seriously. What do you want?"

"You didn't come back!" the kid wailed. "Why didn't you come back?" And then she just stood there, and sobbed even harder.

"Katharine?" I said. She stood there and cried, and then she dropped the club on the floor. It was in fact a flashlight and not a club; another crazy beam of light careened through the room and caught the wall, then the painting, then me in the face. But by this time I was up out of the bed and across the floor. I scooped her up and held her while she cried.

"It's okay, it's okay," I said, while my heart tried to find something approximating a normal rhythm again. "How did you get here?"

"You said you'd come back and you didn't come back," she told me. "And Jennifer won't get out of bed."

"Jennifer won't get out of bed? Why not?" I said, trying to act like this was even a vaguely normal situation while I figured it out.

"She's sad," Katharine told me. "Because you didn't come back."

333

Working as best I could on the shreds of information the unhappy girl could choke out between sobs, I picked up the flashlight and headed toward the front of the apartment. "You said you would come get us," Katharine accused me. "You said we could see your apartment."

"So now, because you are so brave and impatient, you get to see it," I said cheerfully, flicking on the lights as I passed through rooms and hallways. "You are right. I was just too busy and I didn't come back and I promised I would, so now I will show you *everything*. Did you tell your mom where you were going?" I presumed the answer to this would in fact be no, and I was already trying to figure out what on earth I was going to tell Mrs White when I presented her errant daughter to her in the middle of the night.

"How come there's no furniture?" asked Katharine, looking around. "How come the secret room has all the furniture but there's none out here?"

I stopped, and looked at her. "How do you know about the secret room, Katharine?" I asked. She looked back at me, plain, while I figured it out. "Is that how you got in?" I was standing in the great room now, and I could see, in the moonlight, all my locks were securely fastened. "You came in through the secret room, through the trap door!" I exclaimed, like this was the smartest thing I ever heard of, giving her a little poke. She giggled, finally relaxing. "How did you get the trap door open?" I asked.

"We carved a hole in it," she said. "Do you want to see?"

"I do, actually," I said. "I think I would like to see that, a lot."

So I turned around and carried Katharine back through the

hallways and rooms, to the far end of the apartment, as far back as you can get from the front, where the door to the lost room stood ajar, which was not how I had left it.

"Did you open the door?" I asked her.

"I had a flashlight," she said, as if this explained everything.

"Didn't the ghost scare you?" I asked. "I mean, she's not saying anything now"—it was true; she had fallen quite silent—"but sometimes she's really loud."

"That's not a ghost, that's a person," Katharine told me. "She lives in Mrs Westmoreland's apartment."

"How do you know?" I asked.

"Jennifer said it. She figured it out when she was trying to make the hole."

The kid was a fount of information. She led me into the darkened room, past the plundered cardboard boxes, and up to the far wall where a cupboard had been jammed open, barely. Because so many boxes had been stacked in front of it, I hadn't found it yet. "Look," said Katharine. "It's just steps." And sure enough, it was exactly as Louise had suspected so many weeks before: the narrowest of stairways turned and rose within the wall itself.

"Wow," I said. "That is amazing. So you guys worked the plug out?"

"Jennifer did it."

"And how did you get this one open?"

"I just pushed it."

"Did Jennifer help you?"

"Jennifer's in bed."

"Yeah, you said that before," I remembered.

"Can you come talk to her?"

"Well, it's kind of late," I reminded her.

"She's really sad," Katharine informed me again, her eyes wide. "She keeps getting yelled at."

"Why?" I asked. This was not sounding so good.

"Because she won't get out of bed," Katharine reiterated. "*Never*. You have to come *now*."

"All right, all right," I agreed. "You have to go back to bed anyway." Now that I realized how the kid had gotten there, the need to get her back without anyone realizing she was gone in the first place seemed pretty paramount. I most certainly did not want her mother, or her notoriously reactive father for that matter, to stick her or his head in the door to Katharine's room and find her gone into a hole in the floor which in fact led directly into my apartment. I just did not for one moment think that would end up being a good situation for anyone, especially given the increasingly worrisome whispers about the building and its attitude toward me and my mother. Obviously I was not the one who had cracked open the stupid crawlspace, but this whole situation might look alarmingly like I was the one doing the breaking and entering into the Whites' apartment, to someone who was inclined to look at it that way. And I have had enough run-ins with the law to know that appearances matter. I looked up the shaft of the dumbwaiter and then looked back at Katharine, formulating the shred of a plan. "Listen," I said. "Don't tell anybody about this, okay? For right now this has to be a secret, and if your mommy finds out about it we're both going to be in big trouble."

"Why?" said Katharine.

"I don't know, kid. That's just the way it is sometimes," I admitted. "We got to get you back up there and plug the hole back up and then think about this."

The stairs, made of ancient red brick, were curled, claustrophobic and vertical; your hands had to grab onto the steps above you. You could hear and feel small living things moving around that didn't want to know you, and that you didn't want to know. Some of them were not, frankly, so small. I remembered from some grade school history class that people in New York in the nineteenth century didn't have enough milk and so they died young and were really short, which is doubtless how those dead Victorian workmen who used these stairs even managed to fit in there. They also lived in tenements where there were like sixteen people in one hideously squashed room, which is why climbing up terrifying and claustrophobic hidden staircases must have seemed to them like a normal thing to do. Or maybe it's just that being poor in any century sucks and the rule is if you have no money you just have to always do impossible things to survive. Anyway climbing up that walled-up crawlspace certainly seemed impossible, and by the time I tumbled through the hole in the wall onto the floor of Katharine's closet I had broken out into a cold sweat.

"That's kind of scary," I admitted. I glanced back up at the thin snap of the stairwell as it wound its narrow way up the inside of the building and saw the disappearing shape of an enormous rat slowly meandering up above us. "WHOA," I said, then tried too late not to be so loud. "Wow. Whoa, there's, that's scary."

"You said that twice," Katharine noticed.

337

"That's because it's really actually pretty fucking scary," I said. "I know, I owe you a dollar. So. How does this work?" I asked, looking at the wooden slab which Jennifer had somehow crowbarred out of the wall. It was surprisingly heavy. I shoved it in place, carefully. It didn't actually fit into the hole.

"That's not right," Katharine observed.

"Well, show me how," I told her. But she just stood there.

"It's not right," she said. I went back to pull it out again, and reset it into the wall, but the thing of course was stuck now. On one side, several gouge marks revealed where Jennifer had located its weak spot and managed to pry it out, but because I had shoved it back improperly the handhold was now apparently useless.

"You just pull it," Katharine said, yawning. Which I did, I pulled it about twenty times, twenty different ways. Nothing happened.

"Come on, Katharine. You have to show me how," I repeated hopelessly.

"You push it," she said this time, lying on the floor.

"Don't go to sleep. I'm not kidding, I have to go home. You have to show me how to open it. Katharine, open it. Open it." This whole situation just got worse and worse. If she didn't get the thing open, I realized, I was stuck there for good. I could sneak out the front door and take the elevator down to my own apartment but it was locked from the inside, as I well knew. Or I could go back to Vince's apartment, but that move would bring its own problems. I needed to get back down in that crawl space.

"Come on, Katharine, you got to open it for me. Katharine," I hissed, shaking her shoulder.

She looked at me, dopy with sleep. "Jennifer knows how to do it," she yawned. "She's the one who figured it out."

I knew where Jennifer's bedroom was three weeks ago, when I babysat for the Whites, but in the middle of the night and with only the occasional nightlight at floor level as my guide, getting there wasn't the simplest trick to navigate. I took two wrong turns, one of which landed me in the psychotically pink bedroom of the middle-school monsters, both of whom were sacked out and snoring. The other wrong turn brought me perilously close to barging in on Mr and Mrs White themselves, but as I was about to carefully turn the knob on their bedroom door I heard someone moving around, and then Mrs White asked some sort of question, and Mr White answered. A light went on and I nearly cursed aloud, but instead I just took a quick step backward and gave thanks to the crazy genius who invented wall-to-wall carpet. The Whites continued to mumble back and forth to each other as I looked around, got my bearings and headed in the opposite direction one more time, finally locating Jennifer's bedroom at the far end of the next hallway.

Jennifer's bedroom was both adorable and disturbing. Like in Katharine's room the walls had been painted a glowing yellow, and there were again stuffed animals everywhere. But then in the middle of the room there was an enormous bed with a white canopy, and the carpet was a dark and terrifying red.

I crept silently across the blood-red sea of carpeting and knelt down next to the bed, in which Jennifer quite frankly looked like a sleeping princess. "Hey, Jennifer," I whispered. "Wake up. Wake up." She didn't move for a moment. I reached over and touched her shoulder. "Jennifer."

"I'm *awake*," she announced, completely annoyed. I was so startled by the degree to which she really was awake that I jumped a little bit and almost tipped over.

"Well, why didn't you say something?" I asked.

"What are you *doing* here?" she replied, with the authority of somebody who knows she has the better question. "It's the middle of the *night*."

"Katharine opened the door to the crawlspace and came down into my apartment," I told her. Jennifer turned her head a little bit and smiled at this, but still didn't move. "When did you figure out how to open it?"

"A while ago," she said, seemingly losing interest all of a sudden. "I was going to tell you about it. But then you never came back."

"Well, I'm here now, and I closed the door, and I can't get it open again. You have to show me how to do it," I told her.

"Why?"

"So I can get home!" I whispered. "Why do I have to explain this? What's going to happen if your parents find me hanging out in your apartment in the middle of the night?"

"They'll be pissed off," she mused, only vaguely interested in the question. "Or they won't even notice."

"Well, I would prefer it if they didn't notice," I said. "Come on, help me get home. Come on."

She looked at me, and a little spark came back in her eyes. "You were on television. Everybody's mad at you," she informed me. "You're in trouble."

"What else is new?" I sighed. "I'm not kidding, Jennifer. You have to get out of that bed and help me get that dumbwaiter open. We have to do it. Now, right now."

340

"We're all in trouble," she observed, and looked back up at the ceiling.

This is about when this improbable situation started to make some sort of strange sense to me. She was just so non-reactive, as if neighbors routinely showed up at her bedside in the middle of the night. There was definitely a disconnect between event and reaction. And she had the peculiar nocturnal coherence of the chronic non-sleeper. "Katharine says you won't get out of bed," I noted.

She continued to stare at the ceiling. "I get out of bed," she informed me. "I go to school. I come home, and I get back in bed."

"Your mom lets you do that?"

"My mom," she noted, with an evil sardonic edge. "My *mom*?"

I wanted to pick her up and carry her home with me, but I knew that that would not be an effective choice of action. "Jennifer," I said. I let my hand creep up onto the covers and find her fingertips. "Sweetheart, you're depressed. You need help."

"What do you know," she said.

Behind us, a door opened and closed, somewhere else in the apartment. I looked over my shoulder just in time to see the hall light flip on, then shadows rippled across the floor where the light spilled in from the hallway, then the doorknob started to turn. "Shit," I said, and I rolled under her bed just as the door swung open.

"Hey, are you awake?" the hideous Louise asked, peremptory. When Jennifer didn't answer, she asked it again. "Jennifer," she insisted. "Are you awake?"

"If I don't answer why would you ask again?" Jennifer noted, reasonably. "Are you *trying* to wake me up?"

"I asked again because I knew you were awake," Louise observed, unimpressed by Jennifer's reasonable logic.

"Then why did you ask?"

"I heard voices. Who are you talking to?" Louise's question was fluted with suspicion. All I could see from my hiding place was the tail end of a frilly pink-and-white-striped nightgown and her bare feet, which made their way into the room and stopped, then turned and moved out of my field of vision again. I heard a door swing open.

"What are you doing? Are you looking in my *closet*?" Jennifer asked. I was pretty nervous down there under the bed but honestly it felt better to hear her yell at her sister than to watch her lie there like she couldn't bear to sit up and breathe.

"I heard *voices*, Jennifer. I know what I heard. There's someone in here with you." The feet were back in sight and the hem of the nightgown started to lower, as good old Louise, who was starting to seem like the teenage girl version of the Stasi, was in fact bending over to look under the bed.

"Get *out* of here, you freak!" Jennifer suddenly snarled. Her feet appeared by the side of the bed as well, as she inserted herself between me and certain discovery, actually shoving her older sister aside.

"Hey!" Louise snapped. "You are, you're hiding something!"

"You are not the boss of me, Louise!" Jennifer informed her. "MOM!" Okay, this was a little further than I was hoping Jennifer would go in any attempt to protect me, but I was hardly calling the shots at this point. Besides, Mrs White appeared in the room so quickly that it was probable that she had heard the argument and was already on her way to check it out, so I don't know that Jennifer put anything in motion that would not have happened anyway.

"What is going on in here? It's the middle of the night!" Mrs White announced.

"I heard her talking to someone," Louise started.

"She is crazy! I was just in here sleeping!" Jennifer snapped.

"I heard someone. There's someone in here with her," the insanely persistent Louise repeated, but the illogic of her frankly true statement undid her.

"That is ridiculous," Mrs White informed her. "Go back to your room, Louise, and both of you go back to sleep. Honestly. Your father is going to be really angry if he has to come in here, and then we'll all have to deal with it. Go to bed." Her feet stayed in the doorway while she waited for Louise to sullenly drag herself back to her room, and then the door swung shut behind them both. After an excruciatingly long moment of silence, Jennifer's blonde hair swung down over the edge of the bed, and I saw her forehead and then her eyes and then the rest of her face make an appearance. She held her finger up to her upside-down mouth.

Why is it that taking care of other people makes us feel better? The listless despair had evaporated, and she was a different person; her eyes were alert with the delight of keeping my presence there a secret, and then the prospect of getting me home without being discovered by the wearisome Louise was suddenly a fantastic adventure to be had. We waited in alert silence for a full fifteen minutes before she crept out into the hallway, passed

343

by Louise's closed door, passed back again, waited to see if she were awake and reactive, and then when she proved not to be, waved to me in the half light of the hallway to come and follow her. She then led me with assurance through the maze of hallways to the back room of the sleeping apartment, where we found Katharine where I had left her, sleeping on the floor. While Jennifer closed the door behind us, I picked up Katharine and put her back in her bed.

"So how do you get this thing open?" I asked, tipping my head at that blasted plugged up hole in the wall.

"It's really not very hard," she informed me, with a trace of her former arrogance. And sure enough, she squeezed her fingers into the right side of the squared-off piece of wood set into the wall and yanked. The recalcitrant piece of wood popped out as if she had ordered it to. The entire operation took maybe six seconds.

"Wow, that is pretty easy," I agreed.

We both looked at the hidden staircase. I could hear the rats scrambling to stay out of the light.

"She wasn't supposed to try it without me," Jennifer noted, glancing back at the sleeping Katharine. "The little louse. So it does open onto your place?" She leaned forward, trying to see whatever she could in the darkness. There was the barest flicker of light which seemed to touch the edge of that terrifying staircase from somewhere deep in my apartment, but that was all.

"There is a room there," I explained. "Bill and my mom had shoved stuff in front of the door."

"They were hiding it? It's a hidden room?"

"It's more like a forgotten room. There's a bunch of stuff in it, stuff from a while ago, like they needed someplace to put it, so they put it all back there, and then forgot about it. It's like that."

"Like treasure?"

"Well, most of it's junk."

"But not all of it?"

I wish I could say that I was honest with this helpful and lovely young girl. I was not. "It's just a bunch of boxes, Jennifer, just a lot of, you know, stuff people don't want anymore."

"Why didn't you tell me? I was the one who found the door. You wouldn't even know it was there if it wasn't for me. Why didn't you just—call me or something?" She looked at me with such a simple sense of disappointed betrayal it took me a moment to catch up.

"I couldn't," I explained. "Your mom would think it was weird."

"So? You don't mind people thinking you're weird. Everyone in the building thinks you're weird. You make it look okay to be weird." She said it with such sad admiration I felt embarassed and fraudulent.

"Your mother wouldn't let me call you," I told her. "Come on, I have to go home, it's the middle of the night. I can't get caught here! It's like I'm breaking and entering. I could get arrested for this."

"You get arrested all the time. You don't care about being arrested," she observed. "You said it on television."

"I said that on like local access television!" I noted, not without some exasperation. "Who watches that stuff?"

"Everyone in this building watched it tonight. Everybody

345

knows about it. My mom was on the phone with the whole co-op board."

This was not good news. "What did she say?" I asked, worried.

"People think that your mom was a con lady, she made Mr Drinan give her the apartment, the same stuff. Not that they cared about him. They didn't like him to begin with, you know."

"They didn't like the Drinans?" This had never occurred to me.

"They were *Irish*," Jennifer explained, as if this made everything clear. "I mean they liked it that he could do things because he was hooked up with people around the city, but they didn't want him living here."

"Why not? What sorts of things did he do?"

"Look, I don't know, I just heard some stuff while she was on the phone. It's all the same stuff they always say: you're not supposed to be here, your mother was a cleaning lady, they don't like New Jersey, they don't like anybody." Jennifer sighed. The spark was going out of her; you could see it happen even before I was halfway through the hatch. She was sitting on the edge of Katharine's bed, her shoulders hunched over like some sort of old bag lady who didn't even remember how to hold herself up straight anymore.

"Listen," I said. "You have to come to me. You have to sneak out and come down. To the apartment."

"You mean like . . ."

"Katharine did it. You can do it. You just have to be careful. And you have to try and find out what they're doing, like if the co-op board is going to do anything like testify for the Drinans or against my mom or something."

346

"You mean like *spy* on my *mother*?" Jennifer asked.

"No, no, it's more like—yeah, actually, it's like spying on your mother," I admitted. Her eyes lit up, and she sat up for a moment, the wheels turning, as she tried to figure out how she was going to pull this off.

"Yeah," she finally said, with a sort of internal, calculating confidence. She was already working it out. "Yeah, I can do it."

I don't know why it feels so good to help someone else when you're in trouble, but it did. She needed a purpose; I gave her one. Her sly grin bounced back on me and released me into the darkness; I slipped my legs over the edge and scrambled onto that dark and murky staircase, feeling my way back down one foot at a time until I reached my own unknowable home.

CHAPTER TWENTY-TWO

The morning following my nocturnal adventures I found myself completely entangled in about eight conflicting concerns. The biggest problem, as I saw it, was what to do with all the stuff stashed in the forgotten room. It seemed unlikely to me that the room would continue to be overlooked. The first time Lucy invited real estate agents over, they had just breezed through and offered general ideas about how much the place was worth. But now I felt pretty sure that the walk through would be more thorough, and associated with things like the original floor plan, which surely would alert people to the fact that there was another room back there. And once they found the room, all of Sophie's stuff would surely go up for grabs. Including, perhaps, the pearls.

I called Lucy; it seemed the necessary first step.

"Hey," I said, trying hard not to sound too phony in my friendliness. "It's me! I just wanted to call and find out how you thought it went yesterday, with the press conference. I thought it was pretty good."

"Yes, people seemed to feel it was a success. You made quite a splash, as usual," she said drily. "You probably didn't need to share quite so much information about your colorful past, but I guess I'm not surprised that you did."

"Oh, yeah. I'm sorry, Lucy, it just kind of popped out," I apologized nicely, trying to keep things on an even keel for as long as I could manage it. "Listen, I need to talk to you about when those Sotheby's people are going to start showing up and showing the apartment. Is that going to happen right away? Because I'm a little worried about the moss."

"I told you to get rid of that weeks ago, Tina. What is the problem?" she asked, exasperated.

"I know, I know, but it's really important to Len, and he's on the co-op board, and I don't want to piss him off," I explained. "You and Daniel and Alison wanted me to make friends in the building and that's what I'm doing, and I can't just throw it out, I think that would really be counter-productive."

"And he won't move it himself?"

"He's been hard to get hold of lately," I said, dropping a little truth in the middle of all the lies. "I'll keep trying, but it would really help if you could keep Sotheby's from showing the place for a little while."

"I don't know how much flexibility I have on that. The market being what it is, which is obviously not what it should be, we can't afford to set a lot of rules. The kind of buyer a place like ours might attract is not going to come along every day. You don't keep those people waiting."

"Yeah, but the market sucks. You've said so many times, the market sucks. Maybe it makes sense to wait."

"I hardly think you're the expert."

"I didn't *say* I was the expert," I said, trying not to get edgy with her. "I just mean maybe we should wait till next week. So that I can get rid of the moss, and then have a little time to clean the kitchen and vacuum and stuff."

"Sotheby's will take care of the cleaning," she informed me.

"I need some time to get rid of the moss, Lucy!" I finally snapped. "Honestly, I get so tired of the endless go-round a simple conversation always turns into with you! Why do they have to come this week? You keep telling me the market sucks—"

"I also keep telling you to get rid of the moss."

"Oh, for crying out loud. Forget it. Send them over here today. Let's show the apartment with a ton of moss growing out of the kitchen. That'll really sell the place. In this shitty market that'll be a big plus."

There was a tense silence at this. Finally, she sighed, but not a defeated sigh, more the kind of Tina's such a pain in the ass sigh, the one she has perfected and at the ready. "So were you going to tell me about the pearls?" she asked.

This I did not expect. I had to stop myself from blurting out something that sounded utterly defensive and guilty and like I knew that she knew that I had stolen them from a dead woman. Or, that I had stolen them from her and Alison; truth be told that would be what she thought. I rallied my best tone of aggressive innocence. "What about them?" I asked.

"Where did you get them?"

"Where did I get them? Who remembers? Some thrift shop in Delaware," I said.

"You said you left all your things out there, with Darren."

"Well, you know what? That idiot Darren actually got it together to send me a box of my stuff finally. You kept telling me I couldn't have any money for new clothes, so that's what I did, I got Darren to send me my stuff."

"This is the first I've heard of a *package* from *Darren*," she observed, making it sound like the most improbable event of a lifetime, which in fact it would have been, were it true.

"Well, I don't tell you everything, Lucy," I said.

"I know that, Tina, and let me just say, it's a lot of work, trying to figure out what you do tell me and what you don't and what's true and what isn't."

"Oh, for crying out loud," I started. "I'm doing what you tell me. I show up for these dumb meetings. I get dressed up and show up at the press conference. I'm nice to the people in the building. Whatever you ask me to do, I do it! Why am I still the enemy?"

"I didn't say you were the enemy," she responded, with so much undisguised bile it was impossible to mistake her conviction that I was in fact the enemy. "I'm just a little curious about those pearls. Alison said that that curator was very interested in them. She said that he seemed to think they were valuable."

"The *real* estate guy?" I said, inwardly cursing my insanely cocky decision to wear them to that stupid press conference in the first place. "What does he know about pearls?"

"I'm just telling you what Alison told me. She said—"

"I don't know what Alison said, and I don't care," I said, cutting her off. "I got a set of fake pearls out in Delaware at a thrift shop last summer, which is by the way the same place

352

I got the used dress and the cute shoes. You told me to get dressed up, and so that's what I did. And by the way it's a good thing Darren finally sent me that stuff, otherwise I would have nothing to wear because as you have mentioned oh so many times I don't have *any money* and since you don't seem to think giving me money is a good idea, and you also don't want me to get a job, I'm having a little bit of a problem figuring out how to *eat*, much less get dressed up."

"You seem to be doing just fine, Tina," she responded, completely unsympathetic. "I thought you had found some jobs around the building."

"Oh come on, I babysat for the Whites once, and the guy upstairs pays me to let the moss stay here. But you want me to get rid of the moss, so there goes that!"

"That's right," Lucy agreed. "The moss is going. You take care of it or I will, because they're coming over to clean the place on Friday."

"*Friday?*" I said, trying not to panic. "That's in three days."

"Wednesday, Thursday, Friday," she said. "Two and a half."

I had no choice but to keep making phone calls. Len was still not picking up, and neither was Charlie, although at least she had voice mail and I could leave her a message about the increasing complications surrounding this moss situation. I also called the Brooklyn Botanical Garden and left her a message there. Then I spent an hour or so rearranging the storage space and going through the boxes to see if there was anything else I wanted to save. The thought that I was stealing from a dead woman had evaporated; now I just wanted to save some of her stuff, and since I had just concocted the pretty good story about

Darren sending a box of old clothes, I thought I might be able to legitimately do that without having people ask too many questions about where they came from. No one was ever going to do anything except throw her things away; there was no reason I shouldn't get to keep some of them.

So that's what I did, starting with the clothes. Sophie's hippie phase especially had some pretty great moments in it, and, as I had discovered the day before, her clothes actually fit me. So I picked out the best of the Indian print and tie-dyed tops and skirts; there was even a dress with little mirrors all over it. I picked out a couple of pairs of cowboy boots and four or five pairs of shoes. I took out two boxes of yarn and knitting needles with the thought in the back of my head that I had always wanted to learn how to knit. And then I grabbed her old Canon, even though it was an SLR film camera and totally useless.

So I spent the morning and the early afternoon picking out stuff I might be able to use or save and hanging it up or hiding it in my little room. The way Lucy was talking, I thought, there's no telling how much longer I'll be here, and just going through Sophie's things did in fact make me want to turn that sorry old place into a home again. I also found a table and a lamp which were old and beat up enough so they looked like I might realistically have bought them at a stoop sale. I even found a small old Turkish area rug which had funny little animals all over it; when I put it in front of my equally small bed it made the room quite cozy. And since I had already lifted a dozen or so mystery novels from the boxes underneath Mom's bed and lined them against the wall up by the end where I slept, the place quite suddenly looked like a an actual person lived there.

Then I picked up Sophie's alligator clutch from the floor where I had dropped it, wondering where I could hide something that valuable. And then I thought, Oh, it doesn't look that valuable. It just looks like an old purse. Nobody's going to try to steal it. It just looks like an old purse.

So it wasn't a big leap, frankly, to the next step. I was on the verge of money problems. I came to that apartment with nothing, really nothing, and then I was lucky enough to find seven hundred dollars, and then I squeezed another two hundred out of Len, and then another eighty out of the Whites. I had been living on that for almost three months, and that's with at least half of that spent on clothes, because as I said when I got there I had nothing. Things like toothpaste and breakfast and make-up for when you have to go meet lawyers and real estate brokers aren't free. Plant food isn't free; throw-away cell phones aren't free. And when you flip out and have to just get away from your sisters because they've driven you so completely crazy during a meeting or a press conference so you decide to duck in a cab and just pay for it, that's not free either. I was virtually broke again, and that purse was worth at least five thousand dollars. And the dress, I suspected, was worth quite a bit as well. I found a paper bag and I put the clutch in the bottom, and then I put the Balenciaga on top of it. I dropped the pearls in there too.

In the elevator I took a couple of breaths and turned my brain over to reptile mode, which is what I do when I know I'm doing something wrong—like stealing—but I also know that I'm going to do it anyway. Not that stealing is something I make a habit of; if I did I might not be so broke all the time. Or, I might spend more time in jail than the occasional overnight visit. In any case, I don't make a habit of stealing except under the most dire circumstances. On the other hand I wasn't all that bothered about it, either. The person all this stuff belonged to was dead already, and a bunch of people who frankly had no claim on it at all, if you didn't count her sons, which no one seemed to, were about to descend like a murder of screaming crows on it all. What good would that do Sophie, or my mother, or me, if I just left the stuff back there to get grabbed up by lawyers or Sothebys or Mrs Westmoreland or someone else from the building who just might get them because they were part of the plunder, and the plunder was not ours—so they said— why leave it for them? In any event, that is what my determined reptile brain was telling me when I stepped off the elevator: I needed the money, no one else needed the money. No one else was going to help me out; well, Sophie would.

I didn't even make it through the lobby.

The response to our cocky little performance at Sotheby's had been, apparently, swift and decisive. Right there in the Edgewood lobby I found myself in the middle of another press conference, this one decidedly less civil, particularly with regard to me and my family and what in fact we thought we were doing there. The place was packed; there were at least twice as many reporters and photographers as we had the day before and they were shoved together in every available square inch from the elevator bank past Frank's podium all the way to the front door of the building. Everybody's backs were to me as they tried to take photographs and shoot questions toward the small but definite cadre of speakers who were gathered in front of the giant fireplace and yelling back at the questions which were being thrown at them. There were no microphones at this press conference; there was just people speaking loudly and angrily. One person was apparently standing on top of the giant winged chair, but I couldn't see who, as I am as I have mentioned rather short and at a decided disadvantage in a crowd.

"Mr Drinan—Mr Drinan—Mr Drinan!" People were shouting. "Has any court issued a ruling on the status of the will?"

"The Surrogates Court has not issued a ruling, but this morning there has been a cloud placed on the title. The Livingston Mansion Apartment, my mother's family apartment, is not being represented for sale at this time. The announcement that Sotheby's will be representing the Livingston Mansion Apartment is a complete fabrication," Doug shouted, making it clear that that was him up there on the chair. "The so-called heirs of Olivia Finn have no claim on it. The will which purports to bequeath the will to Olivia Finn has been determined to be fraudulent." The alarming and decisive confidence of this assertion pretty much scared the shit out of me for a second, but when I stood on my toes and caught a glimpse of old Doug over the heads of the two gigantic camera guys who were blocking the view, it wasn't quite so clear that Doug knew what he was talking about. His air of frustrated defeat had grown into something like a permanent expression of something beyond unhappiness. His lips had almost disappeared; his hair was disappearing; and his skin was sort of grey-green, which may have been the bad fluorescent light in the foyer but I had seen Frank under those lights a thousand times by now and he always looked fine. Doug looked paunchy and green and mad, and while he sounded like he was winning, he looked like he was losing. For a moment I thought that was a good sign, like it meant we were definitely going to get the apartment. But then Doug kept talking, and I remembered that someone who is losing is usually the worst enemy you could have.

Someone up front asked another question, which I couldn't hear. "No—absolutely not, Sotheby's is not authorized to represent the sale of this property. Everything is frozen as of this morning," some other guy announced, but louder. Seriously, from where I was standing you couldn't see anything but backs. There were more flashes as people took more pictures. Someone else asked another question I couldn't hear, and the guy with the big voice continued to answer. "It's possible that Mr Drinan was never the intended heir in the first place. Upon the death of the first Mrs Drinan we have not been able to ascertain that her will was ever probated. In which case the document being considered by the Surrogates Court at the present time will carry no authority whatsoever; in which case the sons of Sophia Livingston, who grew up in the apartment, are clearly the rightful heirs." There were more mumbled questions, and the guy with the big voice made another announcement. "Why don't we let the chairman of the board answer that question," he declared.

Then he and some other people up there conversed amongst themselves, and then a thin reedy voice started to speak again, but you really couldn't hear. The room was getting hot, with all the camera lights, and honestly people started shoving a bit, because truly it was so crowded and you couldn't see a thing. "We can't hear!" someone in the back yelled. There was more frustrated mumbling, and then the loud voice in the front spoke up again. "Yes, sorry, sorry, here this seems to help," it announced.

358

There was some shuffling that went on up there as Doug stepped off the chair and someone else stepped on it.

I just stared. It was Len. His hair was combed and he was wearing a lovely dark green suit jacket and tie, but his eyes were crazier than ever.

"The Edgewood in no way supports the supposed heirs of Olivia Finn. Our understanding is that contrary to the assertions made by Sotheby's there is in fact a cloud on the title—as of this morning, yes, I am aware of that, yes—but that doesn't matter! It does not matter because in any event the co-op board will in no way endorse any sale at this time. These women are no better than thieves as far as we are concerned. It is disgraceful that they have succeeded in this dreadful misappropriation of property to any degree *whatsoever*," he hissed. "And it will not be allowed."

Then there was some more mumbling at Len's feet which apparently struck some sort of nerve, because it really jacked up the stakes and he suddenly became completely incensed. "Yes there is, there is someone living there who has no rights at all, and the building has very much taken note of it, and she is going to be evicted immediately!" he declared hotly. "This is a landmark building and the indignity—the indignity of this *pretender* and *interloper*—will no longer be tolerated. This is yet another attempt by forces outside the community to take advantage of difficult times for the people of New York, to come in here and remake and reduce a piece of old New York to suit their new and trivial ideas about what the future might be. I say no! No! Unless these people vacate the premises within the week the building will bring its own action against them!"

359

There was some more mumbling, which made old Len even madder. "Legality? There has been too much talk about legality! What about what is historic! What about what is right! What about that!" In spite of the tidy suit Len was starting to look and sound completely psychotic. I couldn't believe it; it was like he was a different person. I wanted to shout at him, "I'm taking care of your moss, you asshole!" But I was well aware that that would not help my situation. His angry exhortations were having their effect on the mood of the room. Some of the photographers in the back were really shoving each other, mostly so that they could get off a decent shot; many of them were just holding their cameras above their heads and firing off their motor drives, hoping that by luck they might end up with something worth printing. But some of the crowd at the back were reporters and they were feeling left out as well, so they started shouting questions really loudly, partially out of frustration, and partially just so they could be heard. "Has the building started eviction proceedings?" a skinny girl in a red jacket shouted. I wanted to hit her, but I also started to worry that someone was going to notice that the evil pretender and interloper was in fact standing right there spying on the proceedings, and mob me.

Which actually is what happened next, just not to me. Someone up front tried to answer the skinny reporter's question with what may have been the last shred of reason in the room. "No one is being evicted!" he shouted, but then there was a kind of swelling up and movement near the front door of the building; someone was coming home and those of us back by the elevators really got shoved. Seriously, it's not like there was a hundred people there—I don't know how many were there, maybe twenty—but the foyer of the Edge is not a limitless space. That one extra person seems to have been the tipping point. Or maybe it was the person who it was. Because suddenly all the reporters started to shout and turn their attention toward the doorway, where the beautiful Julianna Gideon was trying to make her way in.

I had only ever seen her a couple of times, but this crowd was made up of the kind of society writers who know who lives where and how much money you have, and how old your family is and what parties you go to and what charity events you attend. In any case, they all clearly knew who she was, and more importantly, they cared. "Miss Gideon! Miss Gideon!" they shouted, which in the moment honestly seemed sort of obscenely polite, given the fact that they also were shoving around her like a crazed soccer mob and sticking their cameras in her face ruthlessly. "Can we get a comment about the controversy? Have you met any of the women who now claim part ownership of the building? Will you support the co-op board if they attempt eviction proceedings?"

I couldn't even see Julianna at first, but then I spotted that beautiful head of hair, the face ducked down against her shoulder, as she gently tried to make her way through the swarm. She wore a soft rose-colored coat, which had been pulled open by her struggle with the crowd, and she carried a couple of expensive shopping bags which got caught behind her so she had to keep turning back to murmur, "Excuse me, so sorry, excuse me . . ." while she was basically being mobbed. She just kept trying to move forward, then she would get dragged back, people were shouting, and then she threw back her head, releasing her face from all those dark curls with an almost angelic despair. Then her face went all white and her knees buckled and she started to go down.

Who knows what would have happened? She had fainted, there was no question, and people were being careless indeed. But Frank appeared out of the crowd and caught her. She fell into his arms and he picked her up and shouldered his way through the mob, carrying her the last few steps to where I was standing in front of the elevator bank. Her head was tipped back and her curls fell gracefully around the epaulettes on the shoulders of his little doorman's uniform. By this point I had had enough presence of mind to swing the door open for them and swing myself in behind. The reporters were closing in and Julianna wasn't the only one who needed to make an escape. "What floor is she on, Frank?" I said fast, reaching for the buttons.

"Eleven," he told me.

Just then a hand reached in and stopped the elevator door from closing. "No no no no," I begged, half under my breath. I actually smacked the hand, hard, and then tried to pry the fingers off the sliding panel as I shoved my body in front of Julianna and Frank, so that no one could push their way in.

"Would you relax! Tina, *Jesus,* owww." I looked up from the fingers still clinging to the edge of the panel to see who it was blocking the crowd of reporters, which looked small and insignificant now, a bunch of society scribblers trying to make something out of nothing. "You gonna bite me?" Pete asked.

"I was thinking about it."

"I'm sure. She dropped this." He shoved in the two elegant shopping bags—pristine, with corded handles, one from Barney's, the other from Bergdorf Goodman—which had slipped from Julianna's grasp, into the elevator.

"Thanks," I said.

"Wait, wait, this is yours," he added. And then he pushed through the little bag I had been carrying—a brown paper sack wrapped around his mother's Balenciaga dress and alligator clutch and her pearls. I felt myself turning red, but he didn't know; how could he know? "Go on, get out of here," he said, tipping his head toward the bank of call buttons. He turned his back to me then and held up his hands, blocking access to the shouting reporters. "Back up, *back up*, you fucking piranhas," he ordered.

"Is that one of the other heirs?" somebody asked, putting two and two together.

"I don't know, is it?" he wondered. I didn't hear anything further. The door closed, the elevator lifted and we left him and the others beneath us.

CHAPTER TWENTY-THREE

High above the city, with sweeping views of the park similar to my own, the Gideon apartment was a haven of peace and light. Every one of the rooms had been "done", apparently, by some famous designer, in a palate of gold and white. You walked into the living room and felt like you were floating.

Frank was still carrying Julianna in his arms. She had revived to the point where she could insist that he put her down, but not to the point that she could insist upon it with any real force. "I'm fine, really, Frank, I promise, this is so silly," she protested, as she leaned her cheek against his chest. I had opened the door with Frank's set of master keys, which he tossed to me in the elevator with almost alarming speed and accuracy, as if he had been preparing for the moment when he might need to do just that his entire life. In any case, he tossed me the keys and I knew what to do with them. I grabbed her bags and he held onto Julianna and we brought her safely home, where he laid her on a milk-white sofa in front of a bank of windows which overlooked the world.

"I was so frightened," she said, smiling up at him. Frank knelt beside her, and pushed a strand of curling hair off her cheek.

"You're all right now," he said.

"I'm perfect now," she admitted. "Thank you."

She reached over and held his hand. Frank just stared at her, his face so full of wonder you truly thought the universe might stop everything, just to watch this. They had completely forgotten that I was back in the corner by the door; both of them were clearly so content just looking at each other. I almost shouted, "Kiss her! Kiss her!" but there was no need. She reached up, and kissed him.

"What is going on here?" someone announced, behind us. Before I could even turn to say hello, Mrs Gideon with the steely grey hair swept by me to join her daughter on that pristine couch. When Julianna lay on it, it looked like a bed, but as soon as her ferocious mother sat next to her it started to look sort of like a throne. It had strange paw-like feet which you only noticed when Mom was sitting there.

"Oh Mother, I'm fine," Julianna began. Mother cut her off.

"You're clearly *not* fine. Someone just carried you into your own apartment. What happened?" Mrs Gideon continued, turning on Frank and me like we were the problem here and not the solution. She was a fairly frightening person, truth be told. She kept asking questions but they didn't sound a bit like questions; every word out of her mouth sounded like a complete accusation. She was honestly no fun at all.

"There was kind of a crowd down in the lobby. Things were a little upsetting," Frank explained.

"Yes, things are upsetting. People in the building are upset.

My understanding is that it's being handled, Frank. I don't know what it has to do with you," Mrs Gideon snapped, standing. "And I don't appreciate your bringing *her* into my home." She barely flicked her eyes in my direction; I was beneath her, and besides she was having too much fun giving Frank a hard time. "Surely you know that I would consider that inappropriate."

Frank was completely mortified. "I . . . I . . . I . . ." he started, but she was having none of it.

"Please, you've done enough. *Please go*," she ordered.

"Mother." Julianna sat up, her cheeks turning the palest rose. I'm telling you, that girl is someone who knows how to blush. Her pink cheeks were just the slightest shade lighter than her rose-colored wrap. Sitting up alone on that white couch, she looked like a flower. "Frank took care of me. I don't know why you would speak so harshly to him," she said, laughing a little in a way that took all the sting out of her mother's accusations. "I don't know what I would have done if you hadn't been there, Frank. I was really frightened and so silly to faint."

"You *fainted?* I'm calling the doctor."

"I'm fine now, thanks to Frank. I am very grateful, Frank, really I am." She stood now, and held her hand out to him with a simple elegance. He took it in both of his own, too overwhelmed to speak. Honestly, I think if her hideous mother had not been there he would have fallen to his knees in a worshipful daze. But Hideous Mother *was* there. And she was done with us.

"Well, I don't know what happened," she said. "But if you say Frank was helpful I'm sure he was. Here, Frank, wait there for a minute so I can get you something."

"Oh—no, please," said Frank. But Hideous Mother had already stalked to the entryway, where I was still standing and watching, and picked up her purse from a useless-looking sticklike table that was perched just inside the door. She smiled at me tightly as she turned, making sure that I knew that even if I had fooled her pretty daughter I sure wasn't going to fool *her*. But she really didn't have anything to say anymore; she was just ready to get rid of both of us.

"Here," she said, holding out a five dollar bill in Frank's direction.

Frank's face went white, then a deep, truly indescribable color seemed to pass over it like a wave. To give him his due, his expression did not change. But for a moment he seemingly could not speak, or move.

"Mother," whispered Julianna, completely mortified.

"What?" said Hideous Mother. "He's the doorman and he was very helpful to you." She twitched the five between her fingers in an insanely insulting breath of a gesture. "You just said so yourself, sweetheart. I think it's completely appropriate to offer him a tip." She took another step toward Frank and gave the bill yet another little flick. Honestly the whole performance was so shocking you couldn't take your eyes off it.

"You dropped your bags," I said, holding up the Bergdorf's and Barney's bags with a sudden humble but loud goodwill. "I'm going to leave them here by the door, okay?"

"Oh—" Julianna started.

"Frank, you were going to let me into my apartment, remember? I am so sorry, I locked myself out. So stupid. What a great apartment you have. It's so pretty. I didn't at all mean to barge in, I just, Frank was going to help me with my keys and then your daughter fainted." I reached out and grabbed Frank's arm, to get him to move. With a quick, sharp shrug he pushed me aside, but at least it got him going. He strode past the Hideous Mother, and me, with every shred of Latin American pride that was left in him and his uniform. As he clearly wasn't going to pause, I scurried along. He did not give himself permission to look back, even when Julianna called after him.

"Thank you, Frank, thank you!"

"If you want to thank him so much I don't know why you wouldn't let me tip him," Mrs Gideon admonished her, behind our exit. "Honestly, Julianna, your affectations have gotten completely—" The door slammed her voice shut. Frank was at the elevator now, pressing the button with a fierce and uncompromising rage. Blessedly, it was right there, and we didn't have to wait. We both stepped into the elevator and I hit 8. Frank hit L. We traveled in silence for a moment.

"Boy," I finally said. "What a witch."

"Hopeless," he whispered. "Hopeless." He sagged then, leaning against the paneled wall as if it were the only way he could continue to stand. The elevator dinged; we were at my floor. I reached over and pulled him up, put his arm over my shoulder, and half-carried, half-walked him off my landing and into my apartment.

He was mumbling to himself now, some sort of protest I think, but my Spanish is just not all that good when people start talking fast, so I couldn't tell what, exactly, he was really saying. It sounded sort of like you have to let me go I have to get downstairs and do my job but it could just as easily have been a grocery list. In any case he was in no condition what-soever to face anyone down in the lobby, much less that crowd of howling society reporters who were most certainly still on the premises. So I shut the door behind us and pushed him into my sweet empty enormous front room, propping him up against one of the windows that has the really good view of the park. "Here, wait here, Frank. I'm going to get you some-thing to drink, okay?" I said. He just kept talking to himself. I headed for the kitchen, where I knew that there was a nearly full bottle of vodka stashed in the freezer.

As I raced through the little TV area a head popped up off the couch. "Hey, you're home," said Jennifer as she cheerfully set down a mystery novel. I had in fact forgotten that she was meant to show up so her sudden appearance sent my heart rate through the roof.

"Oh, Jennifer," I said, holding my hand to my chest in an attempt not to die from the scare she gave me. "Oh."

"You told me to come," she reminded me, a little worried now.

"No, I'm really glad you're here," I said. "Oh. Really glad." And I was. Even though my heart was still racing, it was not lost on me that finally, maybe, I had an ally. At the very least, for the first time ever in the Edgewood, I had someone to come home to. "Come on," I said, heading for the refrigerator. "Frank's in the front room. He's a complete mess."

"The *door*man?" she said, following me obediently.

We took the vodka to the front of the apartment and I poured Frank a stiff drink. He knocked it back without protest, and I poured him another.

"What's wrong with him?" Jennifer asked.

"It's complicated," I started, but the vodka had brought vitality back to his spirit and he started rambling again, in Spanish. "Frank," I said, taking his hand. "Frank. Speak English, Frank."

"No, it's okay," said Jennifer, calm. "He's upset. He loves her, but it's hopeless, she is a goddess and he is nothing. And his father, there's some—*Que quieres compartir con nosotros tu familia, Frank?*"

So it turns out that a private school education in New York City is pretty thorough. It also turns out that Jennifer was in the Spanish Club so her comprehension didn't actually fall completely apart when someone started talking fast.

"He lives with his father and his two brothers in a one-bedroom apartment in Queens," Jennifer translated. "He came from El Salvador six years ago and sent money to them faithfully but they were never grateful, never—they became jealous. No matter what he sent to them it made them unhappy and greedy for more, and so they came here. He is here legally, but they are not. He can't, they use up all the money—they—" He interrupted her with a long explanation which she asked him questions about before she continued. "He doesn't blame them because the life they had in El Salvador was nothing. There are no jobs there and they want to be men, but they cannot find work, and if the INS finds out that he is, that they're staying with him he's afraid that he can be deported too. He told one of his brothers—*Como se llama tu hermano horrible?*"

"Manuel," Frank answered her, trying to continue and contradict her about the "horrible" part but she cut him off, as she continued to explain it to me.

371

"He has a horrible brother who threatens him. He is supporting all of them and this brother, Manuel, *threatens* Frank that if he doesn't bring home more and more money he'll have to turn himself into the INS and they will all have to go back, even though Frank totally has his green card. I know he does because the building would never hire him if he didn't, and my mom was on the committee that interviewed him. They love him here, they'd never let that happen. Frank," she continued, turning his attention back to him. "*Es impossible, lo que se dice su hermano. El es un mentiroso. Un mentiroso,*" she insisted. He protested firmly, but you could tell he knew that whatever she was telling him was right. "*Porque no ayudan?*" she continued. "*Porque no trabajan, todo su familia viven aquí en Nueva York, aqui nadie le importa si usted tiene una tarjeta verde! Aquí a la Edgewood, sí, es importante but muchas otras lugares no no no. Todos los restaurantes in la ciudad, nadie le importa!*"

He disagreed with her. They argued back and forth. He finally started to cry. She put her arms around him and he wept about his hopeless situation, the trap of his family, his love for a woman who was so far above him the only word he could use to describe her was "*diosa*". By this point Frank was drinking out of the bottle, and by the time we had the whole story out of him he was stupefied with grief and completely smashed, so there was really no way he could go back to work. I got him a pillow and a blanket from my teeny little bedroom, and he fell asleep on the floor, with the light fading from gold to blue all around him.

Jennifer looked up at the changing light and checked her watch. "I got to go," she said, nervous. "I left Katharine playing in her room and we locked the door and she knows not to open it? But she's *seven*, she could just forget and open the door and then anyone could come in and then what would happen?" she wondered. This time I was following her to the back, through the kitchenette and the laundry room. As we moved she quickly filled me in on what she had found out by just hanging around, hiding behind doors and listening in on the flurry of phone calls that went in and out of the Whites' apartment over the past two days.

"People are really mad," she said. "Mom told them that she knows you and you're okay. I told her that she had to tell them that because you were such a good babysitter, but you know there's a lot of rich assholes in this building and they kept talking about you and your sisters and Jersey and like this is such a famous apartment, and you know, um, you know—they can't just let it go down the toilet, shit like that," she told me.

"Oh, that's lovely," I said. "Such swell manners they have up here on the Upper West Side."

"Oh, you know people say things like that, and you know." She shrugged, not knowing how to say what came next. She decided to just say it. "You know, Tina, they didn't like your mom."

"Some of them did. Len did."

"I don't think you maybe should trust him, Tina." Jennifer suggested, cautious. "Mom said, she was talking to him in the elevator? And he said he knew your mom, they had some deal where he kept some plants here and so he came by all the time, and he saw her and Bill together all the time and she just kept Bill drunk, and he saw her getting him to sign things."

373

"He didn't say that."

"That's what my mom said he said. He was the one who is, you know, a real witness. It's not hearsay. Like he says he *saw* all this and he's ready to testify. And he had some idea about some big press conference? To get you out of here?"

"Yeah, I was down there. It's a total scene down in the lobby."

"Well, Mom said that was his idea."

"It was his idea? Len's?" The sheer betrayal of the whole situation hit me like a fist to the stomach. I felt sick.

"That's what she said."

"It's lies. My mom wouldn't, she wasn't like that. She . . ." I stopped myself, completely caught in how much I didn't know about my own mother, and what she might or might not have been doing the last two years of her life. "She helped him," I fumbled. "I don't know why he would do something like this."

Jennifer looked kind of sad, like she was a bit sorry that I wasn't savvier about people like Len. "They're all like that here, come on, Tina. They're all, well, you know. They live in the Edge," she concluded lamely.

I gave her a quick hug goodbye as she glanced into the lost room, through all the junk and the lost details of the lives of the people who had lived there. Katharine was apparently still content, as you could hear her in the distance, chattering to herself in some near corner of her room.

"Frank's right, you know," Jennifer suddenly announced, turning back for a second. "Julianna Gideon *is* a goddess. And I mean, in my social studies class they all talk about democracy and America and immigrants and New York being this big melting pot, but he's a *doorman* from El *Sal*vador and he's got a horrible family and she's like, a *goddess*. And the Gideons just have pots of money, they are truly stinking rich, just like everyone else who lives here. You don't think about things like that. But, you know. It really is hopeless." And with that hopeless remark, she left.

CHAPTER TWENTY-FOUR

In the enormous front room of my apartment under a moonless sky, on top of a bed of horrible mustard-colored shag carpet, Frank slept the sleep of the hopeless and the hopelessly drunk while I considered the set of master keys he had handed me earlier in the day. It was a relatively innocuous-looking set, five in all, two of them larger than the others. Those two clearly had some outdoor use; I was less interested in them. I was, however, quite interested in the three other keys, which presumably would let you into any apartment in the building. Frank had actually just handed me the whole set, and then he had gotten drunk, and now those keys were mine, for as long as it might take him to sleep it off.

Unfortunately all three of them were stamped with the words DO NOT DUPLICATE, so I was relatively quick to assume that any hardware store that didn't take bribes would in fact refuse to duplicate them. Which meant that all I did have was three or four hours before Frank woke up and wanted his keys back. I didn't waste a lot of time thinking about my options.

Abducting that kid's plant back might give me some leverage with Len, which it was definitely looking like I needed. Jennifer's account of his lies along with my own glimpse of his snarling rage was unnerving, and while I didn't know what he was up to I did know I had to get him to back down. I pulled out my throwaway cell and dialed.

"I have a way to get us into Len's apartment," I told Charlie. "How fast can you get over here?"

There was a pause. "Twenty minutes," she said.

"Okay, do you know where the service entrance is?"

"I lived in the Edge for seven years," she informed me. "Of course I know where the service entrance is."

"Well, then, can you tell me?" I asked her. "I think it would be better if I met you there, and we snuck up the back."

Twenty-five minutes later we were on the landing in front of Len's door. Charlie didn't ask a lot of questions about how I had laid my hands on the master keys; she was blessedly uncurious about anything other than getting through the door of her father's apartment and making off with her plant. She stood silently behind me as I lay down on the floor of the foyer and peeked through the crack at the bottom of the door to see if there were any lights on inside. My hope was that Len was still downstairs with the rest of that hysterical co-op board, but I needed to be sure. After five minutes of utter silence it seemed safe to assume we were alone.

So within half an hour of concocting this haphazard plan I found myself standing in Len's silent greenhouse next to his tall, elf-like daughter, wondering what it was, in fact, that we were looking for. The last time I had seen the plant it was quite a small seedling, in a little white plastic cup.

"Do you know what it looks like?" I whispered. A quiet breeze blew through the lush foliage of the deciduous room, but that was the only answer I got. Charlie glided ahead into the night, and before I could find my bearings enough to follow her she was gone.

"Shit," I said, to myself mostly. "Charlie?" There was no answer, and the place was pitch black. I felt a wave of panic; this wasn't the plan, that she would just head off and leave me standing like a dope by the front door. Or maybe that was the plan. I realized that of course we hadn't actually made a plan, and that Charlie must have assumed this would be the best way to proceed, as she did know the layout of the greenhouse since she had, as she informed me, lived there for seven years. So I waited by the door for an exceptionally long period of time, and then I started to wonder if in fact I shouldn't just leave, if perhaps that wasn't the plan, or at least what she assumed was the plan, that I was just going to help her break into her father's apartment and then go.

This is doubtless what I should have done, but I didn't, because it didn't feel right. For a sick moment I realized that once again I had put all my trust in a person I barely knew, and that while Len had surprised me with his many and un-explained betrayals there was really no reason to expect that his only daughter would behave all that much better. What was she doing back there? Why was this taking so long? I also had no reason to believe that she had my back. What if she got caught stealing, and announced to everyone that I was the one who had let her in? "Hey Charlie," I whispered, taking a step forward into the darkness. "Come on. Charlie?" I waited for another moment, listening for any sign of life that was not plant based. There was nothing in return but the sounds of water, and a strange omnipresent sense of things growing. Charlie had completely disappeared, and the fact of her disappearance worked on my imagination like a psychotropic photosynthesis. I took another step forward.

Len had rigged up a series of night lights which cast spooky little glows in obscure corners of the greenhouse, but they were next to useless under the weight of that moonless sky hovering above it all. The lights from the street below were too far away to do any good; the few leaves I could make out were black against black and only my fingers could really discern the subtle differences as I moved deeper into their jungle pathways. My eyes couldn't seem to get used to darkness that dark, so I finally closed them, to keep them from straining for sense. Slowly the logic of the conservatory, room after room, bloomed in my head. The kid had said the seeds were from Africa, and the Latin notes on the woodcut print said something about Malaysia, so there were only a few places in the greenhouse to look, as there were only a few places where Len grew things like that. And there past the orchid room, right on the edge of the poisonous plants room, on a small shrine-like platform lit with a bank of dull purple neon lights was a small tree with fierce shiny dark green leaves, small orange star-like flowers and golden seed pods oozing some sort of sticky white nectar.

"Holy shit," I said.

It wasn't very big—nowhere near as big, at least, as the picture in the mossery indicated it might be; there was no way two grown men could sleep underneath it. It was definitely much more of a shrub than a tree. But in every other way it was identical to the medieval print on my wall. There was something peculiar, almost, in how literally the picture of the plant and the plant itself matched up, almost as if it were a carefully manufactured bonsai version of something much larger but equally specific which had appeared on the earth 2,000 years ago. It was, in fact, the perfect example of the botanist's art; every scrap of knowledge that humanity had attained over centuries of cultivation had been showered on this strange growing thing, and it virtually quivered with its own perfection. That may actually have been the effect of the three separate humidifiers which surrounded its perch under the neon lights and breathed a hissing steam upon its leaves and branches; in any event, there was no question that this piece of greenery was what I was looking for. I reached out to touch it.

"How many times do I have to remind you, Tina?" Len whispered, right in my ear. "It's called a 'poisonous plant' for a reason."

I just about jumped out of my skin. "Man, Len, what the fuck." I threw the words back at him fast, assuming friendly aggression would be the only path available to me in these dicey circumstances. "You're like a fucking snake hiding in the grass. How long have you been here?"

"Since I'm not the one who's been caught breaking and entering I don't actually have to answer that," he informed me, unseen. "And as I recall the snake encouraged Eve to pick the apple, even though it went against her best interests. I'm suggesting quite the opposite."

"I came up to talk to you," I said, tap-dancing wildly. "I've been calling about the moss. You don't even pick up the phone."

"You broke into my apartment in the middle of the night so that you could talk about moss? I don't know that I'd take that approach with the police, Tina, it honestly does not sound very likely. Especially since I can honestly testify that I found you sneaking around my apartment, looking to steal a rare plant which is in fact very valuable to me."

"You know, Len, it's not right that you took that kid's plant. Charlie told me you just took it and now you're what, you're hiding up here, you won't call her back. She's the one who should be calling the police." I looked around, hoping that Charlie would take this cue to reveal herself. She did not.

"She's deluded," the voice in the darkness observed.

"You stole it, Len," I said. He hadn't called the cops yet, and I was starting to hope that maybe he wouldn't. I thought of yelling out for Charlie but she had disappeared so thoroughly that I had no way of knowing if she was even still in there. "Charlie said the kid needs the money. You just said yourself it's worth something, and you just took it from him."

"Spare me the suggestion of moral outrage, Tina. You've been doing nothing but take things that don't belong to you for months, and there's always a good reason isn't there?" he noted, a light and amused sneer curling around the edge of the words now. "You've got a criminal heart vastly more experienced than my own."

"There's nothing illegal about it. My mom, she legally—"

"You might also spare me the drivel about your mother, who by all accounts, including your own, you completely abandoned

382

when she needed you most. Oh, by the way, I thought you looked terrific at that press conference over at Sotheby's. Wasn't that Sophie's dress you were wearing? And her pearls—another lovely touch. Does it make you feel more at home, since you've already stolen her apartment and her history, to steal her things as well?"

"They threw them away," I said, cocky, but my criminal heart was abruptly less sure of its own footing. "They threw her away, too."

"And what do you think you know about that?" he asked, but his voice was hardening.

"What I don't know, I'm learning fast," I tossed back, hoping that I was sounding more secure than I felt. "Charlie brought that plant to you because she trusted you. She's your own kid. You stole from your own kid."

"Oh, parents and children—people take that so very seriously when what is it, really? Just nature in action." Len sighed in the dark. "Of course families betray each other. What would be the fun otherwise? Betraying someone you hardly know, it's not even worth it really."

"Was it fun betraying me?"

There was a kind of gleeful silence at this. "You *are* fun, actually," he told me. "So completely unmoored in the universe. And now you think you've found a home. Only it's someone else's home, someone else's apartment, someone else's clothes, someone else's life. You might just as easily try to understand your own lost mother, or even your lost sisters, but that doesn't attract you. You're too busy coveting . . . us."

"Is that why you're trying to get rid of me now? Because I don't belong? Because a place like this only belongs to the people who had it in the past? You're as bad as everybody else in this stupid building. They just want things to stay the same because they own everything and they think that sharing is for losers. Well, you know what? You *don't* own the Edgewood. Me and Alison and Lucy, we're here fair and square."

"Well, you're not *here* fair and square, Tina. I caught you breaking and entering and trying to rob me. And while I find your philosophical musings about property and identity amusing, I suspect the authorities will not be interested in the least."

"They'll be interested in hearing what I have to say about that plant."

"That *will* be interesting. How many times have you been arrested, I couldn't actually tell from what you said at that press conference. Does your record actually endear you to the police, make them trust you more? When you explain things to them do they actually take your word for it?"

I didn't even bother to answer that one. By this point my heart wasn't pounding as hard; it wasn't pounding at all, in fact. Len *was* having fun; there was no sense of urgency to any of this at all.

"What do you want, Len?" I asked him. "What's the deal going to be?" For a moment one of the shadows shifted, and a hollow glint, the barest reflection of the clustered purple lights, picked up his eyes and then let them slide back into the dark. His hand reached out and hovered over the *Madrigalis* like he was blessing it.

"If she could have made those seeds bloom, you think she wouldn't have?" he asked. "She didn't have the skill. That's what she's angry about. She brought me a boy, she brought me a

384

seed, that's all she brought. A seed is nothing but potential. The rest is mine."

"She's your daughter."

"Don't come back here, Tina," he said, simply. "That goes for Charlie too. My world is off limits. You make her understand that. And maybe you'll be allowed to stay."

"Tell her yourself," I said. "She's right behind you."

The purple glint, which was all I could see of him, shifted to one side, startled, and none too soon, as something long and sharp slashed through the air and sliced in two the space where Len had stood a fraction of a second before.

"Holy shit," I said. "What the fuck."

"Hi, Dad," said Charlie, raising her weapon again. "Nice to see you."

"Put that thing down. Jesus!" I said, really scared that she was going to give it another go. "What the fuck is that thing?"

"It's a pruning saw," Charlie informed me. "I'm going to murder my father with it." And then she brought it down again, barely missing him a second time. Len leapt back, falling into a black mass of something fernlike and dense, but not completely losing his balance, apparently. From what little I could see in the shadows of the obscured foliage, he stumbled to one side, caught himself and moved down one of the black paths which converged on this corner of the greenhouse.

"Your aim is not what it might be, dear," Len called back to her. "There aren't many who would have missed that chance."

"Maybe I'm hoping to drag this out," she countered. "Maybe it might be worth it to me to scare you a few times before I finish you off, you motherfucker." You couldn't see anything, but she was moving fast, after him, down that pathway, holding that thing over her head as she aimed for her third try.

"Stop it, Charlie, man. Come on, I'm a witness here!" I yelled.

"Don't kid yourself, Tina. You're an accessory!" she yelled back. I heard the blade swish again through the night air, and make contact with something plantlike on the other end.

"Not even close," Len hissed, and now he sounded closer, on a different path, in a different direction. It was really so dark in there you couldn't tell where he was. "Your mother will be so disappointed in you," he observed, with real pleasure. Charlie reappeared by my side, still swinging. I had to duck to stay clear of her.

"Mother will delight in every detail of this story," Charlie reported back to him. She swung the pruning saw blindly now, cutting another swath through the unseen foliage in front of her. "Oh, sorry, Dad, I think I just took out your *Heliotropus syncathia*. How long did it take you to root that again? Oh well, you can spend another three years nurturing that one, instead of me. Ooops. You don't have another three years, do you?" She swung the blade again, and I realized that she wasn't blind at all; she knew where every specific plant was in that place, and she was aiming. "Oh dear. There go the Asiatic lilies. Too bad, they are so *pretty*."

"Stop. *Stop*." This time Len's voice came from directly behind me. I didn't know where anyone or anything was, but they did.

"I'm not going to stop, you fuckface!" she yelled, lunging with that thing yet again. And then, under her breath, to me, "Take it. Take it now. Get it out of here."

I didn't need to be told twice. While Charlie continued to destroy her father's greenhouse, I grabbed the *Madrigalis* and stumbled back the way I came. I left the door open behind me, carrying that enormous poison plant with me as I fled. Behind me, the sound of the falling blade continued, cutting down the forest with glee.

Charlie showed up at my door twenty minutes later. "Thanks," she said, abrupt. She had a cut on her forehead, her hands were covered in dirt, and those spooky blue eyes were unreadable. She slipped by me and headed for the kitchen with the innate knowledge that that would be where I had stashed that thing.

"Look," I said, pissed, following her. "I said I'd help you get your plant back. I didn't say you should *kill* him."

"Trust me, if I wanted to kill him I wouldn't have missed," she informed me. She flipped on the lights and looked at the *Madrigalis*, which I had placed directly underneath its picture. "My God," she sighed. "It really is beautiful." She put her arms around the plain terracotta pot which held it and lifted it carefully off the floor and onto the countertop. There she took one of the starlike flowers between her fingers and held it delicately toward the light, so that she could get a better view.

"He got it to flower." she said. "And fruit. He really is . . . amazing."

"You have to get that thing out of here, like right now," I told her. "I'm serious. I can't be seen as an accomplice to this."

"Well, but you are very much an accomplice," she noted, barely glancing my way. "I mean, *I* didn't call *you* and say let's go break into my dad's greenhouse."

"Did you tell him that? Did you tell him that I called you?"

"He doesn't care. All he knows is that you crossed him."

"He crossed me first," I said, sounding like an eight-year-old.

"Seriously, he was out there already, trying to get me kicked out of the building, before I did anything. All I ever did was help him and he—he—"

"Don't tell me about my own father," Charlie said, virtually ignoring me as she examined the seed pods with care. "He probably wanted something out of you, and he got it, and then he wanted something else. He wanted the *Madrigalis*. And you saw me bring it to him. So he had to get rid of you because you knew that he had it, he saw that as threatening somehow. And he was right," she said, finally smiling at me. "You were a threat. You knew what he had, and you knew me, and you helped me take it back. He was right to want to get rid of you." She turned back to the sink and grabbed a small cup, filling it with water.

"So what's he going to do now?" I asked.

"Nothing, right away," she said. She took the pair of Len's gardening gloves which he had left there and slipped them on, deliberate. "Tomorrow, or the next day, I don't know."

"What did you do to him?" I asked, getting a little worried again.

"It's not what I did to him," she responded. "It's what I did to his plants. You can do a lot of damage with a pruning saw. If you're not careful. And I wasn't." She squeezed the seed pod carefully over the water, then studied the effect of the swirling liquid in the cup.

"Oh, you know, that's not—you know, I was trying to *help you*," I said.

"Well, you did," said Charlie. "You helped me a lot." She reached around in the stack of miniature gardening implements on the shelf above the sink and carefully selected one of the larger fertilizing needles.

"Look," I said, finally sick of her and her cool disinterest in the mess she had made for me. "I did this thing for you and that kid. I was trying to be nice and you just, you—you're as bad as he is."

"You actually have no idea how bad he is," she informed me. "I do."

"Then why did you even bring him that plant?" I said. "Why did you ask him for help in the first place? Why did you trust him?"

She looked over at me, unimpressed with the point. "I know a lot of talented botanists, but he is the only one who could have gotten those seeds to grow," she said. She touched the slender, glistening leaves of the *Madrigalis* and smiled with a cloudless and perverse delight. "I never could have done it." She picked up the plant and headed out the door. "Don't touch those things without gloves on," she called back to me. "There is every reason to believe that the sap is really quite toxic."

I didn't know what she was talking about until the next morning, when I glanced into the kitchen and saw what she had been doing while we talked. She had fed her quickly improvised solution from the seed pod and the sap of the *Madrigalis* into the moss's irrigation system. Every tray of moss was dead.

CHAPTER TWENTY-FIVE

It was kind of nice to see old Stuart Long. I hadn't actually laid eyes on the guy since the day we buried Mom, and there he was, sitting patiently in Ira Grossman's glamorous waiting room, looking like a friendly egg, I thought. Then I thought, All eggs pretty much look friendly. But Stuart Long, to my mind, looked particularly so. He was reading a magazine, something that looked financial and boring.

"Hey, Mr Long," I said.

"Hello, Tina," he said, smiling with real pleasure. "It's been a while."

"Yes, a lot has happened," I agreed, sitting next to him. "What are you doing here? Do you have business with Ira?"

"I'm giving a deposition," he informed me.

"Oh, so am I," I said.

"Yes, I presumed so," he nodded.

"Lucy and Alison are doing theirs tomorrow," I observed. "They kind of didn't want me anywhere near the whole deposition thing in general? So we had to sign all these docs saying Lucy was the Administratrix. That's the word, right?"

"I think it's a fine word."

"Anyway, they all decided that she should be in charge since she was more or less in charge anyway. And as I said they pretty much didn't want me anywhere near the lawyers for the other side, because I'm supposedly some sort of loose cannon. But now they say that I have to give a deposition anyway."

"Sometimes it happens that way."

"I don't really follow all of it all that well. I pretty much just show up whenever they tell me to, and do what I'm told."

"Very wise."

"It might be if I really pulled it off. Frankly I understand why they'd rather keep me under wraps. I keep trying, over at the Edge, to be, you know, a good representative for the family. It's not quite going as well as it might."

"Really?"

"Is that a surprise?" I asked, a little surprised at how surprised he sounded.

"No," he said, closing his magazine carefully and setting it back on the table. This is the thing I find curious about lawyers. Even when they want to talk to you, they don't say very much. Mr Long was clearly happy to see me and more than willing to talk to me while we waited to get called in for our respective depositions; it's not like he was trying to ignore me so he could read his magazine. But he really wasn't going to say anything extra. He just sat there. After a moment I got embarrassed and decided to keep this going.

"Are you here for our case?" I asked him. "I mean, I assumed you were, but maybe you're here on somebody else's case."

"I'm here on your case."

"You know, I heard, did I hear that they were suing you? I think Lucy told me that, that those Drinans were suing you."

"Their lawyers have suggested it, certainly. It would be part of the case they need to build around the earlier wills."

"What kind of a case?"

"It's just one among several arguments they might make. That perhaps I was lax in the probating of Mrs Drinan's will. The *first* Mrs Drinan."

"That's so funny, like the first Mrs DeWinter," I said. He smiled but didn't respond so I was pretty sure he had never seen the movie but was too polite to say so.

"I'm sorry about that, Mr Long. I feel bad that you're being dragged into this on our account," I told him.

"Not on your account, no. Bill's wishes were very clear; he meant to leave the apartment and all his worldly goods to your mother, Tina. I am here because legally I am required as executor of his estate to enact his wishes."

"Yeah, but he didn't mean to leave the apartment to *us*," I said. Mr Long tilted his head, like he had to sort of dramatically think about that one, even though it seemed to me that all the legal shenanigans we were about to embark on were pretty much premised on that fact. So it did seem to me that you didn't actually need to act like this is the first time that might have occurred to you.

"Have you spoken to your lawyer about that thought?" he asked me.

"Not precisely," I admitted.

"Perhaps you should, in private," he advised. "Before you give your deposition. Opposing counsel will be present and the deposition itself will be recorded as a legal document. So the question of Bill's intent, as you yourself were aware of it, will surely be raised. Haven't you been prepped on this?"

"They're going to prep me just before I go in. Some underling is going to run through it with me," I explained. But I was kind of touched that he felt like taking care of me, and I also realized that the way to keep a lawyer talking is to act like trials and depositions and what was going to be entered in court were really interesting subjects. "What kind of things do they ask you in a deposition?" I asked.

"Well, they'll probably ask you things about your mother— the last time you saw her, what she told you about Bill, things like that," he reported.

"Oh, no," I said. "I didn't mean 'you' like 'me'. I meant you. What kind of questions will they ask you?"

"Oh," he nodded, as if that were a really intelligent thing for me to be curious about. "Yes, I will be deposed on completely different matters. Although there will be some overlap. I'm probably the only person who really spent time with Bill and Olivia, together. They'll want to know about that."

"You did?" I asked. I don't know why this hadn't occurred to me. From the start everybody told me he represented Bill and his estate. And I remember Lucy saying that he was Mom's lawyer, the day we found out about the apartment. "Of course you saw them together. They had to come into your office and sign things."

"No, no, they never came into the office," Mr Long corrected me. "Bill wouldn't leave the apartment. I went to them."

"You went to them? You went to the apartment?"

"Of course. I had dinner with them many times."

"You had *dinner* with them?"

"Yes, your mother was a lovely cook."

"My mother was not a lovely cook, Mr Long," I told him, almost laughing out loud at that one. "My mother never cooked."

"Oh. Well. She cooked for Bill. And for me, when I would come by with a legal matter."

This was so far out of the realm of possibility I didn't know what to say. "Well, what did she cook?" I finally asked, trying not to sound utterly incredulous.

"She would roast a tenderloin, or a chicken," he replied. "Once we had salmon filets with some kind of sauce. I think it was an anchovy sauce, it was delicious. And Brussels sprouts in a Dijon mustard dressing, she made that once. There were concerns about Bill's diet, which she was quite alert to. No potatoes, wholegrain rice occasionally. Dessert was usually fresh fruit. Pineapple. Strawberries, when they were in season. Or mango! With a little yogurt, we had that several times."

"Were there napkins? Napkin rings? Was there a *tablecloth*?" My incredulity had tipped over into a completely childish sarcasm and contempt. Mr Long the Eggman tilted his head for a moment, thoughtful, and answered the question.

"We used paper napkins. There was no tablecloth because all they really had was that little coffee table next to the television set. I presume you've seen it?"

"Of course I've seen it."

"Yes. That's where we would eat, so mostly we held our plates on our laps. It was quite pleasant, really, sort of like a little picnic, except with lovely food."

"Made by my mother."

"Once Bill made the salad."

"You know what she used to cook for us?" I offered. "Fish sticks. Spaghetti with Ragu sauce from the jar. Hamburgers, the kind that came in those little flat frozen prefab things—like a machine stamped them straight out of the cow somewhere in Kansas. When she really felt like doing something special for us, you know what we'd get? Frozen *waffles*."

"Really?" said Mr Long.

"Yeah, really," I said. I felt like I was suddenly trapped in a cocktail shaker and someone was giving it a go; the inside of my head had completely dislodged itself. "She was still drinking, right? I mean *please* don't tell me, I don't care how shitty it sounds but I really don't want to find out that once she was finished with the three of us my mother actually fixed her life. There was vodka all over the apartment when I got there, just vodka and red wine and and and nothing—like nothing else was there, when I got there. She was still just a big drunk."

"They both drank." Mr Long nodded, and like everything else it just sounded like a fact coming from him. "But I would never have called either of them 'a big drunk'. Neither one of them to my knowledge drank before six." He stopped talking, like that was enough facts for now.

"What do you mean, they didn't drink before six?"

"I don't know if it was true when I was not present. But

whenever I was present they did not drink before six. They had a certain reverence for the phrase, 'cocktail hour'."

"But then they kept drinking."

"We would enjoy wine with dinner, and then I would leave. I don't know if they continued to drink after I left."

"Cocktail hour. When I was a kid, cocktail hour started at noon," I said. I sounded like nothing more than a big whiner, and in fact my voice actually cracked in the most horrifying way, as if I were about to start crying. Mr Long just stared at the floor with a sort of deliberate and embarrassed disinclination to continue the conversation. "I'm happy, no, I mean I'm really happy for them," I added. "You too. I'm happy you got to have these lovely dinners with Bill and my mom. That sounds terrific."

"It was, actually. She was a very good cook. Now that you tell me she didn't cook often, before she met Bill, I understand the pleasure she took in it. There was always a real sense of surprise, that she was good at it. And now I know why."

"Yeah, all those lovely dinners sound terrific," I said, and I picked up one of the magazines from the table so that I could pretend I didn't care. Because like all the rest of the magazines in that swank office it looked boring as hell so I couldn't even pretend to read it; besides which I knew I was behaving hideously so I immediately put it back down.

"She was his cleaning lady. So you knew that, right, before he married her, she was just like his cleaning lady?"

"Yes, of course I did. I was the one who introduced them."

"You *introduced* them?"

"Oh. Yes. It hadn't occurred to me that you didn't know.

Your mother was doing some cleaning for me, and I knew that Bill was looking for someone as well. So I introduced them."

"Well, how did you know her?" I asked, feeling more and more outraged by all this for some inexplicable reason.

"She lived a few blocks away from me, in Jersey City. She advertised her cleaning services in one of the smaller local papers, and I responded to her ad," he reported, plainly, as if reading those small local papers and responding to an ad there was actually a normal and explicable thing to do.

"That's, this is all just—crazy," I reported.

"Why is it crazy?"

"So you *knew* her? You *really* knew her?"

"I knew her in several different contexts, and through several rather significant changes in her circumstances. So I know about those events, and her experience of those events. Is that what you mean?"

"I—don't think—I knew her," I said, a bit lame.

There was silence at this. And why not? I'm sure I was just embarrassing the hell out of old Stuart Long.

"Perhaps you should discuss the gaps in your information with your sisters," he finally suggested. "They seem to have had more consistent contact with her, in the past few years."

"Yes, that's a good idea," I murmured, embarrassed for us both now. "Of course I will look into these questions with Alison and Lucy. That's obviously what I should do. I apologize, Mr Long, really. Please excuse me. I think maybe I need to use the restroom. I don't, actually, need to use the restroom. I'm not kidding, you have to tell me—something. Something more. None of it makes any sense. This is not, no. No." I said.

"And you can say, go talk to Alison and Lucy because they were *around* more? But I sincerely doubt that they were paying attention. Nobody was paying attention, nobody was *talking* to her. You should hear the shit I hear from the people who live in that building. They can't get over the fact that she was a *cleaning lady* from *New Jersey* and so that means something— evil—that she was a thief and a liar and cheating Bill and keeping him drunk. Because there's no way it was about anything except the apartment, but that's not her either, it's not—it's not . . . None of it sounds like anything I remember. None of it. None of it." I stopped, finally. "Sorry," I said. "Sorry. I don't even know why I talk sometimes, I really do sound like an idiot."

I stopped again. Mr Long waited, presumably to see if there were going to be any further useless outbursts. When there weren't, he folded his fingers together and considered his response. And then he considered some more. It was excruciating. It felt like it took him forever to decide what it was he was going to tell me which might rise to the level of some truth about my mother's life.

"She took very good care of him," he finally said. "His health was quite poor those last few years; that was why he never went out. He was afraid to be left alone as well, but she didn't seem to mind, how much he needed her. And he appreciated everything she did for him, very much. He wanted her to have a home, after he was gone. There was nothing dishonest or dishonorable in their relationship. They took great pleasure in each other. It was my impression that they loved each other very much. That at least is what I will report in my deposition."

399

"What was Sophie like?" I asked.

Mr Long looked at me sharply—at least as sharply as a guy who looks like an egg can look. He didn't have a chance to tell me to mind my own business, though. One of Ira's legal underlings suddenly appeared from some hallway and smiled at me from inside his suit. "Tina? Hi, it's Jackson. I'm going to be prepping your deposition today. I'm so glad I poked my head out. No one knew if you were here or not!"

"Yeah, I kind of slithered in, forgot to tell the girl at the desk," I said.

"Not a problem, not a problem," he reassured me, as if I had apologized in theory or in fact. He held out his hand, like he was guiding me to my execution. "Right in here please. We'll just get started."

CHAPTER TWENTY-SIX

Jennifer was not entirely sympathetic to my position about my mother, but that may have been because she didn't understand it. "Okay, so you were mad at her for being a drunk, but now you're mad because she *wasn't* a drunk?" she asked.

"I don't know that she wasn't a drunk," I said. "All he said was she stopped drinking. Which she didn't even, stop drinking."

"But she didn't drink as much."

"That's what he said. When I was a teenager she like drank all the time, and then passed out in the middle of the day. Then we grow up and she suddenly gets it together to fall in love with a total stranger and *not* drink except at like six o'clock, when everybody drinks," I said, pouring a huge shot of vodka over a couple of ice cubes.

"My parents drink wine," Jennifer informed me. She was delicately perched on the minuscule counter in my little kitchen, her plaid skirt falling perfectly over her skinny knees, while she watched me make myself a cocktail. Her geometry book was lying open on the floor, where she left it when I returned from my torturous afternoon. She had paid off Katharine with a series of minor bribes all week—a Tootsie Roll, a blow pop, a two pack of mint milano cookies—so they had worked it out that she could visit for an hour a day, while Katharine played in her room with the door locked. I thought it was a pretty clever bit of plotting, and in addition it had come to seem an unimaginable delight to have her there. Lucy and Daniel and Alison were off giving depositions and living their lives, that cloud on the title had scared off the realtors for the time being, and Len was presumably off plotting revenge on me, so it had gotten pretty lonely in that big apartment. And Jennifer was good company, in a kind of sardonic teenage way.

"So what was this thing you had to do?" she asked. "You were being decomposed?"

"Yes, that's exactly what it was, I was being *decomposed* by a bunch of bloodless vampires also known as *lawyers*," I said. "It was *endless*. This total moron, *Jack*son, that was his first *name*, I hate that when people have first names that are last names. That became cool, *why?* You have to ask yourself. I'm not kidding. This guy, he's got like the most astonishing suit you've ever seen and even though it's *my* deposition, *I'm* the one who's supposed to be answering questions, even so—even *so*—he manages to squeeze it into the conversation that he went to Yale undergrad and Harvard Law. I'm not kidding. Have you ever noticed that, everybody who went to Harvard and Yale and Princeton manages to get it out there in the first five minutes of conversation where they *happened* to go to school and the rest of us are like, do we really need to talk about this?"

"He sounds like, you know, half of Manhattan," Jennifer noted.

"Right? Plus then the whole thing is about him telling me what not to say. They're going to ask you questions about your mother, and these are the things *not* to tell them. You know what I wasn't allowed to tell them? Everything. Seriously. Everything. Every question, he would say 'What's your favorite memory of your mother?' and I would say, 'Her perfume,' and he would say, 'No no, you can't say that,' and I would say, 'But that is my favorite memory of my mother.' "

"She had nice perfume?"

"She had the most expensive perfume in the world," I said.

"Wow," said Jennifer.

"Yes," I agreed. "But she couldn't ever wear it, because it was too expensive, so she couldn't really afford to wear it. Besides, my dad never took her anywhere to wear it to."

"Well, that's a drag."

"Seriously," I said. "So I tried to explain that to this— asshole, *Jackson*—because he's all, 'You have to be more specific.' And then when I tell him that, what I just said, which *is* specific—he's all, 'No no, you can't say that.' And I'm like, 'Well what *do* you want me to say?' And he's like, 'Tell the truth, be specific, but don't give them any rope that they can hang you with.' And I'm like, 'What do you mean, rope?' And he's like, 'They are trying to prove that your mother had a questionable character. You cannot let them prove that.'"

"A 'questionable character'?" said Jennifer. "What does that mean?"

"It means, I don't know, it means—I don't know what it means," I said. "But I've, honestly, I'm really thinking that I just want to do this right. I don't want to screw things up again. My mom—this is my mom we're talking about and, my sisters—and *I*—I love this place! I love it! I don't want to screw this up. I don't want to give them *rope*. There's already been too much—and then of *course* the other lawyer—"

"There's another lawyer?"

"Yes. From the other side, representing the Drinans, who truth be told, I'm sorry but what they did is also not so great."

"What did they do?"

"It doesn't matter. But this other lawyer—the questions—it's all so—the things they said. And tried to get me to say."

"Like what?"

"Nothing. Forget it." I was sick of myself, trying to explain a deposition to a teenager who really just wanted to hang out and blow off her own family for an hour. It all seemed relentlessly stupid, somehow.

"You're in a bad mood," Jennifer observed, and she hopped off the counter and started to look through the cabinets. "How come you never have anything to eat around here?"

"I have things to eat," I said. "There's half a sandwich in the refrigerator."

"That thing is really old, Tina," she informed me. "I looked at it, before you got back, and it is like truly disgusting. Seriously, I'm not saying you're anorexic or anything, but seriously. If I were you I wouldn't wait until I was sixty to figure out how to eat."

I looked at the bottle of orange juice in my hand and actually considered throwing it at her. I'm not kidding, a wave of something truly evil just came over me and I even raised the bottle for a moment and looked up at her with the thought in my heart, *Just throw it at her*. I could feel the rage, physically, rise up the back of my neck; it was what I felt the last time I did something truly worth getting arrested for. And Jennifer saw it in my face that I might haul off and throw a glass bottle full of orange juice right at her head. She didn't freak out, because frankly she was too well raised for that; she just took a startled little step back and held up her hands, confused but sensible. "Whoa, Tina. What's up? Are you okay?" she asked. "I didn't mean anything. I just meant, you should go to a grocery store and get some eggs or something, crackers, carrot sticks, you know, stuff to eat when you get hungry. Or a chicken. Even if you don't like to cook, the grocery stores sell these roasted chickens; they're pretty good."

I could barely understand the words. Honestly, it was so simple, what she was saying, but my head seriously wasn't processing. I set down the orange juice and looked around the counter. "You know what, though, is why, why isn't there a cookbook then?" I asked her. I opened my arms and included the entire kitchen in my conversation, as if it, or Jennifer, or anyone, really, might know the answer to this question. "It's not like I haven't looked! Where are the recipes? How would you know what to do? If you never did it? How would you know?"

"You can buy cookbooks pretty much anywhere," Jennifer told me, strangely and wonderfully knowing what I was asking.

"Then why isn't there one here?" I asked. "Where did she learn how to do it?"

"I don't know," said Jennifer. "Don't people just know how to cook?"

"No," I told her. "They *don't*."

We looked. For forty minutes. We went through all the cabinets, and in all the boxes under the bed in Bill and Olivia's bedroom. We looked under the couch. We looked in closets that had nothing in them; we checked the shelves over the washer and the dryer; we looked under the sinks in the bathrooms, and then we went through all the boxes of books one more time. There were no cookbooks; Olivia seemingly never bought one.

"Or she threw it away, after he died," Jennifer speculated.

Which is finally what made me cry. It just came up, again on the back of my neck, a terrible feeling from somewhere in my DNA which didn't understand itself. It wasn't like I was bawling or anything, but tears just started running down my face and I couldn't seem to stop them. "Oh," Jennifer said, sort of embarrassed and surprised in a sad, sardonic way. "I don't know. I mean, what do I know? Maybe she just never had one. You might be wrong, Tina. Some people just figure out how to cook on their own." She realized she was sounding completely idiotic and so she shut up.

"I'm sorry," I said. "I don't know what's the matter with me."

"No, it's okay. You had a long day," she said.

"You have homework," I observed.

"Yeah," she said. "Okay, I'll see you tomorrow." And with that she turned, grabbed her geometry book off the floor, and fled.

After an hour of sitting in my mother's little living room, in front of the blank television screen, alongside her empty kitchen, I went out and bought myself a roast chicken. I couldn't eat it, unfortunately; once it was in the apartment and on the kitchen counter it just looked stupid to me. So I put it in the refrigerator and channel-flipped half the night.

No matter what you do, it's never enough, I thought.

I lived with the mantra for another whole day. *No matter what you do, it's never enough.* She seriously said that all the time. That was one of my big memories, alongside the perfume she never wore: *No matter what you do, it's never enough.* That's what I did with an entire day of my life: I sat around an empty apartment, counting and recounting the last of my money, trying to think of what I could do to make more, having a cocktail, looking through someone else's photographs, channel-flipping, counting my money again, thinking, *No matter what you do, it's never enough.* This seriously went on for an entire day before I changed the mantra to *To hell with it,* got myself up off the couch and went outside.

They have a grocery store on the Upper West Side called "Fairway". It is in fact famous, as grocery stores go, so that is where I went, and I fought my way through enormous crowds of shoppers while trying to figure out what ingredients to buy in order to make a real meal for myself. And as it turns out, they have little recipe cards perched everywhere, which are free. It's like a service that the store offers for people like me who don't have a clue: You take one of these cards, buy all the ingredients on the card and then take it home and follow the recipe and then, ta da, you've cooked a meal. Buying all the ingredients totally cleaned me out, cashwise, but I did manage to get everything I needed to cook a meal: pasta with scallops and pears in a lemon cream sauce. It sounds fancy, when you read the instructions, but it truly seemed plausible, in terms of my ability to pull it off. I was thinking of inviting Jennifer to stay for dinner. I headed home with no money but big dreams in my head.

Frank was the first to warn me the evening might not go as planned. "Your sisters are here," he informed me, as he reached out to help me carry my groceries to the elevator. Not only was he back to being nice Frank, he was particularly nice to me. We had never spoken about what happened the day he had confessed to me his love for Julianna Gideon, but it was there between us. He knew that the secret of his heart was known to others and the world hadn't come to an end. I think sometimes just that much is enough to give people hope.

"Thanks for the warning," I said, as I held open the elevator door so he could put my bags on the floor in there for me. "Did they say anything?"

"You know what, they did," said Frank. "They wanted to know what apartment Vince lived in."

"*Vince*?" I asked. "What did they want with Vince?"

Frank gave me a friendly little "who knows" gesture at that one.

"I told them I couldn't give out that information but the pushy one didn't believe me."

"She never takes no for an answer," I admitted.

"No, she don't. Anyway she just went through the junk mail I leave by the radiator until she found it."

"Yes, she's clever, too."

"Boy she is," he said, tapping the elevator button and sending me off.

As I opened the door to the apartment I actually felt my heart thump a little in anticipation. It was a surprise, really, but I was happy to hear they were there. I hadn't seen much of them lately, and truly, I was getting lonely. It was hard to sit in that apartment night after night and wonder who you were. Plus things had gotten so complicated with press conferences and clouds and co-op boards all screaming at each other I was frankly hoping for a minute where Lucy might explain to me what was actually going on.

I was also hoping that Alison, maybe, could tell me about Mom. I could make fun of the idea that the two of them knew anything at all, but I suspected that wasn't actually perhaps the truth, as far as Alison was concerned. She was an uptight, nervous wreck of a human being. But unlike Lucy she had a heart. She was the one Mom talked to.

And there she was, as soon as I stepped in; she was in the front of the apartment, for once, scrubbing down the kitchen.

"I see you got rid of the moss!" she exclaimed. I felt a little tug of happiness. I was really glad to see her. She had never given up on her first impression, which told her that the stuff was dangerous and it would cost millions to have it removed, and we could be left on the hook for it, even if we didn't win this case. And now the stuff was just miraculously gone. Once Charlie had poisoned it beyond repair I had tossed all the trays into garbage bags and taken them straight out to the dumpster so that whatever that stuff was that had killed them wouldn't get everyone else in the building. Alison didn't know that, of course, all she knew was that the moss had disappeared. Of course she was cheerful.

"How'd your deposition go?" I asked.

"Terrific," she said. "Just great. I like that Jackson, don't you? He really thinks we're going to win this. He was very reassuring."

"Was he?"

"And so cute! I mean, not my type, I'm happily married! But that doesn't mean I can't look!" This thing she was doing while she wiped down the counters was peculiarly bright and slightly birdlike. I went almost instantaneously from being pleased to see her, to being kind of suspicious.

"What can I do for you today, Alison?" I asked.

"Oh, Lucy and I just thought maybe we should come over and help you keep this place clean," she explained with that cheerful smile. "It just didn't seem fair that you should have to do all the work of keeping this big place presentable, while the lawyers and the real estate people and the people who run the building try and work out their problems. I mean, who knows how long that is going to take! And you're not a slave!"

410

"There's not that much to do, actually," I told her, trying to figure this out. "Most of the rooms don't get used. The moss thing, as you've noticed, has been taken care of."

"So that man who owned it—Len, is that what his name is?"

"Yes?" I said, wondering where this was going.

"Len Colbert?"

"Did I mention his name to you?"

"I just, I saw a Len on the names listed on the co-op board, and I wondered if that were him."

"Yes, that is him. He was the one kind of ranting at that press conference they threw in the lobby, where they told the entire city of New York that we're white trash interlopers. That was his phrase, I think. I think he got mentioned in all the articles. Lucy's friend over at the *Times* gave him an especial lot of ink."

"Well, I didn't read any of it, because I knew it would upset me, but Daniel did, and he did mention that, that this Len person seemed particularly upset." She nodded. "Well, if he's angry already we don't want to make him any angrier. I was going to suggest we should leave the moss where it is."

"No, it's gone."

"Well, maybe you should let him know that if he wants to keep it here he is welcome," she said and she smiled at me brightly again, like a girl scout leader.

"Listen, Alison, is something going on?" I asked. Honestly, she was being so cheerfully weird you finally had to comment on it. But then of course as soon as I did you could see the anxiety bloom in her eyes; it was just right there under the

411

surface of that fierce goodwill and she wasn't going to be able to keep it at bay for long.

"What makes you ask?"

"Oh—nothing," I said. I could tell that she really didn't want to be the one to deliver whatever bizarre news she and Lucy had come to unload on me, so I decided it might be best to spare her for now. "Is Lucy in the back?"

"No, she had to run out for a moment," Alison reported, nervous.

"Really? Frank said she was up here."

"She was. She'll be right back. Would you like some tea? I think I saw some in the closet, in the back kitchen. I would love a cup of tea," she enthused, clearly working to get her act back on the rails.

"Terrific," I said. "Let's go do that then."

We hiked through the great room, and down the endless hallway that led to the other kitchen, in the other half of the apartment. "Hey, Alison, do you remember if Mom ever cooked?" I asked.

"Mom? Cook?" Alison said, startled. The idea seemed as nonsensical to her as it had to me, when I first heard it. "Well, she boiled water for spaghetti, I remember her doing that. But that was pretty much the extent of the cooking."

"Do you cook?" I asked.

"Daniel and I both work, you know that," she said.

"Lucy doesn't cook," I observed.

"When you live on Manhattan you don't have to cook," Alison informed me. "Manhattan is thirty-five square miles of room service!"

412

"Well, I think I'm going to cook tonight," I said. "I bought a bunch of groceries because I thought I'd like to try it. You want to stay for dinner?"

"Oh," she said, like this was really a bad idea.

"You don't have to stay. I mean, you can stay if you want. It's probably going to be a disaster. But you never know. I'm making scallops and pears in a lemon vodka sauce. I read the recipe and it doesn't sound as hard as it sounds. You just boil some pasta, and sear the scallops and the pears. Do you know how to sear?"

"No, I don't, I really don't," she said, getting all upset again, inexplicably.

"It's not that big a deal. I can figure it out," I told her.

"I think that's Lucy," she said, picking up the strange change in atmosphere which occurs whenever someone opens the front door of the apartment. "LUCY! IS THAT YOU?" she asked, and then she scurried away.

Even having been forewarned by Frank, I didn't put together what their plan was. How could you? Lucy had to just come out and announce it to me. She breezed into the kitchen with Alison hovering behind her, and tossed their plan off like a fancy new pair of leather gloves.

"I was just down there on the fifth floor talking to your friend Vince," she told me, as if this were the most natural thing for her to do in the world.

"What? You were what?" I said.

"He really likes you, Tina. Well, we knew that."

"Okay, can we back up for a second. You went down to see Vince Masterson?"

413

"His father is the chairman of the co-op board."

"So?"

"So we—Daniel, and Ira and I, and Alison—think that's a good relationship to build. Obviously no one is happy about the co-op's response to this situation. That press conference they held made a big impression on the media and Sotheby's has, well, I think it's obvious that their interest has cooled. We were all set to move ahead with the renovation and that, all of it, has been put on hold."

"What renovation? You want to renovate this place? With what?"

"There are investors willing to come on board with us. We told you this."

"You did not tell me this."

"If I didn't tell you all the details it's because you can barely hold on to the three or four which are in front of you at any given time."

"Stop talking to me like I'm an idiot, Lucy."

"I'm not talking to you like you're an idiot. I'm telling you the facts. You're angry because we don't always give them to you. Well, I'll give them to you now if you'll stop whining long enough to listen."

"That's charming."

"Please, please don't fight," Alison interrupted, suddenly near tears. "It's terrible, Tina. You don't know how bad things are. We're going to lose everything. We're going to *lose*."

"Relax, Alison," Lucy warned her. "We're not losing anything. It's just going to take a little bit longer to win. We're going to need to be both wily and tenacious, and as you and I both know, Tina is completely capable of that."

"Oh great. I can't wait to hear what I'm capable of," I said. "Keep going, Lucy."

"Vince would really like to have dinner with you."

"So you arranged for that. For me to have dinner with him," I said.

"You have a reservation at Neal's, for seven-thirty. He'll meet you there."

"But then we can cab back home together," I observed, picking up on the genius of the plan fast enough.

"Well, that would be up to you, but since you live in the same building I don't know why not."

"Perfect," I said. "I'm really looking forward to sharing a cab with that octopus."

"He's quite attractive," Lucy told Alison, ignoring my tone. "He looks like a supermodel. I can't believe he looks like that, and he has money! Oh, you put water on for tea! Is there enough for me?" She sailed back into the kitchen and started looking around for extra tea bags.

"Yes, there's water. I don't think it's ready yet, but maybe it is," Alison twittered. "I don't know how long you keep it on."

"You keep it on until it *boils*," I said. "Are you kidding me? You really don't even know how to boil *water*?"

"We don't have tea very often, Tina," Alison replied, with an air of offended dignity. "I just heat up the water in the microwave."

"Well, let me clue you in onto something. The microwave uses up sixty zillion times as much energy as you need and it *doesn't get the water hot enough*."

"Don't yell at her," Lucy warned me.

"How about if I yell at you?" I said, furious.

"What, what?" said Alison. "What's wrong?"

"Oh, stop acting like an idiot, Alison," I sneered. "I'm being pimped out by my own sisters and you want me to act like there's nothing *wrong?*"

"Inflammatory language is not going to be entirely helpful here," Lucy informed me.

"Inflammatory language is *never* helpful. That's not why I use it!" I hissed. "You want me to fuck that guy. I'm supposed to fuck Vince Masterson because his father is on the fucking co-op board."

"He is the *president* of the co-op board."

"No one said you had to sleep with him," Alison protested. "We just thought that since he liked you already, that you could ask for his help, Tina. That's all we were talking about."

"Alison, grow up and get a clue, would you please? Vince Masterson does not want to have *dinner* with me."

"A couple of months ago I almost walked in on you and Vince doing the deed right out front, on that hideous shag rug," Lucy pointed out, unimpressed with my moral outrage. "I don't think it's unreasonable to assume that if you decided to follow through on that impulse it might put things on a friendlier footing. Between us and the co-op board."

"Why don't *you* have sex with him, you think it's such a great idea."

"Well, because you and he have already established such a rapport."

"You don't have to have sex with him, Tina, come on," Alison interjected with a note of pleading. "Just have dinner with him, that's all, and remind him that we're really good people and we want to do what's best for the building and the apartment, we want it to be safe and to go into the right hands. That's really what we want, and they don't have to worry about that."

"Great. That's great. I'm sure that will make a big impression on old Vince," I said, just not really caring momentarily about any of this, I found the whole scenario so depressing. "My sisters are pimping me out," I said to myself. "That's great. My sisters are pimping me out."

"Please stop saying that. That's just not true," said Alison.

"You know, Mom would not want this," I said. "You know that."

"She doesn't get a vote," Lucy said.

"What do you think?" I said to Alison. "You think Mom would want me to do this? Just go have sex with this guy because Lucy thinks that maybe that'll help?"

"It's because of what she wanted, you don't know, Tina, Mom wanted—"

"Alison—"

"No, we have to tell her. If we don't tell her how will she know?"

"Know what?"

Both of them stared at each other. Lucy was clearly both furious and calculating, Alison pleading with her sad and puppy-like eyes. Lucy looked up at the ceiling, like this picture of Pontius Pilate about to dip his bloody hands into a plate of water that my mother actually had hung on the wall of the living room when we were kids.

"Well, now you have to tell me," I pointed out.

"Fine," said Lucy. "Alison, be my guest."

"Mom called me," Alison whispered, grave. And then she stopped.

"Mom *called* you? When, like, last week? From the grave?" I know it was mean but I had really had it with both of them by that point, with good reason.

"Before. Before the grave. But just before."

"What are you—Alison, stop beating around the bush!"

"I'm not, I'm telling you! She called me. She was feeling sick. And she was worried. Because she felt like she couldn't stay here. That she was living in someone else's home. But Bill left it to her, he wanted her to have it and she wanted to stay here and be close to him but she was worried that something might happen to her and she wanted to make a will. And in the will she wanted to make sure, make sure that his sons should get their home back."

This revelation landed, as you might suspect, with some authority.

"She called you? On the telephone?"

"Yes."

"When was this?"

"It was just a few days. Before she died. Like three even," Alison said, the wonder of it still creeping into her voice when she remembered.

"And—"

"Yes. She wanted to make a will but she didn't make a will.

418

We weren't sure. We thought that maybe she called that lawyer—"

"Mr Long?"

"Yes, him. We thought that maybe she had called him and told him?"

"But we've seen his deposition. It wasn't there," Lucy narrated. "And they asked him specifically, did she ever make statements to the effect that she felt that the property was deeded to her improperly. He said no."

"So we think she never said it to him. We think that she only said it to me, then didn't do it."

"And you didn't tell them."

"No, she didn't," Lucy informed me. She went back to the refrigerator and with one icy motion pulled the door open and grabbed the vodka bottle. She pulled the cork out with her teeth. I felt like I was in Russia suddenly. "She didn't tell anybody at first because she didn't know what it meant. And then when Mom died, and we started getting all these phone calls about a house—"

"They said apartment. But Mom had called it a house. That's why I was confused. She said it was a house."

"So you didn't tell them."

"I told Daniel, and Lucy." Alison continued. "But they said not to tell anybody else. Because if Mom really did want to leave it, to someone else, she had plenty of time to do it. Or, she would have called her lawyer. That she could have done that any time. So maybe she was drunk or something. When she called me. And if she was drunk, then she maybe didn't really mean what she said, and that if I told people it would just confuse things."

419

"It doesn't sound too confusing to me," I noted. "You tell somebody what she said, that she wanted the Drinans to have the apartment? That sounds like the kind of statement that will make things significantly *less* confusing. You tell them that, and all the turmoil goes away, Alison."

"Yes, people suspected your rambling conscience might choose to see things that way," Lucy said, taking a straight shot of vodka out of one of my few clean glasses. "Which is why people felt that the right thing to do, to protect you and your interests, was to keep it to ourselves."

"What's that supposed to mean?"

"It means sometimes you get on a high horse and sometimes you get on quite a different horse, and no one knows which on any given day you're going to choose."

"That's not what I do."

"Tina. Your immediate reaction to this story is to run off and tell the lawyers, right? This is what Mom wanted, so that's what we should do. 'It's not confusing.' 'It makes all the problems go away.' But it doesn't. It's hearsay. Alison can't really remember exactly what Mom said. And you weren't on the phone call, you weren't even on the call list, so you don't know what Mom may or may not have wanted. So you can't testify anyway, to what Alison just told you. But if Mom called anyone else?" She shrugged and poured herself more vodka.

"Can I have some of that?" I asked.

"Of course," she said, finding the second clean glass. I waited while she poured the shot, then tossed it back. It tasted good.

"You mean one of the Drinans," I said. "You think she called

420

one of them, and said that she wanted to do the right thing and leave them the apartment."

"Whether or not she did, that will be hearsay too. Unless somebody has something in writing, none of it is admissible."

"Which is why, what? Which is why the co-op board is the bigger problem, today?"

"They're all problems," Lucy nodded. "But today the co-op board is the big one, yes." She poured me more vodka, rather more than I particularly needed. I knew she was just trying to get me drunk so that I'd go along with her crazy plot, but by that point I almost appreciated the gesture. "Listen, Tina," she said. "The Drinans are not going to win this. The one piece of evidence they need—that Mom intended to leave the apartment to them—doesn't exist! So if the building, if the co-op board takes some crazy position against us, it won't do anybody any good anyway. It will just complicate things. And make them messier. You'll be doing everyone a favor if you can straighten this out."

"Lucy says Vince is really nice," Alison said, sadly. "She thinks he wants to help us."

"Oh for crying out loud," I said. Then, "I was going to make a dinner."

"You can do it tomorrow," Lucy told me. "Maybe you could wear that black dress, that you wore to the press conference at Sotheby's. You really look terrific in that."

CHAPTER TWENTY-SEVEN

I went to that restaurant to meet Vince. Why not, I thought. The honest pleasure I had felt when I saw Alison poking around my mossless kitchen had completely evaporated; I didn't want to even try cooking anymore. Really what I wanted to do was just get away from both of them. Plus, while I didn't know what the dead people who had put all this in motion actually did want, I did know that handing the apartment over to the building was what they *didn't* want. Plus the food would be good. Plus I was out of cash, and under the circumstances Vince would definitely have to pay for it.

"Tina, hi." He smiled, as I walked into the bar. He stood up from the barstool and leaned over and kissed me on the mouth. It was quick, but deliberate. There would be no mystery around the given assumptions of the evening. "That dress really is stunning. I was hoping you'd wear it."

"My sister suggested you might feel that way," I replied. "We aim to please."

"And you do," he said, slightly gallant and slightly creepy at the same time. Then he turned to the bartender, who of course was right there waiting for his next command. "A vodka gimlet for the lady," Vince told him. "And can we have some of those cheese things that keep wandering by? I'm *starving*."

Those "cheese things" turned out to be some sort of Cheddar cream puff, which was all we ate while Vince continued to pour vodka gimlets into me, at the bar.

"Aren't we going to eat?" I asked him, as the bartender delivered my third gimlet. "I'm getting drunk."

"But you're so charming when you're drunk," Vince reassured me. "I confess I was hoping to get you a little inebriated and then lure you back into that hot tub. I can still see you there, surrounded by naked men. I can't believe I missed that."

"A little louder, Vince. I don't think the entire restaurant heard you," I pointed out. "And by the way, I do understand what the intentions of the evening are, but can't you at least pretend?" I leaned over the bar and spoke to the bartender. "We're going to be eating at the bar," I told him. "I'd like a big steak, the best one you've got, medium rare."

"Yes ma'am," he replied discreetly. Vince raised his Scotch glass, which was empty for the third time.

"I'd slow down, Vince. You've got a long night ahead of you."

"I'm looking forward to it. You'll not escape me again, Tina Finn, and while we're on the subject, I have a bone to pick with you about that. Why are you playing so hard to get? I know you like me."

"Yeah, I love it when people try to extort me into having sex with them. That's my favorite, favorite thing."

"If your sister hadn't interrupted us, we'd have done the

deed the first day I met you. Nobody was extorting you then."

"What can I say, Vince. Somehow the mystery's lost," I said, but then I glanced over at him, and honestly I had to admit in my heart that maybe he had a point. His jacket hung beautifully across his back, and his blue eyes considered me with a kind of animal intelligence it was hard not to appreciate. The guy just radiated money and charisma. When he caught on to the fact that I was sizing him up he grinned, which made him look both better and worse.

"Extortion my ass," he said, leaning in and kissing me. This time there was nothing fast about it, and it involved a lot of tongue. On top of the three gimlets, it made me see stars, but at the same time I was not ready to just hurl myself down the rabbit hole. I pushed him back.

"Let's get out of here," he said.

"I have a steak coming," I reminded him.

"For crying out loud, I'm jumping out of my skin here," he informed me. "How long am I going to have to wait for this?"

"I don't know, Vince," I said, "but the whining is not actually doing it for me at the moment. I thought we were having dinner. You need to slow the train down."

This pissed him off. "You need to be nice," he said, darkly.

"I *am* being nice," I retorted. "As nice as I get in situations like this. So what is up with your stupid co-op board anyway? Lucy was acting like six years of legal hassle is nothing compared to what those jerks might be upto."

"Well, they're legally evicting you this week, so she might have a point," he informed me, continuing in the tone of careless nastiness which we had both been taking with each other. As soon as he said it he half regretted it, you could tell, but only because it meant he wasn't going to get laid until he explained what that idle, but utterly specific comment actually meant.

"What do you mean, they're evicting me?"

He looked away for a second, annoyed, but it was too late to take it back. "It's in the bylaws of the building," he said, reaching for his drink. He shrugged, like this is common knowledge, and you're so stupid that you don't even know it.

"What's in the fucking bylaws?"

"What I just said! If you don't have any legal standing—and you don't, you have none until they settle all the confusion over the wills—"

"There isn't any confusion over the wills—"

"You have no legal standing, no right at all, Tina, to be in that apartment—"

"Pete Drinan said it was okay. They had an injunction but it got removed—"

"They don't get to say! They have no legal standing either! The building gets to say! And the building wants you out."

"Why? Why?"

"Because you can't just waltz into one of the most exclusive addresses and take it over. It doesn't happen that way."

"I'm hardly taking it over."

"You're living in the Livingston Mansion Apartment. It is not going to be allowed."

"Tell that to the courts."

"You're gone, Tina. Get a clue."

426

"Unless what. I'm gone unless *what*?" I asked, getting a little desperate at the sureness of his absolute knowledge of how places like the Edge worked.

"Unless *nothing*," he said, laughing now. "It's a done deal."

"Then why am I supposed to sleep with you, asshole?" I said. "Why would I do that if they're kicking me out anyway?" Suddenly caught in the mess of lies he had been telling my sisters, and the truths he had been telling me, Vince's mouth dropped open. It was pathetic. "You can't do anything for any of us. Can you?" I said. "And you told my sister, you made my sister think that if I slept with you it would make a difference. You got her to sell me out for nothing."

"No," he started.

"You're a fucking piece of shit, Vince," I told him. And then, louder, as loud as I could, so that the whole restaurant could hear me, "You're a fucking lying piece of *shit*." And with that, I left.

He caught up with me two blocks later, as I stalked up Broadway. I hate heels, they look great on the exit but then you can never keep it up; boots are much better in a getaway. Unfortunately, though, I was wearing those stupid heels because I was supposed to look all beautiful and sexy for that lying shithead, which meant I could hardly walk, which meant that lying shithead didn't even have to break a sweat to catch up with me as I stumbled down the sidewalk.

"Tina, I'm sorry. Tina, stop, just stop and listen to me for a second."

"No."

"Yes, come on, I'm sorry. I exaggerated. It's not true what I told you."

427

"It sure sounded like the truth. At least, it sounded completely different from all the bullshit that comes out of your mouth otherwise."

"They are kicking you out. They had the vote scheduled for it today. But my dad couldn't be there, so they have to reschedule."

"Liar."

"I'm not lying. They need a bunch of signatures when they're engaging in legal action and he's the board president so he had to be there. So I did tell your sister I'd put in a good word—"

"If I slept with you."

"Yes, I did tell her that," he said, having enough of a shred of grace, finally, to be the tiniest bit embarrassed by it. "But the fact is—even if he votes for you, it won't make a difference. They have eleven votes against you. Even if I could swing him your way, you're gone."

"Well then, who owns the apartment?" I asked.

"It will take them years to figure that out, and the longer it takes the better it is for the building. I mean, they never liked the Drinans, either."

"It doesn't matter if they *like* them or not. It was their apartment!"

"It was the *Livingston* apartment," Vince corrected me, quite serious for once. He looked startled, even; there was something about the import of this whole insane situation which I wasn't getting. "Those people, they came into the building, they weren't vetted, they just came in."

"I think they were born there, Vince," I informed him.

"It's not like citizenship, Tina. It's not like if you're *born* in

428

a building you have property rights. I didn't think I'd have to explain that to *you*. And if that first will wasn't probated? The building has more of a claim than anybody. And maybe they should. You know the story about what happened to the mother. They put her in some loony bin and threw away the key, and then she *died* in there. It's totally Victorian."

"It's a Victorian building," I reminded him.

"Well said, but why should they get the apartment? It was her apartment."

"What's your point, Vince?" I asked, although I really didn't want to know.

"My point is neither one of you are going to get that apartment, I don't care how hard you try," Vince said, all convivial now. "It's the *Livingston Mansion Apartment*, Tina! You might have had a chance with one of the minor apartments. But that one, no way."

"I see," I said, although I did not.

"Listen." Vince sighed, suddenly filled with pity and goodwill toward me, God only knows why. "I'll see if I can buy you some time. I really can put in a good word, and it might keep dear old Dad on the fence for a little while."

"How many times do I have to sleep with you for that whopping favor?"

"It's for free," he said, grinning at this. "Come on, Tina, let's grab a cab. You can't walk all the way home in those shoes. I won't bother you. I promise."

"Your promises," I sighed, indicating that I didn't think very much of them. But I wasn't too mean about it.

CHAPTER TWENTY-EIGHT

"So how did it go?" Lucy cooed on the phone the next morning.

"Just great, Lucy," I said. "Vince is definitely on board."

"I knew you could do it," she replied, smug. "Thanks, Tina. I owe you one."

"Anything for the cause," I said. "You need anything else, just let me know."

I hung up and stared at the ceiling. I thought about calling her back and telling her everything that Vince had said, that we would never win this, the building didn't want *any* of us, their goal was to boot both the Drinans and the Finns, and the building was going to win and we needed to come up with a better strategy than having Tina go sleep with everybody on the board. But she never listened. Alison didn't listen much either these days; they both seemed like people I only knew a very long time ago, and then only vaguely. I wondered if that wasn't why I had just disappeared, finally: Because nobody was listening anyway. And then I thought about Mom, and what she would say, and what she would want me to do, and I wished that I had called her just once, from out there at the Delaware Water Gap. The time maybe that she had called to ask me about Asiago cheese, I thought, maybe I should have called her back. Then maybe I would have been the one she called, when she needed to call someone about doing the right thing, and keep that beautiful apartment for the people who had actually lived there. But I didn't call her back; I just never did. I was too busy running away.

There wasn't anything else for it. I went to the 91st precinct and marched myself up to the front desk. "I need to talk to Detective Drinan," I told the desk sergeant. He barely glanced up at me; he was busy opening mail with a plain silver letter opener which looked a little bit like a really boring dagger. He took his time, sliding the pointy end into the top of the envelope and moving it carefully all the way across. I don't know why people think mail is more important than people, but they certainly do. In any case, this desk sergeant, a big fat black guy who was wearing an enormous sweater, like it wasn't 200 degrees in there anyway, finished opening his manila envelope, considered the first three pages of the contents, paper-clipped the docs to the outside of the envelope, and set the whole event down on the other side of his desk. Then he deigned to talk to me.

"He expecting you?" he asked, picking up a phone on his desk carelessly, like he might also make a phone call in the middle of our conversation, that's how unimportant I was.

"I don't think he's expecting me," I said. "But you know, he might be. Actually he actually might be." My fascinating conjectures held no interest for the desk sergeant, who just nodded and hit a few buttons as he shouldered the receiver.

"What's your name?" he asked.

"Tina Finn."

"Yeah," he suddenly said into the receiver, bored as hell, "somebody named Tina Finn is here for Pete." He paused. "Uh huh." Then there was another pause. "Uh huh." Then, another pause. "Yeah, okay," he said. And he hung up the phone and reached into a bag of chips, which was sitting alongside the pile of mail. He put a potato chip in his mouth and then he crunched it a few times, and then he picked up his letter opener and started slitting through the end of another manila envelope.

"So, he, am I . . . should I wait here for him?" I asked. The desk sergeant didn't even look up this time.

"He's not here," he said.

"He's not," I said.

"He have your number?"

"No, actually, he doesn't," I said.

"You can leave it if you want," he said, pulling out some more docs and glancing through them.

"What kind of police station is this?" I said, a little loud. He looked up, raised his eyebrows at me. I swear, I never did know how to talk to the cops. "I could be a *witness* for a *murder* or something and you can barely talk to me!"

"Are you?" he said.

"No," I said. "I am not." And then I held up a brown paper bag which I had brought with me, and dropped it right into the middle of his mail call. "This is for Detective Drinan. This is important. It is important evidence for a case that he thinks is really important and you need to give it to him as soon as he gets back."

"You can wait for him if you want," he told me, completely unimpressed with my theatrics.

"No," I said. "I'm not going to wait. He knows where to find me."

Which he most certainly did. Seven hours later he was at my front door. In his left hand he held a child's green hand-knit sweater with a broken cable on one arm, evidence from a previous life which I had left in a brown paper bag at the front desk of his precinct. "So," he said, "you found the junk room. Is there any reason you need to talk to me about that?"

"You know about that?"

"The room in the back, we used as a storage space?"

"No, of course, of course," I said, feeling stupid now that I thought I had something to show him that he didn't already know about that place. "Well, just, then, come in," I said. He did.

I had spent the afternoon unloading what I could from that room. I thought it was the polite thing to do, somehow: I had taken out everything that I could and piled it all over the little room with the television and the couch and the coffee table. Clothes and shoes, and dishes and books and photos and art projects and knitting, it was everywhere.

"Holy shit," he said, when I walked him back there.

"Yeah, it's a lot of stuff," I agreed.

"You took all this out of the boxes? Why'd you do that?"

"I thought you might want to see it," I said, feeling stupider and stupider. I looked over at him, and there was just a thin streak of color across the top of his cheeks. Other than that, nothing. He looked like he was looking at a corpse. "I really

434

did, I thought this is your stuff, this is your, here, I left a space for you to sit on the couch. I thought maybe you'd want to look at the pictures. There were like four boxes of pictures."

He stared at me, then walked over to the space on the couch which had been left clear for him. In front of it I had stacked the albums neatly on the coffee table, right next to the extra boxes of loose photos and negatives. Pete stood there for a moment, considering the arrangement, then he reached down, and without sitting, flipped open the cover of the first album within reach. Still without sitting, he flipped the first page, and then the second, sort of casually, like he was only half interested in what he saw there. He looked up, and his eyes flicked over the room again, taking in the piles of stuff, the dusty collected bits and pieces of his childhood, and then he wavered for a minute, on his feet, like he was going to fall over maybe.

"Are you okay?" I asked. "I'm sorry. I just I thought you would want to see it. I really, I . . ."

"Yeah," he said, holding up his hand to stop me from talking. "I know. I'm just going to need a minute." And then he turned around and walked back down the hallway.

I felt like an idiot. I sat down in the middle of all the crap and wondered what to do. I wasn't even sure if he was still in the apartment; that stupid place is so big you can't tell half the time if anyone is in there with you; it's like a mausoleum, just a big empty monument to people who came and went. I remembered this thing I read somewhere, when I was a kid, about how once, in America, they tried to make bombs that killed people but left everything else: streets and buildings and cars and equipment, just

435

no people. I thought, Wow, they did it. They set off one of those bombs right here, in my apartment, and nobody knew.

When Pete didn't come back after ten minutes, I went looking for him. If he hadn't left, there was one other place that I thought he might be, and in fact that's where he was, in my room that used to be his room, sitting on the little bed on the floor and looking at the painting of the sunset on the wall.

"I used to dream about it," he said, not even acknowledging me, more like he was just saying something out loud to himself right when I happened to show up. "In all those upside-down ways you dream about things. It would come to life sometimes and try to drown me. She thought it was so cool, when she did it. Far as I was concerned, it was like someone had painted a nightmare on the wall."

"Did you tell her?"

"Come on. She loved it," he said. "And it's really not very good, is it? I mean, really. It's just crap."

"I like it," I said, stepping inside the doorway and considering it. He laughed a little, like he thought I was stupid, but that he appreciated my attempt to say something nice about his mother's dreadful painting. "I do," I insisted. "I'm not kidding. I really do."

"Well, you're wrong," he informed me. "Because it's shit."

"Are those real constellations?" I asked, pointing up at the star stickers on the ceiling.

"No," he said. "We tried. She was all, 'Let's put up the ones no one knows, Taurus and Perseus and the Archer,' only she was so bent on being original it didn't end up looking like anything. It doesn't really mean anything."

436

"But her stuff. I thought you might want her stuff."

"All that shit, in the other room?" he asked me. "Really. You think I might want that?"

"Yeah, well, you know what? It's not all shit," I told him. I went to the closet, picked up that crumpled brown paper bag and pulled out the pearls. I handed them to him. He turned them over in his hand, considered the clasp, and looked back up at me, raising an eyebrow like he was waiting for me to explain this again. "Those are real pearls. Those are worth a fortune," I told him. "I'm not kidding. There's a lot of stuff out there, who knows how much it's worth. There's an alligator purse, someone told me you could sell it for five thousand dollars. And some of her old dresses, they're probably worth . . . Sorry. I'm sorry," I said.

"No, it's fine," he said. "People need money. I assumed you needed money." He continued watching me with those impartial eyes. I wished he would laugh again, but I figured that would be an uncommon event.

"Look," I said, finally. "You should go look through that stuff. Even if you don't want it because of whatever your reasons are, even if it all seems like—nothing, to you—you should go through it. It's yours."

"Our lawyers have been telling us for months it's not ours. According to them, any way you look at it, all of it is yours." He held up the pearls to hand them back to me; they hovered there between us for a moment. He wasn't kidding. I took the pearls, and then I took a breath.

"My mother. Called my sister," I told him. "Before she died."

"So?" he said.

I sat down next to him on the bed. The pearls were lovely to hold, cool and round and heavy. They seemed somehow confident in my sweaty hands, like they knew I could get through this.

"She knew something, that she was, that maybe she was dying," I said. "Anyway that's what I think. I don't know for sure, because I didn't talk to her. She didn't call me. I was out there in hell, down by the Delaware Water Gap. No one knew how to get hold of me."

"But she called your sister," he asked, like a detective to a witness, reminding you to keep the story moving forward.

"She called Alison. She said something like, the wills weren't right."

"No. They were right. He told us, we weren't getting anything. The will was right."

"Yeah, but wait. Mom told Alison that she wanted to make a new will. For herself, so that you and your brother would get it. If anything happened to her. She was going to make a will."

"Did she call a lawyer?"

"I don't know. I talked to that Mr Long, just last week. He didn't say anything."

"He didn't say anything in his deposition, either. I saw it."

"Yeah, but she told Alison—"

"It's hearsay, Tina," he explained, like this was common sense. "It won't hold up in court."

"You don't know that; you're not a lawyer," I said.

"I'm a police detective; I think I know a few things about how the law works. Hearsay is inadmissible. Even if Alison would admit it."

"She admitted it to me."

"She won't admit it in court, and they wouldn't enter it as evidence even if she did. And even if they did, it would only complicate a legal situation that already has way too many complications," he told me. "I wouldn't bring it up if I were you. When did Alison tell you this?"

"Yesterday."

"So she knows how to keep a secret. Good for her. Tell her to keep her mouth shut, in future, about your dying mother's phone call."

"Look," I said. "We have to start getting a clue. The co-op board wants both of us out of here. They're trying to steal it out from under all of us. If we got together on this we could at least—"

"Keep it in the family?" he asked, with a sardonic roll of the eyes.

"I know you have every reason to be mad at me, but I'm honestly trying to do the right thing here," I informed him. "Don't you want this? Don't you want the apartment?"

He looked over at the painting on the wall and his eyes creased with the worry and sadness of the past. You could see he didn't want to think about any of it, but that he also wasn't a coward, when called upon to do so.

"Look, a lot of shit went down here," he said. "So no, I'm not sure that I do want it. And you know, I lived here for a long time, and then I didn't live here for a long time. So I'm not so sure I need it."

"Whether you need it or not, it's worth a lot of money!" I insisted. I was tired of his version of the facts. He kept skipping the one fact that had been twisting through all of it and making it all happen since the day my mother died: the money. "Even if you don't want the stuff, this place is worth a total fortune. It's worth *millions*. You could sell it. If you didn't want it."

"Would you sell it?"

"Me?" I said. "It's not mine to sell."

"So, if you could, you'd just live here forever?"

I thought about this. I had never even let myself think it because I knew from the start it couldn't happen. But if it could? "I like this place," I admitted. "It's beautiful. Things happen here. It's kind of weird, with all the hallways and rooms and hardly any furniture? But I do, I really like living here."

"People don't live here, they die here," he told me.

"People die everywhere," I said. "And this apartment is considerably better than the other places I found."

"Yeah, I've seen your record," he said. "It's pretty interesting."

"I like living here," I said, again, looking around the little room, which was quite cozy now, with the collection of little pieces I had brought together to make a home for myself. "I'm sorry to go."

"I wouldn't be in such a hurry," he said. "It's going to take them years to get this through the legal system."

"No, I'm being kicked out. The co-op board is kicking me out," I told him. "It's part of their big plan to get the apartment. I told you, they want it."

"How is kicking you out going to accomplish that?"

"I don't know. I'm getting all my information third hand. Presumably they have more shenanigans up their sleeves."

440

"Who's behind this?"

"I don't know. They keep saying 'the building' like it has a mind of its own."

"Yeah, they used to do that to us, too," he remembered. "They'd get all bent out of shape about something or other, send notes to my dad, signed 'The Building'. It really pissed him off. My mother screaming all the time, seriously bloodcurdling shit, horrible, and *loud*, and then we'd get these messages from The Building about appropriate noise levels. I think they threatened to kick *us* out a couple times, and her family built the place, like six hundred years ago."

"1879," I reminded him.

"Whatever. Those assholes. And it was always presented in such a creepy way. Like that woman who married beneath her is a little *loud*, when she has her psychotic breaks, but the real problem is those Irish guys who are being rude. They're a bunch of 'feckin' bigots', that was his phrase. He threw in a bit of a brogue around the 'feckin' bigots'." It made him laugh.

"Wait a minute," I said. "You mean he was *really* Irish? Like, Irish Irish?"

"He grew up in Galway. But he was legal, at least after he married her. That was another one they kept tossing around: He only married her for the green card. Somebody, or maybe it was just 'the building,' tried to argue that he wasn't allowed to inherit, when she died. Our lawyers were trying to dig that one up, because if he couldn't inherit it, then he couldn't leave it to your mother, and that meant it came to us straight from her. But there's no legal standing for that one. They may go there anyway, who knows." He looked around the little room, thinking about all this, then he grinned, as a thought occurred to him. "That why you're trying to give it away? To stick it to all of them? If you can't have it, why not me?" This idea pleased him.

"I wasn't trying to stick it to anyone. I'm trying to do the right thing."

"The right thing." He laughed. "You're a criminal."

"Oh, please," I said. "I'm such a dumb criminal. I am the lamest of criminals."

"You have your points," he said. Then he leaned back, considered the stars above, and stretched his arms over his head, happy. He really was one of those guys, the truth made him happy. I had never seen him so relaxed. "I like criminals," he admitted. "I mean, some of them are jackasses and some of them are truly bad people who should not be on the street. The rest of them—they're people who want things. I respect that. I mean, they go too far, they don't understand rules, but they want—life. I get it." He passed the back of his hand across his forehead, like there was something slightly wounding but hopeful in just admitting that much. "I like criminals," he repeated, and nodded, like that was a good thing.

There wasn't any point in waiting for more of an invitation than that. Sitting next to him on that little bed, I felt the same as I had since the moment I first saw him, like I could just leap on that guy, any second. So that is what I did. Or at least, I just reached right over, took his face in my hands, and kissed him.

"Well, hello, Tina," he said, when I let him come up for air.

"I was getting tired of waiting for you to kiss me," I said. And then I kissed him some more. For about fifteen minutes we made out like teenagers on his bed that was also my bed, which is when he stopped for a moment, pushed my hair out of my face, and considered me.

"I'm not sure I want to do this here," he said.

"Oh, yeah?" I said. "When will you know? Because like I said, they're kicking me out any minute now."

And because neither one of us, as it turns out, is all that interested in living in the past, we went ahead and did it, and didn't let the death all around us take the day.

CHAPTER TWENTY-NINE

We spent the weekend in the apartment, and I cooked him scallops, and we got drunk on red wine, and picked through Sophie's treasures. And we lay together in the dark and told stories about our dead mothers, what we knew of them, what we didn't know, how they failed us, and how we failed them.

Reality eventually reasserted itself; Pete took a shower in the bathroom with the good water pressure and then he put his clothes back on so he could head up to his precinct Monday morning. As he was disentangling himself from me at the front door he stuck his hand in his pocket, looking for his car keys, and his fingers curled around something he found there. "Oh, yeah, I thought you might want this," he said, and he handed me a little black bottle of perfume.

"So," I said, "you knew all along that was mine."

"I did know that," he admitted. "That's why I wanted it."

I looked at it. It was cool in my hand, like a big pebble, but black, unknowable. The memory of that one word that had once scrolled across the opaque glass was long gone. I opened it, smelled it for a moment, shook out a drop of the precious oil, and touched the back of his neck with it.

"Oh, great," he said. "Now I'm going to be hearing about that all day."

"I want you to," I told him.

After he was gone, I went back to bed. I woke up to the sound of that throwaway cell, ringing away, as it would for the rest of the day. Lucy and Alison, still in the throes of their concern about the co-op board and what it might be up to, called obsessively.

"Have you heard from Vince?" Lucy started, mid-morning Monday.

"Not since last week, no," I said.

"Have you called him?"

"Well—"

"Tina, you have to follow up! And push a little! Have you met his father yet?"

"No," I said.

"Well, that needs to happen. You can make sure he understands our position, and supports it, and then if he does maybe we can enlist him to speak to other board members on our behalf."

"Ai yi yi, Lucy," I said. "I am not going to sleep with the whole co-op board to get this to happen."

"I would hope that you'll do whatever is necessary," Lucy snapped. "There's fifteen million dollars in it for you. Call Vince right now and let me know what he says." Then she hung up. Then twenty minutes later Alison called.

"Hi, how are you!" she chirped.

"You know, I'm pretty good, Alison," I started. "I had a terrific weekend and I learned quite a bit about this place."

"About the co-op board?" she asked. "Lucy said that you were calling Vince. Have you talked to him?"

"Not yet," I said. "No, I haven't really called him yet."

"Tina, please!" she started, almost crying with frustration. "It is so important to Lucy, and to me, too, to just work with the building a little bit, to get them to have a little bit more openness to our position! It's what Mom would have wanted. I know it."

"Mom told you, specifically, that it wasn't what she wanted," I reminded her.

"She wouldn't want them to have it! She didn't say that, that she wanted the *building* to get it!"

"No," I said. "That's not who she wanted to have it."

"So you're going to call him, right?"

"Who?" I asked, thinking, in some instantaneous fantasy, that she knew about me and Pete and that she was fine with it.

"*Vince*," she said, almost crying again. "For heaven's sake, Tina! This is no joke!"

They called four more times that day, and then twice on Tuesday. I stopped answering the phone again. It had occurred to me that any minute they were going to start coming over all the time to harass me in person and so I needed to pack all Sophie's stuff back into those boxes and haul it back to the storage room. That took most of the day, and by the time I was finished I was exhausted. I took a moment to just sit down back there and think about what I might do next. The boxes were in place. The light was evaporating.

447

I honestly did not know what to do anymore. And then the ghost started up, mournful and frightened and inevitable. She murmured inside the wall, gently complaining about her traps and her losses and the impossibility of her life. She wept and worried in her unknown language, right there with me, and unbearably far away. I let her go on, thinking that maybe she would be able to explain something to me, in spite of the fact that I didn't understand a word she said. She couldn't explain anything at all.

"What are you doing in there?" I asked the room. "Why are you so stuck?"

"I'm not *stuck*," said a friendly voice. "It just takes a minute to get out of here. It's pretty tight." And with that, the ghost disappeared again, and Jennifer clambered into the room, dusting herself off with teenage disgust. "Ugh, it's so gross in there. There are *live things* in there," she informed me. "We have to figure out a better way to talk to each other."

"You could call me on the phone," I reminded her.

"It's too dangerous," she said, quite serious. "Someone might hear me. There's no privacy in our apartment. You wouldn't believe the stuff I heard *today*. They're going to try to kick you *out*."

"I know that part," I told her.

"You do? Because it's supposed to be top secret. Do you know about the big meeting tonight in the Gideons' apartment?"

"It's *tonight?*" I said.

"Like, right now." She nodded. "They're meeting at six. Oh. That's ten minutes ago."

"Thanks for the notice," I said, not sounding particularly grateful.

"I couldn't get away!" she protested. "Louise knows I'm up to something. She's been on my tail like *crazy.*"

I looked up at that horrible, bricked-up staircase, inhabited by rats and spiders and God knows what else was crawling around in those walls. My hands started to sweat. I really did not want to have to do this.

"This thing goes up the length of the building, right?" I asked.

"How am I supposed to know?" said Jennifer.

"Look," I said. "Look. If I don't came back in six hours? Tell somebody I might be stuck in the wall. Tell Frank."

"You're going up there?" said Jennifer.

"I think I am," I admitted. And with that, I hauled myself up onto the ledge of the tiny doorway, put my fingers on one of the steps, crouched forward, and started to climb.

"You don't even know if you'll be able to get out of there!" Jennifer called after me. "Don't you want a flashlight? It's dark in there! What if the Gideons blocked off the entrance? What are you going to do when you get there? What if someone . . ." Her voice trailed off as it became obvious that I was actually going to go through with this idiotic plan.

"Look, just . . . If I don't make it back, tell Frank!" I repeated. And I kept going.

There are advantages to being someone who thinks that rules are made to be broken. Finding yourself stuck in an airless, dank, Victorian crawlspace which very well could lead nowhere is not one of them. Jennifer had obviously opened the wall plug in Katharine's room, but the amount of light which that let in was slight, and once I climbed beyond its friendly solace—and the last moment, presumably, that I might bail out of this completely insane endeavor—it didn't sustain. It was pitch black and things that were used to inhabiting that hideous no-man's-land without any noteworthy disturbance from the likes of me were not happy that I was intruding on their space. I had to lead with my hands, which more than once landed on something crunchy and alive, and then my face went through something weblike and sticky and filled with little nublike things that were probably dead bugs and which got into my mouth when I almost screamed. Then there was the moment when I realized that I didn't know how far I might need to climb to get to the Gideons' apartment, and that in fact I may have passed it. Then there was the moment when I didn't know if I should go backwards or ahead. Then there was the rat I grabbed by accident when I reached over to steady myself against the wall. It snarled, tried to bite me, and then scrambled away. Then there was the moment when, terrified by the rat, I jumped back and hit the wall, which had somehow transformed itself from brick to wood. It made a big thump.

"What was that?" someone asked. The sudden voice might have made me jump again but I was already at the last end of my physiological reactions to fear; there was nothing else left in me.

"Did you hear something?" the voice asked again.

"Margarita thinks there are rats in that old crawlspace," another voice announced. It was old Mrs Gideon, and you could tell even without seeing her that she thought that Margarita was an idiot. "I'll mention it to Frank."

"Frank's the doorman, Mother," the other voice, the beautiful Julianna, replied.

"You really are sentimental about him," her mother replied, with a little sneer.

"I'm not *sentimental*, I'm *respectful*."

"You encourage him, and it's ridiculous."

"We are not talking about Frank, Mother, please! I think I heard something. I know I did. It sounded like a rat, or something, in that old crawlspace. I think Margarita is right, there's something in there. You need to mention it to the super, or why don't you tell the board, since they're all here anyway."

"We are not gathered to talk about rats. Or perhaps we are," Mrs Gideon observed. Then Julianna said something I couldn't quite pick up, as she clearly had moved away from the wall and the giant rats inside it. There was some further murmuring and then silence, as the two women apparently went into the next room, or someplace beyond.

Here is where the true stupidity of my plan revealed itself. I had succeeded in that I had actually landed myself right in the middle of the Gideons' apartment without anybody knowing I was there, but there was no way to get myself out of that wall. I stood there, my heart pounding, with my head leaning against what seems to have been some sort of old cabinet, and let my fingers probe the wood. There was a giant bolt there and no way to open it. My fingers continued to probe it, determined, and I told myself that if I were anything like a functional thief I would have brought with me picks for the lock, but then I thought, It's a *deadbolt*, you can't open it from this side, you'd have to have the equipment to just saw through the wall to get

451

that thing off there, an axe, a short-handled *axe,* or a gun, maybe a gun would do it. I ran through all the possible solutions for opening a deadbolt, none of which were feasible in any kind of reality other than the movies. I was stuck in the wall. There was no way out. I stood in there for quite a long time but there really was no way out. I tried to take a step backwards, wondering if I could just make it back down to the Whites' apartment, but the moving things in the wall started to move again, and I stopped, immobilized by terror. My feet did not know how to go backwards, it seemed, and my hands did not know how to go forward. Then a voice whispered, right next to my head, "Tina? Are you in there?"

It took me a second, honestly. I couldn't quite catch up.

"Tina. Tina. If you're in there, knock or something. I don't have a ton of time."

"Jennifer?" I said.

"Knock where you are, knock where you are, I can't tell, and we have to do this fast," she told me. I rapped gently on the wall several times.

"Okay, that's good, that's good," she said, rapping back on the panel right in front of me. "Is this it? This is the doorway?"

"There's a bolt," I told her. "Right in front of you, they've got a deadbolt holding it shut."

"Yeah, I see," she said, working on it. "It's painted shut. Shoot. It's—oh. Hang on. I have to find something—oh wait. Not so bad, the paint's pretty old. Oh!" And with that, the door swung open three inches and she smiled in at me. "Come on, come on," she said, excited, pulling the door open against the resistance of the paint job which was half of what was holding it in

452

place. She reached in and grabbed me by the arm, forcing me to climb out. "It's a good thing you're little," she observed. "I can't believe grown men used to use that thing."

"What are you doing here?" I whispered. I was shaking, half with relief and half with the sheer terror of what I had just been through. "God, it's horrible in there. Don't go in there anymore."

"Yeah, it's not nice," she admitted. "And I knew you weren't going to be able to get out of there. You didn't think of that. Get down, you don't want them to see you," she advised me. Then she went back to the wall and shut the cabinet door carefully, holding it in place with her shoulder while she flipped the ancient deadbolt back into place. The kid was a marvel. She was grinning with delight at her own cleverness. "Anyway," she said, dropping down to the floor, so she could talk to me, "I just thought I better get up here. So I knocked on the door and interrupted the meeting and said I needed to talk to my mom. So then she came to the door and I told her I had a fight with Louise. She told me that they were busy and to go home, then I said that I needed to use the bathroom which is supposedly what I am doing now. I got to go. They're all in the living room, it's down that hallway, you pass the dining room and some sort of den, and then it's right there. There's a whole lot of them in there. The whole board, and then a couple extra, they look like lawyers. I'd make for the den, you can hide behind the door and hear everything, I checked it out on the way back. Come on, we have to go. I'll make a lot of noise when I go back out through the meeting, so that I can distract them while you're finding some place to listen from. Ready? Let's go."

453

I was still so freaked out by being stuck in that wall for so long my brain was still not functioning fully, so I was glad to have an excited teenager there, telling me what to do. She breezed ahead of me silently, glancing back to make sure I stayed down and hidden by furniture in case anyone suddenly appeared looking for a glass of water or something; then took me into a dark room with plush couches and low lighting, all done in red with the slightest touches of gold sprinkled through. I got nothing more than a sense of its opulence as Jennifer waved her hand behind her, pointing to a corner behind the open door. She stood in the doorway for a moment, waving her hand impatiently, and then she marched deliberately into the next room. I took the hint.

"Thanks for the use of your bathroom, Mrs Gideon," she announced to the whole room. "Mom, can you at least *call* Louise and tell her that I don't *have* to put the middle girls to bed, they're big enough to get themselves to bed *anyway* and it's not my job and plus I have a lot of homework."

"That's fine, Jennifer," Mrs White noted, snappish.

"Well, she's being horrible. Can you call her at least?"

"Jennifer, I said go home," Mrs White told her, with finality.

The door was wide open and there was a couch that stood up against it. Behind the door, and behind the couch, there was a clever little area of carpet, unseen by either room. It was my spot. I couldn't see everyone through the crack in the door— fully half the room was out of my line of vision—but the other half was completely visible. I watched Jennifer scoot into that little hallway by the front door, passing that ridiculous hall table with the spindly legs where Mrs Gideon had given me the evil eye. The sound of the door opening and closing behind her was obscured by the rustle of and settling of fifteen people in the room next to me.

"Thanks to everyone for making this a priority," announced a tall, ridiculously handsome man who was standing and addressing the others, who were all seated around him on elegantly padded dining-room chairs. He was clearly Vince's father; he looked just like him, and carried himself with even more self-involved confidence. Next to him, Vince looked like a cheerful puppy. I immediately understood why Vince hated him so much.

"The petition to have the illegal tenant in apartment 8A evicted is being passed among you for signatures. We have asked everyone to sign it because if there is a lawsuit that results from this action we want to make it clear that the entire board was in agreement and no one can be singled out for culpability."

"Can they sue?" asked someone unseen, from the other side of the room.

"Why don't we let our lawyer answer that one. That's what he's here for," Vince's creepy dad responded. "Gary?"

Yet another good-looking guy in a suit stood up. I swear to God, he looked like every other lawyer I had met during this fiasco, except for Stuart Long who looked like an egg. These guys all looked like the suits they were wearing. Or at least, all you ever noticed was the fabulous suit, and how mean the guy wearing it looked. "From what Roger has told me, and what I've gleaned from phone calls with many of you, these people are aggressive and determined," announced Gary the lawyer. "Under those circumstances, lawsuits are always a possibility. Lawsuits are, however, also expensive. It is clear that they have few resources other than the speculative value of the Livingston Mansion Apartment. We've spoken to the legal department at Sotheby's, and they have reassured us that they will not support any action on behalf of the so-called heirs of Olivia Finn until the co-op has had the opportunity to state its position legally concerning the property."

"Do we have a position?" asked Mrs Gideon, sounding like she was standing right in front of the door. "Other than we wish they would go away?"

"That's what we're here to discuss," Vince's hyper-confident ice cube of a father asserted.

"My husband told me not to sign anything until we have our lawyer look at it," came another voice from behind my sightline. But I recognized this one: It was Mrs White, who sounded nervous and kind of unhappy.

"We can have copies sent to your lawyer, certainly, and wait a few days for your signature," said Mr Ice Cube Masterson. "The reason we asked Gary to be here was to set your mind at rest about the legality of these documents."

"But he's not *our* lawyer and the interests of the co-op are not necessarily *our* interest, are they?" continued Mrs White, insistent. She really sounded bothered and like she might secretly be on my side. That is what I told myself, anyway. I wished I could see her face for a moment. I wondered what color suit she was wearing.

"No one should sign anything they're not comfortable signing," said the suited lawyer, trying to be soothing and looking more like a shark than ever. "I am happy to interface with anyone's attorney around all of this."

"He's already spoken to my guy," someone offered up from somewhere.

"Mine as well," Mrs Gideon purred. "I'm completely satisfied this is the appropriate move to make."

"Look, we can get her out of here with a simple majority of votes, and we don't *need* legally more than six signatures," Gary explained. "But if the co-op wants to send a message to these people, and to the real estate community, and to the city in general, my recommendation is that it be loud and unanimous. That's why I hope to have everyone's signature on the documents of removal."

"I want to support the building, I do," protested Mrs White. "Maybe I could call my husband at the end of the meeting and just make sure it's okay."

"You do whatever you need to, Susan," said Ice Pop. "We all have a lot at stake here."

"Once they're gone, though, does it really change anything?" someone else asked. "I saw all the stuff on television and the papers and it sounds like this fiasco is just going to happen whether we like it or not. These two sets of heirs are just going to fight it out and we're going to be dragged into the press for who knows how long. Is there anything we can do—beyond asserting our right that the apartment remain empty?"

"That's an interesting question, Jenny," Ice Pop agreed. "And in fact, it's why I made sure that all of us could be here tonight. There is something, as it turns out, that we can do. Len, maybe you could explain the situation." He made one of those graceful little gestures that mean "The floor is yours," and Len stepped out of the invisible side of the room and into the front and center side of things. He was wearing the dark green suit coat that I had seen him in at the press conference, and he carried a little cream-colored folder that had some papers in it. There was a big bandage on his left hand. For all her claims that she wasn't really trying to hurt him, Charlie had in fact scored something of a wound, apparently.

But Len wasn't acting wounded. With his calm, treelike posture and wry smile he radiated strength and gentle wisdom to the entire gathering. "I do have some rather interesting— some exceptionally interesting news, about the legal status of the Livingston Mansion Apartment," he claimed. "As some of you know, I was quite friendly with Bill and his wife Sophie for many years before her death. I was in fact a confidant of theirs, and their sons."

"And the second wife, the one who made all the trouble?" someone called.

"I knew her, yes, and yes she was—problematic. Some of the things I saw her doing, to her husband, I was very unhappy, obviously, at the degree to which she was clearly maneuvering him around these questions of inheritance, and the apartment."

"Could you be more specific? You actually saw—"

"I saw a lot, and I'm willing to testify to that," Len claimed, with some seemingly sincere regret. I wanted to rip his face off, or at least give Charlie another go. But before he could continue to tell spectacular stories about how evil my poor lost mother actually was, Vince's dad leaned forward and whispered something to him. Len tilted his head and listened, then

458

nodded with bemused respect. "I quite agree. I quite agree," he murmured. Then he looked up at his audience and held up his little packet of papers. "Our esteemed board president, Roger Masterson, has made the excellent point that a discussion centering on Bill's more recent wife, who actually never held any rights, in regard to the Livingston apartment, is not the most useful way to spend our time together this evening. What's more important, frankly, to all of us, is the status of the apartment as designated by the last will and testament of the first Mrs Drinan."

There was no question something was up. Len was curling his sentences so deliriously on top of each other the whole thing sounded fishy before he had even started telling the story. But everyone else in the room was eating it up. There was a pause and a hush. He sighed and looked down, sad. "Those of you who lived here know that there was some difficulty surrounding Sophie Livingston. Those who knew her remember a woman filled with passion and delight. There were times when she was unhappy. And there were times when her spirit was greatly troubled. We live in times where some might choose to label these fluctuations in temperament as mental illness. And indeed, her unhappiness led her family to make choices for her that were questionable, and questioned."

People shifted in their seats. He was taking too long. I could see old Roger Masterson twitching behind him, trying to figure out how to get him to move things along. But Len was enjoying his moment. "One evening, Bill came to me, explaining his plan, which was to have his wife admitted to a psychiatric facility in the city. I was appalled. My experience with Sophie would never have led me to believe that such a drastic action, a *removal*, was called for. What I could see, from my vantage point, were problems in the marriage, and that in fact what might be the truly rational solution for everyone would be for them to divorce. He was having none of it. What would happen to Sophie, he asked, if she were left alone in that glorious apartment? He was convinced she would do harm to herself. I thought this was nonsense. He didn't want to talk about it; his mind was made up. And he told me that his two grown sons both supported his decision. The most I could do was insist that the facility to which Sophie was taken would be the best possible home for her. I contacted a friend at the university where I was teaching at the time, pulled some strings, and got her placed in a wonderful, wonderful treatment center."

He paused dramatically and considered the documents in his hand. The room was silent, expectant, waiting for the story to fulfill itself. "I would visit her there often," he explained. "Bill and Pete and Doug, her beloved sons, didn't. They moved on with their lives. But I never honestly thought she belonged there. We would have long talks about her life growing up in the Edgewood, the happiest times and memories for her centering on the building, which was so precious to her parents. And I said to her, 'Sophie, you belong in your home, with us.' She felt it was too late for that. But she didn't want the apartment falling into the wrong hands. And so she asked me to help her make a will."

He stopped. He held the little folder up. "Which left the apartment to the building." No one said anything for a moment. Masterson and the lawyer glanced at each other, expressionless.

I couldn't help thinking they were both wondering if anyone would go for this.

"Okay, wait a minute," someone finally said. I was really wishing I could see that half of the room, filled to the brim with people in the building that I knew and didn't know. *What a load of nonsense,* I thought. *I can't believe that anybody is going to fall for this.* But there was money in the air now, and that crowd was particularly attuned to its potential. "You helped her make a will?" the first questioner asked.

"No, no, I am not an attorney, I cannot legally 'help' anyone make a will. But I did alert a member of the staff, who wrote it down for her. She was agitated but definitely in her right mind. So I agreed to serve as a witness, as did the nurse's aide who helped us. And I was given a copy of the document for safekeeping."

Gary the lawyer stood up at this, and presented a stack of papers which he proceeded to hand out to the other people behind the door. "We have copies," he announced. There was a rustle of pages as everyone obediently passed the copies on to their neighbors, and the lawyer took over the narrative for a moment. "We have contacted the other witness on the will, who is of course willing to testify about the legitimacy of the document."

"This counts? It's more like a letter," someone behind the door said, worried.

"It states her wishes clearly. It counts," the lawyer asserted.

"Is this a later will than the one that left the apartment to her husband?" someone else asked, also worried.

"It is the *only* will," the lawyer reassured the room. "There were some questions raised about when and why her will had not been probated properly when she passed six years ago. Because of the recent dissent between the two so-called sets of heirs, investigation was made into the failure to probate any will. Court documents indicate that there was no other will and that the apartment was improperly awarded to the husband as the next of kin."

"If this all happened six years ago, why are we only hearing about this now?" The first unseen questioner was clearly not happy with this whole situation. He was getting pushy.

"That—was—my mistake," Len asserted, with a regretful sigh. He is really a better actor than I'm making this sound. He was even quite deft, during this part of the performance. "Bill was truly bereft when she passed. There was bitterness, and recriminations, so much sadness, and finally real ruptures between him and his sons. For years none of them were speaking to each other! So I confess my friendship to Bill overwhelmed my sense of loyalty to Sophie. I thought, what would be the harm in letting him spend his last years in the home he made with her in better times? He was so lonely. And so isolated there. I thought he would die, eventually, and then I could bring the will forward at that time."

"You were taking a lot on yourself," the angry guy noted, with some asperity.

"Yes, I was, I most certainly was, and I regret it deeply." Len nodded. "I wasn't sure what to do. I consulted several people about the correct course. I spoke to Delia Westmoreland about it at the time; she was such friends with Sophie and I knew that she would understand the dilemma."

"Delia, is that true?" asked Mrs White, as if this possibility might actually change her opinion for the better about this improbable story.

"Yes, yes he did, he came to me, I can't remember when exactly—"

"It was six years ago, just after she died," Len provided.

"If that's what you say, I'm sure that's right, Len," Delia agreed. She was nervous but almost everyone seemed to be going along with things—at least they were listening pretty intently—so she just plowed ahead. "I told him I didn't like the idea of, you know, what he said, holding back information about Sophie's wishes. And I didn't think it was fair of them to put her away like that and then just make a grab for the place. That seemed really bad to me."

"He was her husband," Mrs White reminded her.

"He was *Irish*. He wasn't even American. And it wasn't what she would have wanted. Well, she wrote that down, I guess, that it wasn't what she wanted. And you know she was a feminist, Sophie would never have agreed that Bill could just *grab* her family's heritage, she wasn't into all that male power stuff. That's why it was so terrible, what he did to her. That he and those boys just sent her off to the asylum, I know that's not what they call it anymore but let's face it that's what they *did*. It's appalling really. And you know, her parents never liked him. So I wasn't surprised, when Len told me about this. I thought it serves them right, after the way they treated her, that she would not stand for them getting the apartment too. No, I was not surprised at all."

"Did you see the will? Did Len show you this document, at the time?" prompted Roger Masterson, usefully.

"Yes," said Mrs Westmoreland. "He most certainly did." I was watching her through the door crack; she was right in my line of vision, and she had gotten the hang of this whole thing by then; she was confident and even defiant. "He showed me the will but also he told me his concerns, that Bill wasn't well, and that he didn't have a lot of years left in him and that maybe it would be cruel to just kick him out. Even if it's what he deserved. I mean, I had reservations. But we both, Len and I both thought that he would just *die* soon enough. Certainly no one thought some cleaning woman would show up and try to make off with all of it. It's just appalling, really. That I *know* Sophie did not want."

"But no one else has a copy of this document?" asked the persistent questioner from the corner. "Was it registered anywhere? I just don't think it looks good that someone in the building had it all along and didn't bring it forward before now. That doesn't look right." I wish I knew whoever that person was; he seemed to be the only one in the room with a shred of a clue.

"I think you need to leave that part to the lawyers," soothed Gary the suited lawyer. "Stranger things have happened, certainly, over the years, with regards to wills and inheritances. And we have several witnesses. Len here, Delia, the aide from the nursing home. We can verify the history of the document. Our case is strong."

"I would really hate to find out we were involved in something illegal," warned the voice from the corner. "If that document turns out to be a forgery? The Edgewood cannot be a party to something like that."

"Absolutely not," the lawyer agreed. "Len and Delia understand that they are the responsible parties in this matter. We

464

are taking them at their word. And if anything shows up, we are indemnified."

Boy that's convenient, I thought, without fully knowing what 'indemnified' even means.

"Could you tell us how this would even work?" Len asked, sweetly mystified. "I never really considered the question, even though I helped make it happen. But how can a building own an apartment?"

"We hold it in trust and arrange for its sale. The proceeds go into a fund which we can use as an endowment, of sorts, to support the maintenance of the building," Roger Masterson explained. I thought he was going to start licking himself any second, he was enjoying this so much. "It's quite an exceptional situation. It gives us the opportunity to protect and restore a historic property, and also support our own investment in the building, as co-operative owners of the property. And you should know, Sotheby's, Christie's, Corcoran, all the brokers of important properties have agreed to wait and let us play out our own interest here. No one is going to provide any real opposition to our position. It is not in their interest to do so."

"Isn't that like price fixing?" the malcontent in the corner called out.

"Not at all," Gary said with a cool, knowing smile. "Here, let me walk you through the legalities of a situation like this."

"You have to go," someone breathed into my ear. I almost fell over, I was so startled, but she reached out and held my arm, firm, to hold me steady, and to keep me from giving myself away. I turned slowly. The most beautiful face I've ever seen was right next to my own. "Before they finish," Julianna whispered.

"They can't find you here." And then she stood and silently reached her hand out to me. I took it and followed her back into the kitchen, where she was moving with graceful assurance to the cabinet door that opened onto that terrifying crawlspace. I looked around, only now realizing that of course I would have to get back in there. And then she passed right by the crawlspace, as if it were invisible to her.

"I presume you came up the fire escape," she said, opening the kitchen window onto the night air. "Quickly, quickly!" she urged, looking back at me.

It was significantly easier to climb down the rickety old fire escape than it had been to climb up the twisting nightmare of a staircase trapped inside the walls of the building. The skeletal ladders fit together like a perfect little jigsaw puzzle of wrought-iron perfection, and within seconds it seemed I was on the landing outside the window of my own apartment. The euphoric sense of relief I had experienced as I clambered down the outside of the building waned slightly when I realized that I once again had the problem of not being able to get off the stairs and into the apartment because, not surprisingly, the window was locked. I tried it four times; it was most definitely locked. I peered through the glass and into the lost room, hoping that Jennifer might have predicted the inevitability of this obstacle just as she did the last one, and show up to save me. Which was not, unfortunately, the case. So after a few more moments of considering my dilemma, I looked down at the sidewalk eight floors below and thought about climbing all the way down and letting myself back in the front door. That, I realized, wouldn't work either because the apartment was as usual locked from the inside. I looked up and considered climbing back up a flight and waiting for Katharine to go to bed so that I could talk her into letting me in. That meant I might get caught by the evil Louise, and further it meant that I would have to get back into that crawl-space. Nevertheless it did seem like with the addition of a flash-light this might be the most reasonable of all the solutions, in that it was the only one that actually was a solution. I started to head back up the fire escape. And then I saw the ghost.

She was right there, at the window, looking at me. At first I didn't know what I was seeing; I thought I was looking into a pair of disembodied eyes afloat in an undifferentiated and murky universe. They frightened me so completely that I pulled back and careened for a moment near the edge of the empty space which opened up on the landing beneath; at which point she held up a hand, instinctive, to warn me to be careful. Then she looked over her shoulder, and back at me, and I thought, *The ghost. It's the ghost.* Her hair was pulled back under a kerchief and her skin was as dark as the air around her. I took a step forward and reached my hand up to the window she stood at. There were bars across it. She looked like she was in a cage.

We considered each other for a moment, that was all, and then I knew what to do. "Stay there," I said. And I took off my shirt, wrapped it around my fist, and stuck my hand through my own window, right next to hers. Then I reached in, shoved the window latch open, yanked the window up, climbed inside, and found my cell phone.

"You have to get over here now," I said to Pete, when he picked up. "Now, right now, you have to come *right now.*" Then I ran through the apartment, threw all the locks, and headed down the stairs because I didn't want to wait for the elevator. "Frank," I said. He looked up from his little stand, where he was reading yet another magazine. "You have to come. You have to bring the master keys. There's a person trapped in Mrs Westmoreland's apartment. She's locked in there. You have to help me get her out."

"Tina—look, I don't know," he started. "You know they're saying you're not supposed to be here. I'm not allowed to help you with anything. They told me I could get fired if I did."

"She's an *illegal*, Frank," I said. "Westmoreland's got an illegal up there, locked in a room. She's an *illegal*."

CHAPTER THIRTY

Frank and his master keys got us into Westmoreland's apartment. We found the ghost hiding in a closet and praying to the gods of her homeland to come and save her, so she didn't quite recognize the real thing when we showed up. She fought and cried and insisted in some strange tongue that we had to go, that they couldn't find us there. Then Mrs Westmoreland showed up and threw a fit, insisting that she was calling the police and having me arrested yet again, and then Pete showed up, and I told him what I had seen, that the ghost was a prisoner there, and Westmoreland went into a rage and claimed to have sponsored the ghost, whose name was Gcina, for citizenship, out of the goodness of her heart. In the middle of all the yelling Pete took the whole mess down to the local precinct, where I dragged him into a corner for just a minute so that I could tell him about how I had broken into the Gideons' apartment and what I had heard at the board meeting there. You could tell he didn't believe me, really, but before I could explain it all they dragged me into an interrogation room and asked me about the ghost, and I told them how I had been hearing her in the wall for months and that I knew she was in trouble in there but it wasn't until I saw her that I put it together. Meanwhile Gcina was giving up the whole story in an interrogation room down the hall. And then some cop asked me what I was doing out on the fire escape anyway, and Pete said go ahead, tell them about the other stuff, so I told them all of it, and rather than laughing me out of the room they went back to the building and picked up Julianna Gideon to come down and verify my story. Her mother predictably threw a fit and insisted on coming with her and calling a lawyer and generally screaming at everyone in the most horrible way possible, especially reaming out Frank who honestly was just sitting in a corner quietly waiting to be told he could go home. But then when the lawyer arrived they wouldn't let Mrs Gideon go with Julianna into the interrogation room, where she apparently validated my story about what was said at the board meeting every way she possibly could. Then they took all of that back to Mrs Westmoreland and told her that she was going to be on the hook for all sorts of things, abduction and harboring an illegal alien, but that conspiracy to defraud the courts was even more serious and that if she would flip on the whole cabal of board members at the Edge they'd take that into consideration.

So she gave up everything and got a walk on everything else, because Gcina was from Somalia and no one knew who she was or where her family was and she didn't matter, finally, as much as the Livingston Mansion Apartment did. They started issuing warrants for every member of the board, including Roger Masterson, and including Len, who was in particularly hot water because Westmoreland apparently had admitted the whole fake will scenario and she claimed it was all his idea. Then Gary the lawyer showed up and explained why Roger Masterson was not going to come down to a police precinct in the middle of the night and they could speak to him in his office the next day. Then some uniform officers brought Len in and walked him right by where I was sitting in the waiting room with Pete. Then some lady from INS came up to the precinct and took Gcina off, and when I asked Pete where they were taking her, he admitted that now she would be put in jail, and that they would hold her probably for months and then send her back to Somalia unless she could prove that she needed asylum.

"They can't," I said. "Come on. You can't put her in jail. She's been in jail, for months. We don't even know how long. But at least months."

"I still can't see how you put that together," Pete said, checking his nails. "You really didn't have any evidence, just somebody crying in the next room. You know, if you had brought that to me, I couldn't even get you a warrant on that. It's a good thing you got the doorman to open the door for you. No cop in the city would have done it."

"Because she's nobody?" I said.

"Because you didn't have any evidence."

"I'm on the same landing with them. You could see, when Westmoreland would open the door going out or coming in, the place was getting cleaned every day. And no one ever came. You never saw anybody."

"Still not enough."

"I cleaned houses myself," I reminded him. "I know what

471

it's like to be locked in a trailer at the Delaware Water Gap." And then I went on a crying jag, and so he told me he'd take me home.

Which is where we were, the following morning, when Doug showed up. Unfortunately I had not, for once, locked the door from the inside, both because I was so tired and because I had my own cop and I wasn't so worried anymore about who might just burst into my world. I had not counted on Doug Drinan getting a tipoff from Len Colbert, who used his one phone call to tell Doug that his brother might be here, fraternizing with the enemy, and he might want to come and see for himself.

"I don't believe it," he said. He was standing in the doorway of the bedroom, watching us wake up. At least we weren't having sex, I thought, but Doug didn't actually see the upside of that. He was already in a state. "What the fuck," he seethed. "What the *fuck* are you doing with *her?*"

"Ohhh, shit," Pete noted, groggy.

"*Get up,*" Doug hissed. "Get up, so I can hit you."

"Dial it down, Doug," Pete replied. "I'm still waking up."

"In our room," Doug exploded. "In our *apartment!* With her! You know what she is! You know what her mother did to our family!"

"My mom didn't do anything. She was a really nice person and she took really good care of your father," I stated.

"Tina, stay out of this," Pete warned.

"We know what she did. She stole our home," Doug informed me. "We have evidence, what she was doing, we know what she did and we know what you're doing. At least those of us who aren't thinking with our dicks have something of a clue—"

"Hey hey hey, I said dial it back," Pete repeated. I opened my mouth to say something else which would not have been helpful, but Pete put his hand up, quickly, a fast silencing gesture, as he stood. "We're not going to talk about this, this way, Doug," he stated. "I want you to step out in the hallway."

"Don't you fucking 'cop' me," Doug sneered. "I'm not the crook in this fiasco. I can't believe you're this stupid. Or yes, I can, actually, I can believe it. After what you did—what you did, to Mom—"

"Come on, don't start this again."

"It was your idea! What happened, you were the one who, you and Dad. She didn't want to go. I told you don't do it—"

"That's not the way it went down and you know that—"

"And then she died in there, alone. She was alone—"

"She was there because she needed help! She couldn't stay here! Christ, she tried to kill him, more than once, Doug."

"So he said."

"I saw it! You saw what she would do. You saw the bruises. Come on, man, let's not relive this."

"He made that happen. She was defending herself. He would get drunk and start those fights—"

"I'm serious, Doug. Don't do this."

"*You're doing it! You did it!* You're just like him. She used to say, 'Your brother is just like your father, a a a lowlife, and a drunk'—she would tell me—"

"I know what she said. Come on, Doug, let's take this just down the hall—"

"No! She needs to hear this! She needs to know what you are, what you did. What you—She—" His rage took over as he

473

glanced at me, barely, utter madness in his face. I crept up a little against the wall. This was not a good situation. And it just goes to show, I thought: Pictures don't tell the whole story. I thought of all those photos I went through, of those happy boys and their cool, interesting, rich, hippie mother. They didn't tell this story at all.

"I could kill you for this," Doug continued, pacing. "This was Mom's, everything. This place. And you're just throwing it away! On those—that *woman*, who Dad let *come* in here, like it wasn't hers. When it was only hers. This place is *hers*. It was the only thing she really loved." The words hung out there like a curse, as soon as he said it. I was embarrassed to have heard it. Pete shook his head.

"You know that's not true. She loved us. I remember how much she loved us. That's what I choose to remember from all of it. I make that choice every day."

"That's convenient. Considering what you did to her, what you and Dad—what you *did*."

Pete didn't answer at first. The whisper of loss was rising around them. Doug looked completely spent. He glanced up at the ceiling for a moment, that old trick of raking your eyes frantically to keep them from betraying you. He looked at that idiotic painting of the sunset on the wall and started to shake with a terrible and relentless grief. Pete waited, still, while his brother wept openly for what seemed a long time before he shook himself back into some semblance of control.

"Sorry," Doug finally said, abrupt and ungracious.

Pete nodded, pretending the apology was better than it was. "There was something wrong with her brain," he continued, quiet. Doug accepted the facts, and Pete recounted them. "We talked to a lot of people. You remember this. The chemicals went bad. It wasn't her fault, but it wasn't his fault either."

"She wasn't well."

"No, she wasn't. We got a lot of opinions, Doug. You know we did what we had to do."

The two of them stood there, looking at each other, mournfully resting at the end of an argument they had had far too many times. For a long moment they just looked at each other. Pete reached up to touch his brother's shoulder. And Doug slugged him, hard, right across the face.

CHAPTER THIRTY-ONE

"They're kicking you out, Tina," Frank informed me, under his breath, when I snuck by the doorman's station two days later. "They're real mad at you."

I wasn't surprised to hear it.

The pearls I left at Sotheby's. Leonard Rubenstein, the man who looked like a lion, gave me an official estimate as to their worth, which was somewhere in the range of $350,000. The clasp, apparently, was so much more valuable than the pearls themselves he knew of a jeweler who would take it quickly and essentially break it up for the worth of the parts. He promised to call me by the end of the day with an offer. Then I called Lyle, my friend from the hot tub, who had had the foresight to slip his phone number into that little alligator handbag. He suggested he might come by the apartment and price out the rest of the stuff, so I said sure.

"Really?" he said, almost cooing on the other end of the line. "Can I bring Roger? Or Andrew? Or Steve? They'll kill me, they really will, if they find out that I got to see the apartment and they didn't."

"Whoever wants to come to see the apartment," I said, "is welcome."

It was a good little party. Andrew brought champagne and foie gras and Roger and Steve and Edward and Dave came too, and they loved every square inch of the place; they appreciated every strange corner and disastrous choice. They even loved the mustard-colored shag rug.

"It's so hideous," Andrew said, with an admiring tone. "And who would have thought to use so much? It's a sea of mustard. I thinks it works, I really do."

"You're insane," said Edward, but he kissed him, so I knew he wasn't in love with Vince anymore, which I thought was definitely a good thing.

"Tina, can I talk to you for a second?" Lyle called from the hallway.

He took me back to the storage room so that we could talk business. "All right. A lot of this—everything over here, it's sentimental value I'm sure but that's how you need to see it," he explained, waving at a whole pile of boxes full of things like old shoes, and knitting paraphernalia, and wrinkled cotton skirts. "The Salvation Army maybe would take it off your hands if they didn't have to come pick it up. It's not worth anything. Over here, on the other hand, we have some things that probably are worth quite a bit." He stepped back out into the laundry area and led me around the corner toward the pathetic couch and TV room. There he pointed toward the doorway of Bill and Mom's bedroom, where he had used the arched pocket doors as a frame for a little fashion show.

"What a lovely presentation," I told him.

"Thank you," he said, smiling. "I think it's important, with beautiful things, to display them properly, so we can decide in an aesthetic way what is the best course of action."

"The only course of action I'm really interested in is money," I said.

"Yes, sweetheart, I'm well aware." He nodded. "You can be a philistine all you want. The rest is for me. Okay. The Balenciaga cocktail dress will bring in, conservatively, two thousand dollars."

"Two *thousand*?" I said, hoping that I was hearing this right.

"The alligator bag, I already know who I can take that to, and there's no question he'll pay four. The evening gowns are a little more specific and not quite as classic or timeless as the gowns that bring in the big bucks but they're in good shape, the sea-green one is really a beautiful color, we'll stay conservative and estimate another two for both of them."

"So what is that, eight? That's pretty good. How long will it take to sell them?"

"Wait wait wait. First, my darling, first we have to talk about this." He walked over to the display area, reached up against the wall and presented to me a piece of the ugliest luggage I have ever seen in my life.

"What about it?" I said.

"Do you know what this is?" he asked me.

"You can have it. Nobody wants this stuff," I assured him.

"You know nothing! Nothing!" he informed me, incensed with delight at how much I didn't know. "Six pieces, a matched set of Hermès airline luggage from the sixties. I've never seen even one piece before today! You have a whole set! And it's pristine! It's in perfect condition! I don't know what you might get for it. I just don't even know." He was dialing away on his cell phone, he was so excited.

"But do you know anybody who would buy it?" I asked him. "I need the money fast. They're going to kick me out any second. I have to get this stuff out of here."

"We'll buy it, Tina, don't worry," said Andrew, handing me a glass of champagne.

"*You'll* buy it," I said. "No, no, come on. You don't have to, to to—"

"To take care of you?" he asked. "But we want to take care of you. And if Lyle says it's worth something, trust me, it is. I'm sure it's a terrific investment."

"Do not take less than twenty-five, Tina," Lyle warned me, while he consulted with someone on the phone.

"Twenty-five," I said. "*Thousand?*"

Andrew gave me a check right then and there, and then went with me to cash it. On the sidewalk outside the bank I called Jennifer on her cell; she was just getting out of school and walking home. "You have to sneak out tonight. Tonight's the night," I told her. Be at my place at eleven."

"Eleven, like eleven *p.m.*?" she said, stunned.

"Actually, make it half past ten," I said. "We have a lot to do."

Six hours later there were five gay men waiting for her in the lost room. They helped her climb out of that horrid crawl-space and slip through the darkness into one of the many empty bedrooms, where there was a make-up station, a hair station, party dresses in three different sizes, four evening jackets and eight different pairs of shoes for her to choose from.

"What is this?" she said, laughing.

"It's party time," I told her. "We're going to a club."

She protested, but not too hard. "It's a school night," she said.

"Yeah, you're going to have problems staying awake in history tomorrow," I admitted, picking up a pair of strappy heels, hoping that we got the right size.

"What is this you're wearing?" Andrew asked her, a little worried about that plaid skirt.

"It's a uniform. I go to a Catholic school up on 98th," she explained, eying the party dresses with undisguised hunger.

"Come on," Roger said, his voice drenched in disbelief. "They have Catholic schools on Manhattan?"

We dressed her up and took her out. Edward rented a limo and we went to three separate clubs. Jennifer danced with everyone in our entourage, and then she danced with a bunch of more appropriate college guys, who we then met up with later at an all-night diner in the meat-packing district. There she flirted outrageously with one of them and they ended up making out on a street corner until 5 a.m, at which point I thought I'd better get her home so we could end the evening, perhaps, without parental discovery and Catholic recriminations, in which case it could just be a wonderful night for her to remember forever.

In the car, she threw her arms around me and hugged me with happiness. "Thank you thank you thank you," she told me.

"Thank you, Jennifer," I said. "You did as much for me as anyone I've ever known in my whole life."

"I have to tell you something," she whispered, and her hand slipped into mine, as she put her head on my shoulder. "My mom voted for you."

481

"What?" I said, trying to remember what that meant.

"She voted for you. She didn't want them to kick you out. She said you did a good thing, telling the cops about the phony will, that that was the right thing to do. And she also said you were really nice and a good babysitter. And she voted for you."

The next day, Frank was fired when he told a representative from the board of directors that he would not hire a security firm to help remove me from the building. It didn't matter. I was long gone. And I had a lot of money in my pocket, which came in handy.

A week later, Julianna Gideon bumped into Frank at a restaurant where she was having lunch with her roommate from Princeton. He looked especially handsome as he was wearing an extremely well-cut Armani suit which may have cost $3,000, easily. He explained that he had a new job with a small but well-regarded investment firm which was looking to expand their business in several South American capitals. Julianna's roommate had done her sophomore year abroad in Spain, so she and Frank carried on a quick and intelligent conversation in that most romantic of languages. Julianna was even more charmed than she had been already, and without notifying her mother she agreed to have dinner with him the following week. By the time they had their third date, Frank felt comfortable enough to invite her back to his apartment, which was small but beautifully furnished. He lived alone, he explained, as his father and brothers had recently come into money and returned to their family home in El Salvador. She spent the night.

Gcina Motufe, an illegal immigrant from Somalia, has presented her petition for amnesty to the Immigration and Naturalization Service. She has the best representation that money can buy. Her extremely clever lawyer convinced the INS that since Gcina is actually underage she should be kept in foster care until her case comes up before the courts. She is living with a nice family out at the Delaware Water Gap.

Vince Masterson was angry that once again his father dismissed his son's considered opinion on the matter and voted with the board to have me removed from apartment 8A. He told his father so, rather more forcibly than usual, which his father took poorly, observing that if Vince didn't like living rent-free in one of the most exclusive apartment buildings on Manhattan he was welcome to leave. A few months later, Vince did. He moved to Moscow and invested every penny in his trust fund in the Russian banking system, where he managed to triple his fortune within four years. Every spring he goes golfing in Dubai.

Five months after I left the Edge, I showed up at the Surrogates Court building in lower Manhattan. Our probate, or at least the first of a series of hearings on our probate, was finally on the docket. It was a nice morning in mid-February, one of those odd spring-like days in the middle of winter. The warmth of the air that day seemed mysterious and lively, like something was truly about to be born, if we just had the patience to wait for it. Who would go inside, on a morning like that?

"Well, look who it is." Lucy clipped up the steps like a warrior, her hair pulled back, severe and businesslike as usual in her gray suit. "I guess I'm not surprised."

"Hi, Lucy," I said. "I'm glad to see you."

"You know, Alison's been worried sick," she informed me crisply. "You could have called. We had no idea, no idea whatsoever, where you were."

"Neither of you guys really have room for me, I know that," I told her. "I needed to take care of myself for a while."

"And you couldn't be *bothered* to make a *phone call?*" she snapped.

"I had a lot of things to take care of, and I needed to think," I said. "And you know, could you tone this down for a second? I came here to talk and I don't need you going at me before anybody's even said anything yet, okay?"

"By all means, Tina, tell me how to behave, since you are such an ideal role model for us all," she announced.

"Okay, fine, if that's the way you want it, I guess that's the way things are always going to be," I said. "I'm sorry. I'm sorry we don't understand each other."

"And whose fault is that?" she said, nasty. She didn't even look at me; she was too busy pulling out her CrackBerry to check it.

"Yours," I said. "I think it's yours."

"Of course you do." She nodded.

"Where's Alison?" I asked, looking around.

"She's not coming, she's too upset. She and Daniel are probably splitting up. And of course they were married for ten years so he still expects his share of the apartment and he thinks Grossman is completely incompetent so we have a whole extra set of lawyers to deal with now. That's an utter delight."

"Alison and Daniel are splitting up?" I said.

"Yes, Tina, you might have known that if you had been anywhere reachable, which of course as usual you weren't."

"Well," I said, "I'm sorry to hear it."

"You never liked Daniel," Lucy said, dismissing my regret like yesterday's news.

"No, I didn't like Daniel but I do like Alison," I told her. "So she's not coming today?"

"No," said Lucy. "There's no need. I'm the Administratrix. Neither of you need to be here. As usual, I will do the work." She turned, dismissing me, and headed inside.

"Hey, Lucy," I said. "Count me out. I'm going to walk away from this. Okay? I want nothing to do with it. And you know, honestly—honestly, I think you should do that too."

"What?" she said, like this was the most insane thing she had ever heard.

"There's something wrong with that apartment," I said. "It's like, enchanted. Everything is so beautiful and it's great—it's really great—but you know, there's poison in the walls. You should just walk away."

"Well gee, Tina, thanks for the advice," she said. "As usual, you're so sensible."

"I'm not kidding, Lucy."

"Goodbye, Tina."

"I'm going to call Alison, okay?" I yelled, after her. "Tell her I'm going to call." She disappeared into the courthouse entryway, and she didn't look back.

Pete didn't have any luck with Doug, either. Doug and Lucy, neither one of them was built to walk away from a fight, or

485

the past. As it turns out, however, we were. After six months of wrangling with co-op boards and landlords and mortgage brokers and buildings all over the Upper West Side, we got our own place, further uptown. It's a two-bedroom, with a tiny dining room, a tiny living room, a tiny kitchen, and a sliver of a view of the river, if you kind of stand right up against one of the windows and lean over exactly the right way.

Jennifer White comes over to babysit for us now. Alison comes too, once in a while, for dinner, and she plays with the baby, and then she puts her to bed while I try to finish my homework so I can finally get through college. After we're done sharing our lives with each other, she fills us in on all the legal wranglings and what Doug is up to, and what Lucy is doing, and what clever trick Ira Grossman introduced last week, and what new witnesses Doug found who are willing to state definitively that Mom and Bill were unhappy and crazy and why the one will is meaningless and why the other wills, the crazy fake one as well as the ones that never got written, are not. And then we laugh, and kiss each other good night.

A year after I moved in and out of the Edgewood, the anthropological botanist Len Colbert, who lives in the building's penthouse, was found dead in his home. Apparently he had been regularly ingesting exceedingly rare hallucinogens which police suspected he was cultivating in his extensive greenhouse. Since it was clear that he had died by his own hand, a full investigation was never conducted. The penthouse apartment of the Edgewood was known to easily be worth fourteen million dollars. The estimated worth of his collection of rare flowers and shrubs was put in the range of seven. He did not leave a will.

ACKNOWLEDGEMENTS

My very good agent Loretta Barrett informed me two years ago that writing a second novel would most likely be the most difficult challenge of my writing life. She was right. Since then I have had myriad discussions with dozens of writers about this specific nightmare and while I despaired when Loretta and my excellent editor Susan Watt urged me to just get on with it, I now know that I could not have done so without their pushy support. I thank them for that, and for their mysterious confidence in me. Thanks also to Georgina Chapel, Abi Fellows, Amy Brownstein, Kate Snodgrass, Laura Heberton, Misha Angrist, Bill Rebeck and Susanna Sonnenberg for providing essential pieces to the ongoing puzzle of my life as a novelist. When I needed to be in London, Rima Horton and Alan Rickman took me in with such astonishing generosity I felt like I was in the *Arabian Nights*. Tamara Tunie and Gregory Generet also opened their lives and their home to me in this enterprise in so many sturdy and tangible ways it would take its own book to describe them.

Marisa Smith is my second reader, and Jess Lynn, my husband, is my first. Their unwavering assurance was bracing and cheering and ultimately the thing that kept me on my path.

What's next?

Tell us the name of an author you love

and we'll find your next great book.